THE FOUNDLING'S FORTUNE

RACHEL BRIMBLE

B

First published in 2021 as *Trouble for the Leading Lady*. This edition published in Great Britain in 2025 by Boldwood Books Ltd.

Cover Design by Colin Thomas

Cover Images: Colin Thomas and Alamy

A CIP catalogue record for this book is available from the British Library.

Paperback ISBN 978-1-83703-088-0

Large Print ISBN 978-1-83703-087-3

Hardback ISBN 978-1-83703-086-6

Trade Paperback ISBN 978-1-80656-121-6

Ebook ISBN 978-1-83703-089-7

Kindle ISBN 978-1-83703-090-3

Audio CD ISBN 978-1-83703-081-1

MP3 CD ISBN 978-1-83703-082-8

Digital audio download ISBN 978-1-83703-083-5

This book is printed on certified sustainable paper. Boldwood Books is dedicated to putting sustainability at the heart of our business. For more information please visit https://www.boldwoodbooks.com/about-us/sustainability/

Boldwood Books Ltd, 23 Bowerdean Street, London, SW6 3TN

www.boldwoodbooks.com

1

CITY OF BATH – APRIL 1852

As Nancy Bloom neared the Theatre Royal, she picked up her pace through the chaos of Bath on market day, purposefully averting her gaze from the advertising bills pasted to the theatre's entrance. Would she ever learn to return home to Carson Street via Milsom Street, rather than allow her damn feet to automatically lead her to the one place on God's earth she wished to avoid?

'Hello, darlin'. You lost? Want me to walk you back home for a bit of—'

'A bit of what?' Nancy quickly turned, her smile slipping into place as she faced the obvious ringleader of the three men who stood alongside her. Jauntily hitching her hip, she thrust her bosom forward. 'Tea? A slice of cake? A tinkle on the piano? 'Cause as sure as I'm standing here, you'd have no idea how to act on the lust shining in your cockeyed gaze.'

The man's friends roared with laughter as they pushed and prodded the object of Nancy's jibe, his jowls and potbelly juddering as he was nudged this way and that. Her smile widened as the joker's cheeks flushed red, his face contorted with a scowl as he swatted away the men's hands.

Nancy laughed and wiggled her fingers in the semblance of a wave, glad of the distraction her grimy-faced, almost toothless admirer had provided.

She continued on her way, pushing the man *and* the theatre out of her mind.

The fact she was a whore brought her neither shame nor regret... and what it did bring would remain forever buried within her. No talk of it would pass her tongue; no longing for her futile dreams would she permit to rise in her mind. To do so was stupid, nonsensical and downright delusional. Of course, the pain that writhed in her heart and the scars on her soul were, and most likely always would be, harder to diminish.

Yet, life was good. Her belly was full, her clothes fine and her health better than ever. She wanted for nothing. Some living on Bath's dirty, unforgiving streets could almost be pardoned for believing Nancy Bloom lived the high life. After all, she resided more comfortably than most, housed in one of the city's most esteemed brothels, working side by side with her best friends and earning a lucrative livelihood.

She had neither cause nor wish for complaint.

Her dreams of being onstage were foolish, and she'd fought against them on and off since she was fourteen. Nancy swallowed hard and lifted her chin. What good had it ever done her to keep reliving the longing that burned in her heart, what her instinct told her over and over again was her reason for being here, her calling?

To yearn for such things was futile... and detrimental. She had a job to do and she did it well. Why in God's name was her popularity and success as a high-class whore never enough for her?

Self-hatred twisted and turned inside of her as Nancy marched forward, plastering on a wide smile and tipping winks at each and every labourer, gentleman and youth who slid even the smallest admiring glance her way.

Whether or not she graced the boards of the Theatre Royal or the cracked, grimy pavements of Bath's inner-city streets, Nancy was an actress.

She strode through the maze of streets, hurrying past the abbey bathed in the golden light of the late spring sun and out into the widening road opposite Parade Gardens. Pausing, she looked left and right, waiting for a grand carriage and its preening horses to trot past, followed by a horse and cart carrying potatoes and milk churns.

It never ceased to amaze her how the rich mixed with the poor, the successful with the downtrodden. But this was Bath and these days she could not imagine living anywhere else.

The fact she had lived in places steeped in vice and alcohol, dark back rooms and dank cellars, albeit by force and violence, was neither here nor there. Bath was where she belonged and she prayed almost daily that her fortune would never have reason to abandon her.

She reached Carson Street and hurried up the steps to her front door.

'Evening, Jacob. What are you doing out here?' Nancy tilted her head towards the gardens. 'Thinking of taking Louisa for a walk around?'

The brothel's doorman smiled, his brilliant blue eyes shining with good humour. 'I would if I could persuade the woman to leave her books and spend some time with me. She's been in her study all afternoon.'

'Well, she fell in love with you for a reason, Jacob Jackson. Get in there and use those handsome looks of yours for Louisa's better good. Go on.' She playfully shoved him towards the open door. 'You know as well as I do, she'll not be able to resist you.'

'I'll give her another half an hour and then I'll toss her over my shoulder if necessary.'

'Well, if she turns you down, I'm more than willing to play second fiddle.' Nancy winked. 'A ride on your shoulders is the stuff of many a woman's dreams.'

Jacob shook his head and stared into the distance, his mouth twitching with a smile. 'Get in there and stop your jabbering. There's only one woman for me and well you know it.'

Nancy reached onto her tiptoes and pressed a kiss to his stubbly cheek. 'And I wouldn't have it any other way.'

She walked inside, pleased to see Louisa's study door ajar and her voice filtering into the hallway along with the house's fourth and final resident. Her dear and so serious friend: Octavia Marshall.

Nancy entered Louisa's study and tossed her purse onto the sideboard. 'What's this? A whores' meeting?'

'Ah, the wanderer returns.' Louisa slipped a ledger into her desk drawer and stood, her fingers pushing a stray blonde curl from her temple. 'And where have you been for half the day?'

Nancy dropped into a second chair alongside Octavia, trying her hardest to keep her face nonchalant. Louisa had a knack of looking at her and immediately knowing Nancy struggled with something. She shrugged. 'Just walking about.'

'And?'

'And nothing. Although I do think Octavia and me should go dress shopping soon,' she said, changing the subject. Nancy raised her eyebrows at Octavia's frown. 'What's that face for? You like silk and satin as much as any girl, don't you?'

'Silk and satin do not make a woman, Nancy.'

'No? Then what does?'

'Resilience, ambition and tenacity.'

'Tena... why have you always got to use such fancy words?' Nancy scowled as she unpinned her hat and tossed it onto the desk. 'You might speak as though you were born in a golden cradle, but you and I earn our bread and butter no differently, Octavia Marshall.'

'Ladies, please.' Louisa laughed, her violet eyes shining. 'Stop your bickering. All three of us have work to do tonight and I want both of you at your best. We have two members of parliament paying us a visit for the very first time. We don't want their fantasies about either of you demolished in a cycle of female arguing. Now...' Louisa came around the desk and leaned against it, her hands gripping its edge. 'You still haven't answered my question, Nance. Where have you been, and did you have a nice time?'

Afraid that her earlier thoughts and wasted longings might show on her face, considering how deeply they resided in her consciousness, Nancy forced a wide smile as she stood. 'Nowhere in particular. Just walked about town, flirting and smiling and generally provoking every man in the vicinity into wishing they could afford my company.' She picked up her hat. 'Now, if you ladies will excuse me, I think I'll indulge in a bath before tonight's festivities.'

She walked towards the door, her heart thundering with claustrophobia. Some days her ridiculous dreams came so close to the surface, she feared they would burst forth in a torrent of wailing on her friends' shoulders.

'Nancy?'

Damnation. Why did Louisa have to know her so well?

Nancy turned. 'Yes?'

'You would tell me if anything was bothering you? If you needed to talk? You know I'm always here for y—'

'Of course.' Nancy gave a dismissive wave. 'Don't fret, Lou. You know me. Always happy...' She threw a pointed glance at Octavia. 'Always resilient.'

Leaving the room, Nancy strode along the hallway towards the stairs, her friends' hushed and urgent whispers following her every step. She had no doubt she had managed to rouse both Louisa's and Octavia's suspicion and concern. The sooner she was safely in her room with the door locked, the quicker the tightness in her chest would ease.

2

Frustrated and filled with self-loathing, Francis Carlyle leaned back in his study chair and glared at the play he worked on. The words he'd written taunted him. *His* words. *His* memories. *His* scars. Brought from heart to pen and paper.

Shame and the inability to move on from all that had happened to him in his childhood and adolescence twisted like a knife in his gut. Why did he have the self-obsessed urge to keeping pushing himself back into the hellhole? To revisit his memories of the workhouse and all that he suffered there? Why this insane belief that this play could release him from his mental bondage?

The notion was pitiful, yet he could think of no other way to rid his desperation, to purge everything out of him. To syphon it free as though drawing poison from a festering wound.

'Damn it to hell.'

Ramming his pen into its onyx stand, Francis pushed back strands of dark blond hair from his brow and stood. He walked to the drinks cabinet in the corner of his study, poured himself a large measure of brandy and carried it to the window.

Beneath the glow of the gaslights, the facades of the houses alongside his own on Queen Square shone, the grassed square beyond, developed so painstakingly by John Wood, the Elder, standing empty. The plethora of people who had been outside enjoying the day's sun were now gone, leaving the recreational space empty but for the colourful flowers in the surrounding beds, the full trees once more filled with birds returning to nest.

But the peacefulness did nothing to calm his stretched nerves.

Never would he have imagined that he might one day afford as grand a house as his or own two horses and a carriage, employ a butler, cook and maid. Yet, all was true.

The satisfaction one might expect from securing such achievements had come and gone over Francis's twenty-eight years. The high moments he did his best to savour... knowing the dark, dark lows were never far behind.

Turning from the window, Francis strolled to his desk and glowered at his script once more. Dissatisfaction had become his constant companion. Like a lingering phantom that continued to badger and abuse him. He tightened his fingers around his glass as the need to use his experiences to provoke change within himself, and the world, burned ever hotter. He could no longer live in cowardice. No longer play out every day as the ultimate hypocrite, dressed in finery and mixing in middle-class circles. His table lay abundant with food, his bed bore the softest down and his material existence felt abhorrent.

Inside, he was no different to the boy he'd once been. Still alone, still afraid... still full of dangerous anger. He would always remain 'Little Frank' until he applied all he had learned for the greater good.

Closing his eyes, Francis surrendered to the images that played out behind his closed lids, his heart picking up speed as they passed in a kaleidoscope of brown, black and grey. The thick stone walls of the workhouse, rivulets of damp trailing down the brick, the straw strewn about the floor scratching at the bare soles of his feet as his fingers throbbed from the cuts and drying scabs he'd endured disentangling yards and yards of rope day after day...

The abrupt knock at the door shot Francis's eyes wide open and he quickly snatched up his manuscript and stuffed it into his desk drawer. 'Enter.'

Edmund More opened the door, Francis's valet's perpetual frown more pronounced than usual. 'You will be running late, sir. It's coming up to half past.'

'Thank you.' Hating that his fingers trembled, Francis pulled a script from the corner of his desk and made a show of scanning the dialogue. 'I'll be ready to leave shortly.'

Silence fell, only punctuated by the ticking of the mantel clock. Francis stared blindly at the papers, willing Edmund – more friend than servant – to leave.

Francis raised his head, his temper rising. 'What is it?'

'The theatre will be sending messages if you don't leave now.'

'For the love of God, I'm the damned manager, aren't I? I will arrive when I arrive.'

'As you wish.'

With a dip of his head, Edmund left the room and Francis released a heavy breath. He dropped the script and planted his hands on the desk, his knuckles aching with tension. It was bad enough that Edmund insisted he be called by his surname while in the house, but to shout at the most loyal friend any man could ask for was unforgivable. Yet, more and more often lately, Francis directed his frustration at Edmund rather than at himself within whom the true culpability lay.

Hissing a curse, he checked his manuscript was laid properly in the drawer and locked it, tugging on the handle to ensure it was secure before snatching up the theatre's latest script and the novel upon which the production was based and snuffing out the two candles burning on his desk.

He strode along the hallway to the front door where Edmund waited with Francis's coat and hat.

He shrugged into his coat before facing his valet. 'Apologies for snapping at you. I'll sort my mind out soon enough. Rest assured.'

'I think it might be advisable if we took some time away from the house tomorrow.' Edmund raised his eyebrows, his brown eyes hard. 'A walk in the fresh air will calm things a little, don't you think?'

Francis held Edmund's gaze, torn between rebuffing his advice and heeding it. The man had rarely been wrong in his counsel since he and Francis were children, surviving the cruelties of the workhouse side by side. 'Yes, I think it would. Tomorrow, all right? I promise.'

Francis stepped outside and started the short walk to the theatre. Happy to be alone again, he tried his best to acknowledge the looks of surprised recognition and undisguised admiration as he hurried along. He tipped his hat to the men and women he passed, his smile straining. Every evening, the walk to his workplace felt longer and longer.

Being an actor and theatre manager was not the glamorous role the public assumed it to be. The pride that his audience and stagehands most likely believed Francis took in his success and rise within the theatre had yet to infiltrate Francis's self-worth, despite his unprecedented elevation. The reason lay in his duplicity, in his frustration and continued secreting of a past that persistently haunted him. Something he was convinced would never end unless he brought his own words to life onstage. Played out for all to see and ultimately exorcising the evil from his soul.

Taking the theatre steps two at a time, Francis burst into the lobby and made his way backstage, barely glancing at the workers around him. As it did every night, the theatre's ambience burrowed deep inside him, washing away the self-loathing that ran through his veins. Francis drew air into his lungs and slowly exhaled, tension releasing as the power of his work took over his heart and mind.

His assistant hurried along the darkened corridor. 'Ah, Mr Carlyle. We were beginning to fret you might not make it.'

Francis removed his hat. 'On opening night? I wouldn't miss it for the world!'

Slipping his arm around the other man's shoulders, Francis pushed his selfish wants into submission, his mind and focus once more centred on making someone else's work shine brighter than his own.

3

One... Two... Three...

Nancy took a breath and sighed a long – some might say – entirely theatrical, elongated mew of satisfaction, her fingers clutching the buttocks of the man hovering above her.

Four... Five... Six...

He stilled, his euphorically contorted face freezing before he groaned and then collapsed his full weight onto her naked body, his head falling heavily into the crook of her neck.

She ran her nails up over his back. 'Oh, Mr Jameson...'

He shuddered. 'God, woman. You are a force to be reckoned with. Make no mistake.'

Laughing, Nancy eased him away and he fell to the mattress beside her. 'Oh, I know, but a girl never tires of being reminded.'

'I want to make you mine, Nancy. You know I do.'

She turned her head on the pillow and stared into her favourite client's eyes, her heart softened by the tenderness in his gaze. 'It doesn't matter how many times you ask me to be your mistress, it's not going to happen. I like it here, but it's more than that. I owe Louisa everything. I would never leave her.'

He smoothed his hand across her abdomen and pulled her closer. 'I have money, a nice place across town that you could decorate how you wish. Your every desire would be granted. I've not lain with any other whore but you since the first day I came here over a year past.' His gaze roamed over her face to linger at her lips. 'I'd never forsake you, Nancy. I lo— You mean too much to me.'

For his sake as well as her own, Nancy slipped from beneath the covers and out of the bed. She had lost count of how many clients had declared their love for her. A handful had even proposed marriage, but her heart was armoured in a staunch layer of self-protection. Her mind even more so.

'I know you wouldn't,' she said, plucking her robe from the back of a chair and pulling it on. 'But my place is here. With Louisa.' She walked to her dressing table and sat, picking up a brush. 'Anyway, I'm not sure your wife would quietly accept you keeping a whore, do you?'

'She knows about you, you know.'

'What?' Nancy flicked her gaze to the mirror, meeting his eyes. 'Does she know where I live?'

'Yes, but there's no worry about her ever seeking you out. She's hardly a saint herself. We... have an agreement. She has her lover and I have my mine.'

Strangely consoled that his wife actively sought her own satisfaction, Nancy relaxed her shoulders. 'Well, that's neither here nor there. I'll never be exclusively yours... or anyone else's, for that matter.' She drew the brush through her long strands of auburn hair, her eyes hardening as her determination rose. 'My rejection of your offer is not about me retaining independence either. My motivation for remaining free of a man's keep is about trust. Or shall I say broken trust. Nothing you or any other man can do will change my decision to tread carefully through life.'

'But—'

'But nothing.' She swivelled around on the seat and smiled, his deflated expression provoking her sympathy. 'I like you, you know I do, but I have every intention of living just the way I want to for the rest of my life.' She turned back to the mirror. 'For now, the right way is here with Louisa.'

He stood from the bed and walked towards her. 'You can trust me, Nancy. I'll give you all you want and need.' Mr Jameson stared into the mirror, his hands gentle on her shoulders. 'You could have a hundred dresses, a ton of hats and shoes, your own gig and horse, more money than you—'

'I have all the money I need.' Her patience thinning, she leaned purposely forward so his hands slipped away. 'I've trusted a man before who promised to give me all I ever desired, and it led me into a life of hell.' She swivelled around on the seat a second time, her heart racing as she pointed the brush at him. 'You will be no different as time passes. This – what we do here – would no longer satisfy you and you'd want more. Every man I've had the pleasure or displeasure of knowing has always wanted more.'

His cheeks reddened and his green eyes hardened. 'Not me.'

She held his gaze until he blew out a breath and stalked to the corner of the room where he'd laid his clothes. He pushed his legs into his trousers and Nancy could not help but appreciate the muscles that moved over his back, the sight of his neat, rounded arse and strong, strong legs. The only thing that showed the man's forty years was his slight paunch. But neither Mr Jameson's kindness nor physicality mattered. One day he would look back on his beseeching and realise he'd had a fortunate escape from her.

Nancy pinned her hair and patted some powder on her face.

Satisfied, she stood and tightened the sash on her robe before facing him.

He stared at her, dark green eyes once more softened with admiration. 'You're quite a girl, you know. One of these days a man is going to come along and take you away. There will be no avoiding it. You've a good heart and some lucky fella will get inside it. Whether you like it or not.'

She slid her arm into the crook of his elbow, rising on her tiptoes to press a kiss to his whiskered cheek. 'I very much doubt that but you are sweet to think so. Come, let's go downstairs.'

They walked a few steps towards the door when he tugged on her arm, halting her. 'Is this really it for you? You'll stay at Carson Street and have sex with whomever can afford you?'

There was no derision or disapproval in his tone, only gentle enquiry.

Nancy sighed, burying her desire for the stage, for all the stars and spangles of theatre life that she'd mistakenly fallen in love with so many years before. Tears treacherously pricked her eyes and she blinked them back as she smiled.

'Who knows? Maybe my life will change in time but, for now, I'm happy. Really happy.'

His brow furrowed as he studied her and then he touched his finger to her chin, leaning closer to softly brush his lips over hers. 'You are not happy. Not by a long chalk, but I respect your fervour and I respect you. I will not ask you again to be mine and only mine. Just promise me one thing.'

She swallowed against the dryness in her throat and the sudden, inexplicable sadness in her heart. 'What?'

'That whenever what makes you truly happy appears, you will tightly grasp it and never let go.'

Staring into his eyes, Nancy saw his sincere care for her prosperity, and nodded. 'I promise.'

'Good.' He smiled and patted her hand where it lay on his forearm. 'Then allow me to escort you downstairs.'

Nancy's stomach knotted with the unexpected trepidation that Mr Jameson, her most admiring and loyal client, had provoked in her. She could never be with a man like him, not really. A man who lacked fire for business and success, his income entirely inherited. As much as she liked Mr Jameson, men of his ilk ultimately irritated her and a hundred and one of them walked Bath's streets every day.

Mr Jameson might be kindness personified, but he was also a man who had somehow seen in her exactly what she strived so hard to hide.

Sadness.

And that was something she could not allow anyone to see, lest she crumbled. Enforced bravado had led her to become strong in every way. Enabled her to face every situation with open battle or feigned flirtation. Life skills that had served her well and ones that she had to protect to the bitter end.

But if Mr Jameson sensed even a tiny amount of unhappiness in her, could that mean the true state of her heart was, in reality, exposed to the entire world? That despite her frivolity, laughter and joking, people saw her pain and frustration? Her stupidity and fear? She glanced at him as they slowly descended the stairs.

Well, that could only mean her facade was weakening and she needed to bolster her defences. No man, even the most insightful of men, would ever know the real Nancy Bloom.

4

Standing in the wings at the Theatre Royal, Francis critically considered the set.

It didn't matter how much he stared at the fine table and chairs, the fake dresser complete with porcelain dining set, or the painted backdrop of a sash window and elaborate fireplace, he would never be satisfied.

Colleagues often commented on his need for perfection, his almost obsessive desire for order and complete professionalism and, in turn, he ignored their ribbing. How were they to know his conscientiousness wasn't always born out of commitment to the job, but a trait that had been beaten into him and remained, giving him the certain knowledge that a job done well meant a man stood less chance of criticism or punishment.

He glanced towards the gathering audience as they took their seats, the play due to start in fifteen minutes. Perspiration broke on his palms and he stuffed them into his trouser pockets, inhaling a shaky breath. This play had to exceed the theatre owner's expectations, in execution and ticket sales, if Francis had any chance of Lord Henry agreeing to stage Francis's play... should he ever muster the courage to share it with him, of course.

Urgent whispers and a stifled ruckus sounded behind him and Francis quickly turned, annoyed at the disturbance when the actors would enter from the other side of the stage at any minute.

'For the love of God,' he hissed. 'Will you keep it down... Alfred?' He stopped. 'My God, what happened?'

Francis stepped forward as the musicians' warm-up tune danced across the boards from the music pit.

His second in command swiped his hand over his face, a streak of grey lining his cheek and his black hair uncharacteristically mussed. Alfred was known throughout the theatre for his over-the-top physical perfection. The man liked to think himself the epitome of fashion and sophistication.

'I was ambushed.' He gripped Francis's arm and led him away from the wings and deeper into the hubbub of actors and stagehands. 'Set upon by a gang of ruffians.'

'What?' Francis resisted the urge to reprimand someone walking past with a prop held dangerously high above his head. 'Are you all right?'

Alfred scowled as he released Francis and flung his arms out to the sides. 'Do I look all right?'

Despite his associate's obvious distress, Francis bit back a smile. There was an absolutely firm, undeniable reason why Alfred Dunn was one of the city's most exuberant actors. 'Well, I—'

'Well, I nothing! I was minding my own business, walking past the workhouse—'

'The workhouse?' Francis's humour vanished. 'You were set upon outside the workhouse?'

'Yes, but that's by the by. The point is, what are we going to do about it?'

'Do about it?' A waft of scent and femininity drifted into Francis's nostrils, stealing his attention. He turned to see his star female actress coming towards them. Pulling on his charm, he held out his hands and smiled. 'Eloise. You look wonderful.'

Her cat-like eyes lit with pleasure. 'Like a fearless warrior, I hope, darling.'

'In or out of costume that is exactly what you are.' Francis extended his arm and stepped to the side. 'Your stage awaits.'

She lifted her fingers to his lapel and Francis felt the warmth of her breath on his face. 'I believe we are all retiring to the bar for a drink once the play has finished. I hope you will join me in a glass of champagne... or two?'

Francis fought the urge to step back. Eloise's interest in him had surpassed the professional a number of weeks ago but now he found his recent excuses to avoid sharing her bed again meeting with her resistance. A long time had passed before he'd allowed himself the enjoyment of a casual affair, allowed himself time away from his manuscript and to think of nothing but his physical needs. Eloise had been nothing if not persistent, but their time together was over.

If his aspirations for his play were to be realised, he must concentrate on his labours and nothing else.

He smiled. 'I'll do my best, but—'

Alfred dramatically cleared his throat. 'Your curtain call will be announced any minute, Miss Carpenter.'

'Thank you, Mr Dunn.' She ran her gaze over Alfred from head to toe, her nose wrinkling in distaste. 'You look a frightful mess. I advise against you arriving for this evening's drinks looking as you do. There will be theatre figures of authority there. Your impression would most certainly not aid Francis's desired success.' She faced Francis, her eyes softening. 'I'll see you later.'

Eloise walked away, the sheen of her pale pink dress shimmering beneath the lit sconces lining the corridor and bouncing from her dressed blonde hair. Before the need to write his story had taken over his life, a woman as stunningly beautiful as Eloise, as driven in her aspirations, had appealed to Francis immeasurably. Yet, over the last couple of weeks, Eloise's interest in him had become a distraction he needed to avoid.

'Hello?' Alfred waved his hand in front of Francis's face. 'Remember me?'

Slowly turning, Francis crossed his arms. He didn't have time for Alfred's histrionics. The play was about to start. 'Go and get cleaned up. Meet me in my dressing room in half an hour and I'll pour you a snifter. I want to make sure the play gets off to the best possible sta—'

'Pour me a...' Alfred glared as he theatrically brushed at his jacket and then the knees of his slightly muddied trousers. 'We should be going nowhere but the workhouse.'

Francis stilled, his gut knotting with tension. 'What?'

'They can't get away with manhandling me! My jacket is torn. Look.' He lifted the bottom to show his outer pocket hanging by its stitches. 'I suggest we take some stagehands with us and give those boys a hiding.'

Francis scrambled for words to placate him. The last place he wanted to be was the workhouse. He looked along the corridor. 'I can't leave. It's opening night. Besides, they will be long gone by now.'

Alfred narrowed his eyes. 'Are you too afraid to confront them? Is that it?'

'Of course not.'

'Do you know something?' Alfred's eyes blazed with annoyance. 'Sometimes I wonder what it is to be you.'

'What's that supposed to mean?' Francis pulled back his

shoulders, his irritation rising. 'Is there something you wish to say to me, Alfred?'

'Yes, there is as a matter of fact.'

'Well, I'm all ears.'

'You are one of the most successful self-made men in Bath, Francis. You have women falling over themselves to bed you, men who want to be you. You are handsome as the devil, kind and considerate. Yet, of late, you are not with us as you once were. What is it? Are you tiring of the theatre? Fallen in love with some damsel who needs saving? You always were a choice cut for any woman down on their bloody luck.'

Francis didn't know whether to laugh or punch him. 'Love? My God, man. Do you think I've got time to flirt with such nonsense?'

'Then what is it? Not so long ago, you would've wanted to sort out anyone who as much as looked at an associate of yours the wrong way. Yet, here I am, half-beaten, partially mugged and as soon as I mention where my assault happened, you pale in the face and claim you're too busy to see a wrong put right. Now...' Alfred planted his hands on his hips, two spots of colour darkening his cheeks. 'What the hell is going on with you?'

Swallowing against the sudden dryness in his throat, Francis looked along the corridor a second time. 'How old were these ruffians?'

'What?'

Barely managing to control the anger simmering deep inside of him, Francis glared. 'How old?'

'Well, I don't know. Young. Maybe fifteen, sixteen... that's hardly the point.'

'Isn't it? How do you know what their lives are like, Alfred?' He faced him. 'How do you know when they last ate or slept in a bed?'

'Are you mad? Why on earth would you defend them?' Alfred stepped away, holding his hands aloft. 'You know as much as I what a hindrance to society those sort are.'

'Those sort? Do you mean the poor and starving who walk this city all day, every day, without hope?'

'You have a wonderful life because you worked for it, Francis. The same opportunity is true for everyone.'

'Not always.'

Angry words danced on Francis's tongue, his conscience taunting and molesting him. Every day he strove to keep the shame of his beginnings hidden and now he had brought them to the forefront of Alfred's mind as well as his own. He needed to put a stop to this conversation and the only way to do that was to distract Alfred through placation.

Shame enveloped him as his next words formed like rocks in Francis's throat. He forced a smile and slapped his hand to his shoulder. 'You're right. They're ruffians who deserve the constabulary on their backs.'

'Exactly.'

'Come on,' Francis said, urging Alfred along the corridor. 'Let's watch the play and then we'll have a drink. If you're still riled, we'll see what can be done.'

Alfred's brow creased as he looked deep into Francis's eyes as though checking his sincerity. After a few heartbeats, he gave a firm nod and led the way towards the backstage corridor.

Francis released a slow breath. All was still hidden. All was well. Even if his self-loathing had deepened, his cowardice laid bare for anyone to see if they cared to look at him a little closer.

5

Nancy pulled the ribbon ties on her dress through her fingers, surreptitiously watching Octavia read the novel that had infuriatingly consumed her friend's every free moment for the last five days. It was Monday night and, as usual, the Carson Street house was closed to business. Now they were turning over a decent amount of money, the bills easily settled and their regular customers willing to pay well and immediately, Louisa had slowly reduced their working hours.

Which Nancy appreciated, of course... except for the nights when she was inexplicably, excruciatingly bored. Well, at least she told herself she was bored. But in truth, her thoughts had been enveloped in self-doubt and worry ever since her conversation with Mr Jameson.

Although forceful by nature and necessity, Nancy hadn't liked how easily she'd lost her professionalism with him, whether that had been through her rising temper or how she had most likely said too much, too vehemently. So much so, that he had seen through her tough exterior to her secret vulnerability. She was a fool with foolish dreams and somehow she needed to restrengthen her outer steel.

Which meant paying a visit to the one place she had always fit in so very well.

She dropped her ribbons with an exaggerated sigh, attempting to distract Octavia's attention.

Nothing.

Plucking up her skirts, Nancy made a show of lifting and preening them, smoothing and swishing the satin with as much exhibition as possible.

Nothing.

Infuriated, she stood and started a turn about the room, picking up ornaments and studying them, repositioning the chair at the small writing desk in front of the window. Glancing towards Octavia's bowed head, she walked to the mantel and *accidentally* nudged the vase of flowers on the hearth with her slippered toe.

China scraped against stone and, at last, Octavia lowered her book.

'What is it, Nancy? You have been trying to get my attention like a child from her governess for the last half an hour.' Octavia's eyes shone with amusement rather than reprimand, her lips curved into a small smile. 'Are you bored, by any chance?'

'To the point that I might run naked into the street!' Nancy grinned and raced forward, plonking herself onto the sofa beside her friend. 'Let's go out.'

'What? Where?' Octavia frowned as she glanced at the wall clock. 'It's nearing eight o'clock. By the time we dress and—'

'We're perfectly well dressed for where I have in mind.' Nancy wiggled her eyebrows. 'What do you say?'

Octavia groaned and closed her eyes. 'I am not going to the

White Hart tonight. I know how much you enjoy it there, but it's so noisy. So...'

'Fun!' Nancy stood and gripped Octavia's hand, unceremoniously pulling her to her feet. 'Please. Louisa and Jacob have gone out to dinner. There's nothing to prevent us having a little jolly, too.'

Octavia narrowed her eyes and crossed her arms.

Nancy knew this particular look of Octavia's only too well and fought not to fidget under her friend's scrutiny. Of her, Nancy and Louisa, Octavia was by far the most serious in nature... not to mention the most intelligent, the most well-read and the only one born of a much higher class. The woman was strong, insightful and downright immovable once she had a bit between her teeth.

'What?' Nancy laughed and threw up her hands in supplication. 'I just want to get out of this house for a while. Is that such a crime?'

'You only want to go to the White Hart when you have mischief about you, which means something is bothering you.'

'No, it doesn't.' Nancy's cheeks warmed and she purposefully walked towards the door, avoiding Octavia's study. 'You'll enjoy it once you've had a glass or two of that fancy wine you like.'

'I think it would be wiser for us to take a walk. It's a warm evening, after all. Maybe have some dinner. You know as well as I do that a sojourn to the Hart will mean you indulging in far too much ale, which will lead to you nursing a headache all day tomorrow,' Octavia said, widening her eyes with a pointed look. 'And you really are the worst when you are suffering the after-effects of one of your nights.'

With her back turned, Nancy gripped the drawing room door handle and squeezed her eyes shut. 'I don't want to go for a walk *or* dinner.'

A long silence followed, and Nancy could sense the cogs of Octavia's mind turning and her resistance weakening.

'Fine.'

Opening her eyes, Nancy released her held breath and smiled. 'Fine?'

'I'll agree to *one* drink in the Hart and then we go somewhere else to eat. I refuse to surrender myself to the endurance of another rather suspect pie in that pub as you made me suffer last time.'

Nancy dropped the handle and rushed towards Octavia, embracing her in a firm hug. 'Thank you. Thank you. You are the best friend a girl could ask for.'

'Hmm.' Octavia wriggled from Nancy's arms and snatched her book from the sofa, her cheeks flushed. 'And you, Nancy Bloom, are the most annoying.'

They washed and tidied themselves up and were soon in a hired cab.

Once they were duly deposited outside the White Hart, Octavia handed the driver some coins as Nancy stood in front of the public house and breathed deep.

Despite her increase in wealth and friendship, security and means, she still found herself drawn back to the White Hart, her need to be surrounded by smoke, ale and bawdiness fuelling her soul and never failing to cheer her. She felt such a sense of belonging when she was in a crowd, among the cheering, cursing and laughter. Being here, among the fun-seekers, was where she could be entirely herself without play-acting or behaving to anyone else's whim or request.

'Are we going in?'

She jumped and faced Octavia. 'Of course.'

Nancy stepped forward and pushed the doors wide open,

immediately inhaling the pub's instant intoxication. The place was packed as it always was at this time of night. Old Bill sat in his usual place at the piano, his white hair and whiskers yellowed by the cigar that habitually sat, seemingly stuck, to his bottom lip. The jaunty tune he played swept through Nancy and she grinned as she took Octavia's hand and pulled her through the throng towards the bar.

'A glass of Miss Octavia's wine, if you please, Maura,' Nancy said, smiling at the pub's landlady. 'And a glass of ale for me.'

'Coming right up.' Maura heaved her bosom from the bar top and reached for a pair of glasses hanging on a rack above her. 'Haven't seen you in here all week, Nance. Business good?'

'Can't complain, but I'm glad to get away from the house for a while.' Nancy turned her attention to Old Bill. His knack of tinkling the ivories in such a lively and joyful way had the crowds around the piano dancing a jig, whooping and laughing. 'Has Bill been playing all night? Only I hope he hasn't a mind to finish anytime soon.'

Maura laughed. 'Why? You gonna give us a turn?'

'Oh, Maura.' Octavia shook her head, a line forming between her brows. 'Why on God's earth did you put that idea in her head?'

The landlady grinned and filled a second glass with the sweet wine Octavia liked. 'Sorry, my lovely, but it cheers me and everyone else in here when Nancy entertains us.' She raised her eyebrows at Nancy. 'What do you say?'

Nancy's heart beat a little faster, her toes tapping on the stained and sticky floorboards. She looked from Maura to Octavia, who rolled her eyes. Nancy winked and walked backwards towards the piano, wiggling her fingers in a wave as the music curled around her like a spell, bounding her true self in notes and melody.

'What choice do I have, Octavia?' she shouted above the racket. 'Can't you see my stage is calling?'

She turned and opened her arms wide to the entire pub. 'What do we say to someone romancing this place up a little?' she shouted, and as the pub erupted into cheers and raised tankards, Nancy climbed onto a table, the men sitting there quickly swiping away their drinks before they were toppled into their laps. 'That's what I thought. Give me something to sing to, Bill. Something wise and lovely!'

6

Francis dropped his pencil onto the papers in front of him. Why in heaven's name had he thought coming to the White Hart tavern in the name of research had been a good idea? The revelry and noise of its patrons was damn near ear-splitting.

He leaned his head against the peeling wallpaper behind him and closed his eyes.

A sudden roar of catcalls and whistles erupted, sweeping through the pub on a deafening wave that made him wince. What the hell was going on now?

He opened his eyes.

From his place in the far corner of the pub, it was hard to see anything past the green tiled wall in front of him and the glazed glass panels either side. He had ventured into the Hart an hour before, intent on reminding himself what it felt like to sit and have a drink in a working man's pub, to absorb the sights, sounds and smells of a typical tavern of which many could be found dotted throughout the city.

The fact he was now in a position to drink in gentlemen's clubs and fancy restaurants had become something he took for granted, he realised now, and his arrogance did not sit well in his conscience.

The noise only increased in volume as the old man at the piano struck up a slower, more seductive tune and, judging by the lewd shouts and suggestive requests, a member of the fairer sex had taken up place by the piano for everyone's entertainment.

Francis hunched over the worn and scratched table and picked up his pencil. Sticking his finger in his ear, he tried his best to focus his mind on his work but the cheering only escalated, the laughter ringing louder and louder.

Just as he was about to give up completely, the room descended into sudden quiet, followed by the sweet singing of what Francis could only presume to be an angel. He leaned back and closed his eyes a second time, wanting to savour the heart-rending beauty of her voice and the song's sad melody.

Resisting his every instinct to stand so he could look around the glass partition and view the woman whose voice had struck such an unexpected chord deep in his heart, Francis smiled as she continued to sing, the surrounding silence only adding to the haunting hypnosis she had conjured.

Surrendering to temptation, Francis stood and peered around the partition. He could only see her face and upper body above the crowd gathered around her, but his heart immediately stuttered.

Her auburn hair lay in a thick rope over her shoulder, tied at its end with a simple emerald-coloured ribbon. She wore a straw hat decorated with flowers and berries, the red perfectly matching her devilishly low-cut dress. Her eyes were wide with happiness and dark in colour as far as he could tell from his distance.

He needed to get closer.

Hurriedly gathering his papers and pencil, Francis stuffed

them into his folder and tied the lace that secured it. He pushed it under his arm, took a deep breath and entered the mass of bodies surrounding her, their heads tilted upwards, their faces showing their admiration and the happiness this vision gave each and every one of them.

Her smile was infectious, her eyes were not dark after all, but the most unusual shade of grey and her perfect nose was smattered with a dusting of freckles that suited her immeasurably.

Her gaze caressed the audience as she drew them deeper and deeper into the song's tale. A soft smile played at her lips as she tipped the odd wink, making the recipient dip their head, their cheeks colouring as though it was only he who held her favour. Her power was invisible and undeniable, mesmerising Francis as much as everyone else.

Who in God's name was she? He had to speak to her.

Was such performing normal in these taverns? He had no idea, having not been inside one for so long.

He had left the workhouse to the employment of the shoemaker to whom he owed everything. A good and upstanding man with a wonderful wife. Neither Malcolm nor Winifred Russell, his adoptive parents, would have been seen in one of these places and it wasn't until Francis was older that he'd ventured to the taverns of his own accord.

The song ended and he blinked from his reverie, every nerve in his body stretched taut with the prospect of speaking to this extraordinary beauty. Surely she must be a performer. A street entertainer. Or maybe a warm-up act in one of the city's music halls.

She bowed and blew kisses to the crowd as the applause damn near shook the windows. Taking one of the many male hands offered to her, she stepped elegantly from the table to the floor, pressing a quick kiss to the cheek of the gentleman, who was then enveloped in good-natured teasing from his friends.

Oblivious to the trail of admiring glances that followed her to the bar, the woman accepted an embrace from another woman already standing there, before lifting her hand for a drink.

Francis strode forward, only to be pushed back by the men around him eagerly edging closer to her, their arms and voices raised as they clamoured to be the one to buy her a glass of ale. Determination mixed with annoyance as Francis muttered a curse and used his free arm to elbow the bodies closest to him out of the way, his stare fixed on the woman as she laughed with delight, her grey eyes shining.

Her companion, however, looked less amused by the attention. She shot glares back and forth over the melee, her finger pointed in warning towards anyone who came within a foot of her.

'Behave, all of you,' the auburn-haired songstress yelled, her smile wide. 'I can buy my own drink well enough. If you don't simmer down, then—'

'Aw, come on, Nancy, we mean no harm.'

'It's my turn to buy you a glass, sweet girl. You know you as good as promised me.'

'A pretty voice deserves a pretty drink, don't you think, Nance?'

The good-humoured calls came from every direction as the woman held court. Francis shoved ever closer. Nancy. If he left the Hart with nothing else at least he had her name. Inhaling a deep breath, he pushed between the two men ahead of him and damn near fell against the bar right beside her.

She leaped out of the way, her eyebrows raised, her happy gaze immediately shadowing with a hint of wariness. 'Well, who do we have here?'

Francis stood firm, his feet planted, and his arms crossed over his folder as he braced against the men shoving at his back. 'A man determined to buy a drink for the woman with the most fantastic voice I've ever had the pleasure to hear.'

Her gaze travelled over his face and she took a step back, her eyes steely and body seeming to grow a little stiff. 'Is that so? Well, I thank you, but there's plenty around you looking to buy me a drink and that's not something a girl likes to easily ignore.'

Francis stared into her eyes, fascinated that someone with such a strong, if he wasn't mistaken, Bristolian accent could produce such a soft, sentimental sound when she sang. 'I think it would be wise that you allow me to buy you a drink.'

'You do, do you?'

'Yes, and then we should retire to a table where we can talk further.'

She studied him before she guffawed and turned away to address the rather eager-looking young man standing on her other side. 'Billy, I'll have a glass of ale if you don't mind.'

'Coming right up, Nancy.'

Francis stood like a prize idiot staring at the back of her head, words flailing on his tongue. What in God's name was he supposed to do now? Men jostled and shouted all around him as she engaged in conversation with the lad.

Francis looked to her female companion and was met by her amused gaze as she smiled at him with a certain air of pity.

The challenge was clear.

Riled, yet even more intrigued by the auburn-haired and considerably feisty Nancy, Francis cleared his throat and tapped her on the shoulder. 'I really think you should accept my offer of a drink, miss.'

Annoyance darkened her eyes. 'Is that so? Well, whether you think me rude, ungrateful or just not interested, I don't take kindly to pushy strangers insisting I do anything. So, if you'd like to go about your business, I'll go about mine.'

As she moved to turn away from him a second time, Francis leaned in close to her ear. 'I have a proposition I think you should at least listen to.'

'You really think a lot of yourself don't you, Mr...?'

'Carlyle.' He held out his hand. 'Francis Carlyle. Nice meet you, Nancy.'

She glanced at her friend before tentatively sliding her hand into his and, still looking at him, spoke over her shoulder. 'Sorry, Billy, but I think I'll take a drink from Mr Carlyle here. He seems to think himself someone special.'

7

Nancy walked ahead of Mr Carlyle to a small table in the corner of the pub, purposely sitting on a low stool that allowed her full view of Octavia and vice versa. Who on God's earth was this man? Dressed in a well-cut, navy blue suit and silk necktie, his eyes and dark blond hair glinted beneath the low light. She was used to middle-class men visiting Carson Street, yet she sensed it wasn't sex on this man's mind when he'd been speaking to her but something else entirely. What that was though, she had no idea.

Unease whispered through her and Nancy quickly looked towards the bar lest he caught her studying him.

He cleared his throat. 'So...'

Nancy glanced at his hands as he laid his hat on the table, his fingers curiously scarred with thin, silvery lines but not roughened like he laboured every day... His dress indicated otherwise, too.

She slowly slid her gaze to his, her habitual suspicion growing stronger. 'What is this proposition you seem to think I will find irresistible, Mr Carlyle? Only you should know I am more used to men and their *propositions* than most.'

His blue eyes lingered on hers as he lifted his glass of brandy. 'Oh?'

She would neither explain nor elaborate. There was something about him that unnerved her. Clearly a man of means, yet there was an air of earthiness about him, a worldly wisdom in his gaze, as if he had seen as much evil as he had good and very little surprised or disturbed him. His confidence was something Nancy could only envy.

She hitched back her shoulders, pulling on the persona she had utilised day after day, night after night for more years than she cared to count. 'Just spit it out.' She sighed, wanting to vanquish the soft interest in his eyes. 'My friend is waiting.'

He studied her a moment longer, his attention seemingly stuck on her hair and eyes. At last, he spoke. 'I am the manager at the Theatre Royal.'

Nancy's heart stopped. 'What?'

'I said, I'm the manager... Are you all right?' His gaze filled with alarm and he instantly moved his hand as if to take hers before he dropped it as though remembering himself. 'Your colour has paled.'

Collecting herself, Nancy huffed a laugh and lifted her drink, mortified that it trembled. 'Of course, I'm all right. Pray continue, Mr Carlyle, I can barely stand the suspense of why you should think your position would hold any interest to me.'

His gaze remained on hers as he frowned. 'I'm in charge of hiring actors and actresses for every production and I think you have a talent that can be displayed to its fullest onstage.' He put his hand on the folder he'd laid atop the stool beside him and immediately the light in his eyes dimmed a little, two spots of colour leaping into his cheeks. 'But it's not a play the Royal is producing that I have in mind for you.'

Nancy's heart was damn near beating out of her chest. 'Is this some kind of prank?'

'Of course not.'

'I don't believe you.'

'I swear to you. I work at Theatre Royal and...'

He continued to speak and Nancy stared at his mouth as it moved, but she could hear nothing above the racket of her screaming thoughts. Who the hell was he? Was he connected to the man who'd abducted her years before? One of the men who'd... No, *this* man was but four or five years older than she, and the man who had led her along a path to the pits of hell would be around forty by now. Yet sickness rolled through Nancy and she slowly stood, anger burning like fire in her stomach. She would not be caught again.

'I think we are done here, Mr Carlyle. I have no idea who you are but if you think you can—'

'I am who I say I am.' He rose to his feet, his blue eyes almost pleading with her. 'Miss... Nancy, please, I wish you no harm. The complete opposite, in fact.'

'The opposite? You come into this pub and claim—'

'No claim, I have told you only the truth.' A coolness crept into his gaze, his jaw tightening. 'I am a man of honour, miss. I do not lie, and I do not accost young women with indecent intentions.'

Nancy searched his eyes for skulduggery, insincerity, something. Yet, all she saw was complete and utter candidness. Was the man insane? An escapee from the damn asylum? 'How can you say that when you take one look at me, hear me sing a single time and think I am someone to take a part in a play?'

'Look, we need to talk further. If you will just—'

'No.' Panic and fear hurtled her back to a place she had no wish to revisit, her body trembling. 'I am quite happy with the life

I lead, Mr Carlyle. You are clearly delusional if you think I have any wish to listen to your nonsense any longer.' She shook her head, self-protection shrouding her. It was as though the worst part of her life was repeating itself all over again. Well, this time she was older and wiser. If this man thought he could dupe her with promises of fame and fortune as another had before him, he had another thing coming. 'I've had the displeasure of meeting your type before and I know exactly what you're about. Thanks for the drink, but you've chosen the wrong prey this time.'

She moved to walk away, and he gripped her wrist.

Nancy's heart leaped into her throat as memories came crashing back, sending her back to her fourteen-year-old self and the hell she'd endured for the following two years. Perspiration broke on her forehead and upper lip...

She snatched her arm away, her anger exploding. 'Don't you dare touch me.'

Slowly, he raised his hand, his eyes wide with shock. 'I'm sorry.'

'So you should be.' Shameful, unexpected tears pricked her eyes and she quickly looked to Octavia, who was on her feet and carefully watching them. 'Goodnight, Mr Carlyle.'

Nancy stormed towards Octavia, her legs slightly shaking but her chin high. She gripped her friend's elbow. 'Let's go.'

'Did he grab you? Are you crying?'

Nancy swiped at her cheek, ashamed of the weakness enveloping her, the familiar tightening in her chest. 'Of course not. Come on.'

'But—'

'Not now, Octavia.'

They had almost reached the pub's doors when Mr Carlyle stepped in front of Nancy.

She glared, hating his clothes, his hair, his face, the kindness in his stupid bloody eyes. 'Get out of my way.'

'Please. I am writing a play. Something very dear to me and you would be perfect...' He shook his head and pushed the fallen hair from his brow. 'I didn't expect to find someone so perf— Please, can we talk again sometime? I'll meet you anywhere, whenever you wish.'

Nancy stared deep into eyes, almost mesmerised by the beseeching in his gaze. She could only presume him to be an actor of phenomenal talent. Straightening her spine, she battled against her tendency to seek the good over bad in people.

'No.' She brushed past him. 'I have no interest in listening to what you have to say.'

'Nancy, please. I live—'

'Did you not hear my friend?' Octavia put her hand on his chest and pushed him back. 'She said no. Now, I urge you to leave her be. Otherwise I will not be held responsible for my actions.'

Closing her eyes, Nancy halted and inhaled a long breath in the hope it calmed her racing heart. 'Just leave him, Octavia. He's not worth it.'

But she took Nancy's hand and pulled her forward, so they stood side by side in front of Mr Carlyle.

'What is it you want with my friend?' Octavia demanded. 'We are not the type of women who take kindly to bullying. From anyone.' She looked him up and down, her eyes cold. 'Especially gentlemen who come into pubs they wouldn't normally – like a voyeur taking pleasure in other people's misfortune. I saw you with your pencil, Mr Carlyle. Looking at people, writing feverishly as though you have the right to judge and condemn—'

'You're wrong.'

Nancy stilled. His voice had changed. The amiability had vanished, the softness obliterated and replaced with a cold curtness, his tone low. Dangerously so. Maybe he wasn't the upper-middle class, snotty type she'd assumed him to be but someone who could turn violent on the spin of a coin.

Nancy stepped closer, protection for Octavia and herself burning deep inside. His mentioning the theatre might have given her usually well-maintained defences a wobble, but now they were back in place and she would not be hoodwinked into anything from this man. This stranger.

She crossed her arms. 'I don't believe you, Mr Carlyle. Why would you approach me with such a proposition when you have only just met me? Have you been following me? Do you know where I live?'

'Of course not.'

'Then why—'

'Just an hour of your time,' he said, quietly, his gaze never leaving hers. 'That's all I ask.'

Nancy stared into his eyes looking for any potential danger, any threat of what this man might be capable of. Instead, she saw an almost pitiful sadness that hitched at her chest. Indecision warred inside of her. There was no reason to trust or believe him, but curiosity urged her on, tempting her into something that would undoubtedly mean trouble. Yet...

'Fine.' She exhaled, her shoulders dropping. 'I'll meet you—'

'Nancy...'

'It's all right, Octavia.' She raised her hand, silencing her friend, her eyes on Mr Carlyle. 'I'll meet you at my home but it's going to cost you.'

He frowned, glanced at Octavia. 'What?'

Feeling her strength returning as her tried-and-tested facade slipped over her like a well-worn cloak, Nancy smirked. 'I said, it will cost you.'

Slowly, his frown faded, and his eyes ever so slightly widened as comprehension dawned. 'You're a prostitute?'

'Yes, Mr Carlyle, I am, and my time is money. So...' She stepped back. 'If you want to see me, come to our house on Carson Street and make an appointment. Our doorman, Jacob, will be standing out front from nine o'clock each evening. Come on, Octavia. We're leaving.'

Hooking her hand around her friend's elbow, Nancy led them from the pub. As soon as they were outside and walking along the chilly, dark street, Octavia spoke.

'Are you mad? The man clearly has a screw loose. Did you see the way he watched you?'

'Oh, I saw.' Nancy drew in a long breath. No one had ever looked at her that way. As though she fascinated him, intrigued him... mesmerised him. 'But I doubt we'll ever see him again. Not now he knows we have Jacob looking out for us *and* he'll have to pay for my time.'

'Hmm, I wouldn't be so sure.'

They continued to walk as Nancy's mind scrambled with what Mr Carlyle might or might not want from her and what it was he saw when he looked at her to cause such fascinating certainty in his eyes.

8

Francis paused on Carson Street and studied the wide-shouldered bull of a man standing on the top step of one of the houses. He was dressed entirely in black, suited and booted and hatless. He paced back and forth, looking along the street, his expression more menacing than welcoming.

At least there was no doubt in which house Francis would find Nancy.

Loud male laughter sounded behind him and Francis moved to the side, allowing two gentlemen to pass him. They walked along the street, their good spirits obvious, the reason for their joviality becoming perfectly clear when they stopped in front of the house with the man on its step.

They approached with familiar and happy greetings and a smile even broke the doorman's previous, somewhat foreboding, expression. A few words were exchanged before the gentlemen were welcomed inside with a wave of the doorman's hand.

Francis stepped further into the shadows and battled his infernal indecision.

Was he mad to take this approach with his life story? To have concluded that having a woman play him rather than a man would somehow enforce a distance from himself and his past? Of course, it had been imperative he found the *right* woman...

And then he'd walked into a place a hundred miles away from his normal haunts and found Nancy.

In the three nights since he'd spoken with her, she had filled his mind and soul, propelling his memories and words onto the page with almost feverish ferocity. She had indeed become his muse. Become *him*.

Yet her obvious wariness and deeply embedded street savvy had told him that if she were ever to agree to play the part, he would have to befriend her first. Gain her trust in any way he could.

Francis stared at the house again.

Would she be heading to bed right now with one of the two gentlemen who'd entered? An outrageous possession shot through him as he imagined what it might be like to lie with such a radiant, vivacious woman. Her wonderful voice had caught his attention, but it was her eyes, her hair, her beauty that had secured his fascination.

He inhaled a long, shaky breath. Why was he standing here like a cowardly fool? He was passionate about his work. All he had to do was find a way to evoke the same fervour in Nancy.

Decision made, Francis strode towards the house.

The man outside stopped his pacing and waited for Francis to climb the front steps.

The doorman raised his eyebrows, his arms crossed over his enormous chest. 'Can I help you, sir?'

The affability he'd afforded the two gentlemen who entered previously was entirely absent, his brilliant blue eyes flashing with dangerous suspicion.

Francis was neither perturbed nor intimidated. Not after the necessary fights he'd sustained during his youth and adolescence. He glanced towards the open door of the house. 'I'm here to see Nancy.'

'Is she expecting you?'

Francis held the man's gaze. They were of the same height even if the man's physique was considerably more muscular. He was a giant more suited to a boxing ring than standing outside a brothel. 'No, but it's important I speak with her.'

'Then you'll need to make an appointment.' The doorman glanced past Francis towards the park beyond as though bored. 'Nancy is a popular attraction, Mr...' He faced Francis, his eyebrows raised again.

'Carlyle. Francis Carlyle.'

'Well, Mr Carlyle, if you'd like to come with me,' he said, dropping his arms and turning towards the door. 'I'll take you to Mrs Hill and she'll sort out a time when Nancy can see you. I assume you're in a position to pay for Nancy's time to the amount she's worth?'

Francis nodded.

'Good, then follow me.'

Francis entered a white-painted hallway, the floor a rich, dark wood covered with a long red rug, fresh roses spilling from porcelain vases atop highly polished side tables. As he walked, his austere expression was reflected back to him from the gilt-edged mirrors that intermittently lined the walls, painted landscapes adding just the perfect injection of colour.

A deceptively homely setting to a place that existed for the sole purpose of selling sex.

Muffled conversation came from behind a closed door on his left, which he assumed to be the drawing room, while upstairs... He lifted his gaze just as Nancy's infectious laughter drifted down the stairs, followed by her almighty scream of delight. Francis briefly closed his eyes, the sexual images that immediately rushed his brain neither welcome nor, he supposed, entirely inaccurate.

What was wrong with him? Why in God's name was his instinct leading him to the certainty that a prostitute was the right woman to be his star? It made no sense. Yet he was more certain than ever that Nancy Bloom had appeared in his life for that very reason.

The doorman stopped in front of a closed door at the far end of the hallway and knocked.

'Come in.'

The woman's voice was gentle yet authoritative and the doorman nodded at Francis before opening the door wide so that Francis could enter the room first.

It was the distinct femininity yet understated efficiency of the study that struck him first. A place of work, but comfort too. That, and the interesting way the blonde woman who sat behind the desk looked as at home here as she might sitting side by side with her husband on a parlour sofa, their children playing at their feet.

'Louisa, I have a Mr Carlyle here.' The doorman stared at the woman, his eyes full only of her. 'He wishes to make an appointment with Nancy.'

Francis stood completely still, feeling decidedly invisible as the doorman and the woman stared at each other. Although all appeared professional, a silent sexual tension had come alive in the room. There was little doubt in his mind that they were lovers. He glanced at her left hand. No wedding ring, but Francis was certain of his instincts.

'Thank you, Jacob.' She turned to Francis and stood, her hand outstretched. 'Good evening, Mr Carlyle. Louisa Hill.' They shook hands. 'Won't you take a seat?'

'Thank you.'

Francis sat in the seat on the other side of her desk as the doorman left, quietly closing the door behind him. Above the white-painted ceiling, the muted sounds of creaking bed springs broke the silence, making Francis pull his lips tight against the urge to smile.

This entire situation was completely bizarre. That the woman he wished to star in his play was having sex with a gentleman above his head, that he was sitting in a beautiful study in front of a madam, hoping to secure a night with Nancy, was quite frankly the most surreal of circumstances he'd ever found himself in.

Only last week the height of his thoughts had been entirely concentrated on the play he was producing at the Theatre Royal and the macabre memories of a past he struggled to pen sufficiently onto paper.

Now, he was here.

'Mr Carlyle?'

He blinked. Louisa Hill stared at him expectantly, her extraordinary violet eyes carefully assessing him.

Dragging his gaze from the scar that ran along her cheek, Francis cleared his throat and sat a little straighter. 'I apologise. Did you say something?'

'I did.' She smiled, amusement softening her gaze even as she lifted a finger to hover above the scar before dropping her hand to the desk. 'I asked how you came to learn of Nancy. Indeed, of this house.'

'I met Nancy at the White Hart a few nights back... I heard her sing.'

Louisa Hill's smile widened, and unmistakable pleasure lit her eyes. 'Ah, then I understand entirely why you would seek her out. Isn't she wonderful? Not that she will believe anyone who tells her so.'

Francis sat forward and placed his hat on the floor beside him, pleased that he might learn more about Nancy even if he was unable to be with her... for now. 'She doesn't consider herself talented?'

'With her singing?' She shook her head. 'No, unfortunately not. However, she is sometimes overly outspoken about her other talents. And I presume, it is those that you would like to learn more about now?'

Francis nodded, his duplicity overriding his intention to be honest. It would be bad enough having to answer Nancy's questions about him and his play, but to tell Louisa Hill his true motivation for being here was a step too far.

Shifting back in his seat, he lifted his ankle onto his other knee to portray nonchalance. 'She is quite a lady. I would be willing to pay whatever it costs for a few hours of her time.'

'I see.' Louisa Hill pulled a ledger closer to her and scanned the open page. 'Then, assuming Nancy's agreement, let's see when we can fit you in, shall we?'

9

Nancy led Mr Farlington, one of her regular and most nervous of culls, down the stairs to where Jacob stood at the door, his steady blue gaze sharpened on her face as he sought for any sign of upset she might have suffered.

She endeavoured to allay his fears with a discreet nod and turned her best smile upon her client. 'There now, Mr Farlington, I'd be much obliged if you'd leave your payment with Jacob.' She winked. 'And I hope to see you again at the same time next week.'

'That you will, Nancy.' He shakily exhaled, his gaze flitting to her bosom, the curves of her breasts visible above the loosened laces of her virginal white nightgown. 'Same time, same place.'

He hesitantly turned to Jacob as though it pained him to look away from her, his hand fumbling into his inside pocket.

Nancy swivelled around to head back upstairs for a much-wanted bath.

'Just a minute, Nancy,' Jacob called, halting her. 'Louisa would like a few moments of your time. She's in the study.'

Although her smile remained in place, the warning in Jacob's eyes ignited Nancy's trepidation. Now what?

Knocking on the study door, Nancy poked her head into the room. 'You wanted to see me?'

'I did.' Louisa finished what she was writing and lowered her pen into the inkstand. 'Aren't you going to come in?'

Nancy sagged her shoulders and reluctantly entered, her dream of a bath disintegrating. 'I'm tired and was hoping for an early night. I don't have another cull booked tonight, do I?'

'No, and this shouldn't take long.' Louisa gestured towards the two armchairs in front of the fireplace. 'Take a seat and I'll pour us a glass of wine.'

Nancy's frustration was instantly replaced with apprehension. Louisa always put Nancy's and Octavia's wishes ahead of anything else. Which meant Louisa wanted to speak to her about something important if she chose to delay Nancy's retreat upstairs.

'Is everything all right, Lou?'

The sound of glass clinked as Louisa replaced the decanter stopper. 'I had someone come in asking for an appointment with you.'

Nancy studied her friend's turned back. Her voice seemed to quiver with amusement, her shoulders relaxed. Then, Louisa turned. The woman looked positively elated.

Taking the offered glass of claret, Nancy raised her eyebrows. 'What's going on?'

'Nothing.'

'Then stop grinning at me like that. You look like the cat who got the cream.' She sipped her wine. 'Who was this gentleman? From the way your eyes are lit like lanterns, I'll wonder if it wasn't the Prince of Wales himself.'

Louisa laughed. 'Hardly, but I imagine our visitor will be equally interesting.'

Nancy put her glass on the table beside her and tipped her

head back against the chair, exhaustion closing her eyes. 'Then spit it out. Who was he?'

'A Mr Francis Carlyle.'

Nancy's eyes shot open and she lifted her head so fast something creaked in her neck. 'What?'

Louisa's smile immediately vanished. 'Is he trouble?'

Her heart pounding, Nancy stood and paced a circle in front of the fire. Mr Carlyle had come here? To the house? He'd actually followed up her invitation and was willing to pay money to see her? Dread knotted her stomach and her mouth dried. No, no, no...

'Nance, what is it?' Louisa slowly put her glass down and stared, concern filling her violet eyes. 'Do I need to tell him never to show his face here again or bother you in any way? I thought him quite nice. He came because he heard you sing. I thought that might please you, even if you insist on denying every part of your talent. Mr Carlyle seemed entirely sincere in his admiration of you. In fact—'

'I won't see him. I can't.' Panic swirled inside Nancy like the rough waves of an ocean. She pressed her hand to her stomach. 'What was he thinking? Does he really consider me so naïve that I might believe he thinks me suited to the stage?'

'He said that?'

Nancy inwardly cussed her stupidity at speaking aloud. 'He... mentioned he was a manager at the Royal. That he thought my voice wonderful or something like that.' She waved dismissively and turned to stare into the fire's grate, anything to avoid Louisa's wily study. 'He was full of himself.'

The ensuing silence battered at Nancy's resolve. She could almost hear the cogs of Louisa's brain turning and knew she would not let this be without an explanation... a *full* explanation.

'So...' Louisa cleared her throat. 'It's what he said to you rather than *how* he said it that has you as jumpy as a cat? Or is the real problem that he said something that made you feel hope for something past what we do here?'

Nancy spun around, her anger nicely sparked to a simmer. 'The man did not make me *feel* anything. He is undoubtedly a fake and a fraud. I don't like liars. If he wanted to bed me, then he should have just said as much. He stalked around the White Hart like he belonged there when he quite clearly didn't, considering his obvious success and wealth.'

'And that annoyed you? Since when has Nancy Bloom not been able to handle a man who thinks himself something he isn't?' Louisa raised her eyebrows, her glass at her lips. 'The woman I know would've eaten him for supper. Which means...'

Nancy planted her hands on her hips, her body ever so slightly trembling. 'What?'

'That whatever he said to you struck a chord, that's what.' Louisa put down her drink and leaned forward, concern darkening her eyes. 'Talk to me, Nance. What is it about the man that has shaken you so badly?'

'Shaken me?' Indignation flooded through Nancy as she stalked towards the door. 'Nothing about Francis Carlyle has shaken me. Send him a message. I will see him tomorrow night. Ten o'clock and not a minute later, or else that appointment and every future appointment will be null and void.'

'But—'

Nancy fled the room, bypassing Jacob where he spoke to a gentleman at the door and hurrying as fast as she could upstairs. Once she reached her bedroom, she slammed and locked the door, her hands shaking.

She leaned her back against the door and took a long breath, slowly exhaling as she tried to calm her racing heart.

What was she to do now?

Walking to the bed, she threw herself upon it. What if Mr Carlyle persisted in his claim that he wished to find her a place onstage? What if he didn't want sex, but was actually genuine in his ambitions for her?

She squeezed her eyes shut as a barrage of memories battered her. She could not go there again, not allow her heart to lead her head. She was grown now. A woman with money and a career... of sorts.

If Mr Carlyle told her the same lies made to her when she had been barely fourteen years old, how was she to react this time? Her pulse beat in her ears as she thought how, day after day, she would wander into the theatre and sit on the hard wooden benches to watch whatever matinee happened to be showing. She'd dream of being the actresses who played the female characters, the actresses who played the men. The costumes, scenery and lighting winding deep inside of her and sparking a powerful passion she'd thought would last forever.

Then a monster had come along and enticed her, promised a young, naïve girl the world and had been so convincing not only had Nancy believed him, but her parents had too.

Tears that Nancy had thought long dried slipped from beneath her closed lids onto the pillow. What had followed had been the stuff of nightmares. Nightmares that had haunted her year after year until Louisa had accepted an offer of escape for both of them from the Bristol brothel where they had been working. A man who had once been Louisa's devoted cull. A man who would go on to become her husband. A man who had also turned out to be so much less than he seemed. But only with that man's money and protection had the beatings, rapes and humiliation finally been over.

But, despite all that Louisa had done for her, Nancy had shared only the smallest amount of her past with her, vowing her friend would never look at her as a victim, but as a companion. A friend who was forceful and strong and would forever have Louisa's back.

She could not fall for Carlyle's lies. Not become, once again, overreaching in her ambitions, not allow herself to be hypnotised into thinking – into dreaming – that the destiny she felt deep in her heart and soul was actually real...

Flipping onto her back, Nancy swiped at her damp cheeks and stared at the ceiling, willing her inner strength to the fore. She narrowed her eyes, embracing the fire in her heart that had never fully doused no matter how hard she tried.

Their house on Carson Street was not the theatre. It was a brothel, and here she was in control. Would *always* be in control.

Smiling softly, Nancy slowly nodded. Oh, she would see Mr Carlyle. And, as God was her witness, the minute his cock was in her hand, thoughts of the theatre would be scattered from his brain like gaslights being extinguished one by one in the great Theatre Royal he spoke so damn highly of.

10

Francis approached Jacob Jackson where he stood on the top step of the Carson Street house and hoped to God the nerves clenching his stomach didn't show on his face. He nodded. 'Mr Jackson.'

'Mr Carlyle.' The burly doorman returned Francis's nod and walked ahead of him into the house. 'If you'd like to follow me.'

Francis slowly exhaled through pursed lips as he was led into the parlour. He drew to a stop beside Jacob and forced a smile, the scene in front of him neither expected nor welcome. He had thought he would find Nancy alone. Not taken into a room where not only was Louisa Hill present, but also the woman who had accompanied Nancy to the White Hart.

His heart picked up speed as he looked from one woman to the next, hating the feeling he'd walked into an ambush.

Nancy and her friend from the tavern were dressed in silk robes and slippers, their hair styled and pinned, whereas Louisa Hill was smartly dressed in a navy skirt and jacket, the ruffle of her snow-white blouse pinned with a cameo brooch at her throat.

Two whores and their madam.

Louisa Hill rose from a writing desk in front of the window, her eyes shining with kindness. 'Mr Carlyle. How lovely to see you again. Why don't you take a seat beside Nancy? Can I get you something to drink?'

'Brandy would be most welcome, thank you.' Francis didn't look at Jacob as he left the room; instead, he surveyed Nancy's friend, who sat in a wing-back chair, her narrowed eyes slowly travelling over him from head to toe. Then he turned to Nancy. Out of the two, Nancy's expression was marginally more affable.

He nodded. 'Miss Bloom, it's a pleasure to see you again.'

She smiled, but Francis was discomfited that it didn't quite reach her beautiful grey eyes. God, how he suddenly desperately wanted her to like him. Trust him.

He lowered onto the sofa beside her and accepted the glass Mrs Hill offered him before she discreetly returned to her desk. He sipped his drink and glanced at Nancy's friend, pleased she seemed to be immersed once more in the novel she read.

'So…' He looked at Nancy. 'Have you been well?'

'Incredibly. And you?'

The formality between them was unbearable when he had witnessed the joy and frivolity in Nancy when she danced and sang. That was the woman he wanted to see all the time, if such a thing was possible. Was his being here what made her sit so stiffly? Had his decision to accept her offer to meet her at her place of work been a mistake? The last thing he intended was to make her uncomfortable. He wanted – needed – to evoke the complete opposite in her. He looked at her again and her staid expression told him in no uncertain terms that she didn't want him there.

Did he stay or go?

'So, Mr Carlyle...' Louisa Hill closed her ledger and walked to a beautifully carved bureau in the corner of the room. She opened one of the two front doors and extracted a candelabra. 'I understand from Nancy you are a manager at the Royal. That must be exciting work.'

Francis coughed, all too aware of Nancy's stare boring into his temple. 'It is indeed. I love the theatre and my work there. Having the opportunity to direct and act in plays is a dream I have harboured since I was a child and now I have the means and position to ensure others have that same chance.'

'How wonderful.' Louisa Hill reached into a bureau drawer and took out some beeswax candles. 'I understand from Nancy and Octavia you were quite insistent with your introduction at the White Hart. I hadn't understood when you came here just how persistent a man you are.'

Despite her smile, clear warning shone in Louisa Hill's extraordinary eyes and Francis struggled not to fidget under the weight of her stare. 'I am indeed persistent, madam. I see no shame in that.'

She studied him a moment longer before she grinned. 'Neither do I, Mr Carlyle. Neither do I.'

Francis warmed to the woman who was clearly in charge of the house. A woman who radiated kindness and welcome, despite the shrewdness in her gaze and words. He leaned back into the cushions. 'Nancy's voice was like nothing I had ever heard. Full of depth and emotion. Light and love. In fact, I think Nancy could be—'

'Right, that's enough chit-chat.' Nancy abruptly stood and took Francis's glass from his hand. 'I don't believe you want your hard-earned money wasted talking about me and my enjoyment after one too many glasses of ale.' Her eyes twinkled with enticement and, if he wasn't mistaken, an underlying nervousness. 'Why don't we take your drink upstairs?'

Before he could so much as stand, Nancy was across the room and waiting at the door.

Francis stood, thoroughly enjoying her fire and ferocity. This woman became more and more who he wanted to star in his play with every different side she unwittingly revealed to him.

He nodded at Louisa Hill and then the other woman in the room, who he now knew to be named Octavia. She stared back at him, wariness glinting in her eyes.

'Good evening, ladies.'

Louisa smiled. 'Enjoy your evening, Mr Carlyle. We hope to see you again soon.'

Francis follow Nancy upstairs but, with each step, his confidence turned to apprehension. Christ, he was about to walk into her bedroom. Did he allow her to seduce him? He had no doubt his body would treacherously respond to her touch. Or did he distract her by sharing some of his aspirations? As much as he appreciated her beauty and figure, he had to tread carefully if he was to gain her trust that he had a professional reason for being at the house.

But how could he soften her? Make her warm to him and no longer regard him as the enemy? What he intended for her was entirely honourable and deserved, considering her natural ability to capture an audience... hang it, to capture *him*. But he also respected her suspicion of his motives. How else would a prostitute react to his claims?

He studied her auburn hair, pinned and curled, leaving her nape exposed in all its beauty. Her height didn't stretch any further than a couple of inches over five feet, but Nancy Bloom exuded the confidence and power of a woman so much taller. Her mere presence onstage would undoubtedly quieten even the most boisterous audience the moment she stepped onto the boards.

Every curve of her slender body moved seductively beneath the silk of her robe as she walked along the landing, her every movement sending a twitch through Francis's groin...

She opened a bedroom door and gestured with a wave that he enter ahead of her.

As the lock clicked behind him, Francis took a moment to study her boudoir. It suited her to perfection.

The bed was large and swathed in a satin coverlet and pillows of the deepest emerald green. Matching drapery framed the window and tasselled throws hung over her dressing table and drawers, both littered with a plethora of bottles, jars and boxes. Ropes of pearls and glinting brooches scattered a small side table and an open novel had been laid on each of the bedside tables.

'I always read two books at the same time.' Her voice broke the silence. 'Because I... So I don't get bored.'

The mentality somehow did not surprise him any more than the colours she'd chosen to decorate her room. Everything was so her.

Francis removed his hat and laid it on the bed. 'What do you like to read?'

'Anything and everything.' She lifted her chin, almost in challenge as she came closer, her gaze travelling up and down his body in such a way that could be interpreted as professional: a whore preparing to take her prey. Yet Francis suspected that, if anything, her assessment was born from a need to avoid his eyes.

'But books are not what we are here to discuss tonight. I think there is little need to discuss anything, in fact.'

Her fingers slipped over his jacket lapels and then down to the buttons. She released each one by one before looking into his eyes. A pathetic pleasure rippled through him that she now seemed happier. Almost satisfied they were alone, and she was at work.

But he wasn't here for *that* work. He knew it, even if his damn anatomy did not.

He cleared his throat. 'Nancy, you don't need to—'

'I do, Francis.' The skin at her neck shifted as she swallowed, and a soft pleading shadowed her gaze. 'I need to do this, and *you* need to let me.'

He nodded, any protestation dying in his throat at the sound of his Christian name on her lips. She slipped her hands over his shoulders and pushed his jacket from his body to heap on the floor. Standing on her toes, she lifted her lips to his neck and trailed kisses as light as angels' feet over his skin. His eyes drifted closed and a guttural moan whispered from deep inside of him.

Once she'd unbuttoned his shirt, her soft hands glided over his torso, higher to scale her nails through the hair on his chest. He shivered involuntarily and hungrily captured her mouth, unable to resist any longer. Their tongues met and Francis's erection strained.

God, she was more than he could handle, but handle her he must. She was the one.

She eased back from him and took his hand and, somehow, he managed to open his eyes.

She smiled up at him, her grey eyes alight with satisfaction. 'Still want to waste time talking?'

'You're the one, Nancy.'

A flash of panic passed through her eyes before she blinked as if trying to conceal her brief vulnerability. 'The one what?'

'Just the one.' Before she could respond, Francis swept her into his arms and onto the bed.

She stared up at him, her eyes wide with wonder and shock. 'What are you—'

His bravado rose with his need to match her courage and confidence. 'But you're right, here and now, talking would be wasted.'

Possessing her lips again, Francis surrendered as his entire being filled with want and desire for the irresistible Nancy Bloom.

11

'Will you lower your voice?' Nancy hissed as she glanced around the small but busy dress shop. 'Someone will overhear you.'

'And what if they do?' Octavia's brow creased as she studied the skirt and jacket on the mannequin in front of her. 'Doesn't every woman talk when they are dress shopping? Anyway, if my pressing you about Mr Carlyle's invitation is causing you to be so touchy, it can only mean you are considering saying yes.'

'I am not.' Nancy feigned intense interest in the outfit's sage-green material even though buying a new walking suit barely occupied a second of her scrambled thoughts. 'What on earth was the man thinking by leaving an invitation for me with Jacob? I have no idea why Mr Carlyle would think I would even consider joining him at the theatre and then dinner.'

Octavia stepped towards a glass-topped counter containing a lavish array of gloves. 'Because, my darling, Mr Carlyle likes you, that's why.'

'Hmm, and now Louisa is on the scent like a bloodhound.'

'And as for you...' Octavia turned and looked pointedly at

Nancy. 'I think you didn't entirely hate your time with him last night either.'

Nancy quickly looked away, cursing the heat that rose in her cheeks. The man had been infuriatingly good company. So good that the two hours she'd spent with him passed quickly. Too quickly.

She sighed. 'He was nice enough, but still, I really wish he hadn't spoken to Jacob.'

'Why not? An invitation to the theatre and dinner is the most interesting request.' Octavia raised her eyebrows, her blue eyes curious. 'And the fact it has you in a quandary over whether or not to accept makes it more interesting than ever.'

Nancy turned away from her friend's wily gaze as common sense battled with her need to share why the decision was causing her such difficulty. If the invitation had only been for dinner, and with anyone else, she might have accepted. After all, what whore refuses a night out and being paid for her time without the need to lie on her back?

The trouble was, this invitation had come from Francis Carlyle. A theatre manager. And her pull to the Royal only grew stronger. He interested her, intrigued her and, if that was not dangerous enough, there had been moments... long moments... when she'd been naked with him that she had forgotten she was a whore. He hadn't touched her as so many culls had. He'd been gentle, considerate. Watched her face intensely as though wanting to take note of every change... like a lover who wanted to bring her satisfaction and pleasure.

Worse, she'd forgotten about her own role as a conduit for *his* satisfaction. Instead, she'd revelled in every ounce of erotic pleasure he'd bestowed on her. She had reached orgasm. There had been no feigning, no crying out in exaggerated pleasure. Instead, a soft mewl had left her and then... then she'd whispered his name.

'Oh, for the love of God...' Nancy snatched up her gloves from where she'd laid them on the countertop. 'The man is a pain in my backside. Nothing more, nothing less.'

A quartet of women standing nearby immediately halted their chatter, the small shop seeming to descend into a heavy, ominous silence. Nancy snapped her gaze to Octavia, silently pleading with her that they leave.

Now.

Octavia's brows almost brushed her hairline, her bright blue eyes positively jubilant. 'So it is as I thought,' she said, before facing the women who blatantly stared at them. 'Good afternoon, ladies. You must excuse my friend. She has just realised what it is to be married and thus had the need to expel a little frustration. I'm sure you understand.'

Nancy's shoulders immediately dropped as the urge to laugh out loud trembled in her stomach. For all Octavia's uppity middle-class ways, she was a woman who had known the streets as much as she had undoubtedly known what it was to eat from silver plate. Neither Nancy, Louisa nor Jacob could ever tell who or what would evoke either side of their complex friend.

'Come along, Nancy.' Octavia gripped Nancy's elbow. 'I don't see anything I like, do you?'

Nancy nodded at the women and allowed Octavia to propel her from the shop and out into the street.

Once they were few steps along the road, Nancy burst out laughing. 'Did you see their faces? We should not be allowed in these shops. I know Louisa likes us to dress in a way that reflects the success of the brothel but, my God, we are whores through and through.'

'And proud of it.' Octavia grinned. 'Now, back to business. I am not going to accept your refusal of Mr Carlyle's invitation without good reason. If Jacob is unconcerned by Mr Carlyle's attention towards you and is happy for you to go out with him, why wouldn't you? Why, he's even willing to pay for your time on top of the cost of the theatre and dinner. Why on earth would you not accept such an offer?'

Because I'm starting to like him! Christ, I damn near wanted to eat him when we were in bed together. Nancy cleared her throat and stared along the street. 'Because Mr Carlyle seems just a little too good to be true. Yes, I find him... amiable. But what surprises me more is that you do.'

'I didn't say that.'

'If you're encouraging me to be alone with him, away from the house, it means that you have taken to him. Usually you're more protective of Louisa and me than a lioness with her young. Especially after...' Nancy swallowed '...my attack last year.'

Octavia bristled, her jaw tightening as she stared ahead. 'Yes, well, I sense Mr Carlyle is *nothing* like Mr Chaney.'

Memories filled Nancy's mind. Francis's tenderness, the feel of his lips on her mouth and body, the way he whispered her name over and over again as though she was a goddess... She sighed. 'No, he's no Mr Chaney.'

'Then why deliberate over his offer?'

'Let's go to the gardens and sit awhile...' Nancy exhaled a shaky breath. 'I have something I need to tell you, but you must promise you'll not breathe a word to Louisa. I don't want her looking at me with pity. I couldn't bear it.'

Octavia slipped her arm into the crook of Nancy's elbow, her blue gaze filled with care and concern as she studied Nancy's face. 'Whatever you want. You know that.'

As they walked, Nancy grappled with the words she wanted to say. How much or how little to share in order to obtain Octavia's wisdom but, at the same time, not reveal enough that she would look at her as a victim. As a woman who could not look after herself.

Because she could.

They entered Parade Gardens and found an empty bench. Couples walked back and forth, the women in a pretty array of soft-coloured dresses, their matching parasols open against the early June sunshine. Birds flitted back and forth in the trees and barely a cloud marred a clear blue sky. The day was as close to idyllic as it could be, yet nothing but blackness crept inside Nancy and, once again, darkened her view of the world.

'So, what is it?' Octavia asked, gently. 'What do you want to tell me?'

Nancy stared into her friend's eyes, knowing she could trust her, knowing Octavia would never play judge or jury.

Nancy released her held breath. 'My singing isn't something new. I've always sung. I sang as a child. I would sing when I washed the clothes that my ma took in to clean and press. I sang while I bathed my younger brother and helped prepare the family meal.' She looked across the parkland ahead of them, tears blurring her vision. 'I sang all the time until *him*.'

'Him?'

Nancy faced her, bitterness coating her mouth. 'Whenever I could, I went to the Theatre Royal and sat in the cheapest seats to watch the actors and actresses. I had dreams bigger than the world that one day that would be me. Up there, onstage with an audience clapping and cheering my flawless performance. And then...'

'And then what?'

'And then a man I assumed to be a gentleman approached me. I was fourteen and he told me he knew of a theatre company looking for a young woman just like me to fill a part. Well...'

Nancy huffed a laugh and swiped at a tear that rolled over her cheek. 'I leaped at the chance and when he agreed to meet Ma and Pa, they believed his offer too. He even gave them money, saying more would follow once the show opened.'

'But…' Octavia took her hand and held it tight. 'He wasn't with a theatre company.'

'No, he took me away and I didn't return to Bristol for two years. By the time I was sixteen, I was of no use to him. A girl who looks too much like a woman is surplus to a man who sells children.'

Octavia's fingers tightened on Nancy's and she squeezed her eyes shut. 'Oh, Nancy.'

'It's fine. I'm strong now, but having Francis… Mr Carlyle say the things he said to me. To promise if I trust him, he will see me onstage.' Nancy shook her head, her heart aching with longing and fear. 'It makes me so very afraid of him.'

She swallowed around the lump in her throat as the silence stretched. Her heart weighed heavier and heavier with the shame and humiliation that she had suffered at the hands of the man who'd kidnapped her. That she had seen, heard and done things that no child, woman or anyone should have to endure.

'But you're not a young girl anymore, Nancy,' Octavia said, quietly. 'You can call a stop to Mr Carlyle's attentions whenever you wish to. Whatever he might ask of you, you can refuse. Better still, challenge him. If his intentions for this night out are entirely honourable and without condition, insist that Louisa or I accompany you.' Octavia lifted her thumb to Nancy's cheeks and brushed away her tears. 'You have us and Jacob looking out for you now.'

'I know.'

'Might it not be that it is something more than what he wants that scares you?'

'What else could there be?'

'I suspect you are scared of spending more time with him because of how much you like him. Am I right?'

Denial sprang onto Nancy's tongue, yet she hesitated. She could not lie to Octavia any more than she could Louisa. 'Yes.' Nancy sighed, her pathetic resistance to Francis and what he might be able to give her overriding her good sense. 'You're right.'

'Then go out with him.' Octavia smiled. 'Show him that anything he wants, or asks of you, will be on your terms or not at all.'

Nancy stared into her friend's eyes as the possibility that Francis might be truthful, might be the door to a new life, wound tight in her stomach. What if he was sincere and the life that had been her dream for as long as she could remember had the possibility of coming true at his hands? She was a grown woman now, knew her own mind and relied on her own strength.

He couldn't possibly hurt her as she had been hurt before.

Why shouldn't she take a small step forward and judge for herself how sincere Mr Carlyle might be in his pursuit of her? His soft blue gaze filled her mind's eye and slowly, second by second, Nancy's agreement to their night out rose inside of her. She had never met a man as kind as Francis. Never met a man who seemed so strong yet vulnerable. So admiring of her despite knowing what she did for a living.

His adulation made no sense. *He* made no sense. Yet...

She swiped her fingers under her eyes and pulled back her shoulders. 'You're right. I'm older now. Wiser. I'll go with him and make sure he pays me on top of everything else. The theatre can't scare me. Not anymore. And nor can Francis Carlyle.'

12

Francis stepped from his carriage and stood on the pavement outside Nancy's house. He glanced at Jacob where he stood sentry in his usual place on the top step. The doorman nodded by way of greeting before looking away along the street.

So far, so good.

Inhaling a long breath, Francis turned to Edmund, who sat at the front of the carriage, the horses' reins in his hands. 'I won't be long.'

'Take your time.' His friend and servant looked at the house. 'I understand how *some* ladies can take more time preparing themselves for an evening out than a gentleman originally might imagine. Although as far as the type of ladies who live here are concerned, I have no idea what they do or don't take the time to do.'

Francis crossed his arms. 'Is there something you'd like to say about my being here, Edmund?'

Edmund scowled and stared ahead. 'No.'

'Good, because I would hate to think of you straining yourself unnecessarily by holding back.'

Turning, Francis approached the house's steps. Despite his cool tone with Edmund, unease knotted Francis's stomach. The last thing he needed was his servants discussing his associating with a prostitute. Clearly, Edmund knew the house to be a brothel considering his scathing comments. Unless it was a case of Edmund protesting too much? Indignation rippled through Francis. Well, Edmund could mind his own business as much as anyone else who felt inclined to judge. After all, Francis knew better than most how people sometimes had no option but to do what they had to in order to survive. Neither he nor Edmund knew Nancy, Louisa or Octavia, which meant neither of them were in any position to judge their way of living.

Francis nodded at Jacob before following him inside the house.

'Just wait here and I'll let Nancy know you're—'

'There's no need, Jacob. I'm ready.'

Francis shot his gaze to the top of the stairs and his heart damn near stopped. 'Miss Bloom,' he said, softly.

She descended, her grey eyes on his, a knowing smile curving her lips. Dressed in a plum-coloured dress, she looked radiant. The bodice was cut in such a manner that her shoulders and exquisite collarbones were revealed, her auburn curls pinned high, leaving her neck bare. The black lace at the centre of the gown was accentuated by her black petticoat, jewellery and a trio of feathers in her hair.

Once she stood in front of him, she bobbed a curtsey. 'Will I do for the theatre, Mr Carlyle?'

Somehow, he managed to find his voice. How in God's name was such perfection possible? 'You look beautiful... like an actress, in fact.'

Her smile wavered and the light in her eyes ever so slightly dimmed. 'Thank you.'

'Did I say something wro—'

'We should go.' She quickly turned to Jacob. 'I won't be too late. Make sure Louisa doesn't start fretting if the clock strikes twelve and I'm not home. I have the night to myself, after all.'

Her usual cheekiness had returned, and Francis should have been relieved, but the thought he had upset her with what he'd intended as a compliment harangued him. Tonight was about Nancy. About making her accept how amazing she was; how, with her voice and magnetism, she belonged in his play.

Francis quickly followed her outside to where she stood on the pavement, her stare fixed on the carriage, then the horses, and finally Edmund before she faced Francis.

'Is this carriage yours?'

'It is,' he said, reaching for the door. 'Do you like it?'

'It's... big.' Hesitation flashed in her eyes and she took a tentative step back as though considering whether or not to flee back into the house. 'And fancy.'

He smiled. 'Yes, I suppose it is.'

She looked from him to the carriage then abruptly flashed him a smile before taking his offered hand and climbing aboard. She sat down and stared with wide eyes at the pale blue satin interior.

Francis sat beside her, pleased that the light was back in her eyes and her smile seemingly genuine. Whatever had troubled her appeared forgotten, so he forcefully buried his tension and knocked on the roof, signalling the off to Edmund.

The carriage gave a jolt and the horses' hooves clip-clopped away from the house. Francis inhaled deeply to calm his obstinate nerves, and the light, floral scent of Nancy's perfume infused his nostrils. Roses and something else. Something musky and dangerous. Not unlike her. As desire to kiss her tingled on his lips, Francis pulled them tightly together, resisting the sudden urge to fill the silence with senseless chatter.

Instead, he revelled in Nancy's changing expressions as she leaned closer to the window and watched the passing people, shops and eateries. Her eyes were as wide as her smile, as her little squeaks of amusement punctuated the air as though she was seeing Bath's sights for the first time. Warmth spread through Francis's chest as hope that she was relaxed in his company rose. He couldn't help but wonder how long she had lived in the city. He had assumed her familiar with everything and everyone from their limited conversations, but the excitement in her gaze told him this experience was entirely new to her.

She abruptly faced him, her beautiful grey eyes alight with happiness. 'It's so funny seeing everything from inside a carriage as grand as this. I feel like the Queen.'

Satisfaction rippled through him and he winked, pleased beyond measure that he had brought her such pleasure.

They soon pulled up alongside the Theatre Royal and Francis opened the door, offering his hand as she stepped onto the pavement. She stared up at the theatre's facade and, once again, Francis's heart dropped. Her smile had vanished, her eyes worried.

'Nancy?'

She started and turned. 'Yes?'

'Are you all right?' Francis glanced towards the theatre's open doors as men and women entered, a plethora of shining silks and glittering jewels. 'If you've changed your mind, then we could just—'

'I haven't.' She took his arm. 'I'm glad to be here. With you.'

'Good.' Relieved, he turned to Edmund. 'You can take the carriage back. We will walk to dinner from here and, after that, I will ensure Miss Bloom is returned safely home.'

Edmund's gaze never left the back of Nancy's head, his face unreadable. 'As you wish, sir.'

Annoyed and infinitely curious about his friend's clear disapproval of Nancy, Francis covered her hand where it lay on his arm. 'Let's go.'

When they reached the private box Francis had reserved for the performance, the concern on Nancy's face and the stiff set of her shoulders made him falter. Where his nerves were coming from, he had no idea. For so long, he had thought himself in control, confident and established. Yet, he wanted Nancy so badly to like him, he doubted his every word and action. Had he been too extravagant? The sight of his carriage had certainly unnerved her. Even being here, at the Royal, seemed to be unsettling her.

He gently touched her elbow where she stood at the front of the box. 'Won't you take a seat?' he asked. 'Champagne will be brought to us shortly.'

She looked to the chairs, then the stage, before she gave a hesitant smile. 'Of course.'

Once their champagne was poured, and Nancy had taken a few hearty mouthfuls, she seemed to relax and Francis answered her questions about his work at the theatre, if he knew anyone famous and what production he had planned next. He tried to answer with as much clarity and enthusiasm as possible. Now was not the time to tell her about his real plans. She was clearly nervous, and putting pressure on her tonight would be foolish. Time and again, the look in her eyes mirrored his horses' whenever he thought they might bolt.

The lights lowered and she immediately turned to the stage, leaning forward in her seat, her empty champagne glass clutched in her fingers. She sat, seemingly entranced, as the actors performed the melodrama he had especially selected for her to watch. The play was a mix of drama and comedy. The actors offering skills of every variety and competence. He prayed that by the end of the performance, when he told her what he believed her capable of, she would accept his sincerity. For he had no doubt that Nancy Bloom could outshine even the most seasoned performer given time.

She turned and smiled, her eyes shining as though she fought tears. 'Thank you for inviting me here tonight, Francis. Thank you so much.'

'You're welcome.'

An unexpected lump lodged in his throat as she drew her gaze over his face, her smile faltering as she lingered a moment on his lips before she faced the stage once more. Francis's heart beat faster as a deep certainty that he was destined to meet her whispered through him. Every inch of his soul told him he was meant to go into the White Hart that night, was meant to witness this extraordinary woman singing and entertaining the crowds as only Nancy could.

Her spirit was raw, her beauty unimaginable.

She would evoke emotion in even the coldest of hearts. The perfect vessel to convey his story, to show the world – no, *implore* the world – that things had to change for the poor. That the workhouse and everything it represented could not go on as it had for all these years. Eventually, he would tell her that his play was about him and its events had really happened; no part of the tale fictitious.

But for now, he wanted to be her hero. Strong and steadfast, capable of eliminating anything that might come across her path and dare to extinguish the beautiful, shining light in her eyes. He wanted her to see him as a good man. A man of strength and conviction who held the power to make her a star.

A deep sense of certainty made him sit taller. In time, Nancy Bloom would learn the truth of his beginnings, of his past and his existence amid the cruel events he had now recorded in script.

But not quite yet...

13

The actors took their final bow and Nancy sank into her seat, her palms stinging from her exuberant applause. The play had been astounding. Mesmerising. Entrancing. Everything from the acting to the set, to the music, had caused a sphere of emotions to run through her like a magical river. Everything had been perfect.

Blinking from her stupor, she turned to find Francis carefully watching her, his blue eyes dark with something she couldn't quite decipher, his expression sombre. Yet, unwanted attraction towards this handsome cull stirred deep in her core. Even seemingly annoyed, the man was ridiculously appealing.

'Well...' She laughed as she regained her composure, stooping to the floor to retrieve her purse. 'That was quite the performance. You are an absolute sweetheart for bringing me along.'

'A sweetheart?'

Startled by his curt response, Nancy faced him.

His expression hadn't changed, his jaw still tight. 'I would not have thought that was what you really consider me.'

Unease raised the hairs on her arms. Although she had certainly witnessed moments of intensity in Francis, mostly she had found him to be jovial and happy. Considering their current circumstances, this change in him was more than a little alarming. Her mind scrambled with why such a gentle, offhand remark might upset him. Had he expected more from her tonight? To be a companion this evening in a more demonstrative way? After all, she was hardly a woman of pedigree stepping out on his arm. She was but a whore...

Yet, pride swept through her and Nancy tilted her chin. 'I presumed you only wanted my company tonight. Nothing more, nothing less. Your words to Jacob, Francis, not mine.'

'I do.'

'Then stop looking as though everything about me has disappointed you.' She stood and glared at him. 'The agreement was to the theatre and dinner. If you are regretting that decision, that's your fault. Not mine.' She stepped towards the door. 'Now, if you don't mind, I'm famished, so I suggest we make haste before my rumbling stomach angers you even further.'

'Angers me?'

'Yes.'

He closed his eyes, his voice softer. 'God, Nancy, angry is the last thing I am.'

She gripped her purse, confusion scrambling her brain and emotions as he stared at her again. This time his blue eyes were filled with admiration, his smile utterly disarming.

'Then why look at me so gravely?' Tightening her hand on the doorknob, her heart stuttered. 'I have no idea what sort of game you're playing, Mr Carlyle, but you should know that I am nobody's fool. I might be a whore, but I am a whore who has the benefit of making her own choices and choosing her own company.'

'Did you not hear what I said? I am not angry with you.'

'Oh, I heard you but I know how men work, how changeable

they can be, and so I have no idea of your sincerity regarding how you are feeling about me right now. The way you looked at me before was far from friendly.'

'I was merely thinking—'

'You should know that I thought long and hard about coming out with you this evening, and if I had thought, even for a moment, that your company would be anything less than amiable, I would have flatly refused.' She opened the door. 'Now, assuming tonight is still about you convincing me of my acting talents, I think we should head to dinner, don't you?'

Nancy strode into the busy corridor, her cheeks blazing with the depth of her annoyance, but her chin high. Francis had been looking at her as a woman under his possession. A companion who was his to treat however he chose while they were together. Her reaction had been instinctive and unreasonable, but God damn it, it had hurt to see him looking at her with such blatant irritation. She had so hoped that he might look at her as someone he was proud to be spending an evening with.

'Damn you, Francis.'

Nancy continued along the corridor, but a woman dressed in finery – and unaccompanied – did not go unnoticed and stares burned into her from every direction. Open glances and undisguised disapproval brought forth tuts from elderly well-to-do ladies and smirks from their pretty young daughters.

Nancy swallowed back her discomfort. Somewhere behind her, Francis's raised call echoed from the dark, velvet-covered walls, but she ignored him in her desperation for the exit. How dare he act so kindly, so gallantly, only to expect her to be with him in public as she'd been with him at Carson Street. She was no longer a streetwalker. Her business was done behind a closed bedroom door and she prayed to God that would always be true.

A strong hand gripped her elbow and Nancy fought her every

instinct to snatch it from Francis's grip and turn on him with cat-like ferocity. He would not reduce her to what she'd once been. She was not that person anymore and never would be again.

'Nancy—'

'Can we please just get out of this godforsaken theatre?' she hissed through clenched teeth. 'Anything you have to say to me can be said from across a dining room table.'

They walked outside and, with each step, the erratic beat of Nancy's heart levelled, her inner strength and pride gathering strength. They walked through the gaslit streets towards the restaurant, her arm enfolded in Francis's as he stared ahead, his jaw tight and tension tangibly radiating from him. Maybe her snapping at him could be deemed a little overdramatic, but the need to defend her position had been just. Boundaries were a whore's armour and the sooner he realised that, the better.

She might have put his nose out of joint and maybe he was mad that she'd had the audacity to indulge in an evening for her own pleasure, allowed her attention to wander from the man for what he deemed much too long a period, but that was her right. Irritation bubbled dangerously inside her. Just because Francis had shown her some tenderness during their *paid* sex did not make him an anomaly.

He gently tugged her arm, drawing her to a stop.

Nancy turned to the closed doors of the elegantly decorated restaurant beside her and a shameful ingratitude descended, diluting her anger to a simmer. 'We're to eat here?'

He nodded, his gaze boring into hers. 'Yes, if you still wish it?'

The last of her irritation faltered. Now he looked at her kindly and with admiration... hell, the man could sometimes look at her in the most pleasurable way. Taking a long, deep breath, she sighed. 'If it is your wish, then it is mine, too.'

Taking her by surprise, he leaned closer and pressed a brief kiss to her cheek. 'I'm sorry if I upset you,' he said quietly as he moved back. 'Believe me, that's the last thing I will ever want.'

Words stuck in her throat and her cheek tingled from his kiss as he led her inside the fancy, undoubtedly overpriced restaurant. She stared at his chiselled profile, her stomach once again tumbling with unfamiliar desire, unfamiliar fondness. He was an odd combination of silk and steel. Sometimes he held the vulnerability of a little boy lost. At others, he could stare someone down in a way that spoke of a man capable of pummelling another to the ground without so much as drawing a harried breath.

The combination was entirely intoxicating. And dangerous. Both to Nancy's equilibrium and to Louisa's business. Nancy internally shook herself. If she started to feel anything other than professionalism for Francis, she would have broken the golden rule. Absolutely no feelings for culls. None. Ever.

Such weakness could lead to problems. Financial and emotional.

She had to keep her loyalty to Louisa and Octavia at the forefront of her heart and mind.

Always.

Francis led her inside the restaurant, placing his hand at the base of her spine. Nancy was woman enough to admit she felt herself entirely weakened. He was still set on the notion of her performing onstage. How that would be possible and how true his power to bring such nonsense to fruition was still up for judgement, but the least she could do was listen to him.

It wasn't until their first course was set before them that she managed to coerce her focus solely on the reason she had agreed to come out with him that evening... and it had nothing to do with a glamorous excursion or his determination to court her decision. Rather, her own need to believe what he proposed might have the slightest chance of becoming true.

'So...' He picked up his knife and fork, his eyes sombre. 'I'm afraid I intend to keep asking you to work with me until you agree, Nancy. I want to put you onstage. I want to see you perform my words at the Theatre Royal.'

Nancy reached for her wine and studied him over its rim, quietly pleased that her earlier ill temper and storming from the theatre – his place of work, no less – seemed to have not affected his ambitions for her. In fact, if anything, his gaze now held an avid hunger. As though he'd seen in her what he had needed to see.

She lowered the glass to the table. 'Yet you know nothing about me, and so I fail to understand what leads you to pursue me the way you are.'

'That's simple. You emanate strength and tenacity. There is something deep inside of you that emerges when you are performing.' He took her hand where it lay on the table, his fingers curling around hers. 'I know you will be the most wonderful actress.'

'Why? You have nothing on which to base such an assumption. You have only seen me sing once and that was in the White Hart of all places! How can you be so certain I have any acting talent whatsoever?'

'Because I have watched hundreds of auditions, watched countless actors and actresses work and perform. But you...' He shook his head. 'You have something entirely your own. Something natural and so very, very real. All you need is the opportunity to show what you can do.'

Possibility and excitement warred inside of her. Just to hear him say he thought so much of her had acceptance of his offer flailing on Nancy's tongue. 'I still think you are expecting far too much.'

'I want you to speak my words, Nancy. Convey their meaning. Reiterate their message.'

He was paying little heed to her protestations, yet she couldn't help but ask more of him. 'Which is?'

He slowly slid his hand from hers and glanced around the room, his cheeks slightly reddening. 'All in good time.'

Curiosity rose inside Nancy... along with a hefty dose of wariness. What in God's name was this play about?

He speared a piece of potato. 'My play needs a female lead who has known hardship. Someone who can really understand the emotions of the main character. Of what he... she... is fighting for and against.' He put the potato into his mouth and chewed, carefully watching her. He swallowed. 'What it is to dream of escape, of rescue. Correct me if I'm wrong, but I sense you have felt both of those things.'

Nancy's mouth dried but she forced a smile. 'You've barely known me five minutes and you can see that when you look me?' She picked up her knife and fork. 'Your talents just keep coming, Mr Carlyle.'

'I'm serious.'

She slowly raised her eyes to his. He had no need to tell her that – his seriousness was palpable, and Nancy was beginning to sense that Francis Carlyle was a man who had the innate ability to get anything he wanted. A man of determination, tenacity and feeling. A man like none other she had ever met... and she had met a lot.

But the risk, if she should fall for his words – his promise – was too high. How could she gamble on a dream when she stood to lose everything she now held dear?

She cleared her throat. 'The least you can do is tell me what your play is about.'

'The workhouse.'

She almost choked. That was the last thing she'd expected. 'The workhouse?'

'Yes.' He held her gaze. 'And everything that goes on behind those thick, grey walls.'

'But that must mean the play is a serious drama. You have only seen me sing and lark about beside a piano. Why would you think me the right woman to play such a part? I'm a good-time girl.' She flapped her hand dismissively. 'Good old Nancy. Game for a laugh and a giggle. I don't *do* serious.'

He slowly smiled and leaned forward, his gaze on her lips, her hair and, finally, her eyes. 'Oh, you do serious, Nancy. I've seen it. I've felt it, and I have no doubt it will render an audience enraptured. You are serious and you are passionate. And I promise you, you are perfect.'

She shook her head. Did he think her a fool? 'There must be a hundred women in Bath who can turn a tune at a piano. Why not look elsewhere when I have refused you? You must know a thousand actresses who would bite your hand off for the chance to star in your production. Why me?'

He put down his knife and fork and dabbed his napkin to his lips. 'To be frank, I have absolutely no idea if I am right in putting every ounce of my belief in you, but something is driving me to do just that. When I walked into that pub, the last thing I expected was to see a woman who would make everything I have been writing make sense, but that's what happened.' He leaned forward. 'You are my star, Nancy. I am happy for there to be no other reason than this force in my chest telling me so. Can that be enough for you, too?'

Temptation poked and prodded her, provoked by his seemingly sincere summary of her as a person she could not recognise. But she would neither believe nor trust him... not yet.

Nancy sat a little taller in her seat. 'Well, then. Maybe the future will be brighter for both of us one day, but, for now, we are not writer and actress, Francis, not by a long stretch.'

'Then what are we?'

Nancy stared into his wonderful blue eyes, her heart picking up speed. 'You are my... associate.'

His smile burst like a breaking sun, lighting his eyes with undeniable relief. He picked up his glass and touched it to hers. He winked. 'Agreed.'

14

Francis longed to tighten his hold on Nancy's arm as they turned into Carson Street, half of him reluctant to let her go, the other wanting to follow her up the steps and into the house. He had no idea if he had managed to convince her to trust him, or even if he had stirred any ambition in her of what could be possible. Yet a definite shift had occurred between them.

Something that had brought them imperceptibly closer, which, in turn, had reawakened the desire he'd experienced when he'd bedded her. Yet there was every possibility the flashes of fondness and respect he'd seen in her eyes across the restaurant table could have been little more than his imagination. Well, whether they were or not, Nancy Bloom had well and truly caught his attention and desire.

But as they walked closer to her home, it wasn't just his wish for her to be the heroine in his play bothering him. He also felt a deepening need to spend time getting to know her. To see her laugh and smile and all the while consume every ounce of the joy that emanated from her.

'Here we are.'

Her voice broke through his haze of fantasy and he blinked. For once, Jacob wasn't on the front steps and Francis was thankful for small mercies. He still had so much he wished to say to Nancy tonight and having the doorman as a menacing audience was not his preferred scenario.

She slipped her hand from his arm and glanced towards the closed drapes at the house's window. 'I think Octavia only had two clients expected tonight so the house will be quiet if you'd like to come in for a nightcap?'

The temptation was agony even as Francis shook his head, his eyes taking in every detail of her exquisite face. 'Thank you, but no. I think it best I go.'

A flicker of disappointment flashed in her eyes before she smiled and wiggled her eyebrows. 'You think it best, Mr Carlyle? Are you afraid that I might ravish you on the parlour room sofa? I do have a modicum of self-control, you know.'

He grinned, his groin twitching awake. 'Do you? I did not bear witness to such control when we were last together inside this house.'

'Hmm, you forget I am a born actress, paid to provide a man's pleasure. Anything you witnessed was controlled, have no fear.'

Ignoring the stab of disappointment that jabbed deep in his gut, Francis stepped closer, desperate to kiss her but knowing, in doing so, he would jeopardise the careful shift in their relationship that he so intensely wanted to cultivate. He had to show her that she meant more to him than the physical. That he respected her. Believed in her.

'I will say goodbye but return very soon,' he said, brushing a stray auburn curl from her cheek. 'I won't give up until I have your complete trust. I can make you a star, Nancy, and will do anything to make that happen. Anything.'

She looked deep into his eyes, a line forming between her

brows. 'Is the prospect of us working together all you can think of? Even now, standing here?'

'Yes,' he lied.

'I see.' Regret clouded her gaze and she stepped back. 'Then I will bid you goodnight.'

As she made to walk into the house, Francis's resolve disintegrated. He lunged forward and gripped her wrist. 'Nancy...'

Her eyes burned with the fire he was coming to adore as she crossed her arms. 'I understand what you want from me, Francis, but you will not badger me. I've said I will think about your play. How long I will take thinking about it is my prerogative, so I would be grateful if you would—'

'I wasn't born rich.' The words fell from his tongue before he could stop them, but he had to do something more to bolster her trust, to show he was not a dandy looking in any way to seduce or use her. 'My work at the theatre and my writing are my entire life. Asking you to star in my play is not a frivolous or conditioned request. I have worked hard to get to where I am and I want the same successes for you too.'

'If that is true, you will allow me time to think about all you have said to me.'

Francis closed his eyes, terrified of the compulsion to tell her more, to share a little of the fire in his gut that refused to douse. That only burned hotter and hotter with each passing year that his past life remained hidden.

He opened his eyes. 'I was left in a foundling hospital as a babe and raised in the workhouse. The play... my play... is my story, Nancy. One that means everything to me.' He swallowed against the dryness in his throat as shame ached like a fresh bruise inside of him. 'I...'

'Oh, Francis.'

The pity in her eyes was excruciating and Francis's shame

deepened as she stared into his eyes, her gaze drifting over his face. She stepped closer and raised onto her toes. *Don't kiss me. God, don't kiss me.* She gently gripped the lapels of his jacket and pulled him close, her lips tentatively touching his as though testing his desire, his yearning for her touch.

It was more than he could bear and the first planks of the carefully erected dam around his memories broke, spilling his need for love and understanding like blood from a new wound. He cupped her jaw and kissed her with every ounce of the turmoil that writhed inside him every minute of every day. She had torn the beast from its tethers. A warrior woman not already known to him but one he just happened upon. Their meeting was a miracle. One he had no choice but to pursue to its end.

She pulled back, her quickened breath dancing across his tender mouth before she laid her head to his shoulder, her body softly trembling.

Francis stood immobile, his heart hammering, his body paralysed. What did her trembling mean? Had he upset her? Struck a chord within her that might lead to their union? Or their separation?

Slowly, she eased away from him, tears glistening in her eyes as she softly smiled. 'Goodnight, Francis.'

Physical and emotional sensations rolled through his body as Francis watched her climb the steps and walk inside, closing the door behind her. What happened next, he had no idea, but he'd bared just a little of his pain and he prayed with all of his heart that his exposure would demonstrate his sincerity.

Nancy was a star. *His* star.

15

Nancy looked up from her knitting as Jacob entered the room. His furrowed brow and tight, white lips making him seem somewhat irked. She laughed. 'Good Lord, what on earth is the matter with you?'

'You, as it happens.'

Nancy slowly lowered her knitting. She could count on one hand how many times Jacob had been upset with her since he'd come to work at the house over a year before. 'Me?'

'Yes, Nancy. You.'

She glanced at Louisa, who stood at the other side of the room considering three dresses hung from the bookcases. Seemingly oblivious to Jacob's presence or tone, Louisa's hands remained firmly on her hips as though her choice of what to wear on her sojourn to the Assembly Rooms later was a mathematical equation.

Assuming little support from her friend, Nancy lifted her chin and faced Jacob. 'What's the matter?'

He strode to Louisa, pressed a kiss to her cheek, before standing by the window and looking out along the street. 'Francis

Carlyle, that's what.' He spun around and pinned Nancy with a glare. 'For crying out loud, will you just agree to see the man?'

Nancy returned to her knitting, warmth climbing up her neck. 'I will when I am good and ready. I have things...' She swallowed. 'To consider.'

'What things?'

'Jacob...' Louisa abandoned the dresses and turned, her eyebrow raised and her eyes flashing with warning. 'Will you please calm down?'

'I would.' He glared at Nancy. 'If *she* would just give the man his peace. He's been back here at least half a dozen times since he took you to the theatre and still you refuse to see him. The man has vowed to pay way above the regular fee just to spend a few hours with you.' He looked at Louisa. 'Can you tell me when my position as investor and doorman in this brothel included pacifying men who find themselves half in love with Nancy or Octavia?'

Nancy's heart jolted and she pushed her knitting onto to the sofa beside her. 'What are you talking about? Francis is not half in love with me, he is half mad in the head with ambitions that I'm still not sure I want any part of.'

'Then I suggest you hurry up and decide your mind,' Jacob growled. 'Carlyle is looking to have me put him on his arse if he keeps coming here with his demands.'

Feeling annoyed and cornered, Nancy glared. 'Fine, then my mind is made up. I will tell him I am not interested in his offer and to let that be an end to it. Satisfied?'

'You don't mean that.' Louisa scowled at Jacob before sitting beside Nancy. 'Mr Carlyle clearly has ideas that—'

'That are beyond belief.' Nancy feigned interest in the row of perfect stitches on her needles. 'You can help me write him a message later.'

'And you really do not wish to listen to any more of what he has to say about this play of his?'

'No, I don't.' Nancy forced her eyes to Louisa's, hating the concern filling her friend's violet gaze. How on God's heavenly earth was she supposed to explain how much Francis's confessions about his early life had affected her? How much they had scared her that he might not be the self-assured and ambitious man she'd presumed him to be? 'The man is a law unto himself and I will not be dragged into his madness.'

'Why is his proposal madness? You like the theatre, don't you?'

Panic stirred deep inside Nancy as she looked from Louisa to Jacob and back again. The last thing she wanted was to have to further explain her resistance. They both considered her so strong and to fail in their eyes was the worst possible thing that could happen. If Louisa and Jacob suspected her hidden fragility – her hidden fear that Francis's wish to tell his story might also become hers – then that weakness could soon be suspected by her clients and her allure would all but dry up, leaving Louisa to wonder why she needed Nancy at all.

'I have been down this road before and have no wish to retrace my steps.' Nancy dropped her gaze to her knitting again in the hope they saw she wanted an end to this entirely pointless conversation. 'My place is here with you, not to entertain the plan of a man I barely know.'

Louisa's study bored into Nancy as she tried not to squirm under her friend's scrutiny. She had barely slept since her night out with Francis; had struggled to focus on her ministrations with her clients. Her mind was a mess and her heart heavy with Francis's admission of his dreadful beginnings. She had begun to feel for the man, begun to sympathise with him. Both of which were dangerous and utterly foolish reactions.

'Jacob, could you leave Nancy and I alone?'

Nancy snapped her head up, dread knotting her stomach as Louisa sat back and folded her hands in her lap. Clearly she was in no hurry to continue her task of choosing a dress.

Jacob crossed his huge arms. 'And what if Mr Carlyle decides to grace us with his presence again this afternoon?'

'You tell him Nancy will be in touch shortly.'

Jacob blew out a loud breath and stalked from the room, none too gently closing the door behind him.

Nancy flinched, her annoyance simmering. 'You won't persuade me differently on this, Louisa. Has it ever occurred to you that you might not always know what's best for me?'

Her friend's eyes darkened but Nancy held her gaze. They had known each other a long time and had battled over a hundred different things. It seemed Francis Carlyle had just become the catalyst for another argument. Well, come what may, this was a fight Nancy would win.

'This situation is getting ridiculous.' Louisa's eyes flashed with impatience. 'I want to know what is really going on here, because I have never known you to avoid confrontation with anyone. If Mr Carlyle is harassing you, why do you not just send him away, never to return? When have you ever hesitated from putting someone in their place, gentleman or not? Why this senseless avoidance?'

Nancy's heart raced. She had not seen Louisa this riled since her first husband's betrayal, which meant it was hurting her to see Nancy hiding away. Lately, Louisa's moods had swung from amiable to almost tearful within a blink of an eye, leaving Nancy and Octavia worried and concerned. Whatever bothered her friend, Nancy suspected it to be something personal between her and Jacob because business was booming with the house earning more money than it ever had before.

And now, instead of gently cajoling Louisa into sharing her worries, Nancy was adding another layer of concern to her friend's shoulders.

Guilt flooded through her and Nancy slumped. 'Oh, Lou. The last thing I want is to burden you. You don't seem yourself at the moment and—'

'I am perfectly all right.' Louisa's cheeks slightly coloured. 'It is you on my mind right now, nothing else.'

Their eyes locked, and seeing the stubbornness in her friend's eyes, Nancy relented. 'Fine. Francis Carlyle is... making things incredibly difficult for me.'

'In what way?' Louisa frowned, her gaze and voice softening. 'Let me help you to sort this out once and for all. I hate seeing you like this. Your usual buoyancy feels forced when you're with clients. Your teasing has half the temerity it had before and, frankly... you're not taking care of your appearance as meticulously either.'

Rather than feeling insulted, Nancy smiled wryly. She could hardly argue with that fact, could she? 'You've noticed, have you?'

Louisa smiled. 'Of course I have.'

Nancy closed her eyes, all too aware that if the signs of her inner torment were evident on the outside, then it was futile not to share with Louisa what was going on. She pushed to her feet and walked behind the sofa, gripping its edge. 'I like Mr Carlyle. Probably too much. But his insistence that I am the right person to star in his play is bringing up memories I'd rather forget. Memories that caused me two years of... torture.' Tears pricked her eyes and Nancy quickly blinked them back. She paced the room, her arms crossed. 'Then he shared a little of his beginnings and...' She stopped, faced Louisa. 'They were unexpected to say the least.'

'Well, what did he tell you?'

'He was given to the foundling hospital, abandoned by his mother, and then raised in the workhouse.' Nancy's heart ached for the lost boy Francis must have been as a child. A young child who would have had the same beautiful, deep blue eyes. She buried her sympathy and forced hardness into her heart. 'I can't possibly get any more involved with the man and not come to care for him. You know what I'm like, Lou. I've never been very good at helping other people through their pain. Mr Carlyle must remain a client only, or else seek companionship elsewhere. He has no idea what he is doing to me.'

'You have far too low an opinion of yourself. I have never known anyone so capable of helping others through their pain. Myself included.' Louisa slowly stood and strolled to the window. She looked out into the street before abruptly turning. 'You know very well what you are capable of overcoming. Of how encouraging you are. How you bolster belief in others. Why can you not do the same for Mr Carlyle? I don't understand why his flattering want of you to star in his play is causing you such alarm.'

Words and explanations flailed on Nancy's tongue and in her heart. Secrets she had kept hidden. Shame she had borne alone. But now she had shared her abduction with Octavia and not Louisa. It felt like such a betrayal to her friend, but there was only so much she could tell Louisa without losing the equality between them. She couldn't bear Louisa coddling her if she learned of her past and the stupidity on her part that had provoked the events that followed.

'Look, the whole idea is ridiculous.' Nancy closed her eyes, scrambling for any excuse other than the bare truth. She opened her eyes. 'How am I supposed to even read his play sufficiently? You have been teaching me letters and writing for a couple of years now, but I can hardly read and write well enough to understand and speak an entire script.'

'That is a feeble excuse.'

'It's the truth.' Deciding nonchalance was the best way forward, Nancy shrugged and fought to keep her face impassive. 'And anyway, it doesn't feel right that I might come to have a cull considering me his supporter. He's a paying client, Lou. Our relationship should be professional.'

'And he's asking you to make it personal?'

'Well, no, but if I just remain his paid whore, there would be no issue. Yet, it seems whenever he looks at me his work fills his mind. What does that say about me? About him?' She lifted her hands in frustration. 'The man is not right, Lou. He's... he's...'

'Interesting? Intriguing?' Louisa raised her eyebrows, her violet eyes amused. 'Making you think about him day and night?'

'I am not thinking about him day and night!' Nancy glared, her hands on her hips. 'What I *am* thinking about is why he's decided I am the one to help him.'

'Help him or work for him? There's a big difference.' Louisa strolled across the room and resumed her seat. She sighed. 'Look, why don't you write him a letter agreeing to meet him here this evening? He has already told Jacob he is willing to pay above the asking price to spend a couple of hours with you. If you are here, with us, what can he possibly say or do that will make you feel unprotected?'

Nancy stared, indignant. 'When did I say I feel unprotected?'

Seemingly ignoring her question, Louisa continued. 'If you wish him to leave, you only have to call Jacob.'

'Louisa, when did I say I feel unprot—'

'You didn't, but I know you, Nancy, and something about this man is making you feel vulnerable. Now, you view that as a bad thing, clearly. I, on the other hand, have learned a certain amount of vulnerability is never bad. So, I suggest you invite him here this evening and we'll take it from there.'

Incredulous, Nancy shook her head. 'When did this turn from my problem into our problem?'

Louisa smiled. 'Because that's the way it is between us.'

Nancy opened her mouth to protest but no words came. It had been her and Louisa against the world for so long she could not deny the truth of her friend's words. She blew out a defeated breath. 'How can I send him a letter when I don't even know where he lives?'

'Then address it to him at the Royal.'

'But if I invite him here, isn't that saying yes to his proposition?'

'Not at all. Although, to my mind, I think you're mad not to jump at the chance.'

'How can you say such a thing?' Hurt, Nancy stared at Louisa in disbelief. 'Am I that dispensable to you that you'd see me working away from Carson Street? Earning my money elsewhere and no longer a part of this house?'

'Of course not.'

'Then why are you encouraging me in this charade of Mr Carlyle's?'

'Because you're my best friend and I love you, that's why. This could be your dream come true, could it not? I don't know what happened to you years ago, but you have often referred to it and I know it had something to do with the theatre. If there is even the slightest chance that Mr Carlyle can make your horror disappear, why would you not take it?' Louisa stood and walked to the hung dresses. 'I think you should agree and see where it leads you. I refuse to allow you to make me or this house the obstacle.'

'Louisa, for goodness' sake, you need me here.'

'Of course I do, but we are doing well. Better than either of us could have predicted and I am in position to employ more girls if need be.' She pulled down one of the dresses to hold in front of her. 'Let Mr Carlyle woo you to his request. Make him work for your agreement, if necessary. But promise me you will not turn your back on a potentially better life because of me. I couldn't stand the guilt.'

Nancy walked to the writing desk by the window, her friend's love burning in her heart, her words in her head. 'Fine,' she said, pulling a sheet of paper from a cubbyhole in the bureau. 'I'll send him a message, but nothing is set in stone and he isn't coming here.'

'Why not?'

'Because if it isn't the business we sell from here he's interested in, he has no reason to be here.' Nancy looked at her, steadfast in her reasoning. 'I don't need protecting, Louisa. I haven't for a very long time. If Mr Carlyle is so determined that I am the right person for his play, he can speak to me at his home, not mine.'

'I think that would be a mistake, Nance.' Louisa's eyes clouded with concern once more. 'You don't really know him. He could be—'

'I can look after myself, Lou. You know I can. Please...' Nancy pulled back her shoulders. 'Have some confidence in me.'

She turned back to the desk and lifted the pen from the ink pot, cursing the way her fingers ever so slightly trembled.

16

'And perfect!' Francis clapped as the latest rehearsal at the theatre came to an end. 'Everything is coming along nicely, everyone. There's still a lot of work to do so I would like each of you to work especially hard on characterisation this weekend. These characters are all looking for a way out. Freedom. That needs to be conveyed in every action, facial expression and word. All right then.' He raised his hands. 'You are free to go!'

The actors strolled from the stage alone or huddled in groups and Francis resumed his seat at the front of the stage, the play's script in his hand but already forgotten as the rest of the evening became his own. His thoughts wandered as the tweaks he wanted to make to his own script gathered in his mind. He couldn't wait to get home.

He pencilled a few alterations to some stage direction he thought would benefit the Royal's next play and then stood, gathering his papers and folder.

Muted footsteps came closer and he lifted his head. 'Alfred, my friend. Everything all right? You performed splendidly tonight.'

'Thank you. Here.' He held out a folded piece of paper. 'This was left for you backstage.'

Francis took the paper and opened it.

Dear Francis,

I understand from Jacob that you have been back to Carson Street several times since I last saw you. I think it best we meet...

Unprecedented joy rushed through Francis as he quickly folded the paper from Alfred's curious gaze and stuffed it into his trouser pocket. Desperately fighting his smile, Francis resumed gathering his things. 'Yes, a very good performance tonight, Alfred.'

'What's in the letter?' His associate laughed. 'You look like the cat who got the cream all of a sudden. Lady friend, is it?'

Rare heat warmed Francis's cheeks and he straightened. 'Hardly. It's a summons from my solicitor. He doesn't say what it's about but I'm sure it's something and nothing.'

Alfred raised his eyebrows, the glint in his eyes showing his disbelief. 'I see.'

'So...' Francis picked up his folder and tucked it under his arm. 'If you don't mind, I'm going to have to leave you to sort out the lighting and setting. I'd better get back and see what this summons is all about.'

'Absolutely. No problem at all.'

Francis tossed him a smile and brushed past him, hurrying to his dressing room. Nancy had agreed to see him at last. He had been so close to giving up on her, and almost resigned to the fact that he was left with little choice but to grant her liberty from his yearnings. Yet now she'd requested his company once more.

Entering his dressing room, Francis walked inside and locked the door behind him. Dumping his belongings on a chair, he walked to the small sofa in the corner of the room to read the rest of Nancy's letter.

...it best we meet before you cause Jacob to burst a blood vessel. Ha! If you would be kind enough to write back to me with your address, I will come to your home tomorrow at three o'clock and we will talk further. It would suit me better if we spoke away from Carson Street.

I hope you have been well.

Nancy

Francis grinned as he reread the letter twice more before returning it to his pocket. Tomorrow couldn't come soon enough. And she was to come to his house! The thought of showing her his home and all that he had conquered to be able to live in such a place filled him with pride. Fingers crossed, she'd see he was a hardworking and successful man who must have the spirit to make things possible.

His heart beat fast with the anticipation of seeing her again. Of watching as her amazing eyes revealed the workings of her marvellous mind. She really was the perfect choice for his play... the perfect choice in many ways, even if his personal pull towards her had to be curbed. To bring emotion into his plans would undoubtedly bring about failure.

It was imperative he focused only on how to convince Nancy it was safe for her to move their professional association forward. He bit his bottom lip as he stared blindly ahead. Of course, there was every possibility she'd invited herself to his house with the intention of telling him to leave her be. To never step a foot near her or Carson Street again. That scenario seemed a hell of a lot more likely than the one playing out in his hopeful mind.

Walking to a silver platter on the sideboard, Francis poured himself a glass of brandy and sipped the dark amber liquid as he paced the room. Words, promises and questions reeled in his mind, his body betraying him with his desirous thoughts of touching her again. Her body had filled his dreams, her scent his nostrils, their last kiss yet to evaporate from his lips.

Shaking off his lust, Francis forced his mind to the professional. She wasn't just attractive to the eye of any man or woman; she had a presence. A strong outward appearance that barely concealed the woman she was beneath. A woman that represented so many that were on Bath's streets – the world's streets – as the epitome of human spirit and survival.

Putting down his glass, Francis walked to his dressing table and extracted his manuscript from one of the drawers. He darted his gaze over the opening scene even though every word was imprinted on his brain. The play began with the heroine buying her first grocery shop, just as Francis had done five short years ago, and the audience would immediately understand the heroine's euphoria and sense of accomplishment as she walks out of the vendor's study, the keys to the property clutched in her hand. But then she passes the tall iron gates of the workhouse and the stage is plunged into darkness, the heroine transported back to years before...

Francis inhaled a long breath, the familiar anger and trepidation filling his heart as the set moves to a scene from his childhood. The stage filled with the dark and depressing interior of the workhouse while the heroine looks on in anguish from the side of the stage. She stands alone and afraid, the spotlight telling the audience she is revisiting a past that still clutches with cruel talons in her heart.

Softly closing the script, Francis stared at his reflection in the dressing table mirror. His eyes were cold, his jaw a hard line and lips pinched tight. He closed his eyes, wanting his bitter resentment to end, to somehow find a way to heal the weeping wounds of past events he could neither forgive nor forget.

Sometimes, he felt the answer lay not in purging himself through a play but by taking on some workhouse lads to work for him. Yet how could he do that when he doubted his strength to deal with the inevitable physical and emotional ghosts that would almost certainly haunt and hurt them? He'd yet to assuage his own. God, what a coward he showed himself to be!

Swallowing the lump in his throat, Francis pulled some writing paper from a box on the desk and quickly wrote a note to Nancy telling her his address. He would drop it at Carson Street on his way home. Signing his name with a flourish and a gutful of prayer, Francis carried the letter and his manuscript to the sideboard, placing it on top of the Royal's script. The answer to his healing had to be in the play and Nancy. Why, he could not say, but that was the path he must follow.

He shrugged into his coat, grabbed his belongings and left the dressing room. As he strode from the theatre, determination that Nancy read his play in its entirety filled Francis's heart and soul. She had to understand that his story was not just his but belonged to thousands and thousands of other children too.

Surely then, Nancy, whose heart he sensed was as big as the world, would begin to see that it was her destiny to have met him as he saw it was his to have met her.

17

Nancy slowed her steps as she entered Queen Square, one of the fanciest residential areas in Bath. She stared at Francis's house, nerves twisting in her stomach.

My God, the man must be a millionaire.

How in the world had an actor, theatre manager, or whatever he was, managed to acquire such a property? Was he the son of a baron? A crook? Had he lied to her about his beginnings? Tension inched across her shoulders. Well, whatever had led to Francis living here, she wanted an explanation. If he thought he could hoodwink her into agreeing to his wishes through a glorious home with exquisite sash windows and a ruby-red front door, he was sadly mistaken.

Nancy lifted her chin. Well, she was here now and there was nothing she could do but brazen it out. She ascended the wide steps and raised the brass knocker nailed to the centre of the front door. Brisk footsteps sounded and then the door was swung open and Nancy was met by a smiling housekeeper, her welcome gaze bluer than the spring sky above them.

'Yes? Can I help you?'

Nancy smiled, silently berating herself for expecting a stuffy greeting when Francis was amiability himself. Why would he not employ staff of the same nature?

'Good afternoon. I am here to see Mr Carlyle. I have an appointment.'

'Miss Bloom? Ah, welcome. Please, won't you come in?' The housekeeper pulled the door open wider. 'Mr Carlyle is waiting for you in the drawing room.'

As Nancy was led upstairs, she tried not to be intimidated by the interior of such a beautiful house. Her home on Carson Street was by no means drab or dowdy, but Francis's home was magnificent. The hallway was tastefully decorated in shades of beige and gold, the tiled floor black and white with ornaments and pictures covering every side table and shelf. It was masculine certainly, but also entirely homely.

Not unlike Francis himself.

Nancy purposefully bit back her smile, not wanting Francis to see her delighted face and mistake that for a decided mind as far as his play was concerned. Once they reached the drawing room, the housekeeper pushed open the door.

'Mr Carlyle? I have Miss Bloom for you.' She turned to Nancy and gestured her inside with a wave. 'I'll be right back with some tea and cake, miss.'

'Thank you.' Nancy walked into a beautiful pale green and white room, the oriental rug beneath her feet softening her footsteps. Francis stood in front of the ornate fireplace and studied her, neither smiling nor hostile. Nancy smiled widely with every intention of disarming him... even if her belly was as knotted as coiled rope. 'Good afternoon, Mr Carlyle.'

'Miss Bloom.' He dipped his head and came towards her, his smile slowly appearing. 'I'm so glad you're here.'

His soft gaze wandered over her face and hair before he looked to the sofa in front of the window. 'Won't you sit down?'

'Thank you. This is quite a house.' Nancy sat and arranged her skirts, avoiding his gaze lest her bravery weaken. Why did the man have to look at her as though she was a mirage? A vision? It completely tangled her equilibrium. 'I never would have believed an actor could afford such a place.' She raised her eyes to his. 'Were you adopted by a wealthy family when you left the workhouse? Was this house inherited?'

Amusement danced in his eyes.

'The house is mine. Bought and paid for with my own money.' He sat beside her and crossed his legs, threw an arm across the back of the sofa, clearly relaxed in his own surroundings. 'There will be plenty of time to explain my journey to financial abundance in due course. For today, my intention is to attain one thing and one thing only.'

There was a sudden clatter of china and the housekeeper strode into the room with a laden tea tray, a young maid carrying a sponge cake behind her.

Nancy inwardly cursed as intimidation rose once again. There was every possibility Francis had a team of servants, whereas she, Nancy, Octavia and Jacob purposely ran the Carson house without help. The fewer people who knew about the goings-on inside the brothel, the better. Being surrounded by people at Francis's beck and call felt incredibly humbling when it was hard to imagine a life where maids and housekeepers were a part of her daily life.

'Thank you, Mrs Gaynor. Jane.' Francis leaned towards the table in front of them where the tea and cake had been laid out. 'Miss Bloom and I can serve ourselves in due course.'

'As you wish, sir.' Mrs Gaynor grinned at Nancy before ushering the maid quickly from the room. 'Come along, Jane.'

Heat rose in Nancy's cheeks as they departed. Had Mrs Gaynor already guessed Nancy to be a whore? Thought she was here as a paid visitor? Rare shame unfurled inside Nancy at the realisation she could not disguise what she was despite wearing her finest dress and hat. She hated the thought that she might embarrass Francis in any way or have his staff speculate and gossip below stairs.

'What's wrong, Nancy?'

She snapped her gaze to Francis and quickly smiled. 'Nothing at all. Your staff are lovely.'

But he didn't smile and the concern in his eyes did not lessen. 'I want you to be comfortable here. You look worried. What is it?'

'Nothing.' She set her purse on the floor. 'Shall I pour?'

She reached for a spoon to stir the pot but Francis covered her hand with his, his fingers firm yet gentle as he stared at her. 'I'll do it. Just sit back and relax. Please.'

The skin-to-skin contact sparked an immediate and tangible tension, stirring awake the memories of when he'd come to her bed, the strong feel of his hands, his mouth possessively taking hers... Her stomach quivered and a soft heat caressed the surface of her skin.

She swallowed past the lump in her throat as he released her hand and turned to the tea.

Why in God's name did she have to be attracted to a man who wanted her to do the only thing that would undoubtedly lead to a second ruinous moment in her life? She could not falter in the maintenance of her carefully built defences and agree to what he wanted from her. Yet, she desired him. She wanted him back in her bed as her lover, not a cull. She exhaled a shaky breath. Whatever way she looked at it, Francis Carlyle had got under her skin and now she found herself in the deepest trouble she'd been in for years.

He passed her a teacup and smiled. 'Can I tempt you with a slice of Mrs Gaynor's lemon cake? It's like nothing you would have ever tasted.'

Nancy forced a smile, her mouth so dry there was little chance of her chewing anything, let alone swallowing a bite of cake. 'Maybe next time. I'm still full from luncheon.'

He raised his eyebrows, his gaze filling with satisfaction. 'Next time?'

Damnation. What had caused her to say such a thing? She laughed. 'I'm teasing, Francis. It is highly unlikely there will be a next time. I am here to stop you coming to Carson Street and riling Jacob. It isn't fair to expect the man to act as a guard to me when all you want is to talk. The house is a place of business and if you aren't paying to sleep with me, then Jacob shouldn't be bothered.'

His eyes lingered on hers as his smile dissolved. Exhaling, he sharply stood and strode to a small writing desk in the corner of the room. 'You're right. So why don't we get straight to the point and talk about my play.' He picked up a thick sheaf of papers and slowly walked back as he flicked through the pages. He thrust the stack towards her. 'This is the play in full. I want you to take it home and read it. Every word. Once you are done, we will talk again.'

Of course he would assume she could read and write as well as he. She was a woman of some twenty-four years and as worldly-wise as someone twice that age. She pulled back her shoulders as humiliation washed over her. 'I... I can't—'

'But you can, Nancy.' Francis strode forward in three long strides and sat beside her, the pages clutched in his lap and his beautiful blue eyes beseeching her. 'Just read it and you'll understand why I have to see this play through to fruition. Why I believe in my heart and soul that it has to be you who plays the lead.' He lifted the stack of papers. 'This is my only copy. It's so precious to me but I am entrusting it to your care. Surely by my willingness to do that, you can see how much I want to have you agree to play Martha?'

'Martha?'

'Sorry, I'm running away with myself.' He smiled wryly. 'As you will learn I am very apt to do. Martha is the heroine. You. Please just read it and we will talk further. I am confident you will change your mind. You and I...'

Unable to bear the desperate excitement emanating from him, Nancy touched his jaw, part of her wanting to halt his gushing, another part wishing he would never stop. Their shared passion for the theatre was too alike... too connecting. 'You and I what?'

He lowered the manuscript to his lap and took her hand from his cheek, kissed her palm. 'You and I were meant to make this happen together. This is the story of my life and of a thousand others. You will feel it and want to share in its message, I know you will. Will you read it? For me?'

Nancy eased her fingers from his and slowly slid the manuscript from his lap into her own. She nodded, tears blurring the top page as she stared at the neatly written words. How was she to tell him how little she could read? There were thousands of words in these pages, half of which she would never decipher.

'I'll read it but no promises.'

'Thank you. You see...' He pushed some fallen hair from his brow. 'My deepest wish is that this play touches the hearts of those who can help change the conditions at the workhouse. If my story can go some way to raise more awareness and care among the gentry, then I really think I could start a ball rolling that won't stop until those children are given better food supplies, the opportunity for exercise and time outdoors.' He shook his head, his eyes burning with frustration. 'I see no other way that I, personally, can move things forward other than through the theatre.'

Understanding dawned and Nancy smiled softly, wanting to diminish some of his anguish. 'Which is wonderful, Francis, but I still very much doubt that I am the right person to star in something of such great importance. I am not an actress.'

'But you could be.' He took her hand. 'If I can obtain permission to produce this play, you will be surrounded by a cast who will help you. From whom you will learn. The company at the Royal are extraordinary and I already have in mind who I'd like to work alongside you. They are good, people, Nancy. I promise you.'

'You promise me?' The weight of what he asked of her was heavy, the overwhelming prospect of working with strangers only serving to escalate her insecurity. 'Please, do not promise me anything.' She abruptly stood, suddenly wanting to leave, to escape the entrapment of his sincerity. 'I should go.'

He immediately rose to his feet, hope shining in his beautiful eyes. 'Do you have to?'

Care for him twisted Nancy's heart as she walked towards the door. 'Yes, but I'll be in touch.'

'Can't you at least stay for tea?'

'No, I must go.'

She hurried from the room and down the stairs, thankful that neither Mrs Gaynor nor Jane was present to bear witness to the tears that had dared to fall down her cheeks.

18

Francis stood in his dressing room and shrugged on his jacket, doing his best to dispel the heavy melancholy hanging over him. Tonight's performance had been another resounding success and the theatre's owner had begun making comments about paying Francis handsomely to take charge of the Royal's next production.

By rights, Francis should have been elated. His hard work and dedication at the theatre were paying off and his dreams of one day owning the theatre grew closer every day. Yet as proud as he was of his achievements, his consciousness would not lessen its hold on his demon memories of the workhouse. Until he had done something to make a change there, done something so that today's children weren't left with the same deeply embedded scars he carried, his theatre work would count for little.

A burrowing sense of right and wrong lingered, telling him his experiences were meant to mean something. That God had chosen him to make some real societal changes to what happened in the workhouses and find a way to ensure innocent children were not left feeling nothing but despair about their fragile futures.

He sat to tighten the laces on his boots as a horrible sense that he was wrong about his play making a difference reared its head. But what else could he do? He had no other talent than his pen. No other talent than instinctively knowing what would or wouldn't work onstage.

He had not heard from Nancy for days and her silence only deepened what he already suspected. That the play and his writing were, in fact, mediocre at best. She could have concluded by now that his dreams made him little more than a delusional and, frankly, pathetic thespian.

Blowing out the candles on his dressing table and bureau, Francis walked to a shelf to snuff out the final candle when there was a firm knock on the door.

'Come in.'

'Francis, I'm so glad I caught you.' Eloise strode into the room on a cloud of sickly-sweet scent, her face still caked in theatrical makeup, which made her almost ghoulish in the semi-darkness. 'You've been so hard to pin down lately. A girl might think she was being avoided.'

'Not at all,' Francis lied as he crossed his arms and forced a tight smile. 'What can I do for you?'

She raised one pencilled eyebrow. 'Do for me?' She strolled closer and drew her finger down his chest, her bright green eyes predatory. 'You can take me out for something to eat and then I thought we could spend some time in my bed as we have before... on occasion.'

Francis gently lifted her hand away and stepped back. The only woman he'd wanted to be in bed with – the only woman he'd thought about – for weeks was Nancy. The mere reality that he'd slept with Eloise now made him feel like a cad. 'I think it best we keep our relationship strictly professional from now on.

Things are going well for you, me and the theatre. To jeopardise the production's success, or even ours, by causing any hint of scandal would be senseless.'

'Scandal?' She laughed and waved dismissively. 'Do you really think our spending time together would cause people to talk? I'm an actress, Francis, nobody expects anything different from women like me. Don't you know I am already tainted in the eyes of society? Anyway...' She studied him, the flirtation in her eyes dimming to irritation. 'We had an agreement.'

'An agreement?' Francis tried to think of a subtle way of urging her towards the door. 'I don't think so. Now, if you don't mind—'

'Fine.' She walked to his dressing table and pushed some papers to the side so that she might lean against the table edge. She slowly laid down her purse. 'Maybe it was a silent agreement but an agreement all the same. Our... relations are beneficial to us both.' Her eyes glinted with coyness. 'Or were you feigning your pleasure and satisfaction every time you... you know.'

There was a reason Eloise was consistently cast as a femme fatale, her frequent conquests making her performances far from stretching. He opened his eyes and pinned her with a glare. 'It's over, Eloise. Now...' He walked to the door and opened it. 'If you don't mind, I was about to leave for the evening.'

Her cheeks mottled and her eyes filled with venom before she stormed to the door. 'You'll regret this, you know. You are not the only one who has influence around here.'

'Goodnight, Eloise.'

She returned to him, standing so close that he felt her breath on his lips. 'What in God's name has happened to you, Francis? You used to laugh and joke. Play the fool occasionally. Whereas now all you do is work and then high-tail it out of here as though you have somewhere else more important to be. You used to be an inspiration to the company, buoy our spirits. God, I considered myself lucky that I was the only woman in this theatre who had lain with you, seen that fine body of yours without clothes. Now you're all stuffed up as though you can barely stand to look at me.'

Francis trembled with the effort it took not to grip her arm and manhandle her from his dressing room, but he'd yet to put his hands on a woman in any way other than genially. There was no way in hell Eloise would be the one to change that.

'I've realised it's time to get serious about what I want to do with my life. That means making this theatre, its productions and my work the best it can be,' he said. 'To concentrate on that and not coddle actors and actresses' self-esteem as they constantly hanker reassurance and praise.'

She smirked and put her hands on her hips, walking a line back and forth in front of him. 'That's rubbish. Something has changed in you.' She abruptly stopped and narrowed her eyes. 'God, you haven't fallen in love, have you?'

Nancy rushed into his mind and Francis's heart picked up speed. He huffed a laugh. 'No.'

'Hmm, I'm not so sure.' Her eyes glinted with satisfaction. 'Let me guess. She's a young slip of a thing. Daughter to a respectable and, no doubt, wealthy gentleman whose association can help with your so-called ambitions.'

'I said I am not in love.'

Unease coiled in Francis's gut. He most definitely wasn't in love with Nancy, but he did admire, desire and respect her. All things that had every possibility of leading him down a path he had not intended.

He held Eloise's gaze, tried to keep his expression impassive.

'It's no use trying to wheedle something out of me that isn't there. I just want to make my work here a success. To create opportunities that will improve the theatre and its reputation. That means no more tomfoolery or wasting time. Including sleeping with you.'

The ensuing silence pressed down on him, but Francis refused to falter. He strode to the door a second time. 'Leave, Eloise. I'll see you tomorrow.'

She considered him a moment longer before snatching her purse from the dressing table. Pushing it under her arm, she walked to the door. 'I'll go, Francis, but hear this. I have seen the *real* you. You swan around the theatre as though you own the place. Think yourself the king of the castle in that fancy house of yours. Yet the truth is you are little more than a fake. A man masquerading as confident and successful, but you and I know you are nothing more than a little boy. Terrified and cautious.'

Angry, Francis gripped the chair beside him. 'What is that supposed to mean?'

'It means that you have all this vision, this desire, yet when it comes down to seeing the solutions that are in front of you, the ones that will really make your life as successful as you seem to want it, you shy away, decide that the riskier route isn't the way forward.' She smirked. 'That is not the mark of a man willing to put everything into what he wants, Francis. That is the mark of a man hiding behind fear.'

Francis's cheeks burned with anger. 'That's rubbish and you know it.'

'Is it? I think you are terrified that one day your true self will be revealed to the world and every single person will look away in disappointment or disgust.' Her green eyes were dark with malice. 'Have a good evening, won't you?'

Exposed and shamefully afraid, Francis's heart hammered. 'Goodbye, Eloise.'

She stalked from the room and Francis gripped the door handle, his entire body paralysed with the fear that had once overtaken him daily. He tried to fight it, tried to prevent it from burrowing deep inside his mind, but it was futile. Eloise's words had done what they were meant to do and reduced him to who he really was.

Little Frank.

Afraid and weak.

A nothing borne from nothing.

Squeezing his eyes closed, Francis breathed deep. After a few moments, his heart began to slow, and he blew out the final candle before leaving his dressing room.

He burst through the theatre's double doors onto the street, inhaling the cool evening air until the screaming in his head subsided. He had to see Nancy. He had to be reminded of the reason to keep strong in his belief that he was fighting for something bigger than himself.

As he strode along the street, he pulled out his pocket watch. It was around the same time he'd found Nancy at the White Hart. It was Monday. The same day, too.

Maybe she would be there again tonight.

Picking up his pace, Francis made for the pub and, hopefully, Nancy. As he got closer to the river, the tall, imposing building of the workhouse came into view and Francis averted his eyes from its grimy, menacing windows and iron railings. He had to *do* something. The nagging responsibility never ceased. Was Eloise right to cite him as a fake?

Time and again, the notion of sponsoring a child from the workhouse niggled at his conscience yet he'd done nothing about it. Over and over, he'd thought about going to the workhouse to learn of the current conditions and speak to the some of the children imprisoned there. Then he'd change his mind, his fear taking over. Self-loathing shrouded him. The time had come to prove Eloise wrong. To stand up and do what was right.

If it came to pass that his script was not to be, he would damn well ensure he did *something* to help.

19

The White Hart's stone floor swayed beneath Nancy's feet, and she gripped the bar. Maybe it had been a mistake partaking of three glasses of the wine Octavia seemed to prefer, but – Nancy briefly closed her eyes – at least she was keeping to her vow and taking this evening to wallow in her indecision. She stared, somewhat blurry-eyed, across the smoky pub, revelling in the shield the mass of drinkers and noise provided.

Nothing but Francis and his play seemed to be on her mind and in her heart, and her obsession with both was beginning to rankle.

She lifted her hand towards Maura. 'Another, sweetheart.'

Maura came closer and slapped her cloth to the bar, her eyes steely. 'Not another wine, Nance. Trust me, you do not want the headache that stuff can give you if you aren't used to it. I'll get you a glass of ale.'

Nancy opened her mouth to protest and then slumped. 'Fine. A glass of ale will finish the night off perfectly.'

She turned to survey the throng. Bill was in his usual place at the piano, playing a lively tune that had the punters kicking their heels and clapping. Usually, she would have been alongside the pianist belting out a song. Not tonight. Her mood was far too melancholy to even think that she might...

'Oi, Nancy. Come on, ain't it time you gave us a song?'

She faced the young whippersnapper. Two older men held him up with a hand to each of his elbows, their eyes just as glazed as their charge's. She scowled. 'Unless you're in the mood for a ballad, I won't be singing. There won't be any dancing tunes from me tonight.'

'Play a ballad, Bill!'

'We want to hear Nancy. Come on, Bill!'

Nancy inwardly cursed as the pub erupted into a barrage of pleading and temptation. Even if singing was the last thing she wanted to do, the urge to perform was always too strong to ignore.

She took a hefty gulp of the ale Maura had placed on the bar and swiped her fingers over her lips. 'Fine. Let's be having you then.'

The men opened a path for her and Nancy approached the piano as she adjusted the neckline of her dress and smoothed her skirts. Bill struck up the opening bars to one of her favourite love songs. Softly melodic, it suited her voice and was a punters' favourite. A familiar sensation that she was doing what she was destined to do whispered through her and the effects of the drink she'd consumed began to subside, replaced by an increasing thrum of inner confidence.

She started to sing, basking in the silence that fell in the candlelit pub. The music swept into her heart and Nancy closed her eyes, drawing in every lyric where she could keep the dream of true love alive and not acknowledge that such a truth would never be possible for a whore like her. For Louisa, yes. Octavia, too, she had no doubt. But Nancy wasn't quietly shrewd or well-spoken, she was brash and had far too much spunk. Traits no man in his right mind would ever want...

All too soon, the song came to an end and applause washed over her. Smiling, she took a theatrical curtsey and threw her arms out to the sides, her balance only slightly tipping.

She straightened and laughed. 'Well, that's your lot for tonight, gentlemen. Clear the way, won't you? A girl can only go so long without watering her voice.'

It wasn't until the crowd parted and Nancy was given unhindered access to the bar that she saw a familiar figure standing there, one arm on the counter as bold as brass, seemingly right at home and watching her with hooded eyes. Her heart stumbled.

Francis.

Her mouth dried as a treacherous flutter took flight in her stomach. Pushing her feet forwards, she kept her focus entirely on him as she approached. He was dressed in a dark blue suit that she knew would only serve to accentuate his wonderful eyes, his hat set at an angle as he studied her with an intensity she could fool herself into believing was for her and her alone.

She came to his side and lifted her drink, pleased that her hand didn't tremble. 'Well, Mr Carlyle, this is a surprise.'

'Is it?'

His gaze bored into hers and Nancy's body instantly responded to the desire swirling in the dark depths of his eyes. Her core tugged with longing and her nipples tingled. What in God's name was wrong with her? Since when had she so ardently wanted a man? After years of paid sex, the yearning Francis evoked in her was confusing and terrifying.

She turned away and concentrated on the bottles lining the back of the bar. 'Yes, it is. Considering the hour.'

'The theatre is closed for the night and I needed to see you.'

'Needed?' Shameful hope rose in her chest that he might be

coming to care for her as much as he wanted to use her for his ambitions. 'That's a strong word. What do you need me for?'

'You sang that song hauntingly,' he said, ignoring her question as he glanced towards the piano. 'It was beautiful.' He faced her. 'Your talent continues to astonish me.'

She sipped her drink, dragging her defences back into place. It didn't matter how much Louisa encouraged her, Nancy could not risk believing in Francis's sugar-coated flattery and finding herself back in a position where she had no control, where she allowed her dreams to skew her self-respect and intelligence. 'Well, that's very nice of you to say so, but what is it you want with me tonight?'

'All I want with you is *you*, Nancy. And I fear that desire isn't going to go away anytime soon.'

She closed her eyes, hopelessness writhing inside of her. A man like Francis would never want a woman like her. Not really. For his own advancement, his own satisfaction, maybe. But for life? No, never. God, why was he evoking such nonsensical thoughts in her head? Why would she even want a man in her life forever? He needed to leave. Now.

Slowly, she opened her eyes and faced him. Annoyance with him – with herself – beating a tattoo in her chest. 'A desire for me to be in your play, I assume?'

'Yes. Have you read it?'

Nancy stared at him, trying her best not to weaken. Louisa had read his script to her and then Nancy had attempted to reread it herself. Every word was perfect. The play was nothing short of a masterpiece in struggle and triumph. It had left Louisa speechless and Nancy holding her breath.

She swallowed. 'Yes, and you are extraordinarily talented yourself. The play was…' She exhaled. 'Wonderful. Truly.'

Two spots of colour darkened his cheeks and Nancy's heart

jolted. To see his relief and pleasure was as beautiful as lying in his arms, as receiving his kiss. He put his hand over hers where it lay on the bar and drew circles on her skin with his thumb. 'But was it enough to convince you that you are Martha?'

She watched his thumb and involuntarily shivered as the memory of him circling her nipple in much the same way burst into her memory. 'Maybe.'

Delight lit his eyes, his finger freezing. 'Really?'

'Yes.' Despite her stupidity, Nancy could not resist his happiness and she laughed, pleasure warming her. 'Is that why you're here? In the hope I might flatter you? That your words have weakened me, enraptured me into submission?'

'I like you, Nancy. A lot. I know, deep in my heart, that you are the only person to tell my story. I can't think of anyone else but you whenever I think of my play onstage. Of you delivering my lines and the audience held silent in the palm of your hand.' He gently touched her cheek. 'You are the woman I've been looking for.'

Pain burned behind her ribcage as Nancy battled to hold fast in the knowledge his words were about the play, not her. She turned from his hand and picked up her glass, drained the remnants of her drink.

Returning the empty glass to the bar, an unexpected and undoubtedly foolish urge to act on her desire for him burst wide open and she took his hand. 'Come with me.'

Surprise flashed in his eyes. 'Where are we going?'

'Carson Street.'

20

Francis followed Nancy into the drawing room and removed his hat. The May evening was warm, and Nancy had worn neither coat nor hat, her confidence to walk the streets, openly showcasing her emerald green satin dress, matching earrings and sparkling comb in her hair, only further drew him to her. The glimpses of vulnerability she showed were real and intense when they appeared, but then they were gone, leaving behind a woman who knew herself through and through.

She walked to a bureau and poured two glasses of claret. He was attracted to her in a way he had never been to another woman. Whatever gathered strength inside him surpassed the physical. Surpassed his play. The yearning to possess her, to have her work with him, wasn't just about keeping her close. His growing need of her ran deeper. Much deeper.

Her confidence made him want to up his game, be braver and bolder than he'd ever been before.

Yet he had absolutely no idea what to do with the torrent of emotion inside of him. His entire life had been about survival, beating the odds, making his life bigger and better in any way possible. His ambition ran through him like a bulging vein, pulsing with life. Now he wanted something else too. Something with Nancy. Something that might ease a little of the coldness and distrust that filled his inner being as much as his fear of one day losing everything he had fought so hard for.

'Let's take these upstairs.'

He blinked out of his reverie. 'Upstairs?'

The almost hypnotic seduction of her bedroom filled his senses. The soft scent that permeated the walls and clung to the sheets, the candlelit darkness and paintings of half-naked women on the walls...

His cock twitched awake as he took one of the glasses from her. 'Isn't the house open tonight?'

'No, we close for business on Mondays.' She sipped her drink, her eyes on his above the rim before she walked towards the door. 'Octavia will be sleeping, and Louisa and Jacob are almost certainly out doing whatever it is they like to do. Come on.'

Desire twisted deep in Francis's stomach as he followed her from the room and up the stairs. With every step, the danger of what he was doing resounded in his head, but he had been well and truly caught by Nancy and he was a willing victim to whatever unfolded tonight, tomorrow or the next day.

He released a slow, shaky breath and surrendered just a little of his need to control everything around him. They entered her bedroom and she closed the door. 'I think we need to have a serious talk about the play. Also...' Her big grey eyes met his. 'About us.'

'Us?' His heart picked up speed. Could she possibly feel the connection between them, too? Had their time together deepened in meaning for her as it had for him? 'What about us?'

She sat at her dressing table, put down her glass and then lifted her leg to untie her boots. His eyes were automatically drawn to the length of calf revealed to him as she raised her skirts, seemingly oblivious to his study.

'You see...' Her brow furrowed as she dropped her second boot to the floor and massaged her toes. 'As wonderful as your play is...' She met his gaze. 'I'm not an actress, Francis. I'm just a whore.'

Disappointment that she might believe her words to be true slashed across his chest. 'You are so much more than that.'

'I'm not, and it concerns me you are forgetting what is real. I am a whore. Plain and simple.' She stood, turning her back to him. 'Do you mind?'

Every nerve in his body came to life as he looked at the lace ties trailing her back. Swallowing, he put his glass on a table by her bed and returned to her, slowly started to release the hooks to expose her pale skin. 'You have a gift, Nancy. A real, tangible power to keep people's attention. No, *demand* their attention.' He released the last hook and she pulled away the bodice, escalating his simmering arousal. 'Anyway, aren't whores the very best actresses?'

She tipped her head back to stare at the ceiling. Francis watched her, longing to know what new thoughts had entered her beautiful mind, what she thought of his words, of him.

She faced him and his heart twisted to see tears glimmering on her lashes. 'That might be true,' she said, softly. 'But that does not make me the right woman for your play.' She moved away from him and stepped out of her dress, leaving it pooled on the bedroom rug as she untied her bustle. 'You need someone experienced in acting to take on such a poignant role. Martha...' Her gaze bored into his. 'Or should I say *you*, deserves to be portrayed by a professional. Not by someone with no acting experience. It makes no sense for you to keep pursuing me this way.'

His heart hammered. 'So you've decided? Your answer is no?'

'Reading your story made me proud to know you.' She smiled, her grey eyes gentle on his. 'But it also made me wonder why it has become so important to reveal your story to the world now.'

Francis moved closer and turned her around to untie the cumbersome petticoats before tossing them onto a chair beside him. 'The importance isn't the timing. It could have been ten years ago, five or even less if I had actually managed to finish writing it sooner. It took me...' He inhaled. 'A long time to put to paper everything that was trapped inside of me.'

'And when the play is performed, which it most certainly will be, you will be healed of your memories? Of your nightmares?'

'I don't know.'

'No, me neither.'

The ensuing silence made him want to flee the room, flee her canny observations.

'You are who I want to play Martha, Nancy. Professional or not.' His gaze dropped to her breasts, tantalisingly visible through the sheer material of her chemise. His cock hardened and he stepped closer. Cupping her jaw, Francis looked deep into her wonderful eyes, praying she heard him. 'Performing is your passion. I've seen you sing. I've watched you as you've enjoyed a play. I've listened to how you talk about the theatre. It's in your blood. Can you deny that?'

Her gaze flitted over his face as though she was panicked or afraid. 'I can't,' she whispered.

'Can't what?' Her pain was palpable, and Francis circled his arms around her waist and eased her closer so that she might take any comfort he could give her. 'Talk to me.'

'I might have believed your confidence in me was real a long time ago,' she said, quietly, her eyes glinting with unshed tears.

'But now I know better, I do better, and that means I *can't* believe you, Francis. I won't.'

Complete and utter understanding of what she implied washed through him and Francis embraced the similarity between them like oxygen. 'You're hiding.'

'What?'

'You're hiding because you're afraid.'

Her cheeks reddened. 'I'm afraid of nothing.'

'Aren't you? Well, I am.' He pushed his hand into his hair. 'I'm more afraid than you'll ever know. I'm trying to tell you I understand.' He gripped her hands. 'I know better, too, and that's why I must ensure this play is shown and that you are its star. Your time and mine is now, Nancy. More than that, I truly believe we were fated to meet.'

'How can you say that?'

'Because, together, we can make a change. Show the world through the medium of theatre that the children in the workhouse need saving. Not put to work for hours and hours for a frugal revenue of gruel and water.' Passion rose inside him and Francis fought not to tighten his hold on her. 'Please. If you can't do this for me, do it for them.'

Francis studied her beautiful face, scrambling for the words and conviction that would enable her to see what he could. 'Don't you feel it? The possibility of what we could achieve?'

'We are not the same, Francis. I've done things that I'm not particularly proud of but I'm not ashamed of them either. You had a terrible start in life, but you followed a moral path. I didn't.'

'I don't care about that.'

'But if you put me onstage, it will provoke questions. Nudge people and critics to dig into who I am and where I've come from. You will be exposing yourself to everything I have done. To what I still do. Then what?'

'Then I will stand tall and proud beside you. I have never been more certain that I was meant to work with someone. Work with you.'

'Francis, you're not listening to me.'

'We need to at least try to put into the city's conscience that everyone deserves to live the life of their dreams. Deserves to be seen and heard. We have the power to make that happen. I know we do.'

'But will a play really help those children? You are wealthy and successful. Shouldn't you go to the workhouse and use your money to donate food and clothes? Surely that would be more welcome to those poor children than us trying to spread the word of their plight through a play.'

Guilt and cowardice slashed through his heart and Francis dropped her hands, stepping back. 'I will visit. Soon. I have started to think doing that might be an additional way forward, but...'

Words caught like spiked barbs in his throat. It was a lie. He might have decided to see what else he could do to help a child but to step inside the workhouse was a step too far. But what else could he say? Nancy was right and he wrong. To admit how he shook and trembled whenever he thought of returning to that place. How the prospect filled him with debilitating shame. How could he tell her his terror of revisiting all he had once lived, once been, still haunted him to the point of paralysis? He dropped his chin.

She touched his jaw. 'Francis?'

He lifted his eyes. 'For now, all I have are my words.'

Her gaze drew over his face, lower to his mouth, before she stepped closer and pushed his jacket from his shoulders. He stared at her beautiful face as she loosened his necktie and unbuttoned his shirt.

Did she really want him? Or was she halting their conversation via seduction? By returning to a familiar and safe place that had almost certainly saved her before. The thought that he was making her scramble for safety rather than desire made him feel slightly sick.

'Nancy…' He put his finger to her chin and looked into the depths of her sad eyes. And in that moment his intense fondness for her tipped into something more. 'Please, trust me.'

Before she could respond, Francis lifted her into his arms and walked with her to the bed. She looked up at him and Francis lost himself in the desire in her eyes. No fear, no doubt. Just want.

'Make love to me, Francis.'

And he kissed her.

21

Nancy tiptoed towards the stairs, clasping a bed sheet at her naked breasts. Francis followed behind, his boots in his hand. What in God's name had she been thinking by falling asleep with him still in her bed? Not just falling asleep, but blissfully deep in slumber, waking to find her head on Francis's chest, his arm around her as though they were lovers.

She glanced towards Louisa's closed bedroom door and then Octavia's. It was almost eight o'clock in the morning and nearing Louisa's breakfast time. If either emerged and saw Francis leaving, questions Nancy had no idea how to answer would undoubtedly be asked by the two women who knew her best in the world.

Reaching the front door without incident, Nancy tentatively pulled it open with a muted click as Francis donned his boots. She stared at his bent head, silently urging his haste. As she peered outside, her stomach knotted with nerves. Dawn had come and gone, and the street was alive with stallholders trundling their barrows in the direction of the market, their wares like glistening temptation under the early morning sun.

Francis touched her elbow. 'Are you all right?'

Her heart treacherously stumbled as she looked into his brilliant blue eyes. She'd fallen asleep with him. He would have no idea just how significant that was to her, yet something entirely normal to a million others who had spent a night in the throes of passion.

Nancy nodded. 'You'd better go. I'd rather avoid an interrogation from Louisa or one of the others.'

'Of course.' But he didn't step outside; instead, his gaze burned into hers. 'You'll be in touch?'

Fear and indecision twisted and turned inside of her. 'I will.'

He winked, put on his hat, and walked down the steps. Unable to resist, Nancy peeked out a little further so she could watch him as he strode along the street. She softly smiled at the new jaunt to his step before cursing the warmth in her chest that felt far too much like happiness. Just as she was about to step back into the house, a woman further along the street caught her eye.

Damnation. What was wrong with Octavia that she had to be the first at the book stall every Tuesday morning without fail? Octavia's eyes narrowed as she spotted Francis retreating.

Then she turned her wily gaze to Nancy, who braced, clutching her sheet tighter, ready for whatever Octavia wanted to say – or throw – at her.

Octavia slowly walked up the steps, her brows raised as her sombre blue gaze took in the state of Nancy's undress. 'Was that the theatre man? Mr Carlyle, isn't it?'

'Yes.' Nancy lifted her chin, her defences rising. What did it matter that Francis had stayed the night? She was her own woman and could make her own decisions. 'What of it?'

Before Octavia could answer, Nancy strode along the hallway

towards the stairs as best she could manage with a sheet dragging on the floor. Her heart hammered as she grappled with a plausible explanation for why Francis had been there so early in the morning. How on earth could she have risked such interrogation? She hadn't even charged Francis for the night and was secretly pleased that he hadn't offered payment. Their lovemaking had been personal to her, and part of her prayed Francis felt the same.

'I'm going to get dressed.'

'Why don't you join me in the kitchen for a minute?'

'Whatever you have to say can't even wait for me to make myself decent?'

'No.'

Muttering a curse, Nancy pulled up the sheet and laid some of it over her arm before marching into the kitchen. She sat at the table. 'Well? Let's hear it.'

Octavia heaved her laden bags onto one of the counters and turned, her arms crossed. 'Mr Carlyle paid for the night, did he?'

Nancy swallowed. 'What?'

'It seems the man has become rather infatuated with you.'

Nancy briefly closed her eyes, berating her stupidity once more as she inhaled a shaky breath. She could do this. She could deal with Octavia as she would undoubtedly have to deal with Louisa when she heard that Francis had stayed... uncharged.

Octavia turned and began unpacking the bags' contents, neatly stacking tea, sugar and bread in almost colour-coordinated order. 'I'm only assuming it must have been a profitable night's work. After all, it is very rare that a client stretches to additional hours when our fees are so high. Although deservedly so.'

Nancy cursed the tell-tale heat in her cheeks. 'Absolutely.'

'Then again, if, as I suspect, Mr Carlyle is falling in love with you and intends to make his feelings known, then no price would deter him.'

'He is not falling in love with me.' Nancy struggled to keep the deeply treacherous want from her voice. 'He is desperate for me to be in this play of his.'

'I see.' Octavia faced her. 'So, he paid for the night then?'

Nancy purposefully held her friend's gaze. 'No, but that was my choice.'

'Is that so? Well, well...'

Irritation simmered dangerously and Nancy glared. 'This has nothing to do with you, you know. It's up to me how I conduct my business.'

'Is it really? And you think Louisa will agree with that sentiment? Will Jacob?'

Trying to calm her temper, Nancy closed her eyes. She was being obtuse and snarky with one of her closest friends when all the blame for her weakness with Francis lay entirely on her own shoulders.

Opening her eyes, she exhaled a shaky breath. 'Will you sit down? Please?'

With a satisfied nod and a smile playing on her lips, Octavia sat and laid her arms on the table, fingers laced.

Words flailed on Nancy's tongue as her friend stared at her expectantly. *How in God's name am I supposed to explain myself when my feelings for Francis are such a mess of knots and tangles?* It wasn't even about the damn play anymore. It was about her and him. Overnight, they had grown closer and now it was about them and the possibility they could do some good for the children of the workhouse.

'Nancy?'

Nancy started and met Octavia's marginally softer gaze. 'It's complicated.'

'What is?'

'Francis... Francis and me.'

'I see.'

'Do you?' Nancy asked as unwanted vulnerability twisted inside of her. 'Because I don't.'

She and Francis had talked into the early hours about the intricacies of his life as he had written it, how she would play this scene and that. Then he'd begun to speak of the workhouse and how deeply he felt he must do something to alter the state of what went on inside its walls. At first, Nancy had been struck by his passion and obvious pain, but then she had wanted to do something too. Wanted to help and support him so that he might see in himself what she saw in him. Strength, compassion, a quiet gentleness that curled around her heart and made her look at him as she never thought she would any man.

'Nancy? Are you listening to me?'

She blinked and looked at Octavia. 'What?'

'My goodness, he really is someone all of us should be wary of, I think.'

Annoyed with herself more than Octavia, Nancy's defences rose. 'Look, just stop your fretting,' she snapped. 'Francis is someone I happen to like. Is that so wrong? Is it a crime now for a whore to find a cull favourable? Because if that's the case, I really think you should stop showing such humour with Mr—'

'Oh, just stop. We need to be wary of Mr Carlyle if there is even the smallest chance of you losing your heart to him. That's all I'm saying.'

'Well, you can rest easy. That's not likely to happen any time soon.'

Nancy pointedly looked to the window, her heart racing. Now that Francis had revealed his intentions and desires, they had become hers too. Why shouldn't she use her innate determination, brashness and sass to make a difference? The idea filled her with excitement for something new. To have a proper task to accomplish felt inspiring. No, empowering.

If she starred in a play that not only fulfilled her every dream and wish but also encouraged the toffs in the city to reach deep into their pockets, why on earth continue to dither?

Adrenaline pumped through her, her shaky confidence revigorated. 'Fine. The man inspires me.' She faced Octavia. 'Makes me feel as though he is someone worth knowing. Worth learning from.' A slight sickness rolled through Nancy that she admitted such fondness when she and Octavia had each experienced how quickly men could turn from gentle to aggressive. No, she would stand firm. Francis had given her no reason whatsoever to suspect his duplicity. 'He makes me feel special. Like I matter. But…'

Further words stuck in her throat.

Octavia frowned, her gaze clouding with concern. 'But?'

Nancy pushed the hair from her brow, her fingers shaking. 'But he also makes me believe it entirely possible that I could learn to act as well as sing.'

Her friend's gaze softened. 'You said that as though that confidence is a bad thing.'

'Not bad, just immeasurably dangerous. He tempts me back to the place I told you about before. I can't risk that. I won't.'

'And after all that happened to you, I understand. But…' Octavia gently touched Nancy's arm. 'As much as I worry for the safety of your heart, is there a chance if you refuse Mr Carlyle's proposal you might come to regret it? Possibly for the rest of your life?'

Nancy stilled. She would never have expected such a question from Octavia. A stout reprimand of Nancy's foolishness, yes. A demand that she tell Louisa of her past and her growing fondness that had led to Francis staying the night without payment, yes. Even a dressing-down that she had no business falling for a cull's promises when they were working to make the brothel the very best Bath could offer. But a question about her future? A future away from the house? Never.

A horrible realisation unfurled inside Nancy and bitter nausea rose in her throat. 'Do you and Louisa want me out of here?'

Octavia flinched and she slowly pulled away her hand. 'What?'

Nancy hitched back her shoulders, battling to capture every ounce of her practised bravado in a bid to hide her breaking heart. 'Louisa has encouraged me to listen to Mr Carlyle's desires just as you seem to be now. Is this a conspiracy? A joint venture to get me out of this house? If it is, I want to know what I have done wrong. No, I demand it.'

'Oh, Nancy.' Octavia shook her head. 'You really have no idea how much we love you, do you? My concern, and clearly Louisa's, is that you don't refuse Mr Carlyle's encouragement merely because of what we are building here. If it's for other reasons, understandable reasons, then I will respect that.'

Tears pricked the backs of Nancy's eyes as her longings surged forth, almost choking her with their ferocity. 'He has made everything such a mess.'

'Am I right, then? You're falling for him?'

Nancy laughed, her heart beating hard. 'Of course not, and he isn't falling for me either. We... we like one another most certainly, but love? We've barely seen each other more than a handful of times.'

'Which is all it can take.'

'Octavia, for pity's sake. This is real life, not one of your books.'

Octavia glared. 'Yet, he stayed the entire night without charge.'

'That was... foolishness and exhaustion on my part, nothing more. I fell asleep.'

'You fell asleep?' Octavia's voice hitched up a notch. 'Well, then, that's proof enough for both of us.'

Nancy scowled. 'The point is, the man has a genuine care behind his play. He wants awareness of what goes on in the workhouse brought to the wealthy, to the theatregoers who have the money and influence to make a change.'

Octavia studied her, her blue eyes intense. 'And that's bad?'

'No, it's good.' Nancy stood, frustration coursing through her as she walked to the window. She stared out into their back garden, brilliantly beautiful in bloom and greenery. 'But it also means he's making it harder and harder for me to resist buckling to his insistence I could play this part.' She turned and crossed her arms. 'He is a wonderful writer, Octavia. Louisa was overwhelmed, even choked up a few times, when she read his script. The part he wants me to play is an amazing opportunity for any working actor, but to ask me? It's madness.'

'Yet, it's you he wants.' Pushing to her feet, Octavia approached her and cupped her hands to Nancy's elbows. 'Look, I have to agree with Mr Carlyle's intuition about you. Every time you sing in the Hart, the entire pub falls into raptured silence. You light up, Nancy, and the energy in you glides through the patrons, through me. You have something infinitely special that is being wasted here.' She stood back, her eyes lit with fondness. 'Lord knows, I'd miss you if we lost you to the theatre, but to see you onstage? My friend treading the boards? One half of the two women who have saved me? I can think of nothing that would make me prouder.'

Nancy swallowed and swiped at the tear that fell onto her cheek. 'Do you really think I should agree to work with him?'

'You've already said Louisa has encouraged it. Pay no heed to my caution. Life on the streets leaves a stain, but you don't need me to tell you that.' Octavia pressed a kiss to Nancy's cheek and then walked to the door. 'Why not throw caution to the wind and see what happens?'

Octavia left the room and Nancy stared through the open doorway, her mind and heart in turmoil, yet a tangible excitement building inside of her.

22

Francis stood outside the workhouse gates and stared towards the red-brick building that represented the foundation of his endless nightmares. The longer he stared, the more clearly he could see the interior. Smell, hear and feel every aspect, every piece of filth and mistreatment.

Memories flooded his mind as he struggled not to flee, not to walk away from his past as cowardice had caused him to do a thousand times before. The weeks, months and years he'd spent here slithered through him making him want to claw at his skin. The harsh words and disparagement he'd received from the wardens rang in his ears, their frequent lashings stinging across his back and buttocks.

'Are you sure you want to do this?'

Francis breathed in through flared nostrils and turned to Edmund. Pleased that his friend knew that away from the house they were equals: men grown, but also companions who had forged an unbreakable bond behind walls where friendship was discouraged as much as opinion.

'I have to.'

'You have to?' Edmund glanced towards the workhouse, passionate hatred showing in the tightness of his jaw. 'I can't think of a single reason why anyone should have to step inside that place. Even the desperate deserve a different choice.'

'I'm working on something,' Francis said, quietly. 'A play.'

Edmund turned. 'I don't understand.'

Francis blew out a shaky breath. 'It's set in the workhouse. It's my story, Edmund, and yet I have only used my memories as research. If I'm going to get this right, I should know the conditions inside there today, too.'

His friend's ensuing silence only served to ignite Francis's fears that his play, should it come to the stage, might be the biggest mistake he ever made. God only knew how it would be received. If it would in any way make a difference.

Francis smiled wryly, wanting to lighten the tense atmosphere that had enveloped him and Edmund. 'The only scene I am certain I want to share with the world is the one where I take my guardian's hand as he chooses me from a hundred other boys to work in his shop.' Francis shook his head. 'I had no idea how much that day would change my life. That I would be wanted, even loved eventually.' He faced the workhouse and fought the anger bubbling inside him. 'Malcolm and Winnie Russell gave me everything. They taught me kindness and empathy, to read and write.'

'I know they did, and in turn, you didn't forget me either.'

'I just wish I could've done something for you sooner. You left this place because you reached the age that you could no longer stay. I wish I'd had a way of getting you out of there or someone had taken you in as they did me.'

'You didn't have the power to change either.' Edmund glanced at the building, his jaw tight once more. 'Anyway, I held my own well enough. Never in a million years did I think my old friend would come looking for me, but you did, and now we are our own men and happy, right?'

Something in the tone of Edmund's voice made Francis turn. 'Of course. Why do you question it?'

Edmund held Francis's gaze for a second before he stared towards the workhouse, a muscle flexing and relaxing in his jaw. 'I'm concerned about your association with Miss Bloom.'

'Why?' Francis frowned. 'Who I associate with has never bothered you before.'

'Miss Bloom is different.' Edmund's dark brown eyes filled with judgement. 'She's a whore, Francis. I don't understand why you would risk undoing all your hard work, your impeccable reputation, by spending time with that woman.'

'That woman?' Anger curled Francis's hands into fists. 'She is worth a hundred of some of the women I have to work with. You don't know her, so don't judge her.'

'I'm just concerned, as I said.'

'Well, don't be. If I have my way, Miss Bloom will be spending a lot more time with me... and at the house. I would appreciate you making her welcome. She matters to me, Edmund, in more ways than I can explain, or you could fathom. But regardless of that, if I like and trust her, I think that is reason enough for you to do the same.'

'Fine, but you'll not stop me looking out for you.'

His anger dissolved and Francis put his hand on Edmund's shoulder. Now was not the time to tell his friend that it was Nancy who Francis wanted to star in his play. 'I know, and the same goes for me with you, but she's a good woman, Edmund. I promise you.'

Edmund nodded and Francis dropped his hand. 'The need to do more about the workhouses has well and truly got hold of me. It's time to do something big and if the plans I have for my play come to fruition, then I will feel I have done exactly what I was meant to do.'

'I don't understand. How will a play make a difference to those kids?'

Francis was about to respond when a man in uniform approached from the other side of the gates. Francis stood a little taller, sensing Edmund doing exactly the same beside him. The warden was marginally overweight with tufts of grey hair sticking out from beneath his hat, his whiskers bushy and thick.

He reached the gates, suspicion shadowing his gaze. 'Can I help you gentlemen? I've been told you've been standing here a while.'

Francis's hackles immediately rose. He had been beaten, laughed at, kicked and humiliated by workhouse guards for ten years. From the age of four to fourteen, Francis had endured ridicule, been daily entertainment to one warden in particular. He had no doubt the man standing in front of him had it in him to be the exact same way to some other young lad.

'I am interested to know about the children who come here,' Francis said. 'Do you work with children or adults?'

'Children, as it happens.' The man frowned, glanced at Edmund. 'Are you gentlemen considering employing a lad or two?'

Guilt clenched a knot in Francis's gut. He had a nice home, could almost certainly give a boy a new life as his adoptive parents had given him, but fear ran like ice water down his back. His demons were too loud in his head. He heard their laughter and mockery regularly and with brutality. How could he ever be strong enough for any child who had endured what he had?

He cleared his throat. Money would be the first thing the workhouse cared about. 'No, but I am considering donating a large sum to the house.'

'I see.' The suspicion vanished from the man's eyes and he relaxed his shoulders before offering his hand between the bars of the iron gate. 'Then I am pleased to make your acquaintance, Mr...'

'My name is of no importance right now,' Francis said, but shook the man's hand. 'However, I would appreciate you telling me how the children are treated here. Do you think the food they receive is adequate? The punishments just? The hours they work fair?'

The other man's cheeks darkened and he glanced between Francis and Edmund. 'Well, I...' He threw a look towards the workhouse behind him and lowered his voice. 'I don't, as it happens, but I do my utmost to show some kindness to the poor buggers. I oversee boys aged seven to ten but half of them lost their spirits around the age of five, I reckon. Breaks your bloody heart to see them, but at least I can do some good while I'm here.'

Francis tried to keep the relief from his face even if he knew there was every possibility this man lied through his teeth. 'But other wardens don't share your sympathy, I assume?'

'Not all of them, no.'

Edmund stepped closer to the gate and peered upwards at the chimneys. 'How many boys do you having working the rope?'

'The rope, sir?'

'Yes, the rope. My friend here and I know all about working, or should I say, splitting and detangling rope. Spent hours and hours here, in the semi-darkness, doing just that. In fact, we knew the rope in more ways than one.'

Francis laid his hand on Edmund's shoulder, easing his friend back a step. Now was not the time for Edmund to lose his usual composure. Francis pinned the warden with an icy stare, renewed anger flaring in his gut as memories of the torturous work unbinding lengths and lengths of rope bloomed in his mind. 'It's all right, Edmund.'

'I hope you are speaking the truth about your kindness, sir,' Edmund said quietly. 'Because if you aren't, I will be back after nightfall to show you that I haven't quite become the gentleman my friend has.'

The warden blanched and pulled back his shoulders. 'How dare you? I am speaking the truth. I have never so much as raised my hand to any of those boys and neither will I.' He narrowed his eyes. 'And for your information, sir, as much as any donations are welcome, it isn't money these kids need, it's a home, care and guidance. Now, if you'll excuse me, I'll get back to my work.'

Francis briefly closed his eyes as he tried to get a hold of his own temper. 'As hard as it is, we need to take it easy, Edmund. Losing control with the staff won't get us anywhere.' He put his fingers between his lips and whistled. 'Sir. Excuse me, sir!'

The warden halted and slowly turned, his anger palpable across the distance that separated them.

Francis raised his hand. 'Please, sir, just a few more minutes of your time.'

The warden strolled back towards them, his steely gaze boring into Francis's when he reached the gate. 'I don't appreciate being spoken to that way when I am trying my best to do a job that gets harder every day. Now, what do you want? Because I'm busy.'

Francis raised his hands in surrender, burying his pride for the greater good. 'I apologise. Might I ask your name? I would like to speak to you again when I come back here.'

The warden glanced over his shoulder before stepping closer, the suspicion in his eyes returned. 'And what will you be back for? Donations can be sent by post. There is no need to see the governor if your interest is only in donation.'

'Your passion and sincerity have impressed me.' An intention Francis had not foreseen started to gather strength inside him. It was time to face his demons once and for all. 'I would like you to show me around. To help me see what can be done that would be of real value.' Francis looked towards the steel-grey doors of the workhouse, his gut clenching with revulsion. 'But first I need to take some time to consider my next action. Do you have the authority to take me on an inspection?'

The man considered Francis and then Edmund before he stalked forward, his shoulders dropping and his glare softening. 'Yes, I do, and my name is Mr Albert O'Sullivan.'

'Very good. Then, for now, I will bid you good day, but I will return.'

With a shake of his head and a tut, Mr O'Sullivan walked away, muttering under his breath. Francis had no doubt his name was mud in the man's mind. Deservedly so. If he had any hope of pursuing his ambitions for the workhouse, he had to find a way to separate his pain from his wishes.

'So, what next?'

Francis faced Edmund and blew out a breath. 'I'm not sure, but I'm encouraged by Mr O'Sullivan's sincerity. At least we know there is one warden with whom we might be able to work.'

'If there's one, there will be others.'

'Hmm, maybe.' Francis took off his hat and pushed the hair back from his forehead, holding the strands in a fist. 'But first I need to speak with someone I have to persuade to help me. The truth is, I am becoming more certain of her agreement every day but still she resists.'

'Miss Bloom, I assume?'

'Yes, Miss Bloom.'

Francis smiled, more certain than ever that Nancy would come to see that the play had to go ahead. He put on his hat.

Once she knew that beatings and injustice still continued inside the workhouse as it had a decade or more before, it would undoubtedly be more than her kind heart would bear.

'I suspect she has known a life as dire as ours, Edmund. She is the sort of person who makes others sit up and take notice. Her heart is full of passion and she possesses a deep sense of right and wrong. She will come to want change as much as we do. Mark my words.'

'That warden just told you money isn't enough. These kids need homes. Unless you're going to take one or two in, I don't understand how this play of yours will help.'

'Raising awareness is the first step towards gaining the help of others, including those who work in institutions of influence. My words could be what starts the ball rolling with the wider public.' Francis smiled, excitement burning through him. 'People with homes, businesses and opportunities who can give other children a chance as my adoptive father gave me.'

Turning on his heel, Francis walked away leaving Edmund to follow. The play was just the beginning, but Francis grew ever more certain he would come to do more. But what that more would be was anyone's guess.

23

Nancy slipped onto a bench four rows back from the Theatre Royal's stage and nervously glanced either side of her. She had no idea why she was subjecting herself to this again. What was the use in imagining herself an actor one day? Subjecting herself to the pull of a life she knew was nothing more than a pipe dream, whatever Francis might say? She straightened in her seat, clenching her hands tighter in her lap.

Yet how could she not when Louisa and Octavia had set her the challenge to do just that? To come here today and embrace the passion she had never really stopped feeling for the stage.

Her heart lifted as the performers moved and interacted. God, she so longed to be up there. Inhaling a shaky breath, Nancy tried to surrender to inevitable disappointment of such yearning. So much scared her. Francis's confidence in her, the eventual realisation she could not turn her talent to acting, that her limited reading ability would prevent her from ever learning lines...

The blame for her afternoon sojourn lay firmly with her friends. She should not have allowed Octavia to press her even harder than Louisa into accepting Francis's sincerity and agreeing to star in his play. The truth was, no matter how much his pleading and flattery could mean history repeating itself, her pathetic heart would not let go of the unwavering certainty that Francis had come into her life for a reason and, if she turned her back on him, her regret would be eternal.

The obese, stained-shirted oaf next to her burst into a cackle of laughter as he and his companion shared a joke. When he lurched into her side, Nancy elbowed him back with a glare. 'Watch yourself.'

His glazed, half-drunk gaze wandered over her face before he burst into another barrage of laughter. Muttering a curse, Nancy stood and edged along the row before reaching the aisle and heading to the stall exit. She had seen enough of the play to know she had no choice but to see where Francis's promises took her.

It was onstage that she belonged. If there was a chance to put her whoring behind her, then she would take it. Louisa had given her blessing, telling Nancy the Carson Street house was entirely hers and Jacob's responsibility. That none of them owned each other and Nancy's life was hers to follow.

She slowly walked along the empty corridor, her gaze wandering over the drawings and grainy sepia photographs of past and present stage stars. Her stomach knotted with excitement. Could her future be destined for this wall, too? Would she one day see her picture up there, side by side with the others? Guilt pressed down on her, obliterating her selfish excitement. After all that Louisa had done for her, could she ever really leave Carson Street?

But what if she did and reached the heady heights of success? Made her fortune and was able to treat Louisa for all she had done? Pay her friend back in a hundred ways. Nancy smiled. Oh, what it would feel like to buy her best friend in the whole world a pearl necklace or a diamond brooch. To take her to dinner in the finest restaurants and ensure Louisa and Jacob the best seats for every one of Nancy's performances.

'Excuse me, miss?'

Nancy blinked and drew to a stop. She had been so distracted by her daydreaming that she had not noticed the gentleman who had joined her in the corridor. As soon as she looked into his eyes, his lust was clear. Nancy's stomach dropped even as she straightened her shoulders and pulled on her sass like a well-worn shawl.

'Can I help you?'

She lifted her eyebrows and held his gaze. Her smile was so forced her cheeks ached. Yet there was hell's chance of her giving him the satisfaction of seeing the disappointment twisting inside her. Once a whore, always a whore.

'I believe you to be' – he cleared his throat – 'a working woman. Am I right?'

'Indeed you are, sir, but I am no ordinary working woman.' Nancy put her hands on her hips, instinctively thrusting her bosom forward. 'If you like what you see, you can find me at Carson Street... by appointment only.'

'I see.' He had the decency to blush at least. 'I should have guessed you to be out of my grasp. You are quite mesmerising. If I hadn't seen you sitting on the benches, I would have assumed you an actress.' He smiled, the lust in his eyes now replaced with gentleness. 'I will leave you in peace.'

Nancy watched him until he'd disappeared along the corridor. Satisfaction unfurled inside her. He might have mistaken her for an actress. No words could have meant more to her. Feeling more positive, possibility wound tight inside her as Nancy smiled, continuing along the corridor as though she had angels' wings on her heels. Surely the gentleman's assessment was just another sign that she must pursue Francis's dreams with the same determination as he was himself?

She emerged into the lobby and came to an abrupt stop, her heart skipping as Francis swept in through a side door, slightly panting for breath. 'Nancy, I thought it was you I saw in the stalls.' His blue eyes were lit with pleasure, his smile wide. 'What are you doing here in the middle of the afternoon? Were you looking for me? Please, say you were.'

Nancy looked around the deserted lobby before meeting his eyes, trying her level best to maintain her bravado and not fall headlong into trouble by way of his unrelenting, admiring study. 'I am here trying to work out what to do about you and your play.'

'I see.'

How could he possibly *see* anything when she had absolutely no idea how to unscramble her indecision? How to find the courage everyone assumed was natural to her. 'Do you?'

'Of course. I know what I'm asking is a lot but if you weren't so perfect for this—'

'Just stop.' Nancy steeled her spine against the weakness his passion provoked in her. 'I am not perfect for this role, Francis. I have never acted in my life. The truth is, I have been whoring for so long, I don't know anything else. Look...' She exhaled heavily and took his hand, trying her hardest to remain calm. 'If I agree to do this, I will have to be a different person to the one I am now. I will have to be willing to learn, to be taught, to read properly, to speak properly. Why in the world would you want to take on all that as well as producing a play you hope will benefit the children of the workhouse?'

'Because I know all of what you've said, and more, is possible if we do it together. As I've said before, there is every chance a seasoned actress will not understand the hardship, humiliation and hunger of merely surviving. Oh, they could most certainly attempt to act it, but there is no way they would convey that desperation, that loneliness and fear to an audience as you could.' He tightened his fingers around hers. 'You have lived in the real world. Your experiences still haunt you as mine do me. We could produce something outstanding if only you'd trust me.'

'You are asking me to bare my soul onstage,' she said, quietly. 'To expose the pain I bury deeper and deeper every day to an audience of strangers. I don't know if I can—'

'Believe me, I understand your fear, but you are so much stronger than I will ever be.' His eyes danced with his exhilaration. 'Could you spare some time to come backstage? I want you to see it all. It isn't onstage that the magic starts for us, Nancy, it's behind the scenes. It's in the rehearsals, in the costume and lighting areas. It's in all that the audience doesn't see.'

His excitement was contagious. The longer she looked into his eyes, the weaker Nancy's opposition. Hope tugged at her until she grinned, the opportunity to see all that was hidden from public view too much of a temptation to resist. 'I'd love to.'

Relief flashed in his gaze and he winked. 'Good.'

He led her through a side door and down several flights of steps into the bowels of the theatre. On and on they walked, and Nancy's gaze darted left, right, up and down as she took in the working stage, the dressing rooms, the open doorway of a room containing rail after rail of glittering costumes, hats and shoes. Finally, Francis led her past several people scattered around a small space and up a short flight of steps...

Nancy's breath caught and she stared agog from her spot in the wings with an unhindered view of the stage. 'Francis...'

'Look, go on.'

She stepped closer until she was near the edge of the curtain. Staring out into the audience, Nancy looked up at the royal box, the rows and rows of seats in the circle. From here, she could actually feel what the actors felt. Could see what they saw.

'It's amazing. Fantastical,' she breathed as every hair on her body sizzled with belonging. 'It's where I'm supposed...' She swallowed. 'It's beautiful.'

'Say yes, Nancy.' His breath whispered close to her ear, his hands sliding onto her waist. 'Say yes to becoming a star.'

And in that single, magical moment, Nancy could not find an inch of her bravado, not a slice of forthrightness or a single sharp-witted reply. Instead, she turned in his gentle grasp and embraced the most amazing, overwhelming sense of purpose. Of... rightness.

She reached onto her toes and pressed a slow, lingering kiss to his mouth before gently pulling back. 'Yes.'

His beautiful blue eyes lit with undisguised, undeniable pleasure. 'Yes?'

She laughed. 'Yes.'

And then he kissed her in a way that should not have occurred in public, not in the wings of a theatre where her being there had felt an impossible dream for so long and now felt an entirely, ridiculously possible reality.

24

Francis kept hold of Nancy's hand and led her from the stage. As they passed actors waiting to go onstage, stagehands' and runners' curious stares came from every direction. Pride bloomed in his chest. His colleagues' genial waves and greetings to him were fleeting; instead, their inquisitiveness pulled to Nancy, the extraordinarily beautiful, talented and beguiling woman alongside him.

At times, Francis was stopped with a question from someone working production, costume or lighting and he revelled in showing Nancy his knowledge about working behind the scenes as much as onstage. It had taken him years to climb to where he was today, and he was proud of his achievements. He hoped his role here impressed Nancy enough to bolster her trust in him that what he wanted from her had every chance of coming true.

Francis was confident that it would only take a single performance to start Nancy on her path to stardom. And there was nothing he wanted more for her.

'Good afternoon, Francis, and who do we have here?'

Francis halted as dread dropped into his stomach. 'Eloise,' he said, forcing a smile. 'Might I introduce Nancy Bloom.' He turned to Nancy, her grey eyes unreadable as she looked at Eloise. 'Nancy, this is Eloise Carpenter. One of our most esteemed actresses at the Royal.'

'*One* of the most esteemed, Francis?' Eloise's laugh tinkled. 'I think *the* most esteemed.' She extended her gloved hand to Nancy. 'Miss Bloom, a pleasure.' Her gaze travelled up and down Nancy, making Francis desperate to move her away. 'And what are you doing backstage? Are you a friend of our beloved manager?'

Nancy took Eloise's hand. 'I am, yes.'

'I see.' Eloise's smile wavered, her eyes ever so slightly narrowing. 'And might I ask how you met? I do so love discovering more about Francis.' She lowered her voice conspiratorially as she leaned closer to Nancy. 'He is quite the enigma, you know. Or should I say quite the chameleon.'

Irritation simmered hot inside Francis and he shot Eloise a glare. 'Well, we must be getting on. I assume you have all you need for this afternoon's performance?'

'I do, yes.' Her green eyes glinted with suspicion. 'And I very much look forward to hearing all about yours and Miss Bloom's association later.' She beamed at Nancy. 'A pleasure, I'm sure.'

Eloise flounced away, the people around her parting as though she was the Queen walking through the corridors of Buckingham Palace.

Francis glared after her. 'I'm sorry about that. Eloise is insufferable in her perception of her status.'

The clamour around them was painfully accentuated by Nancy's unusual silence. Glancing at her, Francis's heart sank. Her smile appeared forced, her beautiful grey eyes wide with something closer to fear than delight. Clearly, Eloise had shaken Nancy's previous confidence. Either that, or he had misjudged this spontaneous tour and the result was Nancy's discomfort rather than exhilaration.

'Come,' he said, tightening his grip on her fingers. 'Let's go and have some fun.'

'Is Eloise really a star, Francis?'

He stared at her, hating the self-doubt in her eyes. 'In the Royal's current play, yes. Nancy, please, do not let her self-obsession deter you in your decision to work with me. Eloise is a great actress, but she is also intensely insecure.'

'How could anyone who looks like her and holds such a place in the theatre ever be insecure?' She looked along the corridor where Eloise had disappeared before facing him once more. 'She is phenomenal.'

'She is human, that is all. You will get to know Eloise and her ways soon enough as I intend giving her a part in my play, too.'

'I will be working with her?'

'Yes. She will help you.' He smiled and took her hand. 'I will ensure it.'

He focused on getting Nancy through the hubbub towards the costume department. He doubted her enjoyment of their walkabout considering her bewildered expression, but hoped she possessed the same feminine penchants as others and enjoyed clothes, shoes, hats and jewellery as much as the next woman.

He pushed open the door to the costume department, firmly locking it behind him. 'So, how about we indulge in a little dress-up?'

'What?' Her expression lifted, no longer fearful but entirely amused. 'Is this your way of getting my clothes off, Mr Carlyle?'

'Not at all. I merely thought you might enjoy—'

'I'm teasing, Francis,' she said as she put her bag on a stool and plucked at the fingers of her gloves. 'What girl doesn't like dressing up?'

She walked to rail upon rail of jewel-coloured dresses and ran her fingers across them, her gaze darting over the hats and shoes arranged in the three open cupboards to the side. 'Are these set out for each production?'

'They are. So...' Delighted by her smile, Francis walked to one of the long rails and removed a dress of the highest quality, meant for an actress playing a Russian princess. 'Why don't you try this one, your Royal Highness?'

She eyed the dress, her gaze flitting back and forth to his, and Francis marvelled in the indecision reflected in her eyes. He couldn't help but wonder if Nancy had done a single spontaneous thing in her life. Everything he had set before her for as long as they had known one another, she had considered carefully. Nothing was done quickly or with relish. Well, if he discounted her impulsiveness at the White Hart, of course. Which led to his wondering whether her self-control should be admired or sympathised with.

She stepped closer, took the dress and returned it to the rail. 'There will be plenty of time for dress-up whenever we get to that stage of your production.'

Confused, Francis frowned. 'But I thought you said all girls liked to dress up?'

'They do, but...' She turned, her gaze sombre and a little guarded. 'I think it's more important that we talk.'

Dread unfurled in his stomach. 'Talk? If this is about Eloise—'

'It isn't.'

'Then what...'

She walked to a corner of the room and picked up two stools, placed them opposite one another and gestured with her hand that he sat. Feeling like a lamb walking to its slaughter, Francis complied, his back ramrod straight as he waited until she was seated.

'So...' She exhaled a shaky breath. 'Here's the thing.'

'The thing?'

She lifted her chin as though bracing herself, the skin at her neck moving as she swallowed. 'You are quite clearly someone important, Francis. In life and in this theatre. You are rich. Your house is beautiful.'

'What do any of those things—'

'You own a carriage with horses, you have a butler, a cook, a maid.'

'Nancy...' He had no idea why anything she'd mentioned mattered to what they were embarking on, but if they worried her, they worried him. 'Why are any of those things important?'

'Because if your play is about you, I need to know how you have managed to achieve all that you have.' She looked at her hands, clenched and unclenched them in her lap. 'I need to be certain that you are genuine, Francis.' She met his gaze. 'That the boy from the workhouse is real and that your fortune was made, not swindled, stolen or made in such a way that hurt anyone else.'

'What?' Shocked, Francis tried to keep calm. 'You think—'

'I think nothing because I know nothing.' She held his gaze, the fire in her eyes scorching. 'I have been deceived before by a man parading himself in very much the same way as you. That man was neither real, nor kind. He was... a deviant in every possible way. So, unless you want me to walk out of here assuming the same is true of you, I need to know how you came by your successes.'

He fought the defensiveness that rose inside him. Eloise referring to him as a chameleon, an enigma, had to be the cause of Nancy's distrust. Was he to be insulted and angry, or just tell her about his life past the struggles detailed in his play? Tell her of his ruthless ambition and love for his adoptive parents. He certainly had nothing to be ashamed of, but he did not like having to explain himself to anyone. Including Nancy. Yet didn't he owe it to her to at least share something of the man who had evolved from the depravity?

'The play is not enough for you to know I have struggled and my desires now are real?'

Her jaw tightened, her gaze unwavering. 'No.'

Her body was rigid, her chin tilted in a classic defensive pose. The penny dropped. Her questioning him was more about her than him. She had undoubtedly been associated with rogues and scoundrels of the lowliest order countless times, but he could not help feeling irked that she wanted him to prove authenticity so minutely when... He swallowed. When what? When he'd taken her to bed, kissed her, pursued her, begged her to involve herself in a project that was entirely of his own making?

Francis swiped his hand over his face, a sudden and heavy exhaustion pressing down on him. 'Fine, I'll tell you.'

She shifted on her stool, her gaze on his, her face sombre.

He crossed his arms, but it did nothing to stem the vulnerability unfurling inside of him. 'I was taken in by a husband and wife who owned a haberdashery. I came to see them as my parents and I'll be forever grateful they regarded me as their son.'

'Are they still alive? Might I meet them?'

He couldn't have been more surprised by the request than if she'd slapped him. 'What?'

Her cheeks darkened. 'I just want to be sure...'

'That I speak the truth?' He shook his head, irritation burning hotter inside of him. 'Is your trust of me really that minimal?'

Her grey eyes turned angry. 'I told you that I have reason to mistrust what you are saying. This isn't so much about you as about me being certain I am not walking into another mistake.

Please, don't look at me that way. I am not a naïve young girl anymore and, as much as I like you, I must look after my own interests as much as yours. I have people who rely on me...' Her gaze softened. 'People I rely on in return and nothing in this world will make me jeopardise their trust and friendship.'

Francis studied her before pushing his inflated self-worth into submission. He was asking a lot of her and she had every right to ask a lot of him. He could not lose her through his own self-protection.

'The man I came to see as my father passed when I was twenty and he left me the shop. Their business always turned a good profit, and they were able to give me an education as well as expose me to the higher classes.'

'Hence why you speak so posh and read and write as though you were born doing it.'

Ignoring the irony in her tone, Francis continued. 'I worked side by side with my mother, modernising and changing things that would make us money quicker and in higher volume. With my mother's trust, the shop became more and more profitable. So much so, she was able to retire to the country with her sister.'

'I see. So your mother is still alive?'

'She is, and if you really need to meet her, Nancy, I'll take you to her.' He couldn't keep the annoyance from his tone. 'But I'm not sure that she should be treated to little more than a scouting visit, do you?'

'Is that the real reason?' Her eyes blazed with anger. 'Or because I'm a whore?'

'For the love of God, no. Not because you're a whore, but because I have never taken an actress, or actor for that matter, to the country to meet my mother.' Francis was torn between calming Nancy and raging at her. 'The truth is,' he said, firmly, 'I haven't taken *any* woman to meet my mother. Lord only knows what conclusions she'd leap to if we were to turn up on her doorstep.'

She held his glare for a moment before looking past his shoulder, her colour waning. 'Fine.'

Francis exhaled. 'I sold the shop and invested in property. It is in *that* I made my fortune. Bath is a rising commodity and I acted on my instinct as I do with most things. As I am doing with you.' He leaned his elbows on his knees, silently imploring her to believe and trust him but, judging by her set expression and questions, he still had a way to go. 'Once I had the income, I came to the theatre. A place that has fascinated me ever since my father walked me by the Royal on the way home from the workhouse. If I'm not mistaken, your lifelong love of the stage started around the same age, if not earlier. I started at the bottom, wanting to learn everything. And I did. Now you see me running the Royal and loving every single moment of my working life. This' – he raised his hands, encompassing the room, encompassing the theatre – '*is* my life.'

Tears glittered in her eyes and a ghost of smile lifted her lips. 'Your life?'

'My life.'

'And now you believe you could make it mine, too.'

'Do you want that? I mean, *really* want it?' he asked, reluctant to rid himself of his anger just yet. 'Because if you don't, then I was wrong to pursue you as I have. When I saw you in the White Hart, I believed I had found the woman I had been looking for. The star I have been looking for. And I still believe in every fibre of my being that you are her, but if I am wrong, then it's time I accepted that and leave you be.'

The clump of hurried footsteps and chatter filled the corridor beyond the closed costume room door telling Francis that the second half of the play had finished. He and Nancy had very little time left before they would be disturbed.

He raised his eyebrows. 'Well?'

Slowly, she stood, stretching his tension as she smoothed out her skirts, pushed some fallen hair beneath her hat. At last, she met his gaze, her grey eyes twinkling once more. 'Well, then, I think it's time we get on producing the best play this town has ever seen, don't you?'

Francis stood and walked closer to her, lifting a speck of thread from her shoulder, his entire being longing to kiss her, for them to be fully reconciled, but he refrained. 'That sounds an exceptionally good idea indeed.'

25

Once Nancy had left Francis to his work, she emerged from the Theatre Royal onto the street. The bright, sunny day melted the away the remnants of her pessimism, leaving her feeling just a little lighter now that she had shared what was in her heart with him. Even though at first his agitation had been downright palpable, Nancy still felt she had done the right thing by being honest with him about her reservations that had only been made worse by Eloise Carpenter's appearance.

How in the world am I to hold my head high while working with such an established actress?

And what of the others to whom Francis would introduce her?

No, Nancy shook her head. She would be fine. She would ensure she was fine.

Now Francis had proven his integrity by telling her a little more about his parentage, upbringing and the means of his wealth. All of which mattered more to her than he could ever know. The duplicity and betrayal she had endured from men's lies and veiled promises had left a deep, dark stain on her ability to trust. But now, she hoped, she and Francis could move forward with their plans.

She smiled at the people she passed, unable to completely contain the newly lit flame of certainty inside of her that all would be well. Who was to say Francis would not be the key that unlocked fortune for her as well as for the workhouse children? That, together, they would do some real good in the world? Maybe her necessary whoring would eventually fade into the background of her life and remain there as a plethora of lessons rather than something that defined her. Not that she was ashamed of how she made a living or that she had a bad life. Not at all. Due to the success of Carson Street, she dressed as nicely as any other middle-class woman. Her whoring these days was as far away from streetwalking as begging was to fine dining.

Yet what she deemed success did not involve lying on her back – well paid or not.

She turned into Carson Street and drew in a strengthening breath. It was time to speak to Louisa. To tell her best friend that her confidence Francis would not dupe her had been bolstered and Nancy was ready to reach for the stars. After climbing the steps to the house, she let herself in. Louisa and Octavia would most likely be taking tea around this time and Jacob out on his usual fortnightly visit to his previous and much-loved housekeeper.

Entering the house, Nancy closed the door and strained her hearing towards the parlour. She was greeted by her friends' murmured conversation. Humming to herself, Nancy unpinned her hat and loosened the buttons on her jacket before walking along the hallway. She entered the parlour and stopped, her optimism draining away.

Louisa held Octavia in her arms.

Tears slipped over Octavia's cheeks and what looked to be a fresh bruise stood out red-grey on her jaw. 'It's fine. I was shocked, but I handled him well enough. He won't be back.'

'But you, and especially Jacob, should have told me what happened last night. You're clearly upset about it.'

'It's only talking about it now causing my tears.' Octavia pulled from Louisa's embrace and swiped at her cheeks. Her eyes met Nancy's, flickered with almost imperceptible dismay before she defiantly lifted her chin. 'I'm quite all right, honestly.'

Louisa turned. 'Nancy, you're back.'

'I am,' Nancy said quietly as she came closer, unease whispering through her. 'What's happened?'

'Octavia has been—'

'Acting with complete silliness,' Octavia interrupted, her tone firm. 'There is nothing more to be said.'

'Oh, isn't there?' Louisa snapped, her irritation plain. 'I can't believe Jacob relented to your request to keep this from me.'

'I begged him, Louisa,' Octavia said. 'Not asked.'

Surmising that Octavia had been assaulted last night, anger bubbled inside Nancy as she stalked to the sofa and planted her hands on her hips. 'Did some lowlife hurt you despite our usual checks of any gentleman who enters this house?'

'I'm afraid so.' Louisa walked to the drinks cabinet. 'I think we could all do with a sip of wine. Mid-afternoon or not.'

Nancy took Louisa's seat beside Octavia. 'What happened?'

'It was nothing.' Octavia accepted the glass of wine Louisa held out to her. 'He was new, and entirely charmed Jacob, me *and* Louisa. He had what he came here for but when I mentioned payment, he turned.'

'And he hit you?'

'Yes, but only once.' Octavia smiled, her eyes lighting with malice. 'Before I pulled a knife from my side table. Then he shot out of here faster than a rat up a drainpipe and I gave chase.' She grinned. 'Of course.'

'Well, of course.' Nancy laughed. 'And what, he flew past Jacob out the door? I can't believe it.'

'No, Jacob stopped him but as I was naked on the stairs, brandishing a knife and smiling, Jacob let him go on my insistence.'

'Yes,' said Louisa, sitting down, her expression showing she would be giving her beloved Jacob a talking-to when he got home. 'And then he came to bed and never said a word.'

Octavia took a sip of her wine. 'He could well have been in shock seeing me as I was. Go easy on him, Louisa. The man is only human, after all.'

'Human or not, I feel like this has sent us spiralling backwards.' Louisa's violet eyes flashed with anger. 'We have spent months building up the reputation of this house. Have worked hard to make it a safe and good place to ply our trade.' She lifted her fingers to the scar on her cheek before quickly snatching it away again. 'None of us have had to endure any kind of violence for months and now this? There is no way of knowing where this man came from or if more of his ilk will follow.'

Nancy studied her friend, desperately sad that Louisa's own trauma appeared to be haunting her once again. 'What do you want to do, Lou?'

'I don't know. At least, not yet, but I won't have the three of us in any danger.' Her friend's gaze burned into Nancy's. 'We need one another, rely on one another, and there is no way I will go back on my word that each of you will have my protection for the rest of your lives. We work because we stick together through everything.'

'And we always will,' Octavia said, putting her glass on the table. 'It was a single punch and I saw him off. There's nothing more to worry or think about.'

Unease rippled through Nancy. She was an integral part of the house. Likely the most hardened and unpredictable of the household. Excluding Jacob, whose past boxing career made him as temperamental as a dog. But when push came to shove, Nancy was by far the feistiest. The one Jacob had come to see as his right-hand woman if a scrap were involved. How was she to leave her most beloved friends to pursue her own dreams? Her own happiness?

'Nancy?'

She started and flicked her gaze to Louisa. 'Yes?'

'Did you hear what I said?'

'Sorry, I didn't.'

'I asked if you have any ideas what we should do about this man. Do we pursue him or let him go? That's the question Jacob will no doubt be struggling with.'

'I think we let him go. Keep this incident quiet. For now, anyway.' Nancy lifted her wine, took a mouthful. 'As you said, everything will be fine if we stick together.'

Louisa paced back and forth before she stopped. 'And to think this was happening when all I wanted to do today was tell you that Jacob and I... Jacob and I are...' Her cheeks flushed pink.

'Are what?' Nancy frowned and glanced at Octavia, whose expression showed her equal bemusement. 'Lou?'

'Oh, hang it. I am bursting to tell you both.' Louisa came forward and gripped Nancy's hand and then Octavia's. 'Jacob and I are to be married!' She beamed, her smile the breadth of her beautiful face. 'At Christmas.'

'Married?' Nancy's heart raced with shock and pleasure, tears immediately leaping into her eyes. 'Oh, Louisa!'

The three friends embraced, their laughter and cries filling the room and Nancy's heart. 'A wedding. I can't believe it. Who would have thought? A madam and a boxer.'

Louisa laughed. 'Nothing wrong with that. Not at all.'

Nancy closed her eyes and squeezed her friends tight. This was her home. Her life. Right here, side by side with two women who meant everything to her. One of whom was getting married... the other who had been assaulted. There was much left to do at Carson Street. Much left to tackle and conquer, create and enjoy. How could she follow Francis along such an uncertain path and risk not being here when Louisa or Octavia needed her?

She stepped back, her lips ever so slightly trembling with the effort to keep her smile in place. 'Well, this deserves a bottle of champagne. You two stay right there. I'll be two minutes.'

Nancy rushed into the hallway and slowed as she made her way downstairs to the cellar, her heart and mind in turmoil. Louisa would insist Nancy continue on her journey with Francis, Octavia no doubt the same, but Nancy wasn't sure she *could* leave them when they had been her entire world until a few short weeks ago.

Francis was but a man, whether or not she saw and felt more for him. She had come to like him, had made love with him without fee or payment. She teetered on the precipice of what could be her undoing. Yet, deep inside, she wanted to see where the madness would take her.

She stepped down into the cold, dark cellar, indecision clawing at every part of her. Now was not the time to announce her decision to Louisa and Octavia. First, she had to come up with an unshakeable plan for how she could work with Francis without neglecting her friends. Having given her word to him, she wouldn't digress, but she needed more from him than his words and play. She needed reassurance that her life at Carson

Street and that of her friends would also be protected. Nancy stared at the bottles in front of her and slowly a plan began to form in her mind.

The only way she could make everything work was to specify a few terms of her own to Francis. Terms that would benefit him, her and everyone she loved...

26

Francis gripped his manuscript in his lap and met Lord Henry's gaze. 'It's an honour to be a guest in your home again, sir.'

With a grunt, Lord Henry shifted his considerable bulk further back into his wing-back chair. 'Well, I wouldn't normally extend an invitation into my private residence in the middle of the day, Carlyle, but the tone of your letter indicated a face-to-face meeting was necessary. And as I have no desire to grace the theatre...'

Annoyance simmered in Francis's gut. The man practically owned the Theatre Royal and his absence irked more than it pleased. How could someone so financially invested not have a modicum of care for the place? Francis cleared his throat. 'Indeed, sir.'

'I may be the Royal's majority investor, Carlyle, but my tastes in plays are few and far between, as you know. I am guided by instinct and the advice of you and the set designer, very little else in between.'

'I understand.'

'Then why are you here?' Lord Henry's bushy grey eyebrows

shot to the curve of his liver-spotted forehead. 'I haven't time to be bothered with these things. My wife is already getting herself into a state of agitation over our visit to our daughter at the weekend. She likes me to be on hand to help her and now I find an hour of my day taken up talking to you.'

Dislike for the man who held the Royal's reins shifted in Francis's gut. Having to be cordial towards Lord Henry was like playing nice with a cobra.

Francis held out his manuscript. 'This is a play I've written that I would like you to consider for production early next year, sir. It has a message that I think the entire country needs to hear and heed.'

'You consider yourself a writer now? Good God, what next, Carlyle? Will we see you taking a female lead?' Lord Henry gave a bark of laughter, making no move to take the papers. 'What would this message be, eh? Pray enlighten me as to what you think we all need to hear from your lofty place of self-imposed government.'

'It's a message, a lesson if you will, about the workhouse.' Francis leaned forward, determined that the man took his wishes seriously. 'The play opens with a young girl who—'

'The workhouse? God alive man...' Lord Henry guffawed, his smile causing his fat, round cheeks to rise, practically obscuring his beady eyes. 'Do you think people come to the theatre to have their moods lifted or depressed? Who in God's name would pay their hard-earned money to view a story about depression and depravity? You must be mad.'

'If you will just allow me to explain the concept...' Francis lowered the papers to his lap, clenching them so tightly, his knuckles ached. 'The play will be peppered with humour and portray the amazing ability of human beings to see good in others, when all around them nothing but evil seems to reign. It is a story of courage, survival and succeeding against all odds. It's a foundation on which ten more plays could be—'

'Ten more?' Lord Henry bellowed, his cheeks reddening. 'You are indeed mad.'

'Sir...' Francis drew in a long, calming breath. 'I have found the perfect woman to play Martha, the girl whose story this will be. Nancy Bloom is unknown for now but she's perfect for this role. She has a fire inside of her that I believe I can nurture and develop.' Francis's heart beat faster as Nancy and all she represented filled him. 'She is full of bravado that hides a wonderful, generous heart. She is afraid, yet brave. She is—'

'Would you have me believe this *actress* to be a goddess?' Lord Henry raised his eyebrows and smiled wryly. 'No, Carlyle. I do not think this is something the Royal can contemplate. Haven't our recent successes taught you anything?'

'Sir, I really believe this play could be the start—'

'Of the end for us.' Lord Henry stood, waved his hand dismissively. 'I do not wish to hear any more. The answer is no.' He pinned Francis with a glare. 'People do not want this sort of thing dressed up as entertainment. They come to the Royal for melodrama, comedy. I have no desire to listen to you further and even less desire to read your manuscript.' He reached for a bell on the sideboard and shook it. 'Now, I suggest you heed my advice and drop this ridiculous ambition. Focus on what is making us money, Carlyle. That is your job and why you are paid accordingly.'

Francis rose from the sofa and held the other man's gaze. 'If you will not allow me to make plans for this production, to scope actors and actresses and work out an attainable budget, then...' Francis inhaled a long breath. 'I will have no choice but to take my work elsewhere. I am quite sure another theatre in the city will see the profit in it.'

Tension inched along Francis's shoulders as a heavy silence followed, his glare locked with Lord Henry's. The door opened and Lord Henry raised his palm, halting his servant, while his eyes remained on Francis.

'Wait in the hallway, Jennifer. Mr Carlyle will be leaving in the next minute or two.'

'Yes, sir.'

The young girl hurried from the room.

Francis lifted his chin, passion burning deep in his gut. 'I will not rest until my play is shown, sir. Whenever, or wherever, that may be.'

'Is that so? Well, let me tell you something right now,' Lord Henry said, quietly, his eyes burning with fury. 'No one, including one of the best damn theatre managers in the city, threatens me when it is *my* wealth on the line. I am the majority holder of that theatre and it is with me that the final decision lies regarding what my money will be invested in.' He came closer so that barely a foot separated them. 'If you take this play elsewhere, you can stay put elsewhere, do you hear me? You work for *me*, Carlyle, no one else. Otherwise, you do not work for me at all. Do I make myself clear?'

Francis's heart thundered, a thin red mist tinging the edge of his vision. No one had spoken to him in such a derogatory, condescending and threatening manner for over a decade and now he faced a decision that could make or break his future. Did he walk away with no guarantee he would be employed elsewhere in an industry he loved? Or did he agree to abandon his play and maybe attempt to persuade Lord Henry again in a year or two?

Nancy's face appeared in his mind's eye. There was little chance of Nancy waiting on his promises. His plans had to be set in motion now or Francis risked losing her altogether.

'Get out, Carlyle.'

Francis stood straighter and pulled back his shoulders. 'Fine, I will not pursue this with you again, sir. But...'

'But?' Lord Henry huffed a laugh. 'Get out of my house, man, before I lose my temper completely.'

'I have one more question.'

Lord Henry's nostrils flared. 'What?'

'If I finance this play myself, employ the company to the roles and oversee every aspect from setting to costume to production, thus not a penny being spent from your pocket, would you reconsider allowing the play to at least be shown at the Royal?'

'Now you are showing just how little understanding you have of production costs.'

'I have money, sir. Money I am willing to invest in this play, in myself. My belief in my work's success is that strong. If I finance the entire enterprise, do I have your permission for a single week to show the play? Say, in February or March next year.'

Lord Henry narrowed his eyes, his gaze intensely drilling into Francis. 'You have no idea what you are getting into.'

'Maybe not, but what do *you* have to lose if I follow this course? It is the risk to *your* money that concerns you. This way, you will not have any financial obligation whatsoever.'

'February or March gives you eight months to bring this fantasy of yours to life, ensure the productions we have lined up are shown to schedule, prepare a Christmas pantomime and promote anything we have planned for 1853. Balls will be dropped, Carlyle, and that is not something I will tolerate.'

'I can handle it. All of it.' Francis swallowed, the enormity of what he was taking on bringing a burst of perspiration to his upper lip despite his nonchalance. 'I will work harder than I ever have before.'

'I don't like this. Not one bit.'

'Please, sir. Just show me a little faith and you will see that my vision is right. The public will devour this play and want to make a profound change to the way this city is run. This could be the start of something huge.'

Lord Henry stared, his brow furrowed before he raised a hand in surrender. 'Fine...' He strode to the door and opened it. 'Jennifer, Mr Carlyle is leaving.' He motioned Francis forward with a wave of his hand. 'You have my permission for February or March, but you will not see a penny of my money. God give you the strength to wipe the egg from your face should anything, anything at all, go awry in my theatre between now and then.'

Biting back a retort, Francis curtly nodded and followed Lord Henry's young maid towards the front door. Adrenaline mixed with fear, certainty with doubt, but one way or another, he would make his play a reality. Francis smiled. He and Nancy would make it happen together.

27

At Carson Street, Nancy plunged another plate into a sink of soapy water as she contemplated Louisa and Jacob's wedding. There had been a time when she had believed Louisa would never remarry, but her life – and Nancy's – had changed so much since they had first arrived in Bath over a year before. She and Louisa were entirely different women now, their previous reliance on Louisa's first husband a distant memory.

They had triumphed by falling back on their experience. Their past lives in the sex trade a ticket for their futures, using all they knew to their advantage – for their independence. Pride swelled inside Nancy as she put the plate on the drainer. They had already achieved so much, yet ambition still shone in Louisa's eyes as strongly as ever. Something Nancy completely understood. She couldn't help but wonder if they, Octavia included, would ever stop wanting more. Ever stop fearing that everything they now had would be snatched away from them by the turn of a coin or the whim of a man yet unknown. But in Jacob, Louisa had found a man who would never clip her wings, expect her to dress or behave in any other way than how she wished. Nancy smiled. And she couldn't be happier for Louisa and Jacob's upcoming nuptials.

Her best friend and a man she had come to love like a brother joined in matrimony.

'I'm telling you, my man, you are not seeing her while you're riled up like a bloody hound!' Jacob's voice roared along the hallway. 'You come back when you've calmed down or I'll knock you on your arse.'

Snatching a towel from the counter beside her, Nancy hurriedly wiped her hands as she rushed from the kitchen and up the stairs. As she emerged into the hallway, the sight that greeted her would have been funny if it hadn't been Francis who Jacob held by the collar... and if Francis wasn't giving as good back by holding Jacob's lapels in his fists.

'What in God's name is going on here?' Nancy stormed along the hallway just as the drawing room door opened above her, followed by Louisa's study door to her side, confirming her friends were about to join the show. 'Francis, for goodness' sake. What do you think you're doing?'

Neither man released his hold on the other, their cheeks flushed and their eyes glaring. Nancy fought to hide her shock at the unadulterated fury on Francis's face, the way he was squared up to Jacob as though he neither exceeded Francis in height nor width. In fact, Francis's expression clearly showed he would think no more about fighting Jacob than he would taking high tea at the Pump Room.

'Gentlemen!' Louisa shouted. 'That is enough. I will not have you two coming to blows while you are under my roof.'

Still Francis and Jacob held on to one another, their gazes locked in silent battle.

Nancy's heart pounded. Was this stranger the youth Francis had once been? Was this evidence of the anger that lurked beneath the surface of a middle-class facade? One that masked the upbringing and abuses he'd been subjected to? Sadness gripped her heart that Francis might be in a constant battle with who he once was and who he was now.

Swallowing hard, she stepped forward and forced an expression of amusement. 'Put each other down or else I'll put you together in a room upstairs.' She crossed her arms over her racing heart. 'You really do make quite the romantic picture.'

Their arms dropped as though she had shot them with a dual catapult.

'So,' she said, stepping closer and giving Francis a slow appraisal from head to toe, her heart treacherously skipping. Out of order and control he might be, but good Lord the man was as handsome as they come. 'To what do I owe this unexpected, somewhat robust, visit?'

'I need to speak to you.' He threw a pointed glance at Jacob, his jaw set. 'Alone.'

Louisa stepped around Nancy and walked to her fiancé, gripping Jacob's arm and pulling him away. 'I do not appreciate this little display of masculine superiority, Mr Carlyle, but if you wish to speak to Nancy, that is perfectly fine. We will leave you in peace.' She raised her brows, violet eyes flashing with warning at Jacob. 'Will we not, my darling?'

Jacob muttered something incomprehensible and obediently stalked away with Louisa, her study door slamming shut behind them.

Octavia sighed. 'Well, you certainly brightened up an otherwise uneventful afternoon, Mr Carlyle. You know where I am if you need me, Nancy.'

Once they were alone, Nancy brushed past Francis and closed the front door. 'I can only assume your current mood and whatever you have to say has been provoked by an event outside of this house,' she said, staring into his furious blue eyes. 'Otherwise I do not understand why you would resort to grappling with a man of Jacob's size and temperament.'

'The man flatly refused me entry.' He scowled along the hallway towards the study. 'It's barely three o'clock and I am hardly an intoxicated client demanding a session with a prostitute.'

Nancy's amusement vanished like a popped bubble. She did not like the dismissive tone of his voice. At all. She arched an eyebrow, her irritation brewing. 'Is that so?'

'Yes. Now, shall we retire to the drawing room?'

He moved to walk away and she grasped his arm. Gritting her teeth, she spoke quietly. 'Now, you listen to me, Mr *I own a house on Queen Square* Carlyle—'

'Nancy, for the love of God.'

'Don't go preaching the Lord's name at me either.' She poked her finger into his hard, broad chest. 'This is my home. Jacob, Louisa and Octavia are my people.' She glared. 'You are merely a man whose company I happen to enjoy. A man who had no shame in coming to this house and lying upstairs with a whore who works here. So, don't you dare start looking down at this house, at me, or any of us. Do you hear?'

He held her gaze before slumping his shoulders, colour creeping into his cheeks. 'You're right. I'm sorry.'

'It isn't me you should be apologising to, but I'll take you to see Jacob later.' She slipped her hand into the crook of his elbow. 'For now though, let's go into the parlour. I think I need to make a few things clear to you so there is never a repeat of what just happened.'

Once they were in the parlour, Nancy nodded towards the sofa. 'Take a seat.'

Francis opened his mouth as if to protest before he removed his hat, his jaw tight as he sat.

'Good. Now then…' Nancy stood in front of him, her hands on her hips. 'I want you to promise me that you will never come here and start throwing your weight around like that ever again. You were lucky any of us women didn't knock you out, let alone Jacob.'

A muscle twitched in his jaw, his blue eyes glittering with anger. 'Your doorman could do with showing some courtesy when people—'

'Jacob would have been justified in whichever way he spoke or responded to you. He only ever has us and this house at the forefront of his mind.'

'So even without my explanation, you're taking his side?' He sniffed, his anger palpable. 'Well, at least I know where I stand.'

Disbelief wound tight inside her. 'Don't you dare.'

'What? Say what I see?'

'This house and the people in it are my life, Francis. Not you. I am not ashamed of them or what we do here and never will be.'

There was something animalistic – downright arousing – about the way he looked at her in that moment. As though he wanted to either take her or devour her. The trouble was, neither was making her want to reciprocate angrily. Rather it was making her lower regions pull with inexplicable desire.

She lifted her chin. 'I might have agreed to work with you on your play, but before we embark on that somewhat crazy venture, I have a few ground rules.'

He huffed a laugh and sat back more comfortably, his gaze mildly less irritated. 'You and Lord Henry both.'

Nancy frowned and crossed her arms. 'Lord Henry?'

'The man who practically owns the Royal. I had a meeting with him before I came here.' He glared towards the window as if he could see the man he spoke of standing on the other side of the sash window. 'He has refused to finance my play, which means I must fund, organise and see it through to fruition alone.'

His worry and agitation was clear and Nancy's lust for him quieted. Now she wanted to comfort him, tell him everything would be all right and that she would be beside him to the end, come what may.

Yet she held back, self-preservation closing around her heart. 'I see. Well, is that possible? Will you be able to do this alone?'

He abruptly turned. 'I won't be alone. I have you.' His gaze softened, melting the fragile ice around her heart. 'I hope.'

The uncertainty in his voice clawed at her defences and Nancy's bravado faltered but she somehow managed to remain resolute. She had to show him she would not be pushed around or dictated to. 'You do have me... for now, but that may well change if we don't get a few things straight first.'

'Go ahead.'

'First of all...' She hesitated, part of her not wanting to ruin what possibilities were building between them, the other part knowing she must speak up now or forever hold her peace. 'That is the last time you show any inclination to violence in front of me. Ever.'

'Nancy...'

'My life is good now, Francis. I have known violent men my entire life. I have been beaten and worse at the hands of many. Only a few nights ago, a man decided to wallop Octavia—'

'What?' He looked to the door, his immediate anger palpable. 'She was struck? Here?'

'Yes, Francis. It's par for the course for a whore in normal circumstances, but our house is not normal. It was fashioned, promoted and created on a solid foundation of what would and would not be tolerated, and it is that' – she crossed her arms and glared – 'which I will never allow you or anyone else to jeopardise.'

'I would never do anything to threaten you or what is important to you.'

'Then let me make one thing clear before we get any deeper into a future together.' She heard the implication in her words, her heart stirring with desire to be with him intimately. 'I am a whore before I am an actress. This house and my friends have been the making of me, so Louisa, Octavia and Jacob will never veer from my priorities, whether or not we succeed in your play.'

'I understand.'

'While I am working with you, I expect whatever I would have earned here to be replicated so that neither Louisa nor I are out of pocket. Also...' She drew in a long breath. 'If you even think about using my whoring or this house to promote your play in any way, I am walking away and will never speak to or see you again.'

'You think I would do such a thing? This play is about my life and my life only. I would never expose anything about you.'

'Good.' She took a few paces, her mind racing. Abruptly, she stopped. 'Secondly, I am entirely aware of your background and struggles, but I did not like your tone before. You are neither my employer nor my king, Francis. You are my equal. You have told me, and I believe you, that you were a foundling. Left and abandoned. Then you were a child of the workhouse. You have known hardship, known what it is merely to survive.

'Therefore, I beg of you to never forget where you've been or act as though your old life wasn't true. Otherwise, you could one day find yourself unceremoniously kicked from your pedestal. There are thousands of others trying for what you have. Happiness, success, wealth.' She inhaled a shaky breath. 'Myself included.'

Horrified that she had said so much – revealed so much – tears sprang into Nancy's eyes and she angrily swiped at them.

He slowly placed his hat on the coffee table and stood. Nancy's throat ached around the lump stuck there, words dancing on her tongue. Yet, she couldn't speak, couldn't hear above the cracking and spitting of her pathetic passion now that it had erupted uncurbed once again.

He came to her, standing so close, she noticed flecks of silver in the blue of his eyes for the very first time. Noticed the small scar that ran along the hump of his left cheekbone and the first grey hairs that shone at his temples.

She blinked her mind into focus. 'So, there we are,' she said, looking past him. 'I hope I've made myself clear.'

He put his finger to her chin, sending a jolt through her body, every nerve ending traitorously alert as he dipped his head, brushed the softest kiss across her lips. 'Very clear and I will never, ever let you down.' Another kiss. 'Not ever.'

'You can't say that,' she whispered, her eyes closing. 'No one can.'

'As I am standing here now, I believe it will be me who helps you out of the abyss and I pray to God that my instinct is right...' Another slow lingering kiss to her mouth. 'But, for now, I must go.'

'Go?' She snapped her eyes open as he moved to the table and retrieved his hat. Had she really let him kiss her that way and now he was walking away from her? 'You're going? But I'd assumed you came here to tell me something.'

'I did. It was about Lord Henry, but all will be will. I'll be back.' The determined anger had returned to his gaze, his cheeks flushed once more. 'I need...' He looked again to the window. 'I need to do something.'

He left her standing like an alabaster statue in the middle of the parlour before Nancy lowered shakily onto a chair, inexplicable laughter bubbling behind her chest. She should have been mad, kicking herself for allowing him to get so close to her, to stir her enough that she felt he needed a dressing-down. Yet, instead, she felt as though a huge weight had lifted from her shoulders by speaking so honestly to him. As though Francis had just taken her convictions, all that had been a heavy burden for decades, and escaped with it so that he might fix all that worried her.

Her smile dissolved and she looked to the window, her stomach knotting with anxiety. She must never ever believe such a thing could be true. She had to rely on herself only. Always. Yet, as she raised her hand to her lips, her fingers trembled... What it would be, just once, to believe a man could be good. As good as Jacob had proven himself to be for Louisa.

Could she dare to hope the same might be true of Francis for her? Nancy traced her fingers along her jaw. How she could not?

28

Francis gripped his third glass of brandy and surveyed the back room of Tanner's gentlemen's club, derision knotting his stomach. Cigar smoke hung in the air, mixing with the scent of liquor and hair cream. The dark wood-panelled walls and thick oriental carpets annoyed him as much as the lavish chandeliers and silver coffee pots.

He'd had every intention of heading straight to the Royal from Carson Street in order to speak with Eloise and several others whom he envisaged acting in his play. Before he could even begin to think how he would pull the play together in the coming months, he needed the word of those chosen actors that they would willingly follow him in his endeavours, wherever they might end up.

Yet his bravado had faltered somewhere between Carson Street and the Royal and, instead, drew him to Tanner's. A place of which he was no more a part of today than he would have been ten years ago. God, it irked that Nancy had seen through him as though he were a pane of glass. The opaque veneer he thought he wore so well had been cracked by her scrutiny, revealing him for the fraud he was.

After tossing back the remainder of his drink, he lifted the glass to a waiter standing nearby and tipped his head, indicating he wanted another. Francis's vision was slightly blurred, the beginnings of a headache beating at his temples, but he would continue to drink, continue to brood in whatever way he saw fit. He was his own man, built through determination, mindset and an immovable work ethic and, whether Nancy's summary of his duplicity was right or not, she wasn't here now to berate his behaviour.

Another glass was brought to his table and Francis raised the amber liquid to his lips, gritting his teeth as the brandy passed from his throat to his chest in a burning stream. Culpability of how he'd behaved at Carson Street hammered at his conscience – the way he'd fled from there even more so.

Yet, his behaviour had been justified.

As soon as the boor of a doorman had refused him entry, Francis had seen red and there would have been nothing or nobody who would have stopped him from seeing Nancy. Francis smirked around the rim of his glass. And see her he did. He lifted his glass in a toast to himself.

'Someone's looking mighty pleased with himself, I must say.'

Closing one eye against the pain that shot through his temple, Francis lifted his head. 'What are you doing here?'

Edmund raised his eyebrows. 'Shouldn't I be asking *you* that? Mrs Gaynor is likely to throw your steak in your face if she sees you in this state.'

'Why should I care what the cook I employ does with the food I pay for?'

The amusement in his friend's eyes vanished. 'How long have you been here?'

Francis sipped his drink, looked across the room. 'Not long enough.'

The chatter and laughter rang around them as Francis stared into the depth of his glass, trying his best to be impervious to the heat of Edmund's stare burning into his turned cheek. He could count on one hand how many times he and Edmund had exchanged a cross word and now he was subjecting his friend to a public challenge. *Move me or leave me.*

'You need to leave here, Francis. Now.'

Francis met his friend's gaze. 'Is that so?' He lifted his glass to his lips. 'Just go, will you? Eat the bloody steak yourself for all I care. I'll be home when I'm good and ready.'

Francis looked across the room, the suited and booted gentlemen's cajoling and laughter jabbing at him, making him grip his glass tighter. He silently willed Edmund to leave lest the last of his patience snap and he surrender to the violence burning through his blood like molten flames. Francis was not here this evening. Frank was, and he was not a boy to be messed with.

There was a shuffling and a heavy exhalation as Edmund took a step back. 'As you wish, *sir*.'

Francis closed his eyes as his friend retreated leaving an empty, gaping chasm beside the table. Christ, since when did he speak to Edmund like a gentleman to a servant? Since when did he really speak to any of his staff that way? Francis took a mouthful of brandy and reached for one of the complimentary cigars lying on a silver saucer on the table. And then he was toppling...

He landed with an unceremonious thud on the carpet, his breath whooshing from his lungs as the side of his head hit the floor, his chair crashing down beside him. Francis squinted upwards as a waiter came running, chairs being pulled out all around him and shoes shined to an inch of their lives filling his blurred vision.

'All right, sir. I'm the manager, and I think it best you call it night, don't you?' A firm hand gripped Francis's elbow and heaved him to his feet. 'Let's see if I can hail you a cab. Come along now.'

The room tipped from side to side as the men around him stared. Francis dipped his head, his regret and embarrassment immediate as the first flickers of sobriety seeped in. His current state was the consequence of the shame he'd felt when he'd seen the disappointment in Nancy's wonderful grey eyes when he'd been in the Carson Street hallway, the high hitch of her shoulders, her tightly crossed arms...

All the mannerisms of someone under attack.

The manager hauled Francis from the main room of the club and into the corridor and Francis didn't put up a fight. Every ounce of his inner strength wavered along with his certainty about the supposed path he would take to help the poor bastards currently diminishing and suffering behind the workhouse walls.

Nancy's fear and his chat with Lord Henry made Francis doubt the possibility of his play – his goddamn life – ever benefiting the workhouse children. What would his life have been worth if he failed to endorse some right towards obliterating so much wrong? What in God's name was happening to him that his words and actions had become so all-consuming that he was demanding his way into someone's home? Being thrown out of respected establishments that had so long been on his wish list to be a part of?

He stumbled a few more paces and then hitched his arm from the manager's. 'I'm all right. Leave me be. I can walk.'

The man's set and angry face circulated on a kaleidoscope in front of Francis's eyes. 'Are you quite sure, sir?'

'Yes. I apologise for...' Francis waved in the general direction of the club's main room as he stumbled through the lobby. 'It won't happen again.'

The manager curtly nodded, his eyes reflecting his disapproval before he turned and took Francis's hat from a young, uniformed man Francis hadn't noticed standing alongside him. He handed it over and Francis nodded his thanks before stumbling outside.

The night air swirled around him and he inhaled great lungfuls, trying his darndest to clear the fug from his brain. Onwards he walked, his destination imprinted on his mind like an ugly black stain. Putting on his hat, he pulled the brim low, purposefully avoiding the gazes of anyone he passed, his gait slowly gathering traction the closer he walked towards the workhouse.

By rights, he should have been at the theatre and would have to make his excuses tomorrow because, for the first time in a long time, Francis wouldn't be there. The current play had been showing for a fortnight and the cast and stage workers would have all in hand... not that that made it right Francis was absent.

Just another thing to add to his list of misdemeanours today.

The shadow of the workhouse loomed ahead of him and Francis's gut lurched. The place was like a floating phantom. A ghost he needed to exorcise. The only way he'd thought to do that was through his writing and love of the theatre, maybe the future sponsorship of a child. How in the world would any of those things really make a difference?

He grasped the bars of the tall, wrought-iron gates and shook them, frustration and rage rising on a violent wave as Nancy's face swam in front of his eyes. Visions of her singing on the table at the White Hart gave way to visions of her naked in bed, a thin sheet swathed over her legs, her plump breasts revealed to his viewing. He shook the bars again, a pain slicing deep in his heart as he growled aloud, shameful tears pricking the backs of his eyes.

She was a wonder. A woman who deserved the world clapping and cheering her talent. She deserved doors to open to a future that she could not imagine or maybe part of her didn't even want, if it meant leaving her friends and Carson Street.

'I am not wrong,' he shouted, pushing and pulling at the bars. 'I am not wrong about her and I am not wrong about my play.'

Never forget where you've been or act as though your old life wasn't true...

Nancy's words reverberated in his mind. How many times had he denied who he had once been? These days he drank in gentlemen's clubs as though he belonged there. Occasionally ate and drank in Lord Henry's house, sat at dinner with him and his wife. He had been greeted by gentry, even royalty, at the theatre doors, as though he rubbed shoulders with these people at country shooting parties in the grounds of their grand manor houses.

Sickness rolled inside Francis and a bitterness coated his throat. Nancy saw him for what he was – recognised his need to hide what had happened to him in a way that she never would. She embraced her struggles, chose to live by them openly if it meant she ate, laughed and survived for another day, week or year. Bath's streets were paved in gold as much as they were manure, but Nancy had no need to write a play about it, to change the lead from male to female in a pathetic attempt at concealment.

If she had been at the workhouse and grown into the success Francis was now, he didn't doubt Nancy would be inside that dark, harrowing building, taking one child after the other by the hand and leading them to a better place, a happy home and safety.

Francis squeezed his eyes shut as fear clutched like a fist

inside him. A solitary tear rolled over his cheek and he let it fall, his cowardice laughing like a demon in his ears. He opened his eyes and stared at the windows of the workhouse. If he were to step inside there, the memories would claw and tear at his skin like devils' talons until he was torn open, exposed and little more than the scared boy he once was...

And that is why you are you, and Nancy is someone you could never come close to being...

29

Nancy pulled Louisa closer, their arms linked as they strolled along the market stalls on the warmest day of the year so far, the sun shining. 'So, how does it feel to be a bride in waiting? You and Jacob are going to make the most wonderful-looking couple on your wedding day.'

'Whenever that might be.' Louisa sighed as she stopped to examine a length of lace before returning it to one of the wooden boxes on the makeshift table beside them. 'We haven't set a date and I'm not keen to do so until we know how things are going to play out with the house over the coming weeks.'

Nancy glanced at her friend, the hat she was about to inspect forgotten. 'But I thought you said you will marry at Christmas. What's happened to change that?'

'Nothing. Not really. It's just...' Louisa faced her, her violet eyes filled with concern. 'With you almost certainly heading for a glittering career at the theatre, I think it's time I employed some new girls. Not to live in, just work. And that...' she exhaled a shaky breath '...means opening ourselves up to unforeseen problems, no doubt.'

'No problem is big enough for you and Jacob to delay getting married, surely?' Guilt whispered through Nancy that she might have in any way marred Louisa's excitement about her marriage plans. 'I am back in full force, Lou. I've not heard from Francis for days. It could be that any plans he had for me are well and truly quashed due the lack of support from the main man at the theatre.' Forcing herself to bury her disappointment for Francis, Nancy shrugged. 'It's possible that when Francis high-tailed it out of the house last week, he was destined never to return. So, I am thinking of nothing more than our business, you and Jacob, until I hear from Francis. *If* I hear from him. You mustn't waste any more time worrying about your future. It is looking remarkably rosy from where I'm standing.'

'What do you mean your plans are quashed?' Louisa asked as she led them towards a vacant bench. 'I thought everything was going ahead with his play. Surely Mr Carlyle will manage secure funding and whatever else is needed?'

Nancy looked at the abbey, standing tall and magnificent above the square, its turrets glinting in the sunlight. 'Well, as I said, he hasn't returned to Carson Street or even written to me, so I can only assume funding is impossible. It seems God has shown me I am exactly where I am supposed to be.' She turned. 'With you. At Carson Street... and before you start protesting, I am happy with that, Lou. Honestly.'

'Well, I'm not.' Louisa bristled with indignation. 'Mr Carlyle saw something in you. Something important. And I won't let you give up so easily on something that clearly means a lot to you.'

'The theatre does not mean a lot to me, you do. Not to mention Octavia, Jacob and the success of the house.' Uneasy with her little white lie about her dreams at the theatre, Nancy looked down at her lap and fiddled with the strap on her purse. 'The theatre might be a lifelong dream, but there's a very real possibility it is also a futile one.' She met Louisa's gaze. 'It also matters that Francis appears to be just another man who isn't showing his true self to me. I won't be hoodwinked a second time.'

'His true self?'

Nancy's heart twisted with a loss she resented Francis for putting there. 'There are more similarities than differences in our backgrounds, but I've seen that his success means he denies what he once was, and I don't like it. If he truly wanted to see his play onstage for the benefit of the workhouse children, he'd stop at nothing to make that happen.' She shook her head, her annoyance rising as she looked across the square at the people of different classes mixing with and avoiding one another in equal measure. 'When I last saw him, we exchanged... a few words. He kissed me and then left, never to be seen again.' She faced Louisa and lifted her chin. 'I have no wish to see a man like that, let alone work with one. I'm happy at Carson Street. I'm happy with you and that is where I will stay.'

As Louisa's gaze drifted over Nancy's face, she battled not to fidget. Her friend had the uncanny ability to pinpoint Nancy's feelings, no matter how hard she tried to hide them. She had to convince Louisa of her sincerity, otherwise how would she have any chance of believing her words herself?

'So...' Nancy grinned, her cheeks warming as Louisa's silence stretched. 'I'm fully back in the saddle. Have I not been back to my usual self with the culls? Aren't they once more singing my praises? Mr Jameson even proposed marriage again last night. Everything is back as it should be.' She turned from her friend's narrowed eyes and opened her purse, feigning a determined search for something. Anything. 'And I plan to head to the White Hart tonight. It's been too long since I gave a turn. Maura will think I've abandoned her.'

'Have you finished?' Louisa stood and brushed down her skirts, her jaw a tight line. 'Let's continue our shopping, shall we?'

Her friend's agitation was tangible, and Nancy suspected their conversation was far from over. Louisa would no doubt revisit their discussion at dinner when she had the support of Jacob and Octavia. Nancy pulled back her shoulders, mustering every ounce of inner strength she possessed. Well, they could gang together as much as they wanted. She had been less distracted since Francis's unexpected departure and her culls had told her as much. She was back where she should be. The proof could not be clearer.

If she was meant to be onstage, meant to be side by side with Francis, then God would give her a sign. Simple as that.

A bulky shoulder nudged her, and Nancy stumbled.

'Oh, I do beg your pardon.'

'Not a problem,' Nancy said, regaining her footing and glancing at her trodden shoe. 'Good day to you.'

She and Louisa moved to walk on when the woman who'd knocked her spoke again.

'Miss Bloom, isn't it?'

Nancy turned and dread dropped like a stone into her stomach. *Oh, no...* She forced a smile. 'Mrs Gaynor. How lovely to see you again.'

Francis's housekeeper beamed, her green eyes sparkling with friendliness. 'It has to be fate that I've bumped into you.' She laughed, extending a nod to Louisa. 'I'm Mrs Gaynor, Mr Carlyle's housekeeper. How do you do?'

Nancy inwardly cringed, sensing her friend's glee as she took the other woman's hand. 'Louisa Hill.'

'Well...' Nancy tugged on Louisa's arm. 'It was nice—'

'Might I delay you just a few minutes longer, Miss Bloom?' The delight in Mrs Gaynor's eyes faded to worry. 'Only I think you could be of some help to me. Or rather, help to Mr Carlyle.'

Concern for Francis immediately rushed into Nancy's heart, but she fought to keep her face impassive. Her hardened veneer had been jeopardised by the very man Mrs Gaynor spoke of and it had got her nowhere. Cool indifference, detachment and rational thinking were the only way forward. Always.

'You see, he isn't himself at all and hasn't been for days. He's not eating or sleeping. He's drinking as I have never known him to before and, worst of all, he is making excuse after excuse not to be at the theatre.' Two deep lines formed between her brows, her face paling. 'I fear he is slipping into a very dark place, Miss Bloom, and I have no idea why. He has always been such a good, kind employer. Happy and generous to his staff and his colleagues at the Royal.'

Nancy's mouth dried. What did the woman want her to do? As much as Nancy had wanted to get to know Francis, the painful truth was she didn't really know him at all. 'I...'

Louisa stepped closer, laid her hand gently on Mrs Gaynor's arm. 'Might Mr Carlyle have received some bad news?' She glanced at Nancy, her eyes wide. 'A disappointment?'

'That is my suspicion exactly,' Mrs Gaynor said, her gaze sliding to Nancy. 'And I believe it is you who can drag him from the mire in which he seems so determined to dwell.'

'Mrs Gaynor.' Nancy huffed a laugh. 'My acquaintance with Mr Carlyle is hardly sustained enough that—'

'Oh, but it is!' Her cheeks flushed and her eyes shone with sudden exhilaration. 'He speaks of you all the time. "Miss Bloom this and Miss Bloom that". "When my play is shown and Miss Bloom is its star, then, and only then, will the world see what both she and I are made of".' Mrs Gaynor shook head and smiled. 'He is entirely taken with you and this project of yours. You really are the only person to help him right now – I'm as sure of that as I am of my own name.'

Words stuck in Nancy's throat as panic swept through her. She'd told herself that she had no wish to see Francis again, assuming him well, but if he was in the throes of a downward spiral… Her heart pounded, her care for him making her tremble no matter how hard she battled against it. She didn't have the strength of heart to fight his eyes, his mouth, *him* should she see him depressed.

'He disappeared just before I left the house this morning,' Mrs Gaynor continued. 'He was fussing and carrying on, muttering to himself about the workhouse of all things, and then he simply left. Thankfully, he was wearing a nice suit and he'd requested that Edmund shave him but, oh, the rage in Mr Carlyle's eyes was so frightening.'

'Well, then, Mrs Gaynor…' Louisa stepped forward and pushed her arm into Nancy's. 'I will see to it that Miss Bloom stops by to see Mr Carlyle later this afternoon. How will that be?'

'Oh, that would be wonderful.' Mrs Gaynor beamed. She looked at Nancy. 'As soon as I saw you, I knew you'd help, Miss Bloom. Thank you. Thank you so much.'

She hurried away and Nancy stared after her, frozen to the spot by a cloak of fear.

'So…' Louisa pulled Nancy close as they continued along the street. 'We'd better get home so you can prepare yourself to see Mr Carlyle. One look at you and I'm sure whatever ails him will be entirely cured.'

'You shouldn't have done that.' Nancy drew her friend to a stop, anger overriding her fear. 'I have nothing to say that will help him. Nothing I can do to allay his troubles. He told me the owner of the Royal refused to finance his play. It is no doubt that which is bothering him.'

'Well, you won't know until you see him, so you must go.' Louisa's shoulders dropped. 'Nance, I know you're afraid, but I don't believe that you didn't enjoy your time with Mr Carlyle. That his talent and ideas did not excite you. Your life is yours to do with as you wish and if you want to remain at the house, I am hardly going to say no, but...' Louisa cupped her hand to Nancy's jaw, her gaze soft. 'I know you. How will you be able to carry on as you have, now you know Mr Carlyle to be suffering? You might be able to fool others with your self-imposed detachment, but not me.'

Vulnerability twisted and turned inside Nancy as she looked away. 'Fine, I'll go,' she said, straightening her spine. 'But if you think I won't be *detached* with Francis, you can think again.' She faced Louisa, determination whispering through her. 'No one is allowed to wallow in self-pity around me. Francis included.'

Louisa grinned.

Nancy scowled. 'And stop smiling at me like that.'

30

Francis shook the warden's hand as he stepped into the workhouse courtyard, his gut clenched tight with trepidation. 'I appreciate you persuading the governor to see me on such short notice, Mr O'Sullivan.'

'Yeah, well.' The warden sniffed as he led Francis towards the iron door that looked like it belonged on a doll's house considering the mammoth size of the building. 'Mr Greaves's ears soon pricked up when I said you mentioned a monetary donation.'

'It's appreciated all the same.' Francis drew in a long, steadying breath as O'Sullivan opened the door with a loud clang and led him inside. The dank, musty smell instantaneously evoked remembered horrors and Francis's shoulders stiffened, his breathing more difficult. 'Is Mr Greaves an agreeable man?'

'Agreeable?' O'Sullivan smiled wryly. 'I wouldn't think his staff or the poor sods who have found themselves in this place would call him that. But to you? I imagine he'll be as agreeable as they come.' He gestured along the dark corridor. 'Just this way, sir.'

Francis stared at the row of small windows running along the top of the grey walls allowing minimal illumination, the cloying semi-darkness seeping into his skin. He had no doubt he'd be requesting his housemaid run him a steaming-hot bath the minute he stepped through his front door.

With each step, memories bashed and battered Francis's mind, sickness unfurling inside of him as he tried his hardest to block out his nightmares. He could not falter in his facade that the workhouse was nothing more than a building to him. That it housed those less fortunate whom he wished to help but held no affinity with. Anything less would risk the governor suspecting Francis's motives were founded in more than charity. Everyone who had been forced to live and work here learned their time confined never completely washed off. Resentment and vengeance lingered in a boarder's heart like a slowly seeping poison; the antidote unlikely to ever be found.

'Here we are, sir.' O'Sullivan stopped outside a closed, darkly painted door. 'The governor's office. You ready?'

Somewhat surprised by the question, Francis nodded and kept his expression impassive. God only knew what he would see and hear, but he was here now and would see his mission through. 'Absolutely.'

With a curt nod, the warden rapped hard on the door and pushed it open. 'I have Mr Carlyle for you, sir.'

Francis swept past O'Sullivan into the office and tried to hide his shock, bury his distaste and anger. The room was furnished to an almost grand scale, the desk and chairs big and ornate, the walls lined with prints, and an enormous clock hung above the stone fireplace. How could any man – governor or not – spend his days in a space such as this knowing how children lived just metres away?

Clearing his throat, Francis offered his hand to the broad, bearded man who had risen from behind the desk. 'Mr Greaves, sir. It's nice to meet you.'

'And you, sir. And you.' He shook Francis's hand and turned his steel-grey eyes to O'Sullivan. 'That will be all, Albert.'

No thank you. No congeniality or amiability. Francis wanted to wallop the man.

'Take a seat, Mr Carlyle.' Greaves gestured with a wave towards a chair the other side of his huge walnut desk as he lowered his bulk into a leather chair. 'I am pleased to welcome you. It's my understanding from O'Sullivan that you were most insistent that you spoke with me today.'

'I was.' *But not for the reasons you think...* Francis cleared his throat and concentrated on relaxing his hands that had somehow curled into fists. 'I would very much like to contribute to the institution.'

'I see.' Greaves peered over the top of his spectacles, his affable smile no more as his piercing stare burned into Francis. 'And might I ask what instigated your generosity? Although some of our donors like to come into the workhouse, survey the recipients of their philanthropy, that does not happen often. You do know we are happy to receive donations via a written bank note?'

Hmm, because you would rather watchful eyes stayed shut, no doubt. Francis cleared his throat. 'I do, but what I want in exchange for my contribution means I had to be here in person.'

Suspicion immediately darkened Greaves's eyes and he slowly leaned his elbows on his desk. 'Oh?'

'You see, in order to make my donation – my very significant donation – I would like to talk to the children.'

Greaves visibly flinched, colour leaping into his cheeks. 'Talk... I'm afraid that's impossible, sir. Visits of that nature would have to be arranged in advance. At times suitable to both myself and the wardens. You cannot expect that I might allow—'

'But I do expect it,' Francis said quietly, his eyes locked with Greaves's. 'What's more, I expect it to happen today.'

Francis's heart beat steadily, his body rigid. Unless Greaves intended to bodily remove him from his office and march him along the long corridor to the workhouse's front door, Francis would not be leaving without speaking to at least a few of the young boys here. The realisation that it would be seeing and talking to the children that would fuel the fire he needed to ensure that he somehow, some way, found the means to fund and arrange his play had hit him like a lightning bolt that morning. His failure to do just that was not an option.

The clock ominously ticked off the seconds, neither he nor Greaves moving a muscle.

'I'm sorry, Mr Carlyle, but you need to be reasonable,' Greaves growled. 'The workhouse has rules. Regulations and procedures. Anything less means the children slacken in their duties, find their voices and opinions. We cannot allow that to happen without risking anarchy.'

Francis clamped his back teeth behind his tight-lipped smile, not trusting himself to respond. He knew only too well of the rules and regulations in this place, knew only too well how quickly and viciously voices and opinions were dealt with.

'If you wish to see the children, we can arrange a convenient time and I will bring a select few to my office for your inspection. However, I warn you, these children are not normal in any way.' Greaves closed his eyes and inhaled a long breath through flared nostrils. 'They are' – he opened his eyes, his gaze steeped with disgust – 'animals.'

Francis clenched his hands so tight his knuckles ached, his blood pulsing through his palms. He leaned forward and locked his gaze on the governor's. 'I will visit the rooms today, Mr Greaves, or I leave now, a bank draft for £20 remaining in my pocket.'

The man's eyes widened, his neck stretching so far forward it looked close to snapping. '£20, sir? Well, that's...'

'A very generous donation, I believe.' Francis stood and put on his hat. 'So, shall we see the children?'

Slowly, Mr Greaves rose from his chair, his annoyance palpable. 'Well, if you insist, I will take you to see a few of the boys. The girls are an impossibility, which I am sure you understand.'

'The boys will suffice.'

The other man nodded, a vein protruding at his temple confirming his unease and frustration. How misinformed O'Sullivan had been. Money talks and always would.

Greaves stepped into the corridor ahead of Francis. Studying the back of the governor's head, Francis could barely contain his satisfaction at his victory. The first battle had been won, at least. He had no doubt there would be many more to come before he was able to put in place some real change, but he would fight on regardless. The biggest proportion of his challenges would be finding a personal strategy with which to handle his past abuses, rather than anything Greaves might throw at him.

* * *

As Francis followed the governor through a web of corridors, up several flights of iron staircases and through three or four riveted iron doors, the bile in Francis's throat grew ever more bitter. Panic stirred in his gut and claustrophobia pressed down as perspiration broke on his forehead and upper lip. Weakness grew and hatred burned.

Every now and then, Greaves threw a comment over his shoulder, but Francis had no idea what the other man said. His blood pounded in his ears, riddled with echoes of weeping, cries of pain and the growl of empty stomachs. Forcing his eyes to remain open and not squeeze them shut, Francis mentally shook himself into the here and now as Greaves came to a stop beneath an arched doorway.

'This is the boys' workroom,' he said, his gaze unwavering. 'I assume this will suffice for your viewing?'

'It will indeed. And my talking to them, of course.' Francis nodded, his hands itching to curl around Greaves's neck. 'I wish to hear what their days consist of.'

Greaves pushed open the door and gestured for Francis to enter ahead of him.

Inhaling a long breath, Francis stepped inside a room where the windows were so small and few the meagre sunlight only cast occasional spears of dust-moted light over the twenty or more boys, their heads bent to the coils and coils of rope stacked all around them. The air was stale with unwashed, sweat-sheened bodies. Resisting the cough that caught like a hook in his throat, Francis pushed forward and walked among the boys.

He had left here fourteen years ago, but nothing – absolutely nothing – had changed.

The lack of ventilation, decent light and clean clothing was unaltered; the steely-eyed warden, stick in hand, face like a smacked arse, stood in the same place at the front of the room. The boys ranged from the age of eight to maybe eleven or twelve. Some looked up from their work, a visitor so much of an unusual occurrence that a few gave in to curiosity, despite the risk of a beating.

One boy sat back on his haunches, the rope still in his bleeding fingers, his vacant stare locked on Francis. Francis offered the boy a small smile, his heart breaking. The lad continued to stare, his expression frozen in hopeless despondency. Guilt and anger burned inside Francis as he noted the way the boy's bones showed beneath the stretched skin on his face and arms, his thin wrists visible at the frayed cuffs of his shirt.

Tentatively, Francis approached him, and the boy's eyes widened with Francis's every step. He raised his hand in supplication. 'It's all right. You've nothing to fear. I'd just like to sit with you a moment. Would that be all right?'

The boy's gaze immediately shot to the warden and then Mr Greaves where they stood a distance away. Although the workhouse governor and warden were in quiet conversation with one another, their eyes never shifted from Francis or the young lad.

'Young man?' Francis spoke quietly and smiled. 'Don't look at them. They're not much to look at, after all.'

The tiniest spark of light seeped into the boy's gaze. 'No, they ain't.'

'Good lad. Can I ask you something?'

The boy nodded.

'How long have you been here?'

'Since I was five. My mama is here, too. I'm going to see her again soon. I know I am.'

Francis swallowed as a sharp pain seared across his chest. He knew only too well how long children and parents were separated in this godforsaken place. 'I'm sure you will. Do you eat well enough?'

'No, sir. I am always hungry.'

'Seen enough, Mr Carlyle?' Greaves's voice boomed behind him. 'Had your fill of a sight most have absolutely no desire to witness?'

Francis faced Greaves, anger pulsing inside him. 'Will you watch what you say in front of these children? They have more than enough to battle with without your derision.' He turned to the boy. 'It was nice to meet you.'

The boy nodded, his wide eyes fearful as he glanced quickly at Greaves before returning to his work.

Francis straightened and faced Greaves. 'I will have seen enough in a while, I'm sure… but for now I wish to speak to a few more of these children.'

The governor's cheeks mottled, his gaze hard. 'As you wish. Your donation still stands?'

'So far, yes.' Francis turned back to the boy. His head was bowed to his work once more, but Francis caught sight of the tear that dropped unheeded onto the boy's hand. 'But there is still much that needs to be done.'

'What does that me—'

'All in good time, Mr Greaves,' Francis said, brushing past him towards a couple of lads working in a far corner of the room. 'All in good time.'

31

Nancy lifted the knocker on Francis's front door and let it drop. No going back now...

She shifted from one foot to the other, glancing along the street before adopting what she hoped was an expression of complete confidence. Another few uncomfortable seconds passed and then the door was pulled open to reveal Francis's footman. Edmund, if she remembered rightly.

'Good after... Miss Bloom.' With a blink, his expression abruptly changed from amenable to nothing short of suspicious. 'How can I help you?'

Nancy purposefully held his gaze despite her thudding heart. The doubt about coming here that had bothered her for the last couple of hours tripled under the footman's hostility. Yet, if Francis was suffering...

She lifted her chin. 'I am here to see Mr Carlyle.'

'I am not aware of an appointment.'

'Because I don't have one.' Nancy's apprehension turned to obstinacy. One way or another, she would gain entrance, whether *Edmund* liked the idea or not. 'Mrs Gaynor kindly extended an invitation for me to visit with Mr Carlyle this afternoon. Therefore, I would very much appreciate you allowing me that courtesy.'

Nancy waited, slightly appalled that she'd resorted to speaking like a toff for Edmund's benefit but sensing she had no choice but to show a little class in order to convince the man she did not intend running amok in Francis's grand residence once admitted.

He surveyed her from head to toe before slowly standing to the side. 'Then you'd better come in and I will see if Mr Carlyle would like to see you.'

Nancy forced a smile, dropped her shoulders. 'Thank you.'

Left alone, Nancy stared at the paintings on the hallway walls, the trinkets and vase of flowers standing on a long table. She tried to tally Francis's decor and belongings with the man she was coming to know but porcelain dishes and bunches of roses didn't match up. He seemed a busy, efficient man – one with his heart in the past and his head in the future. The softness in the house must be due to Mrs Gaynor's tender, motherly influence.

'Miss Bloom?'

Edmund's voice cut through Nancy's contemplation and she started, immediately kicking herself for showing vulnerability. 'Yes?'

Clear satisfaction gleamed in the footman's eyes, his mouth twitching. 'Mr Carlyle will see you in his study.'

Tossing him a glare, Nancy followed Edmund upstairs to the next floor and into a back room. It was shadowed, the light somewhat dismal on such a grey, overcast day, but Francis's distracted, almost manic expression was clear to see from where he sat behind his desk, poring over some papers.

'Miss Bloom, sir.'

'Take a seat, Nancy,' Francis said, without looking up. 'I just need to...'

Nancy bit back a smile as his words drifted, his attention fully on his writing as he continued to scribble. She met Edmund's gaze, raised her eyebrows. He stared for a second or two before giving a curt nod and leaving the room, quietly closing the door behind him.

It soon became clear that Francis had no intention of halting his work, so Nancy took a moment to take in his dishevelled collar and necktie, the way his usually neat hair stuck up in places as though he had raked it over and over with agitated fingers.

Concern whispered through her. She wandered to the leather-bound books filling a floor-to-ceiling bookcase. 'Are you not surprised I'm here?' She ran her fingers along the spines of the gold-embossed volumes. 'Only I did not come by choice, but rather by Mrs Gaynor's pleading.'

Silence.

A low thrum of irritation simmered in Nancy's stomach and she began to count the number of green books versus brown and red in a bid to calm her too-often quick temper. There was no mistaking the harassment in Francis's expression, but to ignore her did not sit well, whatever the reason.

She abruptly turned. 'Francis, I am giving you three seconds to look at me before I walk out of here and never come back.'

So much for holding her temper...

He snapped his eyes to hers. 'What?'

'If you are too busy to speak to me,' she said, crossing her arms, 'then I think it best I leave.'

He lowered his pen to the desk and folded his hands in front of him, his gaze distracted. 'I apologise. Please, sit down. I'm glad you're here.'

Nancy dropped her arms and lowered into the seat on the other side of his desk. 'Good.' She plucked at the fingers of her gloves, steadfastly avoiding his gaze and the sadness that lingered there. 'Mrs Gaynor is worried about you and under the illusion I might be able to help. Although I have absolutely no idea why.'

'Help?' He smiled wryly. 'Maybe you could if you have a solution that might give a loving home to each of the children in the workhouse.'

'Well, I...'

'No? Then Mrs Gaynor is very misinformed if she should assume for a minute that you can help me. That *anyone* can help me.'

Nancy frowned. She should have guessed the foundation of his clear frustration, the cause of the anguish in his wonderful blue eyes. 'What's happened, Francis? I know the play is currently unfinanced, but I assumed you would somehow manage to find the mon—'

'Maybe I can, but what if the play is not the answer?'

'To what?'

'The children. Maybe you were right. A play for the benefit of the workhouse? It is a ridiculous notion!'

'I never said anything like that.' Nancy placed her purse on the corner of his desk. 'And I hope you haven't been telling others that I have in any way disbelieved your talent or how it could benefit others. Your play is nothing short of wonderful and I will thank you not to put words in my mouth. Now...' She leaned forward onto the desk, mirroring his posture and, hopefully, his pointed glare. 'What has happened?'

He opened his mouth, closed it, opened it again and emitted a heavy sigh before dropping back against his wing-backed chair. 'I visited the workhouse and spoke to a few of the boys there.' He closed his eyes as exhaustion clearly overcame him. 'The place is as dire and hopeless as it was a decade ago.' He opened his eyes, his jaw tight. 'I fear the play is not the way forward, and I am more sorry than I can say now that I have raised your hopes that you would be its star when you were let down before.'

'Francis—'

'Those children need funding, yes, but they also need someone to stand up and speak for them on a government level. Dressing up the system's issues in the form of entertainment is not the way forward.'

Nancy waited for her returned disappointment, the crushing feeling of her dreams being quashed a second time, but neither came. Instead, her heart filled with admiration for the man before her, for the man who wished to do so much good but had yet to find the most effective path.

The problem was, Nancy could think of no way of helping Francis practically or emotionally either. The workhouse was a place that haunted him deeply. A place etched on his memory and living painfully in his heart. She, a whore with no understanding of the institution, no abundance of spare money or skill that might aid his wishes or assist his cause. And, as much as that frustrated her, Francis surely knew that, too.

'But what if your play *is* the solution?' she asked, quietly. 'What if telling your story kicks the good and mighty into action? What if a message delivered in such a unique way breaks through to people of influence?' She sat in the chair opposite him and looked into his eyes, trying to muster the positivity that so often shone from him. 'The theatre is your passion, Francis. Your words, your story. You cannot give up before you've even begun.' She hesitated and tilted her chin. 'I won't let you.'

He arched an eyebrow, his gaze doubtful. 'You won't let me?'

'No. Your plan is a good one and the least we should do is see it through.'

His eyes narrowed before he stood and came around the desk, leaning his backside on the edge directly in front of her, his knuckles white as he gripped the wood either side of him. 'Do you really believe that? That we can make this happen through my play? That it might come to make a difference?'

'Yes. Your story is filled with hope and, God knows, hope is everything. You and I know without that there is little chance of survival in such an unforgiving world.'

The vexation left his gaze as the animation that constantly stirred her excitement filled his eyes. He smiled. 'You're right. Will you come with me to the workhouse so that you entirely understand the children's plight and dying spirits as I do?'

'What?' Panic swept through her and Nancy raised her hand, hating that she was about to extinguish the new happy light in his eyes. Just the thought of seeing behind the brick and mortar of the workhouse walls, to look into the desolate eyes of the young and desperate, set her trembling. She shook her head. 'I agreed to your play, Francis, nothing else. You cannot expect me to come—'

'But you have to.'

Nancy stood and whirled away from him, planting her hands on her hips. 'I do not have to do anything. What do I know of the workhouse? What do I know of children?'

'I am just trying to show you how important you are to me. How I want you beside me through every part of this fight.' He came towards her and took her hand. 'If we do all of it together, I know we will succeed.'

Her heart jolted as words flailed on her tongue. *How important you are to me...* Why was he playing with her this way? Did he think her fondness for him was a game? She a puppet that he might pull this way and that? She snatched her hand from his and stepped back. 'I won't come to the workhouse, Francis. You are asking too much of me before you have even made the first steps towards the play coming to fruition. If you can find the money and others who are willing to be in the production, then I will come with you. Not before.'

'But my asking you to do this is about more than you being in the play, Nancy. You do know that?' His voice softened, his eyes filled with tenderness. 'I've kissed you. Made love to you. Not as someone paying for your time, but as someone who has come to care for you, value and respect you. I thought you felt the same for me. That I was no longer a stranger you met in the White Hart or a paying client at Carson Street.' His gaze dimmed with hurt. 'That is why I hoped you'd come with me to the workhouse. Why I would love for you to accompany me through every aspect of our mission.'

Fear beat hard in Nancy's chest, the beginnings of a tear searing through the place where her treacherous heart lay. 'Why do you want so much from me?'

'Why do you ask that as though I have an agenda, an ulterior motive?'

'Well, don't you?' Nancy demanded, self-protection sliding back into place as the very real risk of him messing with her common sense – with her heart – gathered possibility. 'I am a whore, Francis. Why do you keep making me remind you of that simple fact? It was a far-reaching dream that I might one day act in your play, but to ask me to get involved in seeing and talking to the children at the workhouse is above and beyond.' She stormed to his desk and snatched up her purse. 'I fear you see something in me that isn't there. I don't belong in your world. I belong in mine. In Louisa's, Octavia's and Jacob's. I thought I made that clear from the start.'

'You belong at Carson Street, of course, but you also belong with me!'

Tears pricked the back of her eyes and she urgently blinked them back. 'No, I don't!'

He stepped closer and she mentally willed him back. *Don't you dare touch me...*

His hands softly cupped her face, his brilliant blue gaze boring into hers. 'Tell me you don't feel just a spark of possibility when we're together. Tell me our time together hasn't made you think of a future beside me as I do with you.' His gaze dropped hungrily to her mouth. 'Tell me, when we made love, that the line between professional and personal didn't blur for you until it vanished entirely.'

Nancy trembled, her usual toughness deserting her, fleeing as though God himself chased it away. 'I have my own life, my own work...'

'And now you have me, too.'

'We do not belong to each other. Why are you saying these things?' Nancy closed her eyes, cursing the vulnerability in her voice. She opened her eyes. 'I won't be used, Francis.'

'Oh, Nancy.' He dropped his forehead to hers. 'I'm not using you, I'm asking you to trust me. To work beside me. Not as an actress but as someone who believes in second chances and possibility as much as I do.' He lifted his head and looked deep into her eyes. 'Somehow, I believe I can do anything, be anything, whenever you are beside me. I know we have only known each other a short amount of time and it's almost ridiculous that I feel this way about you, but I speak the truth. When I'm with you, I become a better man than I ever imagined. Please, Nancy...' He shook his head. 'Consider everything I am saying to you. Confessing to you.'

'I can't.' Her voice cracked. 'I'm not as strong as you think I am.'

'You are strong. Have you thought, however briefly, that you might be more than you ever imagined you'd be when you are with me? Never had a fleeting feeling of possibility that we could achieve so much together? If not, then I will never again ask more of you than to act in my play. But, please, speak the truth. Not for me, but for yourself.'

Wetness streaked onto Nancy's cheeks as her cursed tears fell. She did feel it. She believed he was meant to come into her life. Why, and for how long, she had no idea. How could she lie to him? Closing her eyes, she nodded. 'I have felt those things.'

'You have?'

Nancy opened her eyes, looked deep into his. 'I feel, Francis. I feel *us* and that terrifies me.'

He brushed his lips over hers. 'We can overcome any challenges, Nancy. I know we can.'

Surrendering, Nancy stole her arms around his neck and kissed him firmly, her tongue seeking his. She had no idea what she was doing or how her heart had so quickly moulded to his, but the excitement of a life with Francis, of them working side by side to help others, felt like a door opening where a bright light shone clear, pulling her towards a future that knew no bounds.

32

Filled with pride, Francis raised his hands and grinned at the entire company standing on the Royal's stage. 'That's a wrap, people. Well done. That dress rehearsal was the best I could've hoped for. I am confident our next run will be the best yet.'

The company burst into applause, a barrage of slapping shoulders and backs accompanying them as they walked, chattering and laughing, towards the wings. Francis watched them go, his smile dissolving as he sat in one of the seats in the front row. Niggling guilt that hadn't lessened all day slithered into his gut. As much as he loved the theatre's latest production, he craved to start casting the parts in his own play.

But, before he could do that, he had to be certain to weigh up his time and money. He wasn't even sure he could be a good theatre director *and* produce his own work. Everything he wanted to do had felt achievable when he'd wrongly assumed he would have Lord Henry's backing. But to finance, cast and produce alone felt daunting, and now he'd convinced Nancy to come along this path with him, even more so.

'Carlyle, just who I wanted to talk to.'

Francis briefly closed his eyes, his defences rising as Lord Henry lowered into the seat beside him.

Feigning interest in the script he held, Francis cleared his throat. 'Lord Henry, sir. Do we have an appointment?'

'No, but after your visit to my house the other day and a discussion with my good wife your words have been badgering my conscience. We need to talk.'

Francis's heart picked up speed. Had Lord Henry had a change of heart about his play's financial costs? He fought to keep his face impassive. 'Oh?'

Lord Henry glanced at Francis, his stiffness illustrating his discomfort. 'It is not usual that I go back on my words, but I have reassessed this play of yours.'

Francis studied him, trying to decipher what Lord Henry thought and not jump with joy prematurely. 'With regards to what, exactly?'

Lord Henry shifted in his seat, his expression far from a man happy with his decision. He looked at the empty stage. 'I've decided I will finance it after all.'

Unadulterated relief whispered through Francis as he fought the urge to laugh out loud. Just as self-doubt had threatened to consume him and his dreams, the prospect of his play coming to fruition on Bath's most esteemed stage had suddenly become a reality.

He drew in a long breath and slowly exhaled. 'That is good news, sir. Very good news, indeed.'

'Well, considering the way you spoke about your work as though it would cause the whole theatre to collapse if we didn't go ahead with it, I mentioned both the play and your hopes of it benefiting the workhouse children to Lady Henry.' Lord Henry stretched out his legs and glared at the carpet before meeting

Francis's gaze. 'She is very active in her charity work, you see. She damn near bit my head off when I told her I had declined to finance it. It's fair to say I was given very little choice in the matter.'

'Then I am very grateful to your wife, sir.'

'Hmm.'

Francis settled back in his chair, trying his best to remain professional despite wanting to dance a jig. 'In view of this change, I would like your permission to start auditioning and casting as soon as possible. Obviously, the play won't be shown until the new year, but I'd like to get things moving now before the performers I have in mind start searching for new work elsewhere.'

'Permission granted, but...' Lord Henry pinned him with a stare. 'I do not want this affecting any productions and plans already in place, Carlyle. First and foremost, your commitment is to see through what I have paid you for thus far.'

'Absolutely. I will manage both.'

'You'd better.' Lord Henry heaved his bulk from his chair and stood, holding out his hand to Francis. 'Then we have a deal. You are in charge from here on in and I will cover all costs... as long as they are within reason. Agreed?'

Francis stood, desperate to flee from the theatre straight to Carson Street to share the news with Nancy. He clasped Lord Henry's hand. 'Agreed.'

'Very good. Then I'll bid you goodnight.'

As Lord Henry left, Francis looked at the Royal's empty stage, his heart racing with excitement and the need to start work immediately. He looked left and right across the stage's breadth, already seeing the setting he'd need and the people who would play the characters.

Nancy, of course, stood centre stage smiling back at him.

Grabbing his belongings, he hurried from the stalls towards his dressing room.

He and Nancy had spoken into the evening yesterday, and although she had asked him to give her more time, the need to return to the workhouse pulled at him.

It was as though every day he wasn't there was a day wasted. He had squandered thousands of days and there would not be another that passed without him making some kind of progress towards his goal. The help needed for the city's poor was urgent. Desperate. And if he was to ensure his play was the most powerful and affecting it could be, he had to re-immerse himself in a world he had tried so hard to convince himself was buried.

The time had come for him to face every single one of the demons that dwelled inside of him.

33

As Nancy walked down the stairs at Carson Street, Louisa's and Octavia's voices drifted towards her from the dining room. The clink of cutlery against porcelain mixed with her friends' hushed conversation as they breakfasted, and Nancy's stomach rumbled. She was suddenly so hungry, she could eat her own meal and theirs, yet she hesitated as she approached the door.

Closing her itchy eyes, Nancy tried to rid herself of her night of broken sleep, haunted by dreams of destitute children and the phantom adults who loomed above them threatening pain and punishment. She was stronger than this. What in God's name was making her so weak? Francis desperately wanted her help, but the mere thought of seeing what lay behind the workhouse gates ignited a trepidation she'd had no idea she was capable of feeling.

Having thought herself so capable, so brave, the visions of children neglected, abused and hungry brought forth a torrent of anxiety. What if Francis's play did nothing to help them? What if he was wrong and Nancy wasn't the right person to tell his story?

That question did not need answering. How *could* she be the right person? She wasn't an actress. She was barely a singer. For the good of the play – for the good of the workhouse – maybe she should persuade him to consider the actress he'd introduced her to at the theatre.

Eloise. Was that her name?

Her mind reeling, Nancy entered the dining room.

Louisa immediately halted in her storytelling to Octavia and turned. 'Nancy, good morn... My God, are you all right?' Her friend stood and came towards her, gently taking her elbow. 'Here. Sit down. You look as though you've barely slept.'

'That's because I haven't.' Nancy offered a small smile to Octavia as she placed a cup of tea in front of her. 'Thank you. I spent most of the night grappling with the most awful nightmares. You wouldn't believe what Francis asked of me yesterday.'

Octavia frowned. 'That man seems to think he has a monopoly on your time. On you.'

The vehemence in Octavia's tone raised Nancy's brows and concern. 'Are *you* all right?'

'Of course I am. It's *your* welfare that concerns me.'

'Well, my welfare is perfectly fine... I think.'

Louisa gently touched Nancy's arm. 'What is it Mr Carlyle would like you to do now?'

Turning from Octavia's glare, Nancy lowered her cup to its saucer and helped herself to some toasted bread from the rack on the table. 'His play was written with a long-held wish he has to improve things at the workhouse. He hopes, if the play is successful, that people might—'

'The workhouse?' Octavia's eyes widened. 'Nothing and nobody can change the workhouse. It has been the same way for years.'

'Exactly. Which is why I feel so tormented about what he wants me to do in addition to being in his play.' Nancy reached for the butter dish. 'What he has proposed I do in order to carry out my role in his play with all the sympathy and empathy it deserves and, in turn, touch the hearts and minds of the people who can pull strings in this city.'

'And what does he propose exactly?' Louisa asked.

Nancy met her friend's concerned gaze. 'That I go with him to the workhouse, talk to some of the children so I can see what it is really like in there.'

'I see.' Louisa drew in a shaky breath. 'Well, as hard as that will be, I am also impressed by Mr Carlyle's commitment to authenticity if nothing else.'

Nancy chewed her toast, saying nothing. She had thought the exact same thing.

'Are you sure your discomfort is about his proposal? Or could it actually be about him?' Louisa asked, her gaze softening. 'I know you, Nancy, and you make decisions quickly and with conviction. There must be something more to your uncertainty than carrying out something that will undoubtedly make people sit up and take notice of his production. Could it be that you really like Francis? That you're afraid of disappointing him?'

Nancy plunged her knife into the butter and spread it over a second slice of bread. 'I do like him, probably too much, but my hesitation has nothing to do with that.'

'Every man is *likeable* when they want something. It's after they've got what they want that we need to guard ourselves against.' Octavia pinned Nancy with her customary glare. 'I encouraged you to listen to Mr Carlyle when he had aspirations towards fulfilling your lifelong dreams. Helping him fight against the authorities at the workhouse is a different thing entirely.'

'I didn't say anything about the authorities. This is about the children.'

'Then I hope you haven't been blinded by Mr Carlyle. He will show his true colours soon enough. You know that. He's already adding to what he originally asked of you.'

'That's not fair, Octavia,' Louisa said, curtly. 'Jacob is a clear example of how a man can be. Has he ever let any of us down? Caused us harm? No, so don't blight Nancy's feelings about Mr Carlyle until we know more.'

'God, I feel so damn weak for talking to you about this,' Nancy said, annoyed at the frustration and fear Francis's quest had evoked in her. 'There was a time, not so long ago, that I would have exploded with madness at you for even suggesting I might have feelings for a man.'

'I agree, but as you are not leaping from your chair in order to throttle me, I can only assume my presumption is correct.'

Nancy bit into her toast. As she ate, she tried to get her thoughts, feelings and words into some sort of order, despite knowing any clarity was impossible when everything inside of her was such a mess.

She swallowed and looked at her friends. 'I have looked after myself—'

'Looked after me,' Louisa interrupted with a smile.

Nancy's shoulders lowered, grateful for her friend's kindness and eternal loyalty. A loyalty that just might be tested if she was to go ahead, side by side with Francis until his aspirations were fulfilled. 'I was alone for so long and then for years it was only the two of us against the world, Lou, and now we are four. Me, you, Octavia and Jacob. And for a long time, I have felt in control of my life and decisions; now everything feels scattered. Like my head and heart have been jumbled, changed and confused.'

'By Mr Carlyle?' Octavia narrowed her eyes. 'Then it is as I suspected.'

'But he's not a bad person, Octavia,' Nancy protested. 'It's just that something deeper has changed in him. Now his wants are about more than the play, more than the workhouse.'

Louisa touched her hand, her gaze concerned. 'In what way?'

Nancy sighed. 'I think he wants this play to fix all he endured himself when he was in the workhouse, and I am not sure that is possible. At times his enthusiasm inspires me...' She shook her head, her heart aching for a man she was beginning to care for so much. 'Other times, his passion terrifies me.'

Octavia abandoned lifting some bacon from the hotplate at the side of the table, her deep blue eyes intense on Nancy. 'Then you should not see him again. I have nothing against Mr Carlyle at the moment but if he is making you uneasy then he is on his way to making an enemy of me.'

'He is not making me uneasy...'

Octavia lifted her eyebrows. 'Are you certain of that?'

'Yes. And I *want* to see him again.' She held Octavia's gaze. 'And I will continue to do so until *I* decide differently.'

Their eyes locked until Octavia sniffed and returned her attention to the hotplate.

Nancy exhaled a long breath. 'Francis was eventually taken in by a man who he came to love and care for as he would have a father. It is his benefactor that he thanks for his fortune and success.'

'I see. And now he wishes to pay back that fortune,' Louisa murmured, her gaze glazed in thought, her brow creased. 'But that does not mean you have to assist him in his endeavours if you do not wish to.'

'But I think I do.'

'Then why are you so ashen-faced?' Octavia asked, her expression disapproving. 'You cannot possibly be comfortable with Mr Carlyle's wishes and wear such a look of distress. If he is bullying you—'

'He's not, and I do not appreciate your judgement of him when you do not know him.' Nancy snapped, suddenly irritated. 'Francis is the furthest from a bully anyone, man or woman, could be. He is passionate. Strong-willed and determined. He thinks he needs me beside him in his endeavours, but he doesn't. Not really. He is capable of doing anything he wants alone.'

Louisa smiled, knowing clear in her violet eyes. 'He loves you, Nancy.'

'What?' Nancy stared at her friend, her stomach knotting with fear. 'He does not love me.'

'Oh, God, he does, doesn't he?' Octavia rolled her eyes and speared some bacon onto her plate. 'Well, that's it then. You are headed for trouble whatever decision you make.'

Louisa laughed. 'Oh, Octavia.'

'What? It's true. The man has already shown he can be a force by tackling Jacob. If he wants Nancy, I imagine there is little she can do to deter him.'

Nancy's heart raced, hope and maybe even a little happiness warming her cheeks. 'We are just friends.'

'Friends?' Octavia huffed a laugh. 'And here was me thinking Mr Carlyle was little more than an *occasionally* paying cull. Clearly, I was wrong.'

Louisa rose from the table and came towards Nancy, her gaze tender before she pressed a kiss to the top of her head. She wandered to the window and stared out into the street. Nancy's stomach dropped. Louisa might have shown her affection, but she clearly couldn't look at her. Would her growing feelings – her growing foolishness – as far as Francis was concerned come to cause a distance between her and the friend she held above all others?

'Louisa—'

She abruptly turned, and Nancy snapped her mouth closed.

She knew the look on Louisa's face only too well. She was a strong and savvy woman. A businesswoman above all else and her expression now spoke of nothing but business. 'And you really believe it is himself he is trying to heal through his play?'

Her appetite gone, Nancy dropped her bread onto her plate and picked up a napkin. She wiped her fingers. 'Yes. He visited there a few days ago and was shown the boys' workroom. He says nothing has improved at all since he was there himself.'

Sympathy seeped into Louisa's gaze. 'I can understand how that might upset him.'

'It did.' Nancy exhaled, care for Francis twisting her heart. 'And I'm not sure I want to leave him to do this alone when he is so clearly suffering.'

'Suffering?'

Nancy faced Octavia. Her shoulders had lowered and now she watched Nancy with concern rather than disapproval.

Nancy nodded. 'Yes. Whatever he saw there was enough for him to believe that I must see it too if I am to really understand the role he longs for me to play. But it is clear to me now that the workhouse is his nemesis and I am afraid of what returning there has done to him. I have to help him. But...' Nancy closed her eyes, self-loathing writhing through her. 'I am little more than a fraud. Sooner or later, he will see that.'

'What are you talking about?' Louisa demanded, all trace of her previous compassion vanishing. 'You are a person who wears her heart entirely on her sleeve, Nancy Bloom. Never have I known you not fervently challenge anyone who might make the unfortunate mistake of judging you in any way.'

'I am not as strong as I pretend to be, Lou.'

'What are talking about? You—'

'I was taken...' Nancy opened her eyes, tried to ignore the

mortification of her vision blurring behind her tears. She angrily swiped at her face. 'When I was a child.'

'What do you mean? Taken?'

'Taken and beaten, raped, violated...' Nancy's voice cracked. 'And even when I was finally returned to Bristol and given my liberty, I avoided the workhouse for fear of the stories I had heard. I chose a life on the street. I chose to whore myself as I had been whored out by my captor.' Tears fell and this time she let them fall, her past shame finally revealed to her dearest friend. She lifted her chin. 'Francis is braver than I ever was. Stronger than I am today. I am so afraid of failing him and...' She looked at Octavia. 'I don't want to do that to a man I am falling in love with.'

The only sound in the room seemed to be Nancy's breathing. Everything had stilled. She could hear neither the mantel clock nor the street traffic through the open window, only her own shallow breaths as they painfully wheezed in and out of her lungs. Tears burned and she blinked them back, her eyes flitting between her friends.

'Well...' Louisa came forward and took Nancy's hands, easing her to her feet. Her eyes glinted in the sunlight filling the room. 'Now I know you even better and I am glad for it. For years I have suspected something bad happened to you. Something that made you so determined to care for yourself and me without help from anyone else.'

Nancy turned to Octavia as she took her other hand. The three of them stood in a circle, bounded and connected. Nancy looked at her friends, her heart filled to bursting with love and trust for these amazing women. 'You have looked after *us*, Louisa. Not the other way around. But now...' She stood a little taller. 'I must look after Francis.'

Louisa brushed a fallen curl from Nancy's brow. 'Just as I do Jacob. It's all right, Nance. You are strong and you will be all Mr

Carlyle needs. I promise you.' She glanced at Octavia. 'All I want, all *we* want, is your solemn word that helping him is absolutely what you want to do.'

Nancy's throat dried with fear of what might lie ahead. Francis had asked her to step inside the workhouse, see the stricken faces and environment that had terrified her enough that she had lived night after night on Bristol's streets, rather than seek the false sanctuary in what she had heard were nothing more than houses of horror.

'You have my word.' She willed her inner strength to the fore. 'I want to do this.'

'Then you have *my* word that we will help both of you in any way we can.'

Octavia pulled Nancy close, dropped her head to hers. 'We promise.'

'Thank you.' Relief swept through Nancy as she blinked back more tears. 'So much.'

She eased her hands from her friends' and retraced Louisa's path to the window. Far in the distance, the many grey windows of a tall, wide and ugly building struggled to gleam beneath the strong summer sun. If she narrowed her eyes, Nancy could just about see its dirty arches and stone sills, its slate roof tiles and blackened chimneys.

The workhouse had been there all along, but now it was as though she was truly seeing it for the very first time. *I'm coming, Francis, and whatever happens, I will be right beside you through all of it.*

34

Still clutching the message he had received from Nancy, Francis mentally urged Edmund to hurry the carriage towards Carson Street. The horses' pace felt at a crawl and stretched Francis's patience to see Nancy to breaking point. She was to stand beside him. To trust him in all that was needed for her performance to stir even the most sceptical of men and women.

He prayed her commitment to him meant her feelings towards him were as strong as his towards her but, as much as he longed to show her the desire and care he felt for her, he could not linger on their burgeoning romance now. To do so could mean he lost his focus on the workhouse and the urgency that Nancy see it so that she could truly share in his need for what must be done.

In turn, everything that happened to him and everything that Nancy would learn, would hopefully inspire the others he had in mind to help him with his play. He had been busy the last few days enrolling the help of several of the men and women who worked behind the scenes at the Royal and had also managed to secure the commitment of half a dozen actors and actresses.

Next, he planned to speak with Eloise. Not that he was looking forward to it. The woman was unquestionably talented and, these days, more apt to be the star of a show than not. He could not imagine she would take kindly to learning Nancy would be taking that role this time.

Well, if Eloise didn't like it, he would find another, more willing, replacement.

At last, the carriage trundled to a halt outside Nancy's house and Francis clambered out onto the cobbled street. Shrugging the tension from his shoulders, he tugged at his lapels and started up the steps.

When he reached the top, the front door opened and Jacob appeared, his cheek turned as he spoke to someone behind him. 'Well, whatever his plans, he'd better hope your wellbeing is his top priority or he'll have me to answer to.'

Francis inwardly winced, having absolutely no doubt the 'he' Jacob spoke of was Francis himself... and the person behind him was Nancy.

'Jacob. Good afternoon.' Francis looked the doorman square in the eye. 'Rest assured, Miss Bloom will never come to harm when I'm around.'

Jacob crossed his arms, his blue eyes dark with warning. 'Well, anything to the contrary, Mr Carlyle, and I'll make myself known to you in a whole different way than you know me now.'

Francis's hackles rose. Who the hell did this man think he was? Did he think Francis incapable of caring for a woman he was in love with? Francis stilled. *Oh, God, am I in love with Nancy on top of everything else?*

'Cat got your tongue?' Jacob smirked. 'Maybe that's for the best, all things considered.'

Nancy pushed past him with a firm shove to Jacob's trunk-like arm. 'Oh, leave off, Jacob. You know I am more than capable of looking after myself. Most likely more effectively than you and Mr Carlyle put together.' Her scowl turned to a smile, her grey eyes softening as she turned to Francis. 'Francis. I was just coming to see you and here you are.'

His heart tripped in his chest to see her looking so beautiful, her red hair gleaming in the bright July sunshine, her dress the palest blue. Dragging his gaze from her, he couldn't resist a triumphant sneer at Jacob before facing Nancy once more. 'I'm glad. As soon as I received your message, I came straight away. We have much work to do.'

'Good. And I'm more than happy to get started.' She placed her hand on his arm and turned to Jacob, her smile dissolving. 'Behave yourself until my return. If you can.'

He shook his head, his eyes on Francis. 'It should be me saying that to you if you know what's good for you.'

Ignoring him, Francis placed his hand over Nancy's. 'Shall we?'

Leading her down the steps and into the carriage, Francis slammed the door and picked up his cane, banging it to the roof. 'Off we go, Edmund.'

'This is my second time in this carriage.' Nancy sighed, smoothing her fingers over the blue silk wall covering beside her and then over the plush navy seat. 'But it still feels such a thrill.'

'Well, owning it was a long time coming,' he said as he looked around him, appreciating the carriage's interior. Something he was ashamed to admit he hadn't done for a while. 'But I'm as proud to have you riding with me as I was the day I travelled alone having purchased it.'

'I'm glad, because it is really beautiful.' She shifted further back in her seat, her smile impish and her eyes gleaming with pleasure. 'And I am more than happy to pretend I belong in such transportation. At least for today. So...' She looked out the window, enthusiastically waved at some passers-by. 'Where are we going? I assume the Royal.'

Having no doubt his next words would slice through her buoyancy, Francis hesitated. He would have given a hundred pounds to have her portrait painted just as she was in that moment. Everything about her was lit like a shopfront at Christmas time, when all too often she seemed weighed down in worry and concern. More often than not for others, rather than herself.

'Francis?' She looked at him, a line forming between her brows. 'Where are we going?'

Inhaling a long breath, Francis took her hand. 'I have been busy since we last met.'

Her gaze wandered over his face, lingered a moment at his lips. 'And?'

'And as well as securing some stagehands and actors for my play, I have found someone who shares in my, in *our*, desire to make a difference at the workhouse. Someone of influence.'

'I see. And who is this person?'

'Her name is Freda Martin.'

'A woman?' The apprehension left Nancy's eyes and her gaze turned eager with interest. 'And has she made steps towards success? Does she work alone? With a husband?'

Pleased by her animation, relief lowered Francis's shoulders. 'She is a wealthy woman in her own right. Or at least she is now. She was left a fortune upon her husband's death three years ago and has dedicated her life to the welfare of the city's poor ever since. Her main focus is pregnant women and mothers of small children who have been deserted by the child's father. The women she helps have stories of every origin. Some are the shamed daughters of the wealthy who were banished from their homes, some are street women who have no way of caring for their babies. Some...' He stopped, rare heat warming his cheeks. '...prostitutes who have found themselves with child but unable to care for it.'

Nancy's gaze glazed with thought, her happiness doused, before she nodded. 'She sounds like a woman I will like very much,' she said, softly. 'Are we going to see her now?'

'Yes.'

'Have you met with her before?'

'No.' Francis leaned back against the seat, unwanted nerves knotting low in his stomach. 'And I have no idea what to expect or even if she will help us.'

'Then why are we going?'

'Because I feel like a boat capsized in choppy water.' He faced her, drawing forth the courage to show that, in truth, he really had no clue if the result of his play being made public would reap any rewards. 'I might want to help the workhouse children, but it would be foolish to dismiss that there are right and wrong ways to go about it. A single mistake could mean failure, before we even begin.'

'Surely if we are doing something charitable, no efforts, including a theatrical performance, would be considered mistakes.'

'No, but getting involved in what the government consider their business could. We need to speak to someone who has trodden the path before us. Learn from the mistakes they've made and the lessons they've learned.'

'And to do that we must confide in Mrs Martin.' She stared into his eyes before giving a curt nod, her gaze filled with resolute determination. 'I think that is a very sensible course, Francis. And I'm sure she will applaud our mission as much as we will hers. To make a difference to Bath's poor needs an army, not a handful of individuals.'

Lifting her hand to his lips, Francis pressed a firm kiss to her knuckles. 'God was smiling down on me the day I met you, Nancy Bloom.'

She grinned, her eyes alight once more. 'And I you, Francis Carlyle.'

They settled into companionable silence until Edmund pulled the carriage to a stop outside a house on Brock Street, in a beautiful terrace of townhouses that joined the exclusive Royal Crescent with the equally grand Circus. As he took Nancy's hand and helped her from the carriage, Francis was quick to notice apprehension flicker in her grey eyes and the way her fingers slightly trembled as she smoothed her skirts.

'She is just a woman trying to do good, Nancy,' he said softly, tightening his hand on hers. 'You are every bit as good and beautiful as any other woman in this city. No one, no matter how grand, is better than you.'

She nodded, her lips pressed together as though she either didn't trust herself to respond or didn't believe a word he'd said.

'Wait there, if you will, Edmund,' he said, lifting his head to his friend. 'I can't imagine we'll be too long.'

Edmund's gaze lingered on the top of Nancy's head from his high seat in front of the carriage. 'Right you are, sir.'

Annoyance whispered through Francis. He needed to have a brusque chat with Edmund later and quash his suspicion about Nancy once and for all. He and Edmund might be friends for life, but that did not give him the right to look at any of his acquaintances with anything less than cordiality. Francis threw him a warning glare before urging Nancy along the short, flagstone pathway to Mrs Martin's front door.

35

Nancy lifted her teacup and studied Mrs Freda Martin over its rim as she remarked on the day's weather to Francis. To say the woman was of a formidable stature would be an understatement. Round and wide with steel-grey curls wound in an elaborate design of plaits and twists atop her head, spectacles hanging from a length of jet beads around her neck and somewhat flinty eyes as icy-blue as a clear winter sky, Mrs Martin most certainly resembled the epitome of a woman who got things done.

How anyone in authority, or otherwise, would refuse her anything was beyond Nancy's imagination. The woman was as likely to smile at you as eat you.

'And you and Mr Carlyle are in association how, Miss Bloom?' The matriarchal Mrs Martin put on her spectacles and peered at Nancy above the half-rim lenses, her gaze unwavering. 'His description of your friendship is vague to say the least.'

Francis cleared his throat as if to answer but Mrs Martin jabbed her hand towards him. 'I would like Miss Bloom to answer my question, if you don't mind.'

Nancy lowered her cup to the table at her side, her irritation stirring. Bold and matronly or not, no one bossed Nancy around and got away with it. She and Louisa had vowed never to answer to anyone after her husband died. Whether that be a woman who owned a house on one of the wealthiest addresses in Bath or Prince Albert himself.

'We are friends, Mrs Martin. Friends with a common goal to work towards helping the workhouse children.' Nancy held the other woman's steady gaze. 'We are here for your advice. Nothing more.'

'Is that so?' Mrs Martin studied her for a moment before her mouth broke into a wide grin and her gaze glistened with amusement. 'Well, I'm very glad to hear it and mightily heartened by your mettle, Miss Bloom. A woman who doesn't suffer fools gladly, I suspect. Just the foundation of what is needed in a person wishing to tackle the problem of the city's poor.' She glanced at Francis, her smile slowly dissolving. 'What you have decided to embark on is not for the faint-hearted, sir. Now...' She settled into her huge wing-back chair, more throne than furniture. 'Let me start by giving you both a warning. The decrepit, pitiful state of the city's workhouse and the conditions the poor souls there have to endure is nothing compared to what you will discover should you be resolute in your desire to dig beneath the surface.'

Nancy fought not to look at Francis, knowing that Mrs Martin referred to the emotional and mental state of the workhouse residents over the dirt, hunger and hard, ruthless toil they had no choice but to suffer each day.

She slowly nodded, her eyes remaining on Mrs Martin's. 'We understand.'

'Do you?' The older woman raised her brows as her eyes darkened. 'Because I understood nothing of how most of those people are irrevocably changed by their experience. Their suffering often everlasting and instrumental in every part of their futures.'

Nancy turned as Francis shifted forward, his hands tightly clasped between his knees as he stared at Mrs Martin.

'Maybe Nancy will have to come to understand what you are inferring, because how can anyone know without having lived in one of those places,' he said quietly, his jaw tight. 'But for me, Mrs Martin, I have lived the truth of your words when I was left at a foundling hospital and then spent many years surviving at the workhouse. I very much doubt there is anything, whether physical, mental or emotional, those children are going through that I haven't experienced myself or that I can't entirely sympathise with.'

Once again, Francis's stony expression sent a chill through Nancy. Gone was the happy-go-lucky thespian and in his place a man who wouldn't be fazed being faced with an opponent in a bare-knuckle fight. Every time she saw this change in him Nancy doubted that she would ever truly know Francis at all. Was this the real him or the man so alive and in love with the theatre?

The tension in the room had thickened so quickly and intensely that Nancy had the insane urge to leap onto the low table in front of them and dance a jig just to dispel it. Her heart beat a little faster, aching from the clear pain in Francis's voice.

Nancy swallowed against the dryness in her throat. 'Mrs Martin, we—'

'I am sorry for your experiences, Mr Carlyle,' the matriarch said quietly, her gaze softening. 'I see there is little need for me to further explain the children's plight to you. However, I must warn you of the fight I have faced thus far and, should you be determined in your endeavours, you will undoubtedly face, too.' She took a sip of tea and sat back, her wily gaze flitting between Nancy and Francis. 'The governor and the majority of wardens at the workhouse take umbrage with anyone offering help where they believe none is needed. They are a tight unit, bound together in their wish to keep the people they oversee in the cesspit of what they believe to be the residents' just and fair place.' She closed her eyes, the thin lids scattered with tiny blue veins, her cheeks reddening. 'We fight a hard trek, but we will be victorious.' She opened her eyes, icy-blue and steely once more. 'However long it takes. Now, there is much more I must tell you if you wish to poke at the hearts and pockets of the rich in this city.'

* * *

Almost an hour had passed by the time Nancy and Francis took leave of Mrs Martin and climbed into Francis's carriage. As Edmund urged the horses onward, Nancy's mind reeled with all the information and difficulties Mrs Martin had explained to them. The task of provoking charity from the elite appeared to be nothing short of arduous Mrs Martin had described her three years' of work as a deep, boggy mire from which, once immersed, a person struggled to pull themselves free.

Yet a strange adrenaline beat through Nancy's veins, every part of her itching to get started on what would almost certainly be one of the biggest challenges of her life.

The adversities she had faced and conquered, the hunger and desolation she had felt more times than she could count, had faded into insignificance after hearing Mrs Martin's candid and heartbreaking stories of the children she had successfully placed in homes throughout her time struggling with the workhouse authorities.

And, as much as Mrs Martin had taken pains to stress her gratitude for Nancy's and Francis's enthusiasm, she had also given no indication she believed their efforts would be fruitful or even the slightest bit long-lasting.

Nancy turned to Francis, concerned that he had not yet spoken. 'Are you all right?'

He faced her, looking tired and pale. 'I'm fine. Just afraid of how likely it is that my play will fail to inspire or change anything.' He leaned his head back against the seat, his gaze filled with frustration. 'But that possibility won't deter me, and it shouldn't you either. The sooner we can get started with its production, the better.'

Although nerves immediately took flight in her stomach, Nancy gently clutched his hand. 'I agree. You have already started making progress and I have read and reread your script, albeit not every word as I would have liked.'

He lifted his head, his gaze boring into hers. 'You must not worry about how much or how little you can read. The most important aspect of your commitment is the emotion you bring to the role. How you can make Martha come alive. For that, I have no doubt of your capability. None whatsoever.'

Nancy looked at their joined hands as her trepidation rose. 'I can't help but doubt if my co-actors and actresses will agree.' She met his gaze. 'I can imagine it will be a frustration to them and you if I am unable to keep up. I have never done anything like this in my life, Francis.'

'You will be surrounded by people willing to help you. Every single one of them was once where you are now. A beginner.' He tightened his fingers on hers. 'There are, of course, a few performers who behave as though they are entitled and the best artiste to ever grace the Royal's boards, but not many. Most only care for the production as a whole and that means working as a unit.'

Nancy tried to smile but failed miserably. Instead, she purposefully changed the subject. 'Did you like Mrs Martin?'

'There is nothing to like or dislike. She has given us clear warning of what we are facing and I suspect she thinks us wholly inadequate.'

'You're wrong, Francis,' Nancy said firmly. 'She just wanted to ensure we know what's what. Maybe her intention was even to scare us a little. Clearly, making ourselves known at the workhouse will not be in any way welcomed and Mrs Martin wanted to be sure we understood that.' She smiled. 'We are in this now. For better or worse.'

'I sometimes fear I have made a mistake asking you to be a part of this.' He removed his hat and swiped his hand over his face. 'Your life has been far from easy, yet you have risen and become part of one of the most successful and lucrative brothels in the city. You are strong, Nancy, I have no doubt of that, but this is my grievance to conquer. Not yours.'

'Maybe, but when I tell someone – no, *promise* someone – that I will help them, I see that promise through to the end. You do not get to cede on your plea to me whenever it suits you. I am yours to use in any way you see fit from now on.' She locked her eyes on his, his gaze dark with something she couldn't decipher. 'So, you either throw your fears aside or I will have no choice but to see out your mission without you. Which is it to be?'

He stared at her before giving a firm nod. 'You're right, I am also neither deterred nor afraid by what Mrs Martin has told us. In fact, her words and conviction have made me all the more determined. And now I know you are not going into this blindly and still willing to challenge me, then onwards we shall go.' His gaze bored into hers. 'Together.'

Nancy pulled back her shoulders wanting – no, needing – her

confidence bolstered. 'Good, but I need to be convinced that you trust me, Francis. That you see me as an equal. Someone who understands pain and wishes to work with you to do all we can to save as many other young children from suffering what we have suffered.' Heat rose in her cheeks that he would think her, even for a moment, weaker than him. 'I am strong alone, but with you...' Nancy inhaled a shaky breath, slowly released it as passion to do all he believed her capable of onstage burned inside of her. 'I feel stronger than I ever have before. So, now that you have well and truly caught my attention in every way, I need to know we will throw everything we have into your play to ensure the support of others, or so help me God I'll—'

'You'll what?' A smile played at his lips, desire darkening his eyes to midnight blue as his gaze dropped hungrily to her lips. 'What will you do to me?'

His lust-filled stare and the low timbre of his voice stirred Nancy's core and she lifted her hand to his neck and roughly pulled him to her. She kissed him hard, her tongue seeking his with fervour and longing. Pulling back, she laid her forehead to his, their eyes locked. 'For the love of God, let us go to the workhouse before I give your driver a reason that will mean he finds it difficult to look you in the eye.'

Francis eased back, studied her, and then kissed her again. 'You want to go to the workhouse now? Wouldn't it be better if we returned to the Royal so I can introduce you to a few of the people you will be working with?'

Nancy closed her eyes. Why did the workhouse suddenly feel like an easier option? She opened her eyes, forced a smile. 'Yes, you're right. Let us go the Royal.'

He squeezed her hand and then tapped his cane to the carriage roof. 'Onwards to the Royal, Edmund!'

Turning to the window, Nancy pressed her hand to her quivering stomach and breathed deep. She could only imagine the reception she would receive when Francis introduced her – a masquerading whore – into his co-workers' company.

36

Francis handed Nancy a cup of tea and smiled, hating the tension that stiffened her shoulders. 'Now, do you have everything you need? I will gather the people we will be working with onstage and then I'll come and get you.'

Nancy took the tea and Francis noticed the slight tremble to her fingers. She laughed. 'Of course, don't worry about me.' She looked around his dressing room, possibly avoiding his gaze. 'Sitting here, I already feel as though I am part of the theatre.' She faced him, her grey eyes revealing her apprehension. 'I'm looking forward to meeting your associates.'

'They are yours too now, remember.'

She smiled, softly. 'Yes, mine too.'

He pressed a kiss to her cheek. 'They will love you, I'm sure. I won't be long.'

Walking to the door, he looked back at her a final time before striding into the corridor, his heart aching due to the paleness of Nancy's face. He held no fear that most of the cast and crew would accept Nancy on his say-so. For most of them, the guarantee of work in the new year would undoubtedly be enough for them to agree to anything – a new and untrained actress included.

The only person's reaction he wasn't sure of was whose dressing room he headed for now.

He stopped outside Eloise's domain and took a deep breath before rapping on the door, his determination in place and strong.

'Come in.'

As he entered the room, the sickly scent of perfume and burning beeswax candles assaulted Francis's nostrils, mixing with the hovering smoke from the gaslights. 'Eloise, how are you?'

'Well, this is a pleasant surprise,' she said, looking at him in the reflection of her dressing room mirror, a cloth in her hand. 'I hope you aren't here to criticise my performance this afternoon.' She wiped at her cheek, her gaze icy cold. 'Of course you aren't. After all, you weren't here.'

'I've been busy, but I'm here now. I'd like to talk to you about what I have planned for early in the new year.'

Her hand stilled and she stared at him before turning on her velvet-covered stool. 'Oh?'

'Lord Henry has agreed to finance a play that I have written myself. I would very much like for you to be a part of it. I have a specific role in mind for you to which I think you will do untold justice.'

A smile played at her lips, her eyes glinting with suspicion. 'A *specific* role?'

'Yes.'

'I'm fearing this might be an unwelcome proposition, Francis. If the part was significant, would you not have said, "I'd like you to be the star"?'

Tension inched across his shoulders. 'The role is not a starring role, but it is a part imperative to the story. It could bring you much acclaim, Eloise. It is a sombre and demanding part, which I think will bring the opportunity for you to show yourself as a serious actress.'

'And who will be its star? I'm assuming that's a male part.'

'That role is to be played by Nancy Bloom.' He held her gaze, his back ramrod straight. 'And I would very much appreciate you trusting me that I know what I am doing and that she is the right person to play Martha.'

Two spots of colour darkened Eloise's cheeks as she glared. 'The woman you introduced me to? Well, who is she, Francis? I have neither seen her act nor even heard of her being onstage before. Are you throwing roles at waifs and strays you pick up on the street now?' She stood and walked to her wardrobe, flinging the doors open and wrenching a satin robe from its hanger. She faced him, her green eyes flashing with anger. 'Or is it as I suspect, and you are intimate with her? She is the one whose bed you now prefer over mine?'

Francis fought to hold his temper. As much as he wanted Eloise in his play, he would not bend to her tantrums or her will. A will known throughout the theatre. 'She is my choice, Eloise. Your choice is whether to accept the role I have written for you and work alongside Nancy or else refuse my offer altogether.'

Their eyes locked as the seconds passed, Francis's heart beating fast as anger and determination tumbled dangerously inside of him.

'And what is the role exactly?' She turned away from him and resumed her seat at the dressing table, watching him once again in the mirror. '*If* it is as truly important as you say.'

'The story is set in the workhouse and you are to play the wife of a rich merchant doing all she can to help married couples unable to have children to adopt children from the workhouse.

You will be onstage throughout much of the play. The role will be both challenging and rewarding.'

She smoothed some cream onto her cheeks, clearly wanting to make him wait for her decision of whether she would accept his proposal. Francis continued to stare at her, undeterred by her pitiful show of superiority.

'Fine.' She turned. 'I'll take the role... as a favour to you, but I would still like to know more about Miss Bloom.'

'Good, then I suggest you get dressed and join myself, Miss Bloom and the rest of the company I have gathered onstage as soon as you can.'

Leaving the room, Francis quickly chased around the theatre gathering cast and crew, asking that they all be onstage within the next few minutes.

He then hurried back to his own dressing room to find Nancy wandering about the room, her arms tightly crossed and her face etched with apprehension.

Gently grasping her elbows, he smiled, willing his belief of her into her own psyche. 'Everyone is gathering onstage. Are you ready?'

She inhaled a shaky breath, slowly released it. 'As I'll ever be.'

'Good. You're going to be wonderful, I promise.' He quickly kissed her and took her hand. 'Come on, let's go.'

Francis purposefully walked into the main theatre, his head held high and every instinct on protective alert for Nancy. He looked towards the stage, pleased to see everyone standing on the boards, chatting and laughing as they waited. Including Eloise, who held centre stage, regaling a group of male actors with what she clearly found a hilarious anecdote.

Turning, he winked at Nancy before addressing the stage. 'Everyone, if I might have your attention, please.'

Silence fell but instead of the company's gazes falling on him, they all collectively stared at Nancy. Francis glanced at her.

She stood tall and proud, staring at the gathered actors and stagehands, her mouth curved into a smile. Pride swelled inside Francis, searing joy across his heart. She was a woman like no other.

He raised his hands. 'Ladies and gentlemen, thank you for gathering like this on such short notice. I will not keep you long as we have this evening's performance to prepare for.' He lowered his hands and walked a few paces along the front seats before stopping. 'You have all agreed to a part in the production of the play I have written. Now is the time to share with you *why* I wrote this particular story.'

Confident he had everyone's attention – apart from Eloise's, as she seemed determined to look at no one else in the room but Nancy – Francis explained the purpose of his play, refusing to give Eloise the satisfaction of reaching for Nancy as he longed to. One thing he was certain of was that Nancy could look after herself under the most pressured circumstances. If she was so inclined, Nancy could undoubtedly shoot Eloise down with a look, let alone anything else.

'So, my aim is to raise awareness and, hopefully, donors and patrons to implement improvement at the workhouse. Through this play, I hope to start conversation and action among the elite that will lead to significant change in conditions and treatments for the poor children separated from parents or alone in such a place.' He looked along the row of actors. 'Each of you has an important role to play in its success and I hope my passion becomes yours as we produce and rehearse. Does anyone have any questions?'

An older actor of maybe forty years raised his hand. 'Just one, sir. Who is the young lady alongside you? Only...' He stared at Nancy and frowned. 'Only you seem a little familiar to me, miss.'

Dread dropped like a stone into Francis's stomach and he quickly stepped to Nancy. She stared at the man, her smile seemingly frozen in place, her tongue too.

Francis took her elbow and held tight, more than a little afraid she might bolt. 'This, my friends, is Miss Nancy Bloom. She will be taking the starring role of Martha and I would like you all to make her infinitely welcome.' He turned to Nancy, his heart aching to see her face so set with tension. 'Nancy?'

She snapped her gaze to him, her grey eyes wide. 'Yes?'

'Why don't you say hello to your fellow actors?' He nodded, willing her to make this moment her own, to bury her fears and stand proud. 'Is there anything you'd like to say?'

'Well, I...' She tilted her head to look at the stage, her smile still firmly frozen in place. 'As Francis... Mr Carlyle... says, I am Nancy Bloom and I live right here in the city. This... this will be my first acting role so I am excited to get started. I hope I can rely on your help and patience as I learn the ropes.'

Francis dragged his gaze from Nancy to the stage. Some of the company smiled and nodded, others shifted with clear discomfort. As for Eloise, nothing but malice shone from her eyes along with her thin and twisted smile.

'Thank you, Miss Bloom.' Francis clapped. 'I'm sure everyone here will do exactly that. Will we not?'

A ripple of somewhat understated applause rang out before the harsh thump of heavy footsteps fell across the carpet alongside him.

Everyone looked to the left as Lord Henry strode forward. 'So this is the mysterious Miss Bloom, is it?' he boomed, his hand outstretched. 'A pleasure, miss. I am Lord Henry. For all intents and purposes, the owner of the Royal.'

Francis inwardly grimaced as Lord Henry snatched Nancy's hand tightly in his own.

'Pleased to meet you, sir.'

Lord Henry nodded, his leering gaze assessing Nancy from head to breast, his cheeks mottled. 'So I heard Carlyle announce this will be your first acting role. I'm sorry but I can't say that fills me with confidence, Miss Bloom. What did you do before Mr Carlyle offered you this work?'

Nancy stared, her mouth opening but no words forthcoming as subdued talking and stifled laughter came from the stage.

Francis shot a glare towards the company, but they only grinned back at him, their hands at their mouths or on their hips as they waited for Nancy's response.

Anger burned inside Francis and he immediately pulled her away from Lord Henry towards the steps leading onstage. 'I know, why doesn't Nancy show you why I know she is perfect for this role? What it was that led to me casting her? If everyone could move to the side of the stage, please.'

Nancy's gaze bored into his, their grey depths dark with fear. 'Francis, what are you doing?'

'Why don't you sing us a ballad?' He met her gaze, praying that she trusted him. 'How about the one that led me to pursue you so ardently to play Martha?'

'Now?'

He nodded. 'Now.'

Her bosom rose as she inhaled deeply before her gaze slowly changed from fear to ferocious boldness, and Francis smiled.

Giving a firm nod, Nancy strode to the centre of the stage and, without accompaniment or cue, started to sing.

'When a girl's first love takes her in his arms...'

Hush descended, no sound but the sweet, tender perfection of

Nancy's voice filling the vast space, echoing from the set to the rafters, strong, beautiful and unyielding.

Francis looked at the stunned faces of the company, the shocked, wide-eyed gaze of Eloise and down below to Lord Henry, who looked entirely transfixed.

Still Nancy sang, her confidence and voice rising with every lyric until softly, quietly, she brought her ballad to a heart-rending end.

No one spoke, no one moved, and then Lord Henry burst into enthusiastic applause, startling the others from their stupor to join him. Francis grinned as Nancy laughed and plucked up her skirts in a theatrical curtsey, tears glistening in her eyes.

'Bravo, Miss Bloom!' Lord Henry roared. 'Bravo!'

Everyone continued to clap until, one by one, the actors and stagehands gathered around Nancy in congratulation. Hands took hers, smiles beaming down on her... except for one person.

Eloise glowered in Nancy's direction, her eyes narrowed and her mouth pinched.

Francis crossed his arms and stared her down, having absolutely no doubt it would now be Eloise's mission to find out all she could about Nancy.

37

'You don't understand. These children need help, not judgement!' Nancy recited the line with all the passion and frustration Francis's words evoked in her as she glared at the actor playing the role of a workhouse warden. 'Do you not see their faces in your dreams? Doesn't the image of their thin bodies haunt you when you sit at your dining table each evening?'

'Stop there. Perfect!' Francis's voice boomed from the stalls where he sat forward in his seat, the script pages open in his lap. 'Nancy, I need you to confront the warden just like that during every part of this scene. No holding back. No more doubting yourself. That was exactly what I wanted.'

Relief swept through her and she relaxed her shoulders as Francis called an end to today's late morning read-through. Even though the play would not start its official rehearsals until the new year, Francis wanted to be absolutely certain in the decisions he had made in his chosen actors for each role and that they wasted none of the vital time Lord Henry had granted them.

As the company began to disperse, Nancy walked to the side of the stage to collect her belongings, mindful that one day in the not too distant future she would have a dressing room of her own. Something that had been little more than a pipe dream before she'd met and began to fall in love with Francis.

Her heart stumbled. To deny her feelings for him any longer was futile.

'Ladies and gentlemen, before you go...' Francis raised his voice towards the stage. 'I am happy with everyone's casting thus far, so all that remains is for me to find some children to play in the background of the workhouse scenes.'

He turned his gaze to Nancy and the immediate softening of his expression brought heat to her cheeks. She dropped her gaze to the boards lest anyone else recognise his affection as she did.

'Therefore, Miss Bloom and I will be visiting the workhouse tomorrow. I want to speak to the children as well as observe their behaviour, mannerisms and expressions so that I am in a position to direct the young actors I employ. It is more important than I can say that the right amount of care and compassion is stirred in our audience.'

A burst of gasps followed by a barrage of stifled laughter erupted on the other side of the stage and Nancy looked over, somehow not surprised to see Eloise in the centre of the gathered group. Nor was she surprised that her malicious smile and laughing gaze were pinned on Nancy.

Shooting her a glare, Nancy stood a little taller. It had been a week since Francis announced her as the star in his play and, in that time, Eloise's catty behaviour had not lessened.

'Do you have something to say, Eloise?' Francis asked, his eyes flashing with anger. 'Only I cannot understand how my talking about the workhouse would bring forth such mirth from you and your fellow performers.'

Pleased for Francis's intervention lest she storm across the stage and smack Eloise, Nancy crossed her arms. She had just about had enough of the uttered asides and narrow-eyed glances that had come from Eloise and her small group of followers.

As much as Nancy relished the opportunity to finally be onstage, she was not a saint and never would be. Eloise's derision and trouble-making was driving Nancy to breaking point.

'I'm waiting for an answer,' Francis demanded. 'Eloise?'

'Fine.' Eloise flounced away from the group and walked to centre stage before planting her hands on her hips. 'All I asked my friends was whether they think you and Miss Bloom will be visiting the workhouse at day or night.'

Francis's frown reflected Nancy's confusion. What on earth was the woman talking about?

'Well, in the daytime, I should think,' Francis said. 'Why does it matter? Moreover, why does the question cause such amusement?'

Eloise turned and took a few slow, purposeful steps closer to Nancy.

Nancy straightened her shoulders and pinned the other woman with a glare. Enough was enough. If Eloise wanted a fight, she could have one because hell would freeze over before Nancy gave her the satisfaction of wilting under her fame or intimidation.

She tilted her chin. 'Is there something you want to say to me, Eloise?'

Eloise smiled, her eyes icy-cold. 'As Francis seems to need you to accompany him everywhere, I was just concerned that he might not know how busy you are at night.'

Nancy stiffened, warmth travelling up her neck to her face. *Oh, God, she knows about the house. She knows I'm a whore.*

Eloise grinned. 'Cat got your tongue, Miss Bloom?'

A ball of rage rose and sat hot and heavy in the centre of

Nancy's chest. 'Do you really think the fact you have been digging around to find out more about my life bothers me?'

'Whatever do you mean?' Eloise widened her eyes, raised her hand to her chest in feigned innocence. 'It is no concern to me what your current vocation may be, Miss Bloom, but as for Francis—'

'Enough!' Francis stormed up the stage steps, two at a time. 'You either leave this stage right now or you can forget any hope of being in this play.'

Nancy raised her hand, her glare locked on Eloise. 'It's all right, Francis,' she said, pleased beyond measure that her voice was loud and strong. 'I can handle Eloise's venomous tongue well enough.'

'Is that so?' Eloise made a show of studying her nails as though bored. 'I find myself very much doubting you are in charge of little else other than what you do with *your* tongue.'

Nancy's temper snapped, the last seven days of Eloise's caustic remarks and vicious word-dropping gathering like a crescendo inside of her.

She strode forward until barely a foot separated them, taking immense pleasure when Eloise took a step back, colour rushing into her perfect porcelain cheeks. 'I am a whore, yes, and damn proud of it. I am neither on the streets nor in the alleys, but in a fine house that I doubt any man you know would be able to afford to set foot inside of.'

'Is that right?' Eloise looked over her shoulders at her associates, clearly seeking support. When none was forthcoming, she looked to Francis. 'And you were aware of this? You are happy for a whore to perform in a play you say means the world to you? Shame on you, Francis.'

Before Francis could respond, Nancy stepped forward again,

her anger bubbling over. 'Don't talk to him with your filthy accusations; talk to me.'

The skin at Eloise's neck shifted as she swallowed, tears leaping into her eyes. 'Move away, Miss Bloom, there is no need to act as though you might strike me.'

Nancy raised her eyebrows. 'Oh, there is no act. It wouldn't bother my conscience at all to hit you.' She huffed a laugh. 'Not in the slightest, but...' She took a step back, opening the space between them. 'I do expect an apology or, better still, a realisation on your part that your slander and derision bring nothing but shame to your sex.'

'What are you talking about?' Eloise glared. 'I am more of a woman than you'll ever be. Just ask Francis.'

The implication was clear, and the following gasps and giggles left Nancy in no doubt everyone but her knew that Francis had once been – or possibly could still be – intimate with the woman standing in front of her. Humiliation twisted and turned inside Nancy as she fought to maintain a modicum of dignity.

'Go to your dressing room now, Eloise!' Francis demanded, pointing his finger across the stage. 'Do you really think the fact I made the mistake of sleeping with you is likely to affect Nancy or the role she has to play here? The opportunity she is grasping and giving all she has to make a success of? I think not. Just leave before I make sure you never work in this theatre again.'

'You do not get to tell me what I can or can't do, Francis Carlyle. Nobody does.'

Unable to stand her ground a moment longer, Nancy stepped closer to Eloise. 'You have tried so hard to make my time here difficult, but what you have failed to understand is your words, your liaisons with Francis or anyone else, have no bearing on my desire to give everything to this play. Or even affect my relationship, working or otherwise, with Francis.'

'Is that so?'

'Yes, because I'm an adult. An adult who accepts Francis has a past, as do I and as do you. The fact of the matter is, your cattiness only illustrates your pitiful insecurities.'

'What? How dare you.'

'You see, the women I hold in esteem, the women I respect and love, do everything in their power to lift other women up, not gather in corners to rip them down.' Nancy looked Eloise up and down. 'You're an embarrassment to the female sex.'

Francis moved in between her and Eloise and when he looked at her, Nancy's heart twisted to see such beseeching in his eyes. It pained her that he might think that she, a whore of so many years, would linger on his past relations with anyone, Eloise included.

As long as whatever had happened between him and Eloise was over, Nancy would think no more about it and prayed he would offer her the same courtesy about her culls one day.

'All right. That is enough.' Francis looked from Nancy to Eloise and then the rest of the assembled audience. 'I want everyone to listen to me and hear what I have to say for it is the first and last time I will say it.'

Nancy closed her eyes and drew in a deep, calming breath before opening her eyes to see the company coming closer. They all stared at Francis, her and Eloise with varying expressions of admiration, shock or enjoyment.

Ignoring them, Nancy turned to Francis as he continued to speak.

'I have always known of Miss Bloom's occupation and it does not matter as it does not affect her ability on this stage in any way. In fact, I would say her wisdom, experience and day-to-day dealings with people from every class and occupation mean she has the potential to be a phenomenal actress.' He looked around the assembled company, his jaw tight. 'If anyone feels they can no longer work with Miss Bloom, I want you to say so now.'

Silence fell as Nancy's heart picked up speed. The last thing she wanted was for any of the specially selected actors to walk away after Francis had so meticulously chosen them to fill each role.

'Eloise?' Francis pinned her with a glare. 'What about you? Is the fact that Nancy is a prostitute good enough reason for you to walk away from a play that I believe will be career-changing for us and life-changing to hundreds of children?'

Nancy held the other woman's gaze until Eloise faced Francis, looking suitably chastised and maybe even a little sorry.

'No, of course not. I still want to be a part of this production.' She turned to Nancy. 'I apologise, Miss Bloom. There will be no more comment about you from me going forwards. This play matters to Francis and so it matters to me.'

Unable to fully forgive the woman yet, Nancy merely nodded and watched as Eloise turned on her heel and walked away into the wings.

38

Francis could sense Nancy's impatience as she walked behind him along the corridor, Mr Greaves – the workhouse governor – ahead of them. Yesterday's events at the theatre had only served to bolster her confidence to star in the play despite Eloise's blatant attempts to diminish it. In fact, it was Nancy who had insisted they visit the girls' workroom rather than the boys' today so that she might fully imagine herself in these dire and filthy surroundings.

They had talked over dinner and he had told her all about his regretted relationship with Eloise, and Nancy seemed to accept it as history and asked that neither of them mention it again. Once more, she had shown herself to be the most understanding and self-assured woman he had ever met.

But, as much as he basked in Nancy's enthusiasm and optimism, Francis could not dispel the feeling she walked ignorant of what she would witness once Mr Greaves bid them access to the children he'd agreed they could visit.

Dread rippled through Francis at the thought of seeing shock and distress on Nancy's pretty face, of the possible tears that might glaze her eyes. Her heart was the biggest he had ever had the privilege of beginning to understand and he wanted nothing more than happiness for her. Yet he was not offering her contentment in this mission, only certain worry and anguish, but it was imperative she really understood what it was to exist in this hellhole.

He saw the selfishness in his urging her along this path, poking and prodding at her conscience until she saw and felt the degradation of the workhouse as he did. Anything less and the play would not provoke the public reaction he wanted. Of course, it didn't go beyond his own consciousness that he would not have had the courage to revisit this place before he had met her. Somehow Nancy's strength and tenacity had made him strong enough to face his demons.

'Right, here we are.' Mr Greaves stopped outside a closed iron door and turned. His rheumy eyes shifted from Francis to Nancy, a hint of malice in their depths. 'I want to reiterate again just what kind of children our charges are,' he said. 'They are the lowest in society. They know nothing of manners or decorum.' His gaze bored into Nancy's. 'I would really not relish you fainting, Miss Bloom.'

Francis smirked, his hand curling into a fist at his side. 'I have little fear of Miss Bloom tumbling at the sight of young girls or boys in need of help, Mr Greaves.'

The governor continued to stare at Nancy, and Francis glanced at her, his heart damn near bursting with pride as she glared at Greaves, her back ramrod straight.

Slowly, she stepped forward and placed her hand on the governor's arm. The man visibly flinched but Nancy tightened her grip. 'Have no fear, Mr Greaves, there is nothing on the other side of that door that will scare me. Not when I have seen quite a number of men naked with their private parts on display and all too often lacking.' She smiled. 'Shall we go in?'

Without waiting for the pale-faced governor to respond, Francis followed Nancy as she walked into a darkened room, equally musty and dirt-ridden as the one he'd seen on his last visit.

Helplessness threatened as Francis surveyed the bowed heads of at least twenty or thirty girls aged between seven and eleven. They sat on wooden benches or stools, their eyes on their stitching, heedless to the visitors who had joined them. Each face was more ashen and drawn than the next, their workhouse-issued smocks grey and streaked with dirt, their hair tied back and almost shiny with grime and grease.

'Well, then,' Nancy said, beside him, her jovial tone just a little too forced to convince him she was any less distressed than he. 'Why don't we see if we might talk to some of these lovely ladies, shall we?'

'Miss Bloom,' Greaves growled, his lips pinched. 'I really don't think—'

Nancy strode away and approached the nearest bench, settling down on her haunches behind two girls, who immediately turned, their sunken eyes wide as they stared not at her face but her distinctive red hair and pretty yellow dress. A dress Francis was grateful Nancy had most likely selected to procure a flash of sunshine in such a dreary place.

He inhaled a long breath, his eyes fixed on the woman he had fallen so completely in love with. 'If you are busy, Mr Greaves, feel free to leave Miss Bloom and I to get acquainted with the children.'

'I don't think I made myself clear, Mr Carlyle.'

Francis could not drag his gaze from Nancy as she grinned at the girls around the table, gently shuffling them along the bench before lifting her skirts and taking a seat at the table with them. The matron watching over the room looked fit to burst a blood vessel, yet Nancy looked like a woman in her element as slowly the girls' faces softened, their eyes shining just a tiny bit brighter; a few even smiled... a little.

'What do you mean, Mr Greaves?' Francis asked, unable to stem his smile. 'What is there to make clear? I have money and wish to make a sizeable donation to the institution. Is there anything more black and white?'

'Black and white?' The governor huffed a laugh as he crossed his beefy arms. 'Nothing about these youngsters is simple or easy, sir. If you wish to make yourself known to these waifs—'

'I do, Mr Greaves, and that is exactly what will happen before I leave.'

Francis strode towards Nancy, keeping his gaze purposefully on her rather than the girls as fear twisted inside him. Every moment of the years he'd spent in the workhouse remained branded on his heart and mind, lying just beneath the surface of his self-protection, ready to burst forth under the tiniest provocation. Now he was here, walking into the devil's den once more and opening himself up to a risk of the most extraordinary complexity and power. Yet he had no doubt that, between them, he and Nancy would make a difference to these children. Whether this year or the next.

Nancy's voice rang loud and clear as she jested and giggled, clearly trying her hardest to rouse some smiles from the girls; maybe she even hoped for a laugh. Francis's heart bled for her, knowing these young women were a thousand miles from such a wish.

He touched Nancy's shoulder and she started, tipping her

head to meet his eyes. His stomach knotted to see the tears brimming on her lower lashes despite her smile. She was beyond saddened yet determined and brave and, God help him, he fell a little deeper.

'Come,' he said, casting his eye around the table even as the girls immediately dropped their gazes to their work. A man would never be as welcome as a woman in this room and his doubts that he should be here rose. 'Let us walk around.'

A line formed between her brows before Nancy addressed the children. 'I'll be right back.'

As they walked about the dark and dusty room, Francis took in every aspect, from the children themselves to the straw-strewn floor, to the murky windows, to the stinky, fibre-filled air. He breathed deep, forcing himself to remember that his and Nancy's mission was a long one and nothing would be resolved in a day, a week, a month or maybe even a year. What he could not allow himself to think was that one day Nancy might not be beside him working towards his goal, but off on her own revelling in the fame that would certainly come to her once the city saw her perform.

'Oh, Francis...' Nancy's voice cracked beside him, her fingers tightening on his arm. 'Look at her.'

He followed the direction of her gaze.

In the far corner of the room, a young girl stared directly at them, the material in her lap and the needle in her hand seemingly forgotten. Her gaze was unwavering, relentless with barely disguised contempt. She sat alone and Francis was certain it wasn't her slightly older years that set her apart, but the unmistakable wisdom that emanated from her.

A deep knowledge. An ingrained experience. An inimitable and clear presence.

'She's the one, Francis,' Nancy whispered, slipping her hand from his arm and standing taller. 'She will know everything. She will guide me. Teach me.' She exhaled shakily. 'She is the one to whom Martha will be anchored in society's consciousness forever.'

'Just wait, Nancy.' Francis stared at the girl, her eyes unmoving, her strong chin tilted. 'I need... a moment.'

'But you agree? She is the perfect young woman from whom I can embody Martha.'

'Yes, I think I do.'

A certainty wound through Francis as his heart raced, his palms turning clammy. In this young girl, he could see Nancy even as she was today. The sombreness of the girl's steady gaze, the rigid defensiveness of her shoulders. This was a girl who had found herself in one of the worst places in the city, yet her defiance and resilience was tangible. So like Nancy the pair could be mother and daughter, or if not that, then the firmest of friends, the most united of allies.

With this girl, this young woman, it was as though every dark cloud in his mind had broken wide open, allowing him to see his destiny clearly. There were a thousand others just like her who needed help and to be seen but, God willing, this young woman would be the first to allow him and Nancy to hold out a hand to her. To share her story with the powers capable of making a difference, instigating change, that would, eventually, envelop more than just her.

Her cold, untrusting eyes lay sunken in a face stretched over delicate bones, the stiff set of her shoulders and the proud, proud tilt of her chin showed Francis that this girl was no different to how he'd once been.

Bitter. Lost. Afraid and without hope.

The face of his adoptive father appeared in Francis's mind, his determined expression that bleak winter morning when he had walked into the workroom and taken Francis home. Unbeknownst to Francis, that had been the first real day of his life. Swallowing around the lump that rose in his throat, Francis inhaled as an invisible weight gently touched his shoulder.

With his father walking beside him, Francis stepped towards the girl.

39

Despite her absolute conviction the young girl staring at them was the child whose story would enhance the telling of Francis's own experience, when Francis finally brushed past her Nancy couldn't move.

Her every instinct had been primed to act as his protector, to steel herself against whatever she might witness or feel in the workhouse so that she remained strong and stalwart for Francis. Now she found herself very much afraid, the girl's blind stare causing the hairs on Nancy's neck and arms to prickle and her heart to race.

It wasn't that she had changed her mind about acting in Francis's play or lost sight of how she would be helping these children. The complete opposite. It was fear that she and Francis should fail to convince this poor child that by allowing them to get to know her, she was contributing to her liberty and that of the children surrounding her. What if she thought Nancy viewed her as little more than a case study? Little more than someone looking at her in curiosity like a visitor to the circus?

The look in the young girl's eyes was one that Nancy had seen a million times during her time on the streets and, just as it had then, the numbed desolation chilled her to the bone. It had been fear of that look, of that complete and utter cessation of feelings for herself and the entire world, which became Nancy's motivation for not succumbing to the relentless reaching claws of the workhouse.

And she clearly needed to embrace the same resolve now.

Blinking from her reverie, Nancy joined Francis where he stood a short distance away from the girl, his face strained as he tried to engage her in conversation. The girl remained mute as she continued to stare at him in the same soulless way.

Inhaling a strengthening breath, Nancy pulled back her shoulders and purposefully gripped a stool set a little away from the girl. She drew it closer and sat down. The poor child was entirely devoid of any emotion or reaction.

'Hello, I'm Nancy.' She smiled, steadfastly fighting the tears pricking the backs of her eyes. 'What is your name?'

The girl's gaze turned impossibly colder, two spots of colour seeping into her cheeks, but still she did not speak.

Nancy's lips trembled but she dug deep, knowing her calling to be onstage had now merged with a new destiny. And in order to successfully – and gently – break down this young woman's barriers Nancy would deliver her best performance ever.

'Francis,' Nancy said over her shoulder. 'Why don't you tell this beautiful young lady about your work at the theatre. I'm sure she'd love to hear all about the plays and costumes.' She raised her eyebrows. 'Do you know of the theatre and what goes on inside? To be onstage has been a passion of mine since I was a child and Mr Carlyle is a huge part of that world. Or maybe it is something else you dream of?'

Francis came closer and sat on the floor beside Nancy. She battled to keep her face impassive, to pretend it perfectly normal for a man of Francis's stature to sit his arse so easily on a floor covered in filthy straw.

A flicker of surprise flashed in the girl's eyes as she glanced at Francis, her gaze flitting to his hair for just a moment before she returned her focus to Nancy. Her lips remained tightly closed, the disdain showing in her green eyes potent.

Was she more trusting of men than women? The possibility seemed incomprehensible. But what had this young girl's life been until now? How could Nancy even begin to learn of what had made her this way or that?

'What is your name?' Francis asked quietly. 'We would really like to get to know you. As Nancy said, I work at the theatre and have written a play. A play about the workhouse. I...' He exhaled a long breath, the beseeching in his eyes rending a tear across Nancy's heart. '...really need your help so that my play might force the governors, parliament, the people who can help you, to see how you are not living but merely surviving.'

The girl stared at Francis, her lips slightly parting. Nancy held her breath. Then the girl looked past Francis to something behind him. Nancy turned. Mr Greaves approached, the workroom matron right behind him.

Leaping to her feet, Nancy held up her hand. 'We are quite all right, Mr Greaves. We'd just like a while longer, if you don't mind.'

'Your time is up, Miss Bloom.' The governor glared, his eyes flitting from Nancy to the young girl behind her. 'It is quite clear the girl has no wish to speak to you.'

Annoyance simmered inside Nancy at the way he muttered *the girl* so contemptuously. The man was a complete arse. 'Then having us spend a few more moments in companionable silence should be no bother to you, should it?'

Nancy turned on her heel and walked back to the stool.

The girl turned to Francis. 'My name is Alice Smith.'

Nancy's heart kicked, pleasure whispering through her at the sudden breakthrough.

Francis smiled. 'Well, it's very nice to meet you, Alice. Have you' – he glanced at Greaves over his shoulder – 'been here long?'

'Since I was four and, despite your lies that you wish to help me, I won't leave. Ever.'

Nancy stiffened and turned to Francis, who looked unperturbed by Alice's vehement claim. Instead, his brow furrowed and he shifted closer. 'Since you were four? And how many years is that, Alice?'

She gave him another long, soulless look before flicking her gaze to the window. 'Ten.'

'And so you have known nothing else.' Slowly, Francis pushed to his feet and brushed his hand across the back of his trousers. 'I appreciate you talking to us, Miss Smith. We will leave you to your work.'

Disbelief unfurled inside Nancy as she looked from Alice to Francis and back again. 'Francis, what are you—'

'Come along, Miss Bloom,' he said, offering Nancy his arm without looking at her or Alice. 'We must be off now.'

'But—'

'Now, Miss Bloom.'

Barely resisting the urge to stamp on Francis's foot, Nancy threw one last desperate look at Alice, who immediately dropped her gaze to her lap and picked up the pillowcase she darned. Angry that Francis would so easily abdicate their mission to learn from Alice, Nancy marched alongside him past Mr Greaves and into the corridor.

Francis looked at her with pointed warning. 'Do not say a word. I will explain the moment we are out of here.'

With innate difficulty, Nancy clamped her mouth closed and

did as he asked, secretly wanting to throttle Francis with her bare hands as he spoke almost jovially with the governor as they were shown from the workhouse and into its dismal courtyard.

'I will be in touch, Mr Greaves,' Francis said. 'Good day to you.'

Nancy trembled with the effort it took not to snatch her arm from Francis's as they left the courtyard and walked into the street.

As soon as they were a few yards along the busy pavement, she yanked him to a stop. 'How could you do that?' she demanded, her cheeks hot with fury. 'How could you tell that poor, wretched girl that we wanted her help, that we are endeavouring to give her liberty, only to take her at her word that she has no wish to leave? Couldn't you see that she is almost entirely dead inside? How could you just walk away from her? Answer me.'

He gripped her elbow and steered her to the edge of the street, away from the bustling crowds and street traders surrounding them. 'I did exactly what needed to be done,' he growled, his angry gaze boring into hers. 'Didn't you see what I saw?'

'I don't know, Francis.' She snatched her arm from him. 'What did you see? Because I saw a young woman who sees or feels nothing, and I suspect never will if we do not help her. As for you? I have no idea what you just witnessed or even who you are or what you intended to happen when you started me on this path.'

'I saw exactly the same in Alice as you did.' A muscle twitched in his jaw and his eyes darkened with clear distress. 'But we have to play our hand very carefully and gently with her if we have even the slightest hope of her speaking to us. I completely understand why she thinks she needs to stay; clearly you do not.'

Resenting the disparagement in his tone, Nancy planted her

hands on her hips and spun away from him, trying to get control over her too-often impulsive need to lunge at someone rather than listen. Taking a few steadying breaths, she faced him. 'So, what do you plan to do?'

'Alice is afraid of anything else but the workhouse,' he said quietly, his gaze glazed in thought as he began to pace back and forth. 'She is institutionalised and terrified of whatever exists outside of the workhouse's walls. We need to go slowly with her. Convince her she will have our protection, patience and care. If we fail, she will withdraw even harder.'

'What do you mean institutionalised? The place is a cesspit.'

He glared. 'A cesspit that I lived in, if you remember? For your information, Nancy Bloom, I understand more of how Alice feels than you do right now.'

Shame enveloped Nancy and she closed her eyes. 'God, Francis, I'm sorry.'

He touched her cheek, and she opened her eyes.

Francis shook his head, his gaze soft. 'Alice has never known any other environment or life. We must show her compassion and patience.'

Nancy glanced towards the workhouse again, bile coating her throat as her indignation was eclipsed by heavy sadness. 'The poor child.'

'Exactly.' Francis stepped closer, his gaze tender as he looked into her eyes. 'You were wonderful back there. I couldn't have found the courage to speak to Alice had you not been with me. We are a team, Nancy, and I hope we always will be.'

Always? Fear clutched hard and fast at Nancy's heart. 'What do you mean?'

'I mean, even once we have rehearsed and the play is shown next year, I hope that time is just beginning for us. That this is just the beginning of what we could achieve.'

'Francis...' Nancy swallowed, part of her wanting to leap into his arms, that he might find her worthy to work alongside him, might desire her enough to one day want her romantically, but how could she even entertain such a dream when her loyalty would always remain with Louisa? 'I cannot think past the play. I have other people who rely on me to be there for them.'

'Of course you do. As do I.' He smiled, brushed his lips overs hers. 'But doesn't it feel welcome to imagine that we might become about more than this play? That we might have more between us than the theatre and the workhouse?'

Nancy stared at him, words failing her. Didn't she feel similarly about Carson Street and Louisa as Alice did about the workhouse? She would never leave there. Did Francis think there was a possibility that she would come to live with him? To help him further with his campaign? He had mentioned before about finding homes for these poor children. Would that be his next mission? To have her help him and see her every day? It didn't matter what her heart might feel about Alice and her circumstances, Nancy's head was on straight and steadfast.

Carson Street was her only true protection from everything. Including Francis.

She looked to her feet. 'Carson Street is my home, Francis. I will never leave there.'

'Never?'

'Never.'

The silence stretched before he touched his finger to her chin, forcing her gaze to his. 'How can you be so sure? Neither of us knows what the future holds.'

Nancy lifted her chin from his fingers as her self-protective barriers slammed into place. 'I know Louisa will never hurt me. As for you? We are only just beginning to know one another, and I won't forsake what is safe.'

'I understand.' Sadness clouded his eyes before he took her hand, tucking it into his elbow. 'Let me treat you to a drink at the White Hart. We can plan our next step forward. I haven't given up on Alice. Not by a long stretch.'

A little bewildered that he wanted them to return to the White Hart, Nancy allowed Francis to lead her along the street, her mind reeling with all that she had seen and learned today. All of which had provoked an internal battle that she had no way of knowing how to win, one way or the other.

The brash, good-time girl she tried to be day and night prodded and poked at her, making her want to demand so much more from Francis and that damn workhouse governor. The forthright, no-nonsense Nancy was the woman she needed to be if she and Francis had any chance of succeeding with their mammoth mission. Yet it was the aspiring actress inside of her who shouted the loudest, telling her she could masquerade quietly or loudly, in whichever guise was needed to get Alice and as many other girls as possible out of that dreadful place.

But who was the *real* Nancy? That was the answer she really sought.

40

Francis nodded his thanks to the buxom, red-haired barmaid and carried his and Nancy's drinks to where she was seated in a far corner. His gut knotted with trepidation. She stared towards the piano where the old man at the keys sang a jolly song, painfully out of tune yet every patron joining in with an off-key accompanying chorus.

Nancy's expression was etched with anguish and Francis had no doubt that it was his selfish insistence of taking her to the workhouse that had instilled such sadness in her.

Guilt pressed down on him as he slid her beer onto the table and sat. 'Here we go.' He raised his glass. 'To future success.'

She faced him, her glass untouched and her grey eyes dark with defiance. 'Future success?' She sniffed. 'Whatever you say, Francis.'

The look in her eyes indicated no-nonsense, non-negotiation of who Nancy was at her core. Resilient. Self-sufficient. Immovable. Dread deepened inside of him the longer he looked at her. 'Has something happened?'

'Apart from you blurting out that you can see us alongside

one another in the future? Past this play?' She glowered. 'No, nothing at all.'

Unsure why his words had upset her, Francis picked up his drink and took a fortifying mouthful of brandy, wincing as its heat slid down his throat into his empty stomach. 'What do you want me to say, Nancy? Take my words back? Well, I won't. I am... growing innately fond of you and—'

'Innately fond?' She smirked. 'Well, that's nice.'

His annoyance beginning to grow, Francis crossed his arms. 'Fine, then what is it you want me to do?'

She narrowed her eyes, huffed a laugh. 'What do *I* want *you* to do?' She picked up her beer. 'Well, I suppose there is a first time for everything.'

'What do you mean?'

'You are asking me what I want from you, whereas so far it's been all about what you want from me.'

'That's not true.'

'No? Then tell me how I'm wrong. Because from where I'm sitting I think I've summed things up between us pretty accurately.'

He stared at her turned cheek as she glared across the bar. 'Nancy, look at me.'

She snapped her head around. 'Oh, I'll look at you, Francis. I'd look at you all damn day if that was all you wanted, but it's not, is it? You want me to help Alice and a thousand others. You want me to leave my home and friends and help you put together a hundred broken souls who have been through hell and back. Yet...' She gritted her teeth, her grey eyes bright with unshed tears. 'Yet...'

Francis covered her hand where it lay on the table. She trembled and self-loathing burned hot in his chest.

She snatched her hand from his and closed her eyes.

Panic beat a low thrum at Francis's temple. Was she leaving him? Was she right? Had he been nothing but selfish with his demands since they'd met? Christ, he was a damn fool. All he'd wanted was to do enough to convince her of their united success, both with the workhouse and each other. He knew how they could be together. She with her passion and fortitude, he with his money and determination. They would be invincible.

'Nancy—'

'It's time to tell me the truth.' She opened her eyes and glared. 'All of it.'

'About what?'

'About you for a start.' She lifted her pint and drank, wiping the froth from her lips with the back of her hand. 'First of all, why did you bring me back here? Why the White Hart when this place must be as far away from your usual drinking establishments as Tanner's is to me.' Her gaze burned into his. 'Why do you keep pretending to be someone you're not?'

Protestations and excuses clogged his throat as she unwittingly, intelligently and brutally exposed his eternal duplicity. How could she see him so clearly when so many others never had?

Francis opened his mouth... closed it. Opened it again...

'Well?' She raised her eyebrows, her gaze and voice cold. 'Do I leave now? Or will you start being honest with me?'

'I came here because somehow the White Hart has come to mean something to me. It... keeps my feet on the ground. When I am here, I'm reminded of what I should've been. Of *who* I should've been.'

'Who... ah, I see.' Anger flashed in her eyes before she turned away from him, her jaw tight. 'In other words you consider these people less than who you are today. Yet, considering your beginnings, you think these people are *your* people.' She snapped her gaze to him. 'Am I right?'

'You are more wrong than you could ever know.' Frustration twisted inside him, prodding at his own rising irritation. 'These people are more real, stronger, more alive than I will ever be. They are more genuine than anyone I am likely to meet in the middle-class circles I find myself in. I am successful in business, Nancy. Successful at the theatre. But not so in life, and being here, among people I should call my peers, reminds me of who I am really. A poor man from poor beginnings.'

She stared at him for a long moment, the rage in her eyes slowly diminishing until she looked nothing short of bone-tired. Her shoulders slumped and she shook her head. 'You're not fooling anyone, Francis. Especially me.'

Shame brought heat to his face and he looked towards the piano, the upbeat tune having given way to a soulful ballad. 'Meaning what?'

'Meaning...' She placed her hand on his. 'Meaning how is pretending to be someone you're not serving you? Why bother having your big fancy house, your servants and carriage if you take no pleasure in them?'

He faced her, his heart thundering, his brain devoid of words.

Her temper seemingly cooled as she lifted her hand to his jaw. 'Or do you believe you *have* to have those things in order to prove yourself? That they matter because then others will never detect what happened to you in the past? That they serve as evidence of the man you are today as opposed to the boy you once were. If yes, then why not? You should not feel any shame in that.'

'Shouldn't I?' He lifted her hand from his jaw and drained his brandy. 'You are who you are, and the world knows it. You have no desire to put on airs and graces. People can either like you or not. Either way, you face the world with a smile.' He looked at her. 'And that's why I'm falling in love with you.'

Her cheeks immediately flushed pink. 'You're falling...' She looked towards the piano again. 'Don't be ridiculous.'

'Nancy, look at me.'

Annoyance whispered through him. For all of his faults, he was not insincere with words. His actions, his clothes and possessions were more often than not artificially coated in deceit, but never his words.

She turned, her eyes glistening in the gaslight.

Francis swallowed against the sudden dryness in his throat, hating the fear in her eyes. 'I don't expect a response, Nancy. I am just telling you how I feel because I must. My love for you grows every day and not because of how much you have already helped me, but because of the strength you give me to stand taller, to revisit a past I was too afraid to fully face until I met you.' He reached for her hand, pleased when her fingers curled around his rather than pushing him away. 'You are amazing and, yes, I want you beside me in everything I do, but I will never be so conceited to think that you might ever feel that way about me.' He smiled wryly, tipped her a wink. 'Mostly because if I did you are likely to smack me in the face. Which, of course, would be deserved.'

She didn't smile, only continued to stare at him as though he wasn't real. As though she disbelieved all he had confessed to her.

He dropped her hand and exhaled heavily. 'We are both actors in one way or another,' he said, lifting his empty glass and glancing towards the bar. 'But when we made love' – he turned back to her – 'you weren't a whore, but a woman who knows how to accept and give love. When you were at the workhouse, you weren't a woman surviving, but a woman with the heart and care of a mother.' He briefly closed his eyes, opened them again and looked deep into her eyes. 'You are a woman I want to love… if you'll let me.'

41

Nancy stared at Francis as the temptation to confess her reciprocating feelings treacherously danced on her tongue. How could she tell him her heart was becoming his too when there was so much he didn't know about her? So much shame and humiliation that had changed her – moulded her – into a woman who, at times, could be afraid of her own shadow… her own self?

Once again, Nancy withdrew into cowardice.

Forcing a wide smile, she laughed. 'You are too kind, Francis, but we haven't time to discuss such things. We have work to do. Important work.'

'Nancy—'

'If you feel such connection to who you once were, you must keep that in mind, first and foremost. You have risen out of poverty and depravity and are using that accomplishment to the greater good. The children at the workhouse are all we should focus on. No more chattering about us and what we might or might not feel. So…' She drew in a long breath. 'We get to work. First of all, as the play will not been shown until the new year, we should approach someone of influence in the meantime.

Someone who can spread the word about the play and its intention. Someone in the local council with the power and authority—'

'Nancy—'

'First thing tomorrow you must write to our local councillor or member of parliament. Beseech their support.' Excitement built inside of her despite the annoyance shining in Francis's eyes. 'Detail every inch of the poor conditions in the workhouse. From the children to the workrooms. Challenge the meagre food rations and how many hours they are allowed to sleep each night. Hold the man accountable and make him—'

'Nancy, stop.'

He clamped his hand to her forearm, and she froze as his blue eyes bored into hers.

He released her and swiped his hand over his face. 'Why do you always revert to barrelling through things like bullet shot from a cannon?'

'What?'

'Why approach everything with the force of a battering ram?' He sighed. 'Our cause is a delicate governmental matter. If we start making demands of politicians, we will not only face slammed doors, we will also be a laughingstock. For once, I suspect quite possibly for the first time in your life, you must slow down.'

Her defences rose and she glared. 'This is who I am, Francis. Who I thought you respected. Clearly, you only appreciate my forthright nature when it suits you. Well, I'm sorry, but—'

'That is not the case at all.'

'No? Well, when you have...' Nancy faltered.

How was she to tell him of the events and experiences of her past? The things that had made her become the aggressive, hard-headed, hard-hearted woman she was today? How was she to explain why it was necessary to be quarrelsome, quick-witted and sometimes downright belligerent in order to protect herself? To protect Louisa and Octavia? The man had endured hardship and hunger, but he had not been forced to have sex, threatened and used for nothing more than physical gratification.

Francis would not understand anything of what had happened to her. And she wasn't sure she wanted him to either.

Sickness coated Nancy's throat as she defiantly hitched back her shoulders, her gaze steady on his. 'I have learned to adapt to situations with the only weapons I have. Brashness, Francis. Forced joviality and humour.' She drained her beer. 'Maybe you should try those things sometimes to bring about the things you want, too. Mr Greaves and his ilk know nothing else but taking from those less fortunate. Of frightening and intimidating until his imagined power is pathetically and woefully shown to himself and those around him. There is no other way to deter people like that than with aggression. Believe me.'

'I do believe you, but I still think you're wrong to want to start rousing members of parliament before we are ready to—'

'Wrong? Are you really that naïve?'

He flinched and narrowed his eyes. 'Is it necessary that we attack one another now?'

Warmth seeped into her cheeks and she looked past him. He didn't deserve her snappishness or nastiness. Her reaction, her shame to his accusations about her personality, were hers and hers alone.

He blew out a heavy breath, his gaze laced with defeat. 'Look, our entire endeavour needs to be approached with care. None of this is about us, our feelings or histories. It is about those children.' His jaw tightened. 'If you feel yourself incapable of executing a little self-control and patience, then maybe—'

'Maybe what?' Her heart beat fast. 'You'll find the love you claim to feel for me has diminished? Entirely vanished?'

'Nancy, for the love of God...'

Hardening her heart against the tiredness that seemed to suddenly weigh on him, Nancy stood. The things that happened to her – had been *done* to her – pummelled her rationale. 'Things have happened in my life that have taught me if I weaken, even for a moment, it could bring me to being held against my will once more. That I could—'

'What do you mean held against your will?' He abruptly rose to his feet, his hand reaching for her before whatever he saw in her eyes made him drop it to his side. 'What happened to you?'

Fear pounded in her head, terror in her heart. She lifted her chin. 'Events that make me ashamed. Experiences that will never leave my head or heart, the same as yours won't for you.' She swiped at the errant tear that slipped over her cheek. 'But your history was in no way your fault, whereas mine...' She closed her eyes. 'Mine was born of my ambition.' She opened her eyes. 'My belief that I was meant to be onstage.'

'And that meant you were held against your will? I don't understand. Did someone hurt you? Attack you?'

Their eyes locked as Nancy's breath turned harried, tightness forming in her chest.

'Nancy?' Concern filled his gaze and he strode around the table, pulling her to him before she could resist. He whispered against her hair. 'Oh, my love.'

No, no, no. She couldn't lean on him this way. She couldn't need him...

'It's about time both of us buried the past and looked to the future,' he whispered against her hair. 'For our sanity if nothing else.'

Her tears came faster, and Nancy leaned into him. 'I'm not sure I can.'

He eased her back and lifted his thumbs to her cheeks, wiping away her tears, before brushing a soft kiss to her mouth. 'You can.'

Nancy looked into his eyes and fell a little deeper, fear beating through her heart. 'I have commitments to Louisa, and I will never default on them. I owe her my life. I owe her everything.'

'And I respect that.'

His mouth captured hers and the ensuing cheers and shouts around them silenced as Nancy kissed him with all the passion and sadness tumbling through her.

She leaned back and cupped his cheek. 'Louisa wants more for me even now and has given me time to work with you as and when I wish.'

He softly smiled. 'Because she loves you, Nancy. That is what love is. Allowing the people closest to us to reach for the stars, fulfil their ambitions, wants and dreams. I just hope you know I want nothing less for you either.'

The longing in his eyes kicked at Nancy's heart. She was a whore no matter what Francis might see when he looked at her. He thought her capable of charity, love and forgiveness but she wasn't sure that she could deliver his high expectations. She had to abide by the proof that had presented itself to her over and over again. That no man, including Francis, could ever be truly relied upon. Would never really hold her best interests at heart.

'My time will be split between you and Carson Street. I can give you no more than that. Do you understand?'

Disappointment clouded his gaze before he nodded. 'I do.'

'Good.' She smiled despite the sadness pressing down on her. 'Then I think we should say goodnight and each return to our homes. We need to take some time to think about Alice and what we can do next to gain her trust that we are visiting her in the hope of making change. Change for her.'

'And what will you do tonight?'

'I will work.'

Turning away from him, Nancy walked through the crowded pub to the door, still so afraid of not ever being who she truly wished to be. Of not ever being able to stand proud in her own skin when exploitation, sex and ill-gotten gains ran like a mesh of scars through every part of her. Heart, body and soul...

42

Francis entered his house on Queen Square and closed the door, taking a moment to savour its unusual quietness. The muted sound of clattering crockery filtered up the stairs from the kitchen and his stomach rumbled. He could not remember the last time he'd eaten, and he wistfully breathed in the aroma of roasting beef and vegetables.

He would take his dinner in the kitchen tonight and gather his staff. No matter how eager he was to help and, hopefully, rehome Alice and – in time – others from the workhouse, Edmund, Mrs Gaynor and Jane had served him well and deserved the respect of being made aware of his plans. Until now, he had shared little about his play with any of them. Even less about its real purpose.

If everything went as he envisaged, the house would become busier as the months passed and more and more people of influence entered his life. Meetings and dinners at the house would be necessary; maybe he would need to call on his staff to help him prepare for bigger events that he and Nancy could host once the play was being performed.

He would welcome and take on board the views and concerns of Edmund and the others as much as he had Nancy's. Any child given the possibility of escape from the workhouse needed a plethora of support and hope. He had to believe that this house and its occupants would be the beginning of both those things.

Hanging his coat on the stand by the door, Francis strode towards the kitchen, recollecting the disdain he'd seen on Edmund's face more than once when he'd been looking at Nancy. If his friend disapproved of Francis keeping company with her, then Lord only knew what he would feel about the possibility of children from the workhouse visiting the household.

Then again, was Edmund really capable of such hypocrisy? Francis thought not. Therefore, his disapproval of Nancy had to be grounded in something else entirely. Not that Edmund's feelings about Nancy would alter Francis's mission, but he hoped he could allay Edmund's fears, at least. By keeping his attitude upbeat and jovial, Francis would reassure his staff as well as conceal his own reservations.

Entering the kitchen was more often than not like stepping into the midst of battle and this evening proved no different. Francis leaned his shoulder against the doorframe and crossed his arms, thoroughly amused by the scene before him.

'If I've told you once, Edmund More, I've told you a thousand times,' Mrs Gaynor cried, her apple cheeks flushed red as she passed a saucepan to Jane, who set about spooning carrots onto a platter. 'You need to swap that permanent frown of yours for a smile sometimes. There are plenty of young women who would be willing to step out with you if you'd give them a chance.'

Edmund tossed a glare at her and returned to his task of uncorking a bottle of wine. 'I have no damn interest in courting. I only have to be in this kitchen to know the grief that comes with the fairer sex.'

'Is that so? Well, I'll tell you this for nothing,' Mrs Gaynor continued as she turned to a pan of roasted potatoes, 'you've got a face like a smacked arse half the time and that won't do you—'

'Ahem.' Francis coughed and entered the room, grinning. 'I'm not sure I'd use your choice of words, Mrs Gaynor, but I'm afraid she has a point, Edmund. It wouldn't hurt you to be a little more amiable to the opposite sex every now and then.'

All three of Francis's staff leaped to attention as though he was a sergeant major rather than an employer who was always as easy-going as possible.

He laughed. 'As you were, please. I was enjoying your exchange immensely. Good evening, Jane.'

The young girl's eyes twinkled mischievously as she giggled. 'Good evening, sir.'

'Oh, Mr Carlyle, sir,' Mrs Gaynor breathed, her hand at her chest and her cheeks now scarlet. 'What on earth must you think of us? Whatever you need, you only had to ring and one of us—'

'It's quite all right.' Francis walked to the table and pulled out a chair. 'I'm here because I'd like to take my dinner in the kitchen tonight in the hope you are all able to join me.' He looked at his staff in turn. 'Is that possible?'

They all looked at each other with varying expressions of surprise and concern before gabbling a chorus of agreement.

'Good.' Francis smiled. 'Because I'm famished.'

The next twenty minutes passed in a flurry of activity as water and wine were poured and the table laid before being loaded with the magnificent dinner Mrs Gaynor and Jane had prepared. Pleasure whispered through Francis as he glanced around the table at his staff, the gentle ribbing of one another continuing, each of their gazes filled with fondness, their smiles wide. If he did not achieve anything more as a wealthy man, he could at least be proud of the relaxed and happy household he headed.

He constantly felt as though he pursued a never-ending quest for righteousness – a rebirth. Yet, deep down, he knew obliterating his past was an impossibility when his memories remained stained on his consciousness.

Once their plates and glasses were filled, Francis picked up his knife and fork. 'So, the reason I wanted to dine with you tonight is because I have begun work on some plans that will no doubt come to affect you, too.' He met their curious gazes. 'And therefore I want you to voice your concerns without fear of my immediate disagreement. This matter is of the utmost importance to me and I hope that will go some way to convincing you that what I have planned will make this city a better place. Either way, I welcome your opinions.'

Mrs Gaynor's smile dissolved, Jane's eyes widened with near-terror and Edmund's narrowed to slits. Francis tried not to laugh at the contrasting personalities of the staff, who somehow worked together methodically and, for the most part, harmoniously.

He speared some beef and potatoes and chewed, carefully watching Edmund. He would be the most likely stickler about Francis's ambitions rather than Mrs Gaynor or Jane.

His friend met his gaze, his food untouched, his hands clasped around his knife and fork. 'And I presume these plans have something to do with Miss Bloom?'

'To an extent, yes. However, they were made on my own initiative long before I met Miss Bloom.' Although he somewhat lied, Francis kept his expression firm. He would never have gone along the path of visiting the workhouse and speaking to the children without knowing Nancy would be there for him to call on when he walked back into the outside world. He was more aware of that than anything else. He cleared his throat. 'However, you can expect Miss Bloom's attendance at the house more often from now on.' He exhaled. 'At least, I hope you can.'

'Oh, well, that's wonderful.' Mrs Gaynor beamed. 'She is lovely young woman, sir. A kind heart that you can see clearly in those stunning eyes of hers.'

Francis grinned, his faith in Mrs Gaynor's judgement as steadfast as ever. 'She has a good heart indeed, which is why I asked her to accompany me to the workhouse today.' His smile wavered as he faced Edmund. His friend stared back at him, the disbelief in his gaze shooting across the table. 'It is mine and Miss Bloom's intention to do all that we can to instigate some changes in the conditions at the workhouse and my first step is to spend some time getting to know a young girl there.'

Edmund closed his eyes, his jaw tight.

Francis turned to Mrs Gaynor and then Jane. Their eyes were wide with shock as they stared back at him. Dropping his attention to his plate, Francis ate through the silence, wanting to hear their responses before he elaborated further. That way, he would know exactly what he was dealing with.

'If I may say something?' Edmund's tone was distinctly clipped.

'Of course.'

'Children from the workhouse are... I mean, I have been told the children there are rarely from stable backgrounds. What is your reason for getting to know one of them? Surely, it isn't wise to embark on any kind of relationship with this girl only to turn around and disappear from her life further down the line?'

Francis lowered his knife and fork and held Edmund's heated stare. The concern in his friend's eyes heartened Francis rather than deterred him. Edmund had known the demands and drudgery of the workhouse longer than Francis and it was that experience and the time it had taken Edmund to get over his abuses that would be on his friend's mind.

Guilt pushed into Francis's heart, but his determination was stronger. He had to do this.

'I agree,' he said, reaching for his wine. 'And I have no idea where our conversation will lead us as far as Alice is concerned, but speaking to her and possibly others is a necessity.'

'Because?'

Francis reached for his wine. 'Because I have written a play that will be showing at the Royal in February or March. The story is about the workhouse and it is my hope it will stir change from the gentry, men of influence and wealthy women involved in charity. Miss Bloom will be playing the main part and anything Alice can tell us about the workhouse today will be imperative for an authentic performance.'

Mrs Gaynor sighed. 'Which is wonderful, sir, but Edmund is right. What about the hopes your visiting might bring to this child?'

Francis looked between Edmund and Mrs Gaynor. What more did they want him to say? His plans had not stretched beyond progression and research. 'What else can I do but pray that one day Alice will come to escape the walls of that vile place and build a life free of abuse and neglect?'

'If I might make an outlandish...' Mrs Gaynor's cheeks flushed '...but fair comment, sir?'

'Of course. Anything you wish to add will be of value. That is why I wanted us to discuss this together. As a unit, if you will.'

'Then...' Mrs Gaynor glanced at Edmund and Jane before facing Francis. 'Maybe, in time, you could suggest to the girl that she might like to come here as a maid?'

Any possibility of a coherent, articulated response flew from Francis's head like a flock of migrating birds. 'What?'

She shrugged and cut into her beef. 'Is it not a valid possibility? I've not known you to take interest in the workhouse children before,' Mrs Gaynor said, as she continued to load her fork. ''Course you've got a generosity that's a credit to you and it by no means surprises me that you want to help those less fortunate, but on top of that...' She smiled, the glint in her gaze making her eyes shine like cut diamonds. 'I also haven't known you to ever look at anyone quite the same way you do Miss Bloom.'

Francis stared at his cook in disbelief, not really certain of where Mrs Gaynor was heading with her observations. 'And that has some bearing on Alice?'

'Maybe.' Mrs Gaynor kept her concentration on her plate. 'I mean, I assume the girl is young? Maybe thirteen or fourteen. She could quite easily become part of this household.' She finally looked up. 'Part of yours and Miss Bloom's life, in fact... a surrogate daughter if you will.'

Jane giggled and looked to her plate. Francis swallowed, his mouth draining of moisture as he looked at Edmund. The vein bulging at his friend's temple looked fit to burst.

Francis quickly faced Mrs Gaynor. 'My goodness, you are running ahead with some outlandish romance, are you not, Mrs Gaynor? My plan is to help Alice. Nothing more. As for how I look at Miss Bloom...' He glanced around the table a second time, his heart hammering but a desire to share his growing feelings for Nancy also vying to be heard. 'She is a wonderful woman whom I am enjoying getting to know. What the future holds is anyone's guess but, for now, we are nothing more than friends. Good friends.'

Edmund reached for his wine glass, his eyes unwavering on Francis. 'The company you are choosing to keep of late becomes more and more surprising, *sir*.'

Annoyance stirred in Francis's gut. 'Indeed. Well, if you have something substantiated and proven to tell me about Miss Bloom that you think best advised I know, then now is the time to share it. If not, I suggest you have enough respect and like of me to trust that I know my own mind and instinct when it comes to our fellow man or woman.'

Tension stretched between them and Francis sat rigid, waiting for Edmund to contradict him, maybe even argue with him if the man's rising colour was anything to hold measure by. The seconds passed until Edmund took a hefty gulp of wine and slowly lowered the glass to the table.

'I will stand by any and every decision you make, you know that,' Edmund said, his dark brown gaze boring into Francis's. 'I just want you to be certain you are doing the right thing by getting involved with the workhouse. That you are doing the right thing by becoming closer to Miss Bloom.'

Mrs Gaynor guffawed. 'What's that supposed to mean? I have never known you to be so haughty, Edmund. Miss Bloom is a wonderful woman. If you know anything different, then I think we all have a right to know.' She raised her eyebrows. 'Well?'

Francis's heart beat hard as he glared at Edmund, silently imploring him not to share Nancy's occupation. He had no right to tell his staff something that Francis had chosen to keep secret. If anyone was going to tell Mrs Gaynor and Jane about Nancy's prostitution, it would be Nancy herself.

'No, Mrs Gaynor,' Edmund said quietly, picking up his cutlery. 'I have nothing else to add as far as Miss Bloom is concerned.'

Francis slowly released his held breath. 'Good. Then all that remains is for Miss Bloom and I to convince the young girl Alice that she will always be safe in our company. As for her coming to this house in the future, Mrs Gaynor' – Edmund inhaled a deep breath – 'it is something that I might well consider... in time. But for now, let us eat before our dinner gets cold.'

Mrs Gaynor immediately turned to Jane, regaling her with a story about an overturned wagon in the market square that morning. Francis looked across the table at Edmund. His friend held Francis's gaze for a long moment before dropping his attention to his food.

Swallowing hard, Francis did the same. He had no idea what just happened but suddenly the idea of giving Alice a home as his parents had him felt a very real and exciting possibility.

43

Nancy glanced around the breakfast table as Louisa, Octavia and Jacob discussed every subject from the weather to the fight one of Jacob's friends might or might not accept. She had not an inch of care for the sun or a boxing match. Was she the only person in this household who cared about the real problems in this city?

'Good Lord, Nancy.' Jacob laughed across the table. 'I hope to God it's not me you're thinking about. The look on your face can only mean someone or something is in for a pasting of some sort.'

Nancy glared at him, her hands curling into fists in her lap. 'I *am* thinking about you actually. You and your interest in a fight that might never happen.' She snatched a bread roll from the basket in front of her just for something to busy herself with rather than reaching for Jacob's neck. 'Isn't there anything more interesting we can talk about over breakfast?'

The silence was sudden and deafening.

Splitting her roll with shaking fingers, Nancy battled the angry tears burning her eyes. Couldn't her friends see how the world suffered? How much children, young and older, sought solace and comfort? Couldn't they hear the cries of hunger, disappointment and abuse that screamed throughout Bath's streets?

'Octavia? Jacob? Would you mind leaving Nancy and I alone?'

Nancy muttered a curse as Louisa's stern and curt demand practically bounced from the silk wall hangings and hitched Nancy's frustration further. Now she would be in for a questioning that would know no bounds. Louisa was like a rabid dog once she suspected one of her pack was unhappy.

Chairs were pushed back and napkins tossed onto the table, and Nancy kept her gaze locked on her roll and knife as she haphazardly plastered it with butter. Her stomach lurched at the mess, her appetite non-existent, but she could not find the strength to look Louisa or anyone else in the eye.

The door slammed unceremoniously behind Jacob and Octavia.

Louisa rose from her chair and walked the length of the table before taking the seat beside Nancy. 'Well?'

Closing her eyes, Nancy abandoned the bread and slumped back against her chair. 'I'm sorry.'

'For?'

'Everything.' Nancy opened her eyes and her friend's violet eyes shone with a blend of annoyance and care. 'I shouldn't have spoken to Jacob like that. I shouldn't be airing my frustrations and I shouldn't be giving you cause to worry about me.'

'Is there a valid reason for me to worry?'

'No.'

'Don't lie to me, Nance. We promised we'd never go there, remember?'

Nancy swiped her hand over her face before blowing out a heavy breath. 'God, what's happening to me, Lou? Where has my humour gone? My laughter? I don't know what I'm doing anymore. The person I always thought I was, who I was comfortable being, is slipping away.'

Louisa took her hand and held it tight, her face set with concern. 'Has this got something to do with Mr Carlyle?'

'It's not Francis. Not specifically anyway.' Nancy shook her head, her heart filling with love for Francis even if her mind was a mess. 'He makes me feel things I have never felt in my life. He makes me wonder if I might come to love him but, as terrifying as that is, I don't want to lose who I am in the process.'

'Why would you? Is he expecting you to change? Be someone you're not? Because if he is, he is not the right man for you, Nance, and he never will be.'

'No, it's not that.' Nancy slid her hand from Louisa's and stood. She circled her chair and gripped the back. 'It's just... I feel like I've done it again.'

'Done what again?'

Nancy closed her eyes as she struggled to find the right words to explain what was going on inside her, the conflicting thoughts and feelings that had taken over every hour throughout the night and into this morning. She'd always stood proud in whatever measures she'd taken to survive, but lately her whoring felt wrong. Like by choosing to sleep with her clients, she betrayed Francis – betrayed herself.

'Nance?'

She opened her eyes and swallowed. 'Francis's intentions for the workhouse are truly inspiring, Lou, and I want to be part of his plans.'

'Which is wonderful, though I sense a but coming.'

'But when I was with him last night, I had the horrible feeling of being a pawn in someone else's desires.'

'I don't understand. If you want to work alongside him, how can you be a pawn? You can walk away whenever you want to.'

'But it's about more than choice. It's about my own desires and weaknesses. My own independence. I allowed Francis to convince me he would help me fulfil my dream of being onstage. Just like I did with the man who kidnapped me. My dream once more blinded me to the dangers of trusting in someone. Of believing that maybe, just maybe, I have a talent worth pursuing and another person recognised that.'

'You do have a talent.'

'You don't know that.' Nancy pushed away from the chair and strode to the window, frustration building inside of her. She abruptly whirled around. 'What if my talent doesn't lie on the stage, but in my stupidity to want to do right by other people? To bolster others as I should be bolstering myself, and now... now... I've...' She spun around to the window, gripping the wall beside her as she glared into the street. 'Now I've fallen in love with a man with worse insecurities than me. Not only that, the pair of us have become immersed in the lives of children.' She turned again. 'Not just children, but desperate children. What in God's name am I doing, Lou?'

Louisa stood and came towards her, her gaze softened with concern. 'What children? You're not making any sense.'

'Francis took me to the workhouse. He once thought his play, his own story of his time there, would help others to see something had to be done about that place, but then he decided that in order for me to play the heroine of his play with absolute sincerity, I needed to speak to some of the children.'

'And that turned out to be a bad thing?'

'Well, not bad but...' Nancy swallowed. 'All-consuming. At least for me. I spoke with a girl named Alice. She seems so desolate, so quietly resigned to what she clearly thinks is the rest of her life.'

'But it's Francis's intention that change, is it not?'

'Yes, but—'

'Nance, don't you see? If Francis sees you as an integral part of that happening, then you are most definitely not a pawn in his eyes. If he values your opinion, he is not taking advantage of you. You must see that?'

'But how can I be sure? And now there are to be children involved. What if I mess up?'

'You won't. You must start believing in yourself.'

'But I look into his eyes and I know his play is just the beginning. He wants to help as many of those poor souls as he can, one by one if necessary. I'm scared, Lou.' Nancy's voice cracked as panic gripped her. 'Because I actually believe him capable of doing just that. I believe in him and all he wants to do. And... and...'

Louisa smiled. 'And what?'

'And I want to be right beside him in all of it. Help him in any way I possibly can.'

'Oh, Nance. That's good.' She pulled Nancy into her arms and kissed her temple. 'Why are you hating yourself for such a thing?'

Like a breaking dam, tears flowed over Nancy's cheeks and she pulled back, swiping at her face with trembling fingers. 'Because how can I help him? What do I know of charity, children or being strong in the face of others' suffering? I belong here. With you. My ambitions for the stage could fail and so could any future ventures Francis might propose. Why expose my weaknesses in such a way? I have all I need here.'

'Do you? I think not. You are looking for something past Carson Street. Something extraordinary.'

Nancy stared at her friend, realisation dawning. 'What are you saying? That I will never be truly happy?'

'Of course not.' Louisa shook her head and smiled. 'Reaching for what seems impossible is exciting. Something that you must keep within yourself always. You don't owe this house or me anything. Including your time. You will always be my friend, always be welcome here, but if you are to give up whoring and be beside Mr Carlyle in his work, in his life, so be it. I will support you however you need me to. Octavia and Jacob will, too.'

'I don't know.' Nancy closed her eyes. 'It's not just me, it's what Francis is surrendering, too.'

'What do you mean?'

Nancy opened her eyes. 'I mean I am not sure if he even knows how much his vision could consume him. How it could bring up terrors and memories that are best left buried.'

'I think you are doing him an injustice. He will know all of that, Nance, and is still pushing forward. His tenacity is something to be admired, not cautioned against.'

'Maybe, but I can't help being afraid for him.'

'Which only serves to prove your heart. The decision to forge forward is Francis's choice.'

'Yes, but...' Nancy pursed her lips, unsure what she was feeling and desperate for her friend to help her decipher the mess inside her heart and mind. 'If Francis and I both love the theatre, both believe in its magic and possibilities, is it right that we begin to interfere in government decisions, politics and such?'

'Why not? You are strong, and you are forthright. All that you want will come to you in time.' Louisa's determined glare bored into Nancy's. 'But, for now, you must wait until this new work is done and then, eventually, yours and Mr Carlyle's love for the theatre will come back to the fore. I promise. You will make it so.'

'But how can I tell him that stardom still burns in my heart when he is trying to do so much good? He will turn away from me, Lou, and I wouldn't blame him.'

'He won't. Not when he sees you want to work beside him in

his philanthropy *and* the theatre. That's what you want, isn't it? You want to do everything with him.'

'Yes. Yes, I do.'

Louisa grinned and took Nancy's hands. 'Then tell Mr Carlyle you will help him with whatever he wishes at the workhouse and with the children, but you also believe in his writing and, most importantly, in yourself.'

Nancy stared. Is this what love did to a woman? Made her suspect herself to be neither good nor strong enough? Made her fear that in loving another she risked all love of herself?

'Love is about compromise, Nance,' Louisa whispered. 'It's not about giving up all you want. It's about coming together to ensure both your and your lover's dreams and aspirations are worked towards with the same commitment. Believe me, being with the right man, the right person, is the most wonderful and powerful thing in the world... if it's right.'

'And if it's wrong?'

'You learn from your mistakes. That's all any of us can do.'

Nancy nodded, her inner strength stirring. She wanted to be with Francis, wanted to see where the future might take them, whatever the obstacles. 'You're right.'

'I know I am. Go and find Francis,' Louisa said softly, her violet gaze shining. 'Tell him everything that is in your heart.'

'Everything?' Nancy arched an eyebrow, a tentative smile pulling at her lips. 'Even that I know without any doubt that I will one day be a star?'

Louisa grinned. 'Especially that.'

Laughing, Nancy pulled her friend into her arms and held her tight. Maybe one day she and Francis could have it all. How and when evaded her, but if they just took one small step at a time, surely anything was possible?

44

Francis entered the bar at the Theatre Royal and stretched his neck, his tie feeling distinctly tighter than usual. The cryptic message he'd received from Nancy that afternoon lay in his pocket, still not revealing any idea why she would ask to meet him here of all the alternative places for them to spend an evening in Bath.

Yet, here he was. A man running to the woman he loved as soon as she bid him.

The pride he felt in such action was questionably misplaced, yet Francis basked in the feeling regardless. Being in love, being with Nancy, suited him more than anything ever had.

Scanning the room, he caught a flash of familiar auburn hair, although tonight it was dressed with amethyst-coloured stones and a pearl comb. His heart swelled in his chest as he shouldered his way through the throng, the clink of glasses and raised voices seeming to fade as his focus remained on Nancy while she chatted and laughed with the barman. The young sap looked half in love... or maybe lust.

A wave of ungentlemanly possession whispered through Francis as he sidled up beside her. 'Is this seat taken?'

She started and turned, her eyes filling with a flash of love that was quickly replaced with flirtatious desire. 'Well, no. It isn't.' She turned to the barman. 'Would you kindly pour this gentleman a glass of brandy, young man? It seems he wishes to join our company.'

Francis fought his smile as he met the young lad's scowl before he turned away to get Francis's drink. He slid onto the stool beside Nancy and drew his gaze over her beautiful face. 'You look stunning.'

'Thank you.' Her smile was wide and confident, despite the faint blush at her cheeks. 'I thought I would wear one of my most expensive dresses considering we are celebrating.'

'Celebrating?' Francis smiled, unable to drag his gaze from hers. 'Has something happened?'

'Yes.'

Before he could ask her to elaborate, the barman returned with Francis's drink. 'Thank you.' He handed over a cash note. 'Keep the change.' He picked up his drink and sipped. 'Well?'

Nancy lifted her champagne glass to her lips, her eyes shining with mischief. 'Everything has become clear since I last saw you,' she said. 'Starting from tonight, all we both want will happen, Francis. All of it.'

An inexplicable tension crept into his gut, unease inching across his shoulders. 'What do you mean?'

'I mean, I have spoken to Louisa and now everything makes sense as to how we go forward. Have you spoken to your staff? Told them about Alice?'

'Well, yes, I—'

'And I have told Louisa of our work for the workhouse and she is supportive. Told me to do whatever we have to so that your dreams come true. But, of course, you and I know it's about so much more than *your* dreams. It's about' – she grinned – 'our dreams. Dreams for creating a better life for those children, for banishing your ghosts, for seeing your play onstage and...' She shakily exhaled. 'And it's about me becoming the star I've always believed I would one day be. Now that you have shared your beginnings with your staff, and they know where you have come from and why it is so important that you do this work' – she took a hefty sip of champagne – 'nothing can stop us, Francis. In confessing your past, you have liberated yourself in every way just as I have by telling Louisa what I genuinely want to do. What's more' – the skin at her throat shifted as she swallowed – 'I have told her who I want to be with... hopefully forever.'

Francis sat immobile, words abandoning him as he looked into her grey eyes so heartbreakingly filled with hope and optimism. Shame and a familiar sense of humiliation stirred inside of him as Nancy stared at him, her wonderful smile beginning to falter. God, he was an imbecile. A coward of the highest order. Tell his staff of his beginnings? Never. How in God's name would Mrs Gaynor and Jane ever look at him or Edmund in the same way? Believe that Francis had any right to be their master?

'Nancy...' He briefly closed his eyes before opening them again. He took her hand. 'I will never tell my staff of my beginnings.'

Disappointment flooded her gaze. 'Why not?'

'Because...' Words and excuses flailed on his tongue. 'I couldn't.'

She stared at him before taking another sip of champagne and slowly returning the glass to the bar. 'Why are you so determined to keep pretending, Francis?' She lifted her eyes to his. 'Why not take what you want to do at the workhouse as a chance of liberty? Not just for the children, but for you too? I don't understand. This is the chance you've been waiting for. Every bit as important as your wish to see your story told onstage.'

He swiped his hand over his face. 'That's why you brought me here, isn't it? You think it is here that your dreams will be fulfilled as well as mine.'

'Yes.' She gave a firm nod. 'The theatre is what brought us together and is what will keep us together.'

'You're wrong.'

'What?'

'I'm sorry.' He stood, disillusionment replacing his shame as the future he had hoped he'd found with Nancy slowly began to disintegrate. 'The work I want to see done at the workhouse, for the children there, no longer seems enough. Mrs Gaynor...'

'Mrs Gaynor what?'

'She said something... suggested something that has been preying on my mind ever since.'

'Well, what did she say?'

Francis looked deep into Nancy's eyes. How could he tell her about his consideration of offering Alice a place in his home and Nancy not run for the hills? Her dream was stardom, not watching him employ or even adopt a young girl he barely knew.

She would think him mad – as he did himself.

He shook his head, glanced about the bustling bar before forcing his gaze to hers. 'Mrs Gaynor suggested that I might consider bringing Alice into my home.'

Her eyes widened. 'Into your home?'

'Yes, as a maid, but that doesn't feel right somehow.'

She covered his hand where it lay on the bar, the surprise in her eyes giving way to care. 'What are you saying, Francis?'

He blew out a breath. 'I don't know. At least not yet, but what I do know is my staff have no need to learn of my beginnings.'

'Of course they do.'

Annoyed, Francis glared at her. 'Why? I pay them to—'

'What? To cook and clean for you? Serve you?' Sudden anger blazed in her eyes, her cheeks reddening. She lowered her voice. 'They are there to support you. That's what people in service are truly doing, Francis, and if you can't see that, I have no idea what it is you would want for Alice or any of the other children you claim you wish to help.'

'I want nothing but to help them,' he hissed, his pulse thumping in his ears as curious gazes turned their way in his peripheral vision. 'And, what's more, I am now determined to get as many children as possible out of that place and into loving homes where they will thrive. Just as I did.'

'Which is wonderful, and I want that too, but I also ask you this: did your father ever treat you like a servant when he took you into his home? Or did he train you, inspire you, encourage and love you?'

Guilt slithered into his gut. His adoptive parents had done all that and more, not once making him feel inferior or like an asset to their prosperity.

He swallowed and faced the people staring at them before turning back to Nancy. 'Let's get out here. Go somewhere quieter where we can discuss this prop—'

'Is there really anything more to say?' She drained her glass and stood, pushing her purse high under her arm. 'I have never felt so alive or free as when I confessed my true soul to Louisa today, but now everything I said to her about our future, about your work, about you, feels coated in pretence. Constructed in duplicity.' She stepped back from him. 'And I'm sorry, Francis, but I have no wish to be around a man who cannot be honest with himself about who he is. If you find that so impossible, how will you ever be honest with anyone else?'

She stormed away from him, shoving through the crowd

without apology. Tall, strong, impenetrable. A woman who had been through hell and back yet owned her every experience like a badge of honour. Who wished to continue reaching for her dreams and what she wholeheartedly believed to be her destiny.

And what of him?

Shame grew until he caught the eye of the barman, who smiled, his gaze clearly showing his glee that Francis, a man who appeared so high in station, had just let the most priceless jewel be stolen through his own stupidity.

'What the hell are you looking at?' he snapped at the barman. 'Don't think for a minute I'd ever let a woman like that slip from my fingers. She's worth more than anything or anyone. You hear me?'

Francis swiped his hat from the bar and shoved his way through the accumulated audience of gawping spectators.

45

Nancy fled further and further away from the theatre and marched along the street towards the workhouse.

She needed to look at that ugly stone building and remind herself of what she had committed to after meeting Francis, after believing in him, in some ways more than she ever had anyone else. Maybe even more than she had Louisa. Which now felt incredibly shaming.

After her conversation with Francis – or maybe their first real argument – she felt if she didn't once more picture the conditions and the faces of the children living there, she would lose all the compassion and love Francis had evoked in her. His care for those children was the new and abiding factor he stood for in Nancy's eyes and heart. And, God help her, she feared returning to the hard-heartedness she'd lived by before meeting him.

But now she wondered if he had just shown her who he truly was: a man living a lie. A man hiding behind finery and pomp.

Anger and confusion beat through Nancy, pushing her forwards, fuelling her resentment towards a man who had coerced her into caring about children, caring about someone else's future other than her own and that of her friends at Carson Street. Francis had widened the scope of her heart and heightened her ambition and then slammed the door shut again with his stupid male pride.

'Nancy, wait!'

She halted, closed her eyes, tipped her head back. Couldn't the man take a clear rebuff?

Turning, she crossed her arms and glared as Francis slowed to a stop in front of her. 'Go away.'

'No.' He held her gaze, his jaw set. 'We are not finished. Not by a long shot.'

'Is that so?' She huffed a laugh. 'You really have no more idea of who am I than I do you. You are not the man I thought you were, Francis. Not if your elevation in society has made you forget who you once were. I thought I made that clear before, yet here you are—'

'I don't need to tell my staff that I was once at the workhouse to carry out the work I want to do. Have you stopped to consider that maybe your continuing insistence that I bare my soul to the whole damn world has a lot more to do with you than me?'

Shocked by his words and their vehemence, Nancy stepped back, vulnerability tip-tapping along her spine. 'What's that supposed to mean?'

'It means…' He clutched her elbows in his hands, his brilliant blue gaze boring into hers, his frustration palpable. 'You say all you want in life is to be onstage, to be a star, yet over and over again you talk about your whoring and Louisa. Which really matters the most to you? Don't you see that those lives are intertwined?'

'Of course they're not. Nothing could be more different.'

He shook his head. 'You're wrong. There are enough people who consider any woman who chooses to perform onstage a whore. This world you want so much to be a part of is as hard and unforgiving as the world you live in right now. Just as cruel and exhausting. It's time for you to wake up from this dream of yours, Nancy. The theatre is cut-throat, and even though I have no doubt at all that you will handle it well enough, I do doubt your visions of what this desired stardom will actually look like.'

Her heart pounded. This was the side of Francis that showed his core was as steely as her own, that he had been subjected to cruelty and abuse just as she had. They were tough and maybe even a little twisted, but that just made her want him more.

They were also full of pride.

Snatching her arms from his grip, Nancy glowered at him when really all she wanted to do was slam him up against the wall beside them and have the bastard give her such a seeing to she saw stars. Possession and passion, love and desire whirled like a maelstrom inside of her, exciting her, frightening her. How could she want someone so much yet also be so immeasurably frustrated by him?

'Do you know why I was so happy when you met me tonight?' she demanded, her body trembling. 'Do you know why I was sitting at that bar itching for you to come through the door? No, you don't, because you seem to think it is a sworn thing that I will help you without condition now that I've been to the workhouse. Now that I care about Alice and the other kids there. But that is not true, Francis.' She planted her hands on her hips. 'This is just as much about what I want as it is about what you want.'

'I know that.'

'Do you? Because it seems to me you think me incapable of caring for those children *and* reaching for all I've ever wanted. Well, you're wrong. I can do both, Francis, and if you can't see that, maybe I will achieve your dreams and mine without you.'

His steely gaze locked on hers, his jaw tight. 'Why is being onstage so important to you?'

'What?'

'You heard me. What is the real reason you want to be a star, Nancy? Why does it matter to you so much that you are on Bath's stage and have all the city admire you?'

Tears stung her eyes, her humiliation rising as he forced her to admit what she had always desperately desired deep inside. What she needed so that all that had been done to her during her abduction was washed away on a tide of applause and she could be fresh and clean once more – could just be Nancy.

She planted her hands on her hips, her cheeks burning. 'Because then people will really see me. The real me! Not Nancy the whore, but Nancy the woman. Nancy the girl who made her dreams come true.'

The smoky night enveloped her, stealing the air from her lungs. Frustration and love swirled in the depths of Francis's eyes, but she would not falter.

She had laid her truth bare.

'For the love of God, woman,' he said, softly. '*I* see you. Is that not enough?'

A lone tear slipped over her cheek. 'I wish it was, but it's not, Francis. I'm sorry. Too many people have dismissed me. Too many have seen me as little more than a way of making money. I can sing and I can dance. I can make people laugh and smile. I truly believe all will be made well inside of me if I am onstage.'

He stepped back and whipped off his hat, pushed his hand into his hair. 'Then we must endeavour to do both.'

'And we will, if you promise me that you will share your own beginnings publicly. Confess that your play is not fictional but a true story. *Your* story. Please, promise me you will do that. If not today, then sometime soon.'

He briefly closed his eyes before opening them again. 'I promise.'

She stared into his eyes, unable to tell whether he spoke honestly but afraid to press him further and have him sever their relationship. 'Good, then I am certain Alice will help us with your play and maybe even set us in the right direction for what must be done at the workhouse. She is the key, Francis. I'm sure of it.'

He stepped closer and drew her into his arms. Nancy shook as she clung to him, fear and love mixing until she had no idea where one emotion ended and the other began.

46

'I am somewhat surprised to see you back here again, Mr Carlyle.'

Francis looked Mr Greaves in the eye and stepped closer to the workhouse governor's desk. 'I don't see why. I said I would be back, did I not?'

'You did.' Greaves dropped his attention to the papers in front of him. 'But you and Miss Bloom soon left once you had spent some time speaking to that young girl.' He lifted his gaze, a sneer twisting his mouth. 'I'd assumed she'd deterred you from your charitable endeavours. There is no shame in your newly discovered disgust of these urchins, sir. None whatsoever.'

'My...' Enraged, Francis curled his hands into fists at his sides. 'I am far from disgusted, sir. I have returned with the sole intention of speaking with young Alice again.'

The governor's eyes widened, his cheeks mottled. 'Whatever for?'

'Because that is my wish, and it will continue to be my wish for however long I see fit. After that, I may well be back again as I am also considering employing Alice.' Francis walked to the office door and opened it. 'So, shall we go along and speak to her?'

'There are procedures and regulations—'

'That I will be more than happy to adhere to once I have put my proposal of employment to Alice and she is happy to pursue a new life working for me. Until then, I won't be signing any piece of paper, considering any rules or regulations – and, more importantly, neither will I be signing a cheque.' Francis raised his eyebrows and gestured into the corridor. 'Shall we?'

Greaves eased his bulk from his chair and rounded the desk, tugging at the hem of his uniform jacket and eyeing Francis over the rims of his half-spectacles. 'These youngsters are not normal, sir.'

'Normal? And what is normal, Mr Greaves?'

The governor only grunted before he led the way along the dark corridor towards the same workroom where Francis and Nancy had met Alice before. As they entered, the dank and musty stench drifted into Francis's nostrils. Each child seemed lost and alone in their small space, their faces pale and devoid of emotion. Every one of them far too thin, their government-issued clothes hanging from their malnourished bodies like adult clothing over a child-size mannequin.

There seemed to be even more children sewing, knitting and mending than when he'd last been here and the enormity of his mission threatened to overwhelm him once more. Francis pulled back his shoulders and fought the despair that threatened to devour him. One child at a time. That would remain his mantra until he and the other men and women he intended recruiting over the coming weeks were triumphant in their work to close this godforsaken place down.

No matter how long that might take.

Francis glanced at Greaves as he and the female warden overseeing the workroom walked towards him, their stony expressions making them look as welcoming as two lions poised to slay their next meal.

Determined that the two of them would in no way affect his purpose, Francis smiled. 'Good morning, Mrs...?'

The woman narrowed her eyes, her hands clamped in front of her. 'Heffer.'

Considering the woman was stick thin, her skin stretched tight over sharp cheekbones, the name didn't exactly suit, and Francis struggled to retain a snort of laughter. He quickly faced the room and spotted Alice, once again working alone, this time in the opposite corner from where she'd been seated last time. 'Well, Mrs Heffer, I'd like to speak to Alice, if I may?'

She frowned. 'Alice?'

'The girl in the corner over there.' He stared at the warden. 'Surely you know these children by name?'

Greaves guffawed. 'As if we have time to care, sir. No, they are numbers and crosses on a list. Nothing more. Now, I will leave you to speak with Mrs Heffer and, in turn, the child you wish to employ. Once you are done, Mrs Heffer will ensure you are escorted back to my office.'

'Very well.'

Francis glared after Greaves as he gave a disgruntled appraisal of the room before turning abruptly on his heel. Arsehole.

'Mr Carlyle?'

He turned. 'Yes?'

Mrs Heffer smiled, her face transformed as her blue eyes turned soft with unexpected kindness. 'Would you like to speak to just Alice? Or maybe speak with some other children, too?'

Francis stared, entirely confused by the woman's turnaround in demeanour. 'You disapprove of Mr Greaves, I assume?'

'Disapprove and despise.' She sniffed and tossed a glare

towards the closed door. 'The man is a snob at the best of times, but I tolerate him, act polite and indifferent to the children whenever he is around so that he might leave me to do my job. However...' She studied Francis through narrowed eyes. 'The man is also partial to allowing all and sundry to come and look at these poor mites... for a price. There are men who like children, sir. Really like them, but my instinct tells me you are a fine, upstanding gentleman. Your intentions honourable.'

Sickness unfurled in Francis's stomach. 'Of that, I can absolutely assure you.'

'Good, but I still want to know what it is you want with Alice. The girl has been through enough here and where she was before. She doesn't need any more terror in her life.' She looked Francis up and down, her gaze steely. 'Whether that terror comes dressed in riches or rags.'

'My intention with Alice and, I hope, others is to give them a chance of forging a good and honest life away from here. I have strength and fortitude as well as money and influence. I can make a difference.'

'Hmm. Maybe you can, but why Alice?'

Francis stared across the room to where Alice worked and once more the affinity he and Nancy had felt when they'd first looked at the girl returned. 'I just have a feeling about her. She is the one with whom I wish to begin my endeavours.' He faced Mrs Heffer. 'She seems wiser than her years. Hardened. Experienced.'

'You'll forgive me my scepticism about your good intentions, sir.' Mrs Heffer inhaled a long breath, then slowly exhaled as she glanced towards Alice. 'I can't believe anyone would truly want to make a difference, or really understand what these poor wretches have endured, unless...'

'Unless what?'

She faced him. 'Unless they've experienced the workhouse for themselves.'

His argument with Nancy resounded in his head as panic sped Francis's heart. *Tell her. Tell her, you bloody coward. Tell her...*

'Hmm.' Mrs Heffer hitched back her shoulders and gave a curt nod. 'Then it is as I thought.'

Francis's face burned with his cowardice, Nancy's scowling face appearing in his mind's eye. 'Mrs Heffer, I...'

'Say no more, sir. I understand enough to know what you're all about, but you'd be best advised to leave things alone unless you are in this fight heart and soul. Getting Alice out of here won't be easy and she doesn't deserve to have her hopes raised only for them to be dashed further along the line. The girl has been through enough.'

'I more than have the means to ensure she is cared for. I will ensure she is fed, clothed—'

'That's not what I mean.' She glanced across at Alice again. 'There's something you should know about her and Mr Greaves.'

Francis frowned, disturbed by the way Mrs Heffer's face had paled but for two spots of colour on her cheeks. Her gaze flitted over his face, hatred clear in her dark eyes. 'She is one of two girls that are... special to Mr Greaves, sir.'

Anger and revulsion ignited as Francis clenched his jaw. 'Special?'

'I think you know what I mean.' She stared towards Alice. 'If you get that poor girl out of here, then you promise me you'll give her a life the poor mite could never have imagined considering all that she goes through day after day.'

Francis looked across the room. Alice had stood from her stool and her stare bored into him from across the space that separated them. Her sad, emerald green eyes flashed so clearly in Francis's memory, it did not matter that the girl stood so far away.

Sadness twisted inside him at her possible fear rather than pleasant surprise that he had returned. Without Nancy beside him, he looked no better than Greaves, interested in her for unsavoury reasons.

He turned to Mrs Heffer. 'When I was here before, Alice seemed more willing to talk to me than Miss Bloom. Considering what I think you are telling me about Mr Greaves, why would that be?'

'Because she isn't used to women showing her any more kindness than men and would have assumed, out of you and Miss Bloom, it was you pulling the strings. It would have been Alice's intention to deter you without any regard for Miss Bloom's importance past decoration.'

'I see.'

'After all, in this world it is the men who make the decisions, sir. Well, at least, they do outside of the home. These children have learned the same is true in the workhouse. Men are the ones they fear but Alice has, unfortunately, been here long enough to know she has nothing to gain from befriending women either.'

Anger simmered inside Francis that Alice was fourteen years old but had not yet been given a single reason to trust an adult, whether male or female. He looked across the room and Alice stared straight back at him. 'She said she had no wish to leave.'

'And nor will she unless you can completely convince her that you will keep her safe. This is her home. She's not used to anything else.' Mrs Heffer's eyes widened with warning. 'But you could change that, Mr Carlyle. I hope, forever.'

Francis swallowed against the sudden dryness in his throat. His motivation to do more was as strong as ever, but his fortitude had been shaken since Nancy had shown her disappointment through his lack of honesty with his staff. She was the power between them. She was the one with the big, open heart and laughter that could shake even the most dejected from their misery.

Surely only with Nancy's support would Alice ever be happy in his home? Or maybe Mrs Gaynor and Jane's guidance and humour would be enough to show the young girl she was wanted?

He looked to Mrs Heffer. 'I will return in due course.'

'As you wish, sir.'

Francis looked at Alice one last time. She kept her eyes on his for a long, heated moment before sitting slowly back down on her stool, her face devoid of expression but her slumped shoulders and tapping foot seeming to say so much.

Was she relieved he was leaving? Or merely angry and entirely unsurprised?

47

'I'm sorry, Miss Bloom. You are not what we are looking for at this time.'

Humiliation burned hot at Nancy's cheeks as she dipped her head in a semblance of a thank you and walked from the music hall stage. This was the fifth hall she had auditioned at over the last week, not to mention four theatres. No one wanted her. Not even for the smallest part or the shortest act.

Shame and disappointment twisted inside of her as she pushed her way through the other women waiting in the wings to be called onstage. The place was a dump. Peeling patches of chipped paint flaked from the walls, the floorboards beneath her feet sticky with God only knew what, yet still she could not get even a five-minute slot.

After blurting her conviction to be onstage to Francis in such an entirely uncensored way, she realised it was neither fair nor right to completely rely on him to furnish her dreams. The rehearsals for his play would not begin for weeks yet, so she had decided to test the waters solo.

The trouble was, it had become more and more obvious she lacked any real talent past what was acceptable at the White Hart.

The stars in her eyes were fading, her certainty of her destiny once more decomposing on the slag heap as it had so many years before. She had no proof of her talent, only an unfailing voice and feeling deep inside that told her to keep pushing forward. That she was a star waiting to be born.

That was not enough. Had never been enough.

She burst through the dance hall's doors onto the street and breathed in the chilly night air. Wanting a drink and adulation in equal measure, Nancy headed for the Hart. At least there, she was blessed with a modicum of appreciation.

The pub was packed to the rafters and Nancy closed one eye against the volume of booming laughter, wolf-whistling and general hilarity. Her head thumped with the tension that had been beating at her temples through most of the day, her heart heavy with disappointment. She was hankering for a fight and woe betide the next person who in any way annoyed her.

Shouldering her way to the bar, she slapped her arms onto the counter and leaned forward, trying to see where Maura was serving. The woman was right down the opposite end.

Nancy blew out a breath. 'Damn it.'

'What you having, Nancy? And watch your mouth.'

Her heart and agitation lifted at the sound of Jacob's voice. He stood with his arm slung around Louisa's shoulders, Octavia standing behind them, her back ramrod straight and her face twisted with disapproval as she glanced around her.

'Well, aren't you three a sight for sore eyes.' Nancy laughed and reached up on her toes to kiss Jacob's cheek. 'I'll have a glass of ale, fine sir. Thank you very much.'

Jacob winked and released Louisa. 'Go and find a seat and I'll join you ladies as soon as I can.' He leaned closer to Nancy's ear.

'Louisa is fit to bursting with worrying about you. It's time to make up your mind about things, my girl.'

Nancy's smile dissolved as she looked around Jacob towards Louisa as she followed Octavia to a corner table. 'What do you mean?' She defiantly lifted her chin. 'I've not given Louisa any reason to worry about me. She knows I've been to the music halls.'

'Yeah, but she also knows you've not seen Mr Carlyle for the last few days.' Jacob raised his hand to get Maura's attention. 'It's that worrying her, Nance. Go and set her mind at rest.' He lifted his eyebrows. 'One way or another.'

'Francis and I are perfectly well.'

'Yet you seem to be on a mission to do everything your own way, with or without the man beside you.'

'That's not true. We are still working together, side by side.'

'Good. Then go and speak to Louisa.'

Nancy reluctantly walked to the table where Louisa and Octavia sat talking. The last thing she needed was a dressing-down from her friends when she already felt like a pile of manure. But needs must and she needed her friends.

'So...' She exhaled a long breath and slid into the velvet-seated booth beside Octavia, meeting Louisa's steady gaze across the table. 'Jacob's given me earache already and the three of you haven't been here longer than two minutes.'

'I'm glad.'

Nancy quirked her eyebrow and grinned, hoping her humour might lessen the annoyance in Louisa's eyes. 'That you've not been here longer than two minutes?'

'No, that Jacob has given you earache.'

Nancy looked towards the bar, her throat parched with need for a drink. 'I'm all right, Lou.'

'*You're* all right.' Octavia sniffed. 'But where does that leave us when you're coming and going? One day a whore, the next an actress.'

'I'll answer anything Louisa wants to ask me, but you and Jacob have no claim on me and never will.'

Their glares locked and Nancy narrowed her eyes until Octavia looked away – even if her fist remained clenched on the tabletop.

'Now, now, girls,' Louisa said, her tone cold. 'I won't have you falling out.' She focused on Nancy, her violet eyes blazing with annoyance. 'When Jacob gets back with our drinks...' She looked to the side. 'Ah, here he is.'

Jacob placed four glasses on the table and Nancy immediately reached for her drink. Taking a hefty swallow, she swiped the back of her hand across her mouth and let out an exaggerated sigh. Her enforced bravado felt strangely alien as opposed to comfortable as it had been for most of her life. The reason for the transformation scared her. She was changing, both inside and out. What in God's name was she supposed to do to stop that from happening? She needed to be sassy, strong and steadfast. Anything else meant weakness, and falling in love with Francis had shown her how unnerving that could be.

'So...' Louisa cleared her throat and pinned Nancy with a stare. 'Is it safe to assume that you and Mr Carlyle have parted ways?'

Nancy sipped her drink, trying not to squirm under the intense scrutiny of her friends. 'Not at all. We... had words but I'm sure we'll work things out.'

The noise around them intensified and when a great bulk of a man nudged into Nancy's elbow, splashing her ale onto the table, she was grateful for the distraction. 'Hey! Knock it off. Get out of here.'

Surprised that Jacob hadn't joined in the fracas, she slid her gaze to him.

He stared back at her, seemingly impervious to the interruption. 'What?'

'That man... my drink.' Nancy glared. 'And you call yourself our protector.'

He arched an eyebrow. 'Do I?'

Octavia sniggered and Nancy shot a glare to her friend. 'Something to say, Octavia Butter-Wouldn't-Melt?'

Her friend narrowed her eyes. 'If you're looking for a fight—'

'Enough.' Louisa scowled at them before looking at Nancy, her violet gaze assessing. 'This moodiness of yours is driving me mad, Nance. Now, if you and Mr Carlyle are finding it impossible to admit your feelings for one another and work together for the benefit of the workhouse, then might it not be best if you parted ways? You are turning into a complete grump.'

Nancy blustered, heat rising in her face. 'A grump? Why wouldn't I be grumpy if Francis gave me an opportunity to believe I might have a modicum of talent yet I can't find any performance work without him? I am not denying how much I like him, but the man is a—'

'Complex individual, of the type you have never had the opportunity or want to become close to before.' Louisa sighed. 'Maybe Mr Carlyle has stunned you with his attention as my first husband did me, Nance, but whereas I was grateful for Anthony's interest, you do not need a thing from Mr Carlyle and that is making you afraid to rely on him too much. I understand that. You do not wish to sacrifice your pride and say it was him who made your dreams come true. Why would you?'

Nancy stilled. Why did she suddenly feel as though Louisa's words were laced with something else... something that made Nancy feel like a fool rather than a conqueror?

She looked at Jacob and Octavia, who both wore such knowing expressions that Nancy leaped to her feet. 'You can all go to hell if you think I have that kind of pride. How I feel about Francis has nothing to do with my so-called success. I love him, all right? He is kind and decent, hardworking and foolishly generous and I love him.' She poked a finger at Louisa. 'And I have no shame in admitting that. I haven't seen him for these past few days because he won't allow the world to see how he has suffered and that infuriates me. He is hiding behind what I believe will one day be the finest and most affecting play Bath has ever seen. The man is gifted and brave. He is strong and willing to put his heart and money on the line for others. Why in God's name wouldn't I admit to loving a man like that?'

Louisa smiled and raised her glass to Jacob and Octavia. 'She's going to be just fine.'

Nancy's mouth dropped open, but words failed her as she gaped at each of them in turn. 'Was this some kind of intervention? My God...' She picked up her drink and took a hefty gulp. 'Pathetic. That's what you are. All of you.'

Jacob stood and put his hand on her shoulder, his brilliant blue eyes shining with amusement. 'So, you're just letting the toff simmer awhile. Fair enough.'

'He is not a toff.'

His smile widened, the knowing glint in his eye burning ever brighter. 'I apologise. You're letting the *gentleman* simmer awhile because he won't shout from the rooftops that his play is really about him, right?'

Nancy gave a firm nod, hating the feeling that this conversation was making her look more and more like a buffoon. 'That's right.'

'But he's not abandoned the workhouse children?'

'Well, no. Of course not.'

Nancy's heart picked up speed. Her avoidance of Francis sounded so selfish when Jacob put it like that.

'Then the problem is, he's a man whom you still don't fully trust.' Octavia sighed. 'Well, I can't say I entirely blame you for that. I would most likely feel the same.'

'Exactly.' Nancy gave a curt nod. 'I'm glad somebody—'

'But I wouldn't have walked away from helping him when he has not wavered for a single second from his hope for those children.'

Once again, Nancy opened her mouth, but words stuck in her throat. The three of them stared back at her, their eyebrows raised. Nancy's heart thundered and perspiration broke on her forehead.

'Oh, God.' She closed her eyes. 'I've done it again, haven't I? Jumped on the defensive, stormed off as though I know best.'

Jacob nodded. 'Yep.'

Louisa grinned. 'You're just being you, Nance.'

'Only a whore like you could be so narcissistic.'

Nancy glared at Octavia. 'Narcissistic?' She drained her glass. 'Why can't you talk like a normal person?'

Storming from the pub, Nancy headed for Queen Square and Francis, right where she should have been these last four days.

48

An urgent knock on his study door jolted Francis from his concentration. 'Come in.'

The door opened and Mrs Gaynor entered, her eyes shining and her smile wide. 'You have a visitor, sir.'

'A visitor?' Francis feigned interest in his papers. There was only one person he was in the mind to see and there was little chance of her appearing anytime soon. 'It's almost eight o'clock in the evening and I have no wish to entertain anyone without notice. Send them away.'

'Are you quite sure, sir? Only...'

Impatience hummed through him and Francis raised his head. 'Only what?'

Mrs Gaynor beamed, her gaze triumphant. 'Only, it's Miss Bloom.'

Francis froze. Well, his body did, even if his heart danced a jig. 'Miss Bloom?'

'Yes, sir.'

He quickly stood and brushed at the lapels of his smoking

jacket, smoothed his hair. 'Then, send her in. Send her in. We'll... um, have tea. Yes, tea.'

'Right away, sir.'

Francis rounded his desk and once again smoothed his jacket, lifted his chin this way and that, regret he hadn't shaved today niggling at him. A few seconds passed and then he heard a tip-tap of shoes on the hallway tiles before the door was pushed wider and Nancy entered.

She stood just inside the room, her eyes on his. Wearing a navy blue dress, with her auburn hair pinned and twisted, held in place with pearl-tipped pins. She looked as astoundingly beautiful as ever and any notion she might have lacked sleep over the last few nights, as he had, vanished. Why on God's earth he thought a woman like Nancy might pine for him, he had no idea.

'I'll be right back with your tea, sir.'

Francis blinked and cleared his throat. 'Yes. Thank you, Mrs Gaynor.'

The door closed and Francis waved towards the leather sofa beneath the study window. 'Won't you sit down? Or we could have tea in the living room, if you prefer.'

'In here is fine.' She walked past him, making no effort to remove her coat or put down her purse as she sat. 'I don't want to disturb you for too long.' She dipped her head and then looked at him from beneath lowered lashes. 'Considering how I've been purposefully avoiding seeing you.'

Francis's heart beat faster, his hands itching to touch her. He lowered onto the sofa beside her. 'If that was because of my inability to be honest with myself and others, then I understand why.'

'Do you?' She smiled wryly, her gaze once more dipping to her purse where it lay in her lap. 'My friends didn't. Which is why

I'm here, and now that I see you again, I am grateful for their bullying.'

Pitiful hope that maybe she had missed him sparked in his chest. 'Their bull—'

The door opened and Mrs Gaynor came in with a tray laden with a teapot and cups, a plate of biscuits and, for some reason, a slim vase of daisies. 'Here we go, a nice cup of tea will smooth everything over just right.'

Francis glowered at her turned cheek as she placed the tray on the table in front of him.

'Thank you, Mrs Gaynor.'

'Would you like me to pour?' She beamed at Nancy. 'It will be no bother.'

Francis glanced at Nancy as she shook her head, her grey eyes soft with fondness. 'I'll pour, Mrs Gaynor. Thank you.'

'As you wish, dear.'

Dropping a semi-curtsey to Nancy and then Francis, Mrs Gaynor left the room and Francis shook his head. 'I have absolutely no idea what is wrong with her.'

Nancy smiled. 'I do.'

'You do?' Surprised, he lifted the lid of the pot and stirred. 'Then, pray, enlighten me because the woman looks fit to bursting.'

'She's a woman, Francis.'

'And?'

'And she can see how we feel about one another.'

He stopped stirring and slowly laid down the spoon. He looked deep into his heart, love for this woman damn near choking him. It had been so very long since he'd touched her. 'Is that why you're here?'

'Because of how I feel about you?' She nodded, briefly closed her eyes. 'Yes. That and your dreams for the workhouse. I shouldn't have walked away from you. From the children. I'm sorry.'

Joy swept through him as he smiled. 'If anyone should be apologising—'

'I was wrong to think so much of myself and my talent.' She dropped her gaze once more. 'All week I have been around and around the theatres and music halls looking for work. Any work. But I've not been accepted or been given a chance anywhere.' She lifted her eyes to his and laughed, the sound hollow. 'I think my talents are only seen by you and felt in my heart, which is not enough for hopes of stardom. Not by a long shot. But—'

'Rubbish.' Protectiveness towards her rose inside him. 'You are extraordinary, Nancy, in every way. You will be successful. I know it. I have worked with hundreds of actors and actresses with half your talent and magnetism. It will take time, but—'

'Then I can wait, can't I?' She lifted her hand to his jaw, her study grazing his face to linger at his lips. 'I want to help you with the workhouse, Francis. I want to love you.'

Shock and happiness rolled through him even if he dared not hope that this wise, voracious, beautiful woman was really here to stay. 'There's something I need to tell you.'

She slipped her hand from his face and frowned. 'What?'

'I returned to the workhouse today.'

He reiterated his conversation with Mrs Heffer and how she had made clear she could not accept anyone's motives for adopting the children being pure unless they had experienced workhouse life for themselves. Then he told her about his failure to confess his past to Mrs Heffer and the nature of Greaves's special relationship with Alice.

'He...' Her cheeks reddened and rage darkened her eyes. 'He touches her? Uses her?' She closed her eyes. 'I'll bloody kill him.'

'Nancy, listen to me.' He gripped her hand, felt her tremble. 'We are going to get Alice out of there, but I can't do that without you. You were right. I have to own my story in every way and I think it will be telling my truth to Alice that will convince her to leave with us and come here.'

'But surely if you could not tell Mrs Heffer when she suspected that you might—'

'I couldn't. Not even under those circumstances.' He abruptly stood and strode to his desk. He snatched up his manuscript and shook it. 'I read and reread my story today and it is deep and unyielding inside me. I know if we go back to the workhouse together, I can stand in front of Alice, in front of Mrs Heffer, and share my story. As for Greaves...' Anger clogged Francis's throat. 'One way or another, I will see him removed from there permanently.'

Nancy rose from the sofa and came towards him. He looked deep into her eyes, and Francis's heart raced as she eased the papers from his hand and laid them on the desk.

'Nancy, I understand if asking you to stand beside me when I talk to Alice is too much, but—'

Her mouth pressed hard against his, her tongue slipping between his lips. She ran her hands over his upper arms to his shoulders, her nails digging in and pulling him so close, her breasts pressed firmly against his chest. Love and passion burned through him and Francis gripped her tight, kissed her back possessively.

Arousal shot through him, his erection straining as they kissed harder, deeper. His fingers moved over her body and he pushed her coat from her shoulders, his heart pumping.

'Nancy...' he whispered against her mouth. 'I love you so much.'

'And I love you. You are not alone anymore.' Her grey eyes

were sombre and heated with desire. 'Tomorrow we begin our life together. Tomorrow we go to the workhouse and bring Alice home.'

He nodded, dropped his lips to her jaw, her neck...

'But right now, Francis Carlyle,' she breathed, clutching the back of his head, 'you need to lock the damn door.'

49

A MONTH LATER...

Francis fought to get a grip on his nerves and placed his hand on the small of Nancy's back as Albert O'Sullivan, the workhouse gatekeeper, led them into the building and along the maze of corridors to the governor's office.

Today was the day that he and Nancy hoped Alice would agree to Francis not really employing her but adopting her. Nerves dried his throat as he glanced at Nancy, who stared straight ahead, her expression resolute. He would not be doing this without her, although she begged to differ.

For the last few weeks, they had talked all day and late into the night about Alice, the workhouse and his play. Their words and aspirations tumbling over each other as their mutual desires blended and bonded in what Francis now believed to be an unshakeable pact.

Words, conditions and money had been exchanged with the workhouse and now all that remained was to convince Alice that his and Nancy's numerous visits over the last few weeks meant they cared for the young girl and were committed to giving her a future free of fear and desolation.

But that did not stop Francis from worrying that he would not be all that Alice deserved. He knew only too well the mental and emotional scars the workhouse could leave on a child, and Alice had been there a decade. He clenched his teeth behind tight lips. Plus, Alice had endured Greaves's 'special attention' day after day, week after week.

Albert stopped outside Greaves's office and rapped his knuckles on the door before pushing it open. 'Mr Carlyle and Miss Bloom to see Alice Smith, sir.'

'Ah, show them in, O'Sullivan. Show them in.'

Nancy entered the room ahead of Francis and he closed the door before sitting beside her in front of Greaves's desk. Hatred rose bitter in Francis's throat as the man slid his rheumy eyes over Nancy's face and chest.

'Mr Greaves,' Francis snapped, leaning forward in his seat. 'Shall we get started?'

Greaves smirked at Nancy before lifting the papers in front of him and laying them out in a row in front of Francis. 'The official adoption papers, sir. Miss Smith will not be leaving the workhouse with you today unless all are signed, and the final payment made.' He sat back in his seat and looked at Nancy. 'I assume you have something to do with Mr Carlyle's change of heart from employing the girl to adopting her?'

'There has been no *change* of heart, Greaves, only a deepening.' Francis snatched the first paper from the desk. 'As for why Miss Bloom is here, that is none of your business.'

'Maybe not, but I find it interesting that you are not married and wish to adopt Miss Smith as a single man... Very interesting.'

Rage swept over Francis in a dangerous wave and he snapped his gaze to Greaves. 'I know just what you—'

'Mr Greaves...' Nancy lowered Francis's raised finger and held it on his knee. 'Does it really matter to you whether or not Mr

Carlyle is single? Does it matter the nature of my relationship with him or my involvement in Alice's adoption?' Her grey eyes bored into Greaves. 'Because what *should* matter is that the adoption is carried out to the official letter, you receive due payment and we walk out of here with Alice.' She released Francis's hand. 'Now, I suggest we move this along before Mr Carlyle cannot contain his disgust with you any longer and does something that I will absolutely relish, and you will regret.'

Francis pinned the governor with a glare. 'Shall we move this along, Greaves?'

Greaves nodded towards the papers. 'Not until you've signed all that needs signing. How do I know you won't tire of the girl once you've had your fill of her?'

'That's enough!' Francis's temper snapped and Nancy started beside him as he leaped to his feet, slammed his palms flat on Greaves's papers. 'You take us to Alice right now or I will shove these papers up your arse. We are here with every intention of changing that girl's life for the better and you sit there like we're bartering for wares at a bloody market. Unless you want me to walk out of here and return with a constable to ask you questions about how you are running this place and your involvement with Alice and undoubtedly other young girls, I suggest you shut your damn mouth and lead us to the workroom.'

Francis shook with fury as Greaves, his face now mottled red and his eyes bulging with anger, stood from his chair. 'I'd be very careful about threatening me, Carlyle. Very careful indeed,' he growled as he rounded the desk. 'I have been running this house for—'

'Too long.' Nancy stood and strode to the door. 'But we'll worry about that once Alice is settled in Mr Carlyle's home.'

She walked into the corridor and Francis held Greaves's glare before following her outside. As Greaves led them to the workroom, Francis looked at Nancy and she smiled, tipped him a wink. Returning her smile, Francis stood taller and inhaled a strengthening breath.

The purging of his demons had begun with his confrontation with Greaves and now, with Nancy beside him, he was certain all the ugliness, all the poison for both himself and Alice would be extricated. As for Nancy? He glanced at her again as she scowled ahead at the governor's turned back… He hoped that one day in the not too distant future she'd agree to leave Carson Street and become his wife.

The dream was probably too much to ask considering her passion and fervour for Louisa Hill, her friends and the Carson Street house but, in time, he would propose anyway.

'Right, then.' Greaves stopped outside the workroom, his gaze flitting between Francis and Nancy. 'I'll leave you with Mrs Heffer. She will see you back to my office when you are ready.' His gaze burned into Francis's. 'The papers will be waiting.'

With a brusque nod of his head, Greaves brushed past Francis and marched along the corridor, his boots thudding against the stone floor.

'Arsehole.'

Nancy laughed. 'Absolutely.' She tugged on his sleeve and inhaled a shaky breath. 'Are you sure that you do not want Alice to know you are adopting her?'

'Not yet.' Francis glanced towards the workroom door. 'We have only just managed to persuade her to work for me. The mere mention of adoption might scare her. I will tell her when the time is right.'

Nancy nodded, her grey eyes concerned. 'If you think that best. Come on, let's go and see her.'

They entered the room and after a brief chat with a very happy Mrs Heffer, Francis led the way across the stinking room to where Alice, once again, sat alone in a corner. Her fingers moved nimbly across the material in her lap, her needle a blur as she worked. Although she was yet to lift her head, Francis had no doubt she was aware of his and Nancy's approach. He had an assured feeling that there was little Alice was not aware of – and wary of.

'Good morning, Alice.' Francis smiled. 'How are you?'

'Fine.'

Even though she didn't meet his eyes, Francis pushed on. 'I've brought Miss Bloom with me again. We'd really like to persuade you to leave the workhouse and come home with me today. To come and work with my staff as a maid.'

Nancy pulled a vacant stool closer and sat down. 'Won't you look at us, Alice?'

Slowly, the girl raised her head, her startling green eyes alert and intelligent on Nancy. 'I don't understand why you want to help me.' Her gaze hardened. 'I won't go somewhere else to... be treated the same by someone different.'

The insinuation was clear and sickness coated Francis's throat as Nancy looked at him, her eyes wide, encouraging him to say something.

Taking a deep breath, he lowered onto the floor as he had before. 'Alice, you will be treated well in my home. I live in a nice part of the city and have a valet, cook and maid who are waiting to welcome you. We are a family, and I would like you to be a part of that family.' He softly smiled. 'It is also my wish to hear your experiences and any ideas you might have for how things could be made better here. For the children, the conditions, the food, everything. Miss Bloom and I...' He looked at Nancy. 'We wish to make a difference and, in order to do that, we need your help. Who better than you to tell us what is needed most urgently, what happens here that is immoral and unlawful?'

She stared at him as she digested his words and, hopefully, his honesty and conviction. She turned to Nancy. 'And will you be there? At the house?'

Francis stilled, his eyes on Alice as he waited for Nancy's reply. It could be on Nancy's answer that Alice's decision hinged as to whether or not to come home with him. The young woman might believe that it was only men who held any sort of power, but Francis could not believe it would not matter to Alice that as many women as possible were present whenever she was with him.

Nancy leaned forward and smiled. 'I think I need to tell you who I am, Alice. What I do.'

Alice studied her before slowly nodding.

'I... I'm a whore.' Nancy exhaled a long breath. 'And proud of it. I work in a brothel with two wonderful women who are my dear friends, but Mr Carlyle has written the most wonderful play and believes I can star in that play. I have dreams to be an actress and I pray they will come true but, for now, all me and Mr Carlyle want is to change things in the workhouse, which has been his dream since he left here many years ago.'

Alice seemed unperturbed and unsurprised by Nancy's admission. Instead, it was the revelation about Francis that had clearly shocked her. She faced him, her eyes wide, two spots of colour at her cheeks. 'You were here?'

'Yes. Nancy has told you who she is and what she does, now it's my turn.' Francis drew in a long breath, slowly releasing it as Nancy's hand covered his. He kept his gaze on Alice. 'I was left at the foundling hospital as a baby and then brought here when I was about four years old...'

50

Nancy sat bolt upright in Francis's drawing room, his staff standing in front of him as he told them Alice's adoption had been approved and she would be returning with him to the house that very evening. Pride beat through Nancy as she watched him speak, his gesturing hands and lively face showing his happiness.

She prayed that what she had to tell him once they were alone would not send his happiness crashing to his expensively carpeted floor with a resounding, unforgiving thud.

She glanced at Edmund, resisting the temptation to stick her tongue out at him. He clearly regarded her as beneath Francis's company. It irked a little, but not enough that Nancy would consider walking away from Francis, their love or Alice.

As for Mrs Gaynor and Jane, they seemed happy with Nancy's visits and greeted her enthusiastically.

'And so, the guest bedroom needs to be prepared for Alice's arrival. She will live and work here, but I would very much like her to eventually see this house as her home. She has made it very clear that she will not stay here without working and I have, of course, agreed to whatever preferences make her feel the most comfortable.'

'Oh, Mr Carlyle, sir,' Mrs Gaynor exclaimed. 'I cannot wait to meet the young lady. Don't you worry at all about her not being made to feel welcome.' She looked at Jane and then Edmund. 'We'll gather around her, won't we? She'll soon come to see how much love there is within these walls. Make no mistake.'

'Good.' Francis grinned. 'Now, back to your work while Miss Bloom and I further discuss our plans.'

Nancy sat back as Francis's staff left the room. 'I'm exhausted, but so entirely proud of you, Francis.'

'Proud?' He strode to the drinks cabinet and held up a decanter of claret. 'I know it's early, but…'

'Um… I…' Nancy nodded. 'All right. Just a very small one. We've earned it.'

He poured them each a glass and returned to the sofa, passing her a drink before sitting down. 'Are you happy?'

'Happy? I'm ecstatic.' She sipped her wine and put the glass on the table beside her. 'Alice is a wonderful girl and I hope she is the first of many youngsters we can help. I understand now that Alice was looking for more from us. It occurred to me that she had no reason to trust us unless we demonstrated that trust with complete honesty. How could we expect the same from her if we were not willing to show ourselves? Warts and all.'

'Indeed. Alice is intelligent, wise and savvy.' Francis stared into the distance. 'I don't doubt for a minute she'll keep me on my toes.'

Nancy laughed before leaning forward and pressing a lingering kiss to his lips, her heart filled with love for this extraordinary man. 'I am so proud of you for telling her your story.'

'You were right all along. Every obstacle I have faced, every rejection and fear, has been made by my unwillingness to openly admit my history. My pride overtook everything the more successful and wealthy I became.' He sipped his drink and shook his head. 'And for that, I am ashamed.'

Nancy grasped his hand and squeezed. 'We all have lessons to learn and I'm learning more about myself every day. I don't even know if I...' Nancy stopped, her cheeks heating. Was she really going to blurt out what she had been thinking since they left the workhouse? Could she really confess all as he had? Her hand drifted to her stomach. 'If I...'

'What is it, my love?' Francis frowned and put his drink on the table. 'If you are worried about anything, then you must—'

'I'm not worried, Francis.' Nancy inhaled a long breath and smiled, excitement about their future together knotting her stomach. 'Far from it.'

'Then what?'

Nancy stared deep into his eyes. No matter what unfolded once she told him her news, she would be keeping his baby. There would be no abortion attempt, no shame. She had yet to tell Louisa and the others, but if they could not support her decision, then she would leave with her savings and start afresh somewhere new. God knew she had the heart and strength of a hundred men, and no one would keep her down.

'I'm with child, Francis,' she blurted, her heart pounding. 'I am carrying your baby.'

'What?'

'I'm going to have your baby.'

His face had paled, his blue eyes wide with shock. The seconds passed, words to alleviate the confusion in his eyes dancing on her tongue. She should not have just dumped such a revelation in his lap. Once Alice arrived, his household would undoubtedly be turned upside down.

She swallowed around the unexpected lump in her throat, her eyes stinging. 'There is nothing you need do or say, Francis. I just wanted you to know and accept that I will be keeping this child and raising it as my own. I have money, but hopefully Louisa will be happy for me to—'

'A baby? My baby?'

Nancy nodded, her heart thundering and then her smile widened as the shock left his face and his eyes lit with undisguised pleasure. He leaped to his feet and pulled her up, yanking her against him and kissing her hard on the mouth. Nancy blustered and shoved him backwards, her breath harried. 'Good God, Francis, are you trying to suck my blood?'

He roared with laughter and pulled her close once more as Nancy laughed right along with him.

'Well, what I had planned to ask you in a week or two can no longer wait,' he said, dropping kisses along her jaw, nipping lightly at her bottom lip. 'The time is now.'

Nancy tipped her head back, the pulling sensation he evoked every time he snuzzled her neck rising with astounding force. 'What were you planning to ask me?' she breathed. 'Because whatever it is, you'd better get on with it while I can still concentrate. Why do I always want to fall into bed with you whenever you kiss me, Francis Carlyle?'

He smiled against her lips and she kissed him deeply, rejoicing in the way his hand moved between them so that he might trail fingers back and forth across her stomach.

'What was your question?' she murmured.

He looked deep into her eyes, their dark blue depths growing sombre before he dropped on one knee to the carpet.

Nancy's heart raced, tears leaping into her eyes and she shook her head. 'Francis, no. There is no need for you—'

'Didn't you hear me? I had planned to ask you anyway. This is not because of the baby. This is because of you and all you mean to me. I love you. I want to be your husband and love and protect you for the rest of my life.' He lifted her hand to his mouth and pressed a lingering kiss to her knuckles. 'Will you marry me?'

She couldn't breathe. She couldn't think. How could he propose to her? Nancy Bloom. Crass, impulsive, foolhardy dreamer. Whore...

'Francis...'

'No.' He shook his head, his jaw tight as his brilliant blue gaze bored into her. 'Don't think. Just feel. Yes or no, Nancy? Do you wish to spend the rest of your life letting me make you happy?'

Nancy stared into his eyes, her heart fuller than she could ever have imagined as she nodded. 'Yes.' Tears slipped over her lashes. 'Yes. Yes. Yes.'

Grinning, he stood and embraced her, his lips coming down on hers as Nancy clung to the man she loved, knowing deep in her heart that her feelings for Francis would never ever falter.

They would live and love. Welcome children. Their own and so many others.

* * *

MORE FROM RACHEL BRIMBLE

ACKNOWLEDGEMENTS

I would like to thank Boldwood Books for republishing Nancy's story and all the wonderful readers who have read my books over the last eighteen years. I love setting my stories in the wonderful city of Bath and imagining new ways to reach every part of society during whichever period I am writing.

The Victorian period is a particular favourite of mine and I am grateful for the authors of the many books I read about boxing and prostitution during this period while writing this book. And finally, a big thank you to the wonderful archivists at the Swindon & Wiltshire History centre who found some fabulous original documents from the period which I drew inspiration from more than once!

ABOUT THE AUTHOR

Rachel Brimble is the bestselling author of over thirty works of historical romance and saga fiction. The first book in her series, *The Home Front Nurses*, is set in Bath.

Download your exclusive bonus content from Rachel Brimble here:

Visit Rachel's website: www.rachelbrimble.com

Follow Rachel on social media here:

facebook.com/rachelbrimbleauthor
x.com/RachelBrimble
instagram.com/rachelbrimbleauthor
bookbub.com/profile/rachel-brimble
tiktok.com/@rachelbrimble

ALSO BY RACHEL BRIMBLE

The Home Front Nurses Series

The Home Front Nurses

Dangerous Days for the Home Front Nurses

Winter Wishes for the Home Front Nurses

The Pennington's Shop Girls Series

A New Start for the Shop Girls

The Shop Girls Get the Vote

A New Start for the Shop Girls

Christmas for the Shop Girls

The Shop Girls' Farewell

The Ladies of Carson Street Series

The Widow's Vow

The Foundling's Fortune

The Wife's Reputation